Clare Dowling was born in Kilkenny in 1968. She trained as an actress and has worked in theatre, film and radio. She has had drama and children's fiction published and she writes scripts for Ireland's top soap, *Fair City*. She lives in Dublin and is married with one son and one daughter.

Clare Dowling's previous bestsellers include *My Fabulous Divorce*, *No Strings Attached* and *Going It Alone*.

TOO CLOSE FOR COMFORT

There's nobody like your sister when things go wrong. At least that's what Ali hopes, as she flees America in the dead of night after sixteen long years, leaving a bit of a mess behind. Emma will surely take her and her (slightly fractious) kids in, and it'll be just like old times. But the last thing Emma needs right now is her family tramping all over her cream-coloured carpet, and her well-ordered life. Not when things are quietly imploding all around her. And how is she going to explain about fiancé Ryan, and why she suddenly had to boot him out? Ali and Emma want more than anything to pick up where they left off — but not before it all comes out in the wash.

Books by Clare Dowling
Published by The House of Ulverscroft:

MY FABULOUS DIVORCE
NO STRINGS ATTACHED
GOING IT ALONE

CLARE DOWLING

TOO CLOSE
FOR COMFORT

Complete and Unabridged

CHARNWOOD
Leicester

First published in Great Britain in 2011 by
Headline Review
an imprint of
Headline Publishing Group, London

First Charnwood Edition
published 2011
by arrangement with
Headline Publishing Group, London

British Library CIP Data

Dowling, Clare.
  Too close for comfort.
  1. Sisters- -Ireland- -Fiction. 2. Single mothers- -
  Fiction. 3. Love stories. 4. Large type books.
  I. Title
  823.9'2–dc22

  ISBN 978–1–4448–0867–4

Published by
F. A. Thorpe (Publishing)
Anstey, Leicestershire

Set by Words & Graphics Ltd.
Anstey, Leicestershire
Printed and bound in Great Britain by
T. J. International Ltd., Padstow, Cornwall

This book is printed on acid-free paper

For Margaret and Pamela

Acknowledgements

Thanks as always to my talented and enthusiastic editor, Clare Foss, and all at Headline. Thanks also to my agent Darley Anderson, and to Breda Purdue and the team in Dublin. Special thanks to Margaret and Pamela for the firsthand knowledge of sisterhood. And a big thank-you to Stewart, Seán and Ella.

Prologue

26 August 1991

Dear Ali,

Have you lost your mind?

Please, please say that this is just some stupid joke. Please say that you were drunk, and it seemed like a great idea to go ringing Dad up — reverse charge too; he was ripping — and tell him that you're not coming home. He was in the middle of his dinner. His birthday dinner. Yes. Even Liam remembered, and got him one of those desk jobbies — you know the ones, where you get to drop a little silver ball against a row of other silver balls, and watch the domino effect? Dad was the happiest we'd ever seen him. Until the phone rang, that is.

Mam's been crying all day. Dad can't even speak. I know this isn't what you want to hear. But we all just want you home. Me especially. It's been dead around here all summer without you. Worse than dead. Putrefying.

I'm going to keep this short, for maximum impact. Also, I know for a fact that you skip over bits in my longer letters, because you never once mentioned my Clairol disaster.

PLEASE, COME HOME.

A very shocked Emma xx

1

PS. Don't go ballistic. But Mam asked me out of the side of her mouth if you wanted to 'tell her anything'.

31 August 1991

Emma —

Assure Mam that absolutely everybody over here practises safe sex, including me. Well, obviously don't tell her that. Tell her I haven't had sex since I arrived. Out of her womb, that is. Do not at any point mention Troy to her.

Has Dad calmed down at all? I really wanted to speak to you on the phone the other night but he wouldn't let me. He said that he'd wasted enough money on a college course for an ingrate degenerate (steady on, Dad!) without having to foot a massive telephone bill too. But honestly, at what point in my childhood did he actually think I would make a good dental hygienist?? He's a lovely man, and he was very kind to us when we were growing up, but he's completely delusional. You know you agree.

I didn't plan this whole thing. I just want you to know that. Otherwise I'd have brought my hairdryer out with me in June. Last weekend I dragged out that massive suitcase Mam made me bring, and started packing to go home and everything. I even went and had my final turkey sub in the deli down the road (six hundred calories each!!! Mental. I sent on those things to Mam, by the way. Could you please watch her the first few times to make sure she doesn't

2

overdose? You know the way she needs glasses, only she won't admit it). But then I started thinking about college, and going back to sit in that awful, depressing lecture hall, looking down on Una Brady's roots, and listening to Horse Hannigan droning on about enamel and receding gums and God knows what else, and me usually having had no breakfast, and I just fell into the pits of depression. This wasn't my usual depression. This time I was actually crying and stuff, and having thoughts about 'ending it all'. I honestly think I'd be seriously tempted if I wasn't having such a good time over here.

I can't go back to college, Emma, I just can't. And, please, don't go on about my dyslexia — I think at this point I've got as much mileage out of that as I decently can. If I'm being straight with you, I'm not even sure I *have* dyslexia. I think I'm probably just slightly thick. And no, this is not a cry for help. There's no need to dash off a letter back giving me a massive pep talk about how great I am, if I'd only realise it. Because do you know something? I don't care any more. I've had enough of books. I mean it. I don't even fancy opening a *magazine* any more, that's how bad things are. (Although you would absolutely love the *National Enquirer* over here. Totally scurrilous. Also, curiously fixated with UFOs. Apparently, something like one in ten Americans has seen one. It makes our moving statues look completely normal.)

While I'm on the subject of college, I'm going to give you some advice (brace yourself). When the time comes to fill out your application form, go off to Auntie Pat up in the mountains for the weekend — she'll put you up if you bring her a bottle of something — and ask her to leave the dogs out to keep Dad away. Then spend some time thinking about what you'd actually like to do, as opposed to what the last three generations of the Kenny family have achieved with the sweat of their brows. (And I'm not belittling it — Dad's very happy there — but a small dental practice in Blanchardstown?) If you haven't a clue, take a year off and work with the children in Calcutta — I think they would really appreciate it — and come back older and wiser. Or don't come back at all, like me. Although that would probably kill Mam and Dad altogether. With me, they kind of expect it. At least, I was the only one of us they ever put that kiddie harness on, even while I was only hanging around the house.

Tell Mam not to worry. Macy's seem to think I'm a productive employee, although I'm pretty sure they're mixing me up with Fiona, and have said they'll keep me on 'off the books'. Troy has heard about two Irish girls who have a room to rent long term in their apartment. Or it could have been that the apartment has only one room. But I've taken it anyway. So tell her I won't be on a street corner selling my wares or anything like that. Although if I had to, at least nobody would recognise me over here. Not like at home, where the first punter would probably be Davey Brennan, or Paddy Sheahan. Mental altogether.

I'm going to go now, because I'm starting to get very nostalgic. Apparently this is the constant

4

scourge of the ex-pat, and you just have to grin and bear it. Right now I'm imagining you and me lying on our beds, our hair fanned out on the pillows like we've just tragically died (it was always drowning so there wouldn't be a mark, remember?) and being prayed over by hundreds of distraught people who cannot believe how flipping gorgeous we are, even in full rigor mortis, and I swear, I'm going to cry at any minute.

Keep my side of the room warm! And do not use my bed as a handy wardrobe for things you can't be bothered to hang up. I'll be coming back for a visit at some stage, you know, and will need somewhere to lay my weary head, not to mention that fabulous pair of leather trousers I got for half nothing due to my staff discount in Macy's.

Love and hugs!

Ali xxx

PS. Did Dad say anything about the birthday present I sent him? You might have reminded me in time, you lick-arse.

6 September 1991

Dear Ali,

I got your package (next time will you use plain brown wrapping so that I can face the postman). The information leaflet inside is very suspicious. You're supposed to take two at mealtimes, and they bind to the fat in the food, 'thus rendering it unavailable for absorption by the gut'. So far, so good. I'll still be able to fit into my wedding dress on my fiftieth birthday next year, says I. (Sophia Loren eat your heart out!) But then, turn over the page. There, in much *smaller* print, it tells you that they're only to be used as part of a calorie-controlled diet, and that, as in any weight-loss programme, you should *exercise* and consume a *low-fat diet*.

How much did you pay for these pills? Because I think we might have been sold a pup. But just as a test, I took two at lunchtime, and then ate a large toasted cheese and ham sandwich, followed by a couple of bourbon creams. Will keep you posted!

I have to go. Here's your father home. To be honest, it's very hard living with him since you threw your education back in his face, and I have to placate him constantly. If I could eat a few bars of chocolate and have the calories rendered unavailable for absorption by my gut it'd be a great bloody help.

That was Mam dictating the above, by the way. She feels she can't write to you separately, or it would be betraying Dad. He's insisting they have to show a strong, united front, like the time they found that six-pack of Heineken in the airing cupboard. And sorry about having to refuse your phone call on Friday, too (though it might help a bit if you didn't always try to reverse the charges). Dad was standing over me like some angel of death, his hand hovering near the wall plug. His genius plan is that if none of us has any contact with you, then you'll 'come to your

6

senses'. The blank postcard you got of the spring lambs gambolling around lush, Irish fields is all part of the offensive too, by the way. The next one is going to be of the Cliffs of Moher. He's quite excited about it. Liam said he'd be better off sending one with a picture of Dublin's most popular pubs. Liam says hello, by the way. At least I think it was hello. You know the way he never really moves his mouth when he speaks. Anyway, I saw Dad come home yesterday with packets of Tayto crisps and a box of Barry's Tea, so don't be surprised if you get those in the post too.

I'd better tell you about Mam now. I know she's on about diet pills and pretending everything is fine, but underneath it she thinks that you're impressionable and have fallen in with the wrong crowd. That's what she told Auntie Alice on the phone, anyway, when Dad had gone to work and she could have a good cry over the whole thing without him looking for the nearest window to throw himself out of — you know what he's like around crying women. Anyway, Auntie Alice suggested that Mam talk to the parents of the other girls who went out with you in June, in case it was some kind of collective madness, and you'd *all* fallen in with the wrong crowd, probably a street gang or something. This cheered Mam up greatly, and she was beginning to make plans for all the fathers to go over *en masse* and drag the lot of you back by the hairs of your heads. Except, of course, that when she rang the other parents, she found out that their lovely, sensible, sane daughters were all coming

7

home next Friday as planned, all ready to go back to dentistry/law/nursing after a lovely summer away experiencing a different culture. That it's only you.

'I'm ringing her this minute,' she told Dad with great determination. 'I don't care any more about your stupid plan to freeze her out. She won't even have noticed anyway.'

'Unhand that phone, Madam,' he shouted back. (We're doing *King Lear* in school at the moment. The whole class is going around saying to each other, 'I do declare I fancy a Mars bar from the royal tuck shop, noble sir.' Well, we think it's funny. But then again we're a whole two years younger than you, and so are much more immature.)

Anyway, there was a bit of a tussle over the phone, and Liam had to threaten them with a bucket of cold water unless they broke it up. Not that there was any danger of him getting off his behind. You can actually see the indentation in the couch from where he sits watching MTV all weekend. Dad keeps trying to see the news, but Liam always has the remote control, and Dad has to wait until Liam goes out to the loo to agonise over his spots before he can scramble to turn it over. Then Mam comes in and starts giving out that the television is on twenty-four hours a day, and that nobody speaks to each other any more, or at least no more than strictly necessary. She finishes up by saying that it was no wonder that you upped and left, and that if she had her own money (which she does, she just doesn't want anyone to know about it), she'd be right there after you. This is just an idle threat, of course, but it's enough to bring everybody down, and make us even more discontented with our little corner of the earth here in Dublin.

So, for the sake of us all, can you get some kind of coded message to her about the street gang thing? Just to cheer her up. It's weird to see her and Dad fighting all the time. I can't even go down the town any more to escape them because I have to study. We got the whole 'you only get one lick of the lollipop' speech from Sister Joan on Tuesday. She clearly doesn't have a clue about our class. Emily Hunt went to *grind school* during the summer — can you believe it? We don't even know where she found one. And Alison is already studying until eleven o'clock every night; she doesn't even break off for *Baywatch*. It's Valium Sister Joan should be handing out, not whipping us up into a further frenzy. I'm trying not to worry too much about the whole college applications thing yet. I'm just going to keep studying like a lunatic and hope that my life's path suddenly becomes clear the night before I have to fill the blooming thing in.

Can I ask something? If you hate your course so much, why not just jack it in? Why not change to one you *do* like? Is this a really stupid question? Dad will come to terms with it in time. In fact, he's already started grooming Liam; leaving dental moulds lying casually around the place, that kind of thing. Liam keeps looking at him suspiciously, and making his usual mutterings: 'No way . . . not going to . . . fucking hell . . . my life is terrible . . . leave me alone . . . hate everybody.' Mam says he must be going through the longest period of teenage angst in history. Then she says to Dad, thinking no one was listening, 'Thank God we've got one normal one.' And they both turn to look at me!

You can stop laughing. I need to make one thing crystal clear right now: there's no way I'm staying around to look after them in their old age. I saw the look in their eye. We either club together to put them in a nursing home, or else one of us is going to have to kill them.

I'd better go and post this before Dad comes home from work and sees me. Hopefully he'll come to his senses in time. I know I've been poking fun at him, but he's actually very upset about the whole thing. I know this because I caught him with one of the photo albums out the other night, and he was looking at a baby picture of you. God, you were fat.

Oh, would you not change your mind and come home? We'll all do our best to be happy and exciting and make you glad you did. Well, Dad will probably be the same, but Mam and I will try. Promise!

Love & hugs,

Emma xxx

PS. Dad hasn't put on the stetson yet. I don't think he's sure if it's a joke or if he's actually meant to wear it. Neither are we.

10

Hi Emma,

Fiona's gone home! And Anne-Marie and Jo! Am distraught and upset! And, it has to be admitted, slightly squiffy. (Are you getting these letters, or is Dad ripping them up upon arrival? I hope he's not reading them first. Dad, you're despicable. And yes, the stetson was a cruel, cruel joke.)

I went to the airport earlier to see the girls off. Fiona was crying her eyes out, mostly because of Kyle (Texan, six foot two 9.7 on the Richter scale) who hadn't even shown up to say goodbye. Then didn't Anne-Marie start up about her job in Maud's Ice Cream Parlour, and the Puerto Ricans. (They all used to insult each other at work to pass the time — taking off each other's accent, that kind of thing, and telling each other to feck off back to where they came from. It was vicious, but great fun.) I had to ease them all to the departures gates and hand out tissues, thinking, hang on, shouldn't *they* be comforting *me*? Still, such is the cross I have to bear to remain in the land of sunshine and cheesy popcorn. Yum. Seriously, though, it was awful once they'd gone. I hadn't really thought about it before, but there I was, in Logan Airport, knowing absolutely nobody. Not even Troy any more. That's a long story, not worth repeating, and certainly not if Dad is intercepting these letters — I wouldn't want to be the cause of any kind of cardiac incident. Anyway, I burst into tears too, big eejit that I was, right there in the airport. It wasn't like at home, where ten people would be rushing forward to ask you where you'd hurt yourself. Here, everybody just walked around me in a wide circle, looking at me like I was mentally unstable, and that's when I thought: we're not in Kansas now.

You know the way I've always really wanted to say that line? If you want to know, it wasn't all that satisfying in the end.

Guess who walks by then. Nobody other than Fiona's fella, Kyle. He'd run all the way from the car park to the departure gates, and he was devastated to learn that he'd missed Fiona by seconds. We both stood there, quiet as anything, but we couldn't even hear her bawling any more. I knew they'd probably headed straight for the bar on the other side for a few scoops and probably a basket of chips, but I didn't say that to Kyle in case he thought Fiona didn't care.

Finally he seemed to realise that I was completely on my own. 'Y' all look like you could do with a coffee,' he said at last (a terrible crutch, the accent, but he seems to bear it bravely enough). So we went for one, and he gave me loads of tips on how to manage without a social security number, and he told me where all the expats drink. All good, useful information, and I really wish I'd written it down at the time. Then he was really sweet and dropped me off at the new apartment on his way home.

I'm sitting on my new bed right now. I use the term 'bed' loosely. There's no furniture here either, so it's sleeping bags again. The girls seem OK, but Eileen got really excited because I ate

12

one of her cheese slices this evening. We all have a shelf in the fridge each and apparently aren't allowed to share anything. This is a bit of a problem for me as I don't get paid until Friday. And neither of them has mentioned yet the huge hole behind the sink in the bathroom, or the little bowl of pellets beside it . . . Any ideas??

I don't suppose there's any point in telling you to take it easy on the study front. You're old enough at this stage to recognise your obsessive-compulsive streak, and your insane desire to make up for my and Liam's shortcomings (joke! joke!). If you look in the top of my side of the wardrobe, you'll find a bundle of study notes on *King Lear* that I was saving for you. In it is everything you ever wanted to know about the poxy man, including exam papers going right back to 1972, and loads of sample answers. You'll hardly even need to read the play at all. I certainly didn't.

Write back, won't you? Please? Mam rebelled yesterday and made a sneaky phone call to me just before I left the old apartment. It was great to hear her voice, even if she spent most of the conversation advising me that a cooked chicken can last a whole week, if properly covered. And she wants more pills. She must be throwing them back like Smarties. The girls in work are on new ones. Apparently you can eat what you want, so that'll cheer her up. I'll send a batch on.

I'd better go. The girls have got in a crate of Bud Light to welcome me to the apartment — apparently we're allowed to share alcohol — but we're only halfway through it so have got some serious work to do. Also, am feeling *very* tipsy now.

Love Ali xxx

PS. A moral dilemma — would it be wrong to go out for a drink with Kyle? Just as friends, seeing as I haven't any left over here now. I haven't told him yes yet. Would Fiona take it The Wrong Way?

20 September 1991

Dear Ali,

Look, Dad was only trying to frighten you. I heard the whole thing in my bedroom. There are hundreds of thousands of illegal aliens in America. There's absolutely no reason why they should specifically target you, and 'hunt you down like an animal'. And they certainly wouldn't throw you in a maximum-security gaol to be carved up by the inmates. Mam told him that she thought the whole thing was very low of him. Now they're not talking. The flipping drama.

I think he's just in a bad mood because Mrs Meagher didn't go to him for Jenny's braces — you know Jenny, she's the one with teeth like Cilla Black's. Even Dad said that, and he's always really prim and proper about not commenting on people's teeth in public. Anyway, Mrs Meagher took Jenny to Jim Hegarty (I know, the butcher) instead. I think your phone call might have come in the middle of a rant Dad was enjoying about all the

14

low-down, nasty, ungrateful people in his life. Also, it probably wasn't the best timing on your part to ask for a loan. I think he just flipped and thought that if he put the frighteners on you, then you'd pack up and come home.

Anyway, don't worry about it.

Love Emma xxx

11 October 1991

Dear Ali,

OK, you've made your point. And nobody can blame you for playing Dad at his own game. But at least think of poor Mam. She's in a terrible state. Every time the phone rings she runs to it like a crazy woman, and shouts into it, anguished, 'Is that you, my precious baby?' But it's nearly always Auntie Alice or someone from Dad's work, and we're having to try to get there before her now to avoid any further embarrassment.

It's been three weeks now without a word from you. Dad got on to the Embassy yesterday. They were very helpful until they realised that you weren't really missing at all, that the two of you had just had a row and that you were refusing to contact anybody. He was hoping that they could track you down at Macy's, or else send a 'cop' around to your apartment. They told him he'd been watching too much *Hill Street Blues*, and that he should chill out and give you some space. He's been going around the place very quiet and sad-looking since. I think it's pretty genuine.

Mam has started to lie on your bed for hours on end, sniffing your pillow, only I explained to her that it was difficult for me to get any studying done, what with all the noise, and so she only does it now during school hours. I don't want to steal your thunder or anything, but unless you want me to flunk my exams, would you ever cop on and give us all a ring?

Your (patient, sort of) sister

Emma

25 October 1991

Dear Ali,

This isn't even funny any more.

Emma x

29 October 1991

Dear Emma,

Just in case I didn't sound urgent enough on the phone earlier, I'm following it up with a plea to put a rocket under Dad. Things are desperate here. We think we have it cornered in the kitchen, but we're all so petrified that we're taking it in turns to stay awake and watch over the other two in case our toes get chewed off in our sleep.

Oh, I wish I was at home in my own bed, across from you. This is horrible.

Ali xx

Dear Emma,

Thank you, thank you, *thank you*. And to Dad. Whatever else I say about him, he always comes through in a crisis. I've sent him a pair of Levi's as a thank-you. I honestly think he would look good in them.

We're all slowly getting over the fright of things here. It was Eileen who was in the bath, shaving her legs, when it came out from under the sink. It wasn't even afraid, she said, just kind of lounged there while she screamed her lungs out. It was the size of a small cat. I am not exaggerating. American rats are bigger built than the ones back home. This lad had clearly been coming out to stuff himself with Eileen's bread and crackers every night in the kitchen, and all the time she'd been blaming me. Anyway, the sight of Eileen trying to squeeze out the bathroom window, buck naked, must have unsettled him because he eventually turned and headed for the living room, where me and June were trying to glue together some fake ID so that we could get into the bars over here. June actually fainted. I couldn't believe it. She just passed out cold and cracked her head on the mantelpiece, and had to go into work the next day with a chipped tooth and a big bandage wrapped around her head (she's an assistant at a beauty counter).

I was pretty scared but managed to hold on to my nerve, and draw upon my experience of finding a ferret in our prefab in school that time.

I threw empty beer cans at him until he retreated to the kitchen — reluctantly, I might add, and June said he was hissing and spitting — and then we slammed the door on him and barricaded him in with a chair. 'All our food is in there,' Eileen raged. She meant hers, because June and I had only a box of cereal between us. She was still naked at this point. Anyway, I left the two of them armed with bottles of Mr Muscle in case he got out, and I went out to a phone box to get hold of the landlord. It just rang out, like usual. We think at this point he's probably emigrated because Eileen says he hasn't collected the rent in two months. Which is great, as we really need a television, and so we're going to spend the money on that instead, and a set of speakers as we're having a party next weekend. So all's well that ends well, really, on that front.

Will you tell Dad thanks again? We tried to get June's dad to help first, but he kept telling us to try and trap it in a wellie. As if any of us owned a pair of wellies. Eileen said we should call Pest-O-Kill ourselves, and wait until they'd trapped the rat before breaking the news that we didn't have the money to pay them. As she said, what were they going to do, *release* the thing? But then June started to look all watery again, and that's when I made the decision to swallow my pride and give Dad an opportunity to make amends for his vile threats. Anyway, Pest-O-Kill wouldn't come until someone had paid by credit card up front.

Tell him we'll pay him back, every cent. Obviously it'll have to be in instalments. I'm enclosing twenty dollars. He might want to wait until the exchange rate is a bit better before lodging it.

I'm really glad we're all speaking again. Tell Mam I'll give her a phone number as soon as we get a line installed. This is harder than you might think, because none of us has a social security number and they're really picky about things like that. But Eileen has some kind of plan. I'm not sure it's entirely legal, but anyway . . .

I keep thinking about the rat. I wish we'd given the wellie thing a go first before calling in the exterminators, but Eileen says I'm just soft.

Thanks again!

Love Ali xxxx

2 December 1991

Dear Ali,

I've sent you a plum pudding in the post. I put it in a Roses tin with lots of foil around it and Styrofoam chips. Emma says it'll probably set off alarms in the post office!

We're still hoping you'll make it home for Christmas. But obviously not if you have to crawl back in on your belly over the Canadian border under cover of darkness. That image has stayed with me, by the way. The thing I want to know is, have you not had your fill of that place yet? I'm not trying to put pressure on you, darling. But your bed is still here for you, and I could keep an eye out for a job for you here, just until you get back on your feet. A nice little

19

number in Dunnes Stores maybe . . . ? I'm not without contacts, you know.

All right, look, I know it's depressing here. The country is a shambles. Don't get me started. Your dad says that people are now leaving it up to fourteen months between their annual checkups, in the hopes of saving money on a visit further down the line. And three or four of the neighbours have organised 'hair salon' nights at each other's houses — they dye each other's hair to cut down on hairdressing bills. I haven't signed up yet because they're all looking a bit orange, if you know what I mean. Anyway, one of them made a crack along the lines that we must be loaded, what with the price your dad charges for a simple filling. Well, I wasn't having that. I broke down the cost of it for her, and told her that hers were more expensive because she has such a big mouth. The look on her face! I'm laughing now even thinking about it.

But enough of all that. I need you to have a word with Emma about all the studying she's doing. She's so focused and determined, completely unlike the rest of us. Sometimes I wish she'd sneak out and find an unsuitable boyfriend, or take up drinking. At least we have some experience of *that*. Often when I look at her I get the impression that she has this whole business of life sussed, and it's quite unnerving for your father and me. She doesn't even openly disrespect us, although it's not as if she hasn't been set an example by you and Liam.

'Come out to the cinema with us,' we tried to encourage her the other night. There was some mindless action movie on that other, normal children enjoyed. 'I'd love to,' she said — sincerely — 'but I have to do this essay on what role I think the media has in creating the news, as opposed to simply communicating it.'

'What?' said Noel. With a really dim expression on his face, I have to say.

'It's all right,' she said. 'I don't understand it either.'

But she did! She was just being nice! Sparing our feelings. Let's face it; she's smarter than the rest of US rolled into one, unless Liam is going to stun us all yet.

My main worry is that she's aiming for medicine, or law. Not that she would dream of letting us in on any future plans she might have for herself. But I'm just thinking, the *points* she'd need. Clever and all as she is, supposing she misses out by a fraction? What then? Knowing her, she'd doggedly repeat those exams over and over until she achieves what she wants, and frankly I don't think the rest of us are up to it. Anyway, she might listen to you. At this end, we're just not sure where we've gone *right* with her.

By the way, what's in those last diet pills you sent me? Don't get me wrong — I feel marvellous on them. Much better than the old ones. I have so much energy that I could hoover the house all day long! In fact, I feel a bit jittery if I don't. And the weight is falling off. No, the only hiccup is that I find it hard to sleep at night — I'm writing this at three in the morning

— and my heart goes like the clappers sometimes, like I was on speed or something. Anyway, I'm just wondering.

Much love,
Mam

Dear Everybody,

I know this is going to come as a bit of a shock. But I'm getting married. So at least now you won't have to worry about me any more. Kyle is very, very nice, and he's a Christian, Mam, which I know is not the same as a Catholic, but it's close enough. Even though we haven't known each other very long, I want to stress that we are both very happy about this. So are his parents. His family has a plastic packaging business in Texas and we're flying down so I can meet everybody over the weekend. We're going to stay in Boston for the moment, as Kyle is studying, but hopefully we'll move to a bigger apartment with a spare room if anybody wants to come over for a visit.

We've decided to get married as soon as possible — we both just want a quiet wedding, with no fuss — so there won't be a chance for you all to make it out in time. But maybe in the summer. Or else we will try to come home in the late autumn so that you can meet him. I'll be legal then, so there won't be any problem. All in all, everything has worked out well for me over here, so I don't want anyone to worry about me.

I'm going to give you some time to digest all this, and then I'm going to ring on Saturday so that you can talk to Kyle. He really is very nice.
  Lots of love,
  Ali

1

Ali

Travelling with three children in tow wasn't any fun. Especially when the children in question didn't actually want to *go* anywhere, except back to bed, which was where they belonged at five in the morning.

'I need a coffee,' said Anto, bleary-eyed. He was ten.

'Shut up,' said Erin crossly, 'or I'm going to start wanting one too.' She was seven.

Where did I go wrong? Ali wondered fruitlessly, as she negotiated the streets in the dark. It wasn't that hard, as most law-abiding people were tucked under their duvets and the only other vehicle in sight was a police car idling at a drive-thru, its occupants munching on quarter pounders and fries.

Ali drove past the car, making sure that she stayed within the speed limit.

'Why are you ducking?' demanded Erin. You could get nothing past her. The boys wouldn't notice if Ali sauntered by them buck naked and twirling the American flag over her head.

Just for the record, she did not walk around in front of her children naked. It was just an example. However else her parenting skills might fall down, she usually managed to keep her clothes on.

She met her daughter's eyes in the rear-view mirror now. 'I am not ducking.' It was always best to speak in a firm, grown-up voice to Erin; to at least try to give the illusion of being in charge, even if nobody believed it.

Erin eyed her back for a moment — what do you take me for, a bloody fool? — but it was obviously too early in the day to mount a full-blown challenge, thank God, and so she sank back in her seat and looked out the window. Beside her, Anto dozed. It must be the lack of caffeine.

I am a crazy woman, Ali thought. But she'd been driven to it. It wasn't as though she'd woken up an hour ago, and on a whim thought, feck it, I'll just reef the kids from their cosy beds on a school day and we'll all pile in the car and go on a madcap adventure together! Although there were plenty of seriously unbalanced mothers living not too far from her who did just that. You could usually spot these types by their moustaches. And their habit of ending a lot of conversations with the words 'praise the Lord'.

But a good number of people in the South thought that way. Not so much in their part of town, but move a few blocks north and you were into serious God-fearing territory. When Ali first moved down to Texas, she wondered whether in fact America was just a dream, and that really she was back at home, having been frog-marched to Mass at some unearthly hour of the morning by her mother, and force-fed Father Eamon's

26

croaky pleas for intercession on behalf of whatever scut had spray-painted the side wall of the oratory with the unholy words 'Tommy is Gay'.

Father Eamon wasn't a patch on some of the women Ali had met at Jack's first playgroup. Along with regular churchgoing and charity bake sales and making up shoeboxes for the homeless children in Africa, they thought nothing of a dawn hike up, say, the nearest ridge of mountains with backpacks full of cupcakes and home-made seed bars, their bearded spouses in tow (the husbands usually had a lot of facial hair too).

Ali had been invited on one of those expeditions shortly after joining the playgroup. She'd thought it might be a good way to make friends. New girl in town, and all that. And seeing as she had yet to set foot in the white clapboard church at the top of the town (the sign outside saying 'Come Sing with Jesus!' always put her off), she figured a nice walk up a hill with the new neighbours would be just the thing to help her settle in. Besides, it would be great to get away from Kyle's parents, Ethel and Hal, for an hour or two. Oh, they were lovely people, and had been extremely welcoming, despite their only son having to abandon a brilliant future in college in favour of a hasty marriage and early fatherhood (secretly, they thought of Ali as vaguely sluttish, an opinion helped along by her continued penchant for miniskirts at the age of *thirty-four*). But, God, their *yard*: a square of lawn and pavement in front of the house that

Hal worked on incessantly. He swept and planted and weeded and pruned, and, just for a bit of excitement, occasionally scooped up a bit of litter from the pristine lawn, which he would hurry in to show Ethel.

'Look at this!'

They would gather round, turning the litter this way and that, and eventually declaring. 'That's from the doughnut shop.' The fact it had 'Dee's Donuts' emblazoned on the side was usually a clue.

'Again! We're always finding their litter on our lawn.'

'They should send somebody around the neighbourhood to pick it up, like the burger places do.'

The evidence would be bagged and tagged, and then Hal would put on his red checked bomber jacket and baseball cap. 'I'm going to go around there right now.'

'Don't spare your words,' Ethel would encourage him.

So it was great to get away for the day, even if it was on a nature walk instead of to the pub. Kyle was working and couldn't come, so Ali baked some muffins with enough linseed in them to ensure regularity for a week, and off they set, her and little Jack, dangling precariously from her chest in a sling. It all felt very homespun and nice, despite her constant fear that somebody would break into a rendition of 'The Lord is my Shepherd' at any moment. Nobody did. In fact, everyone was so normal and pleasant that she wondered whether she'd misread these people all along. Who did she think she was, anyway, coming from the city and looking down her nose at these simple, yet honest people, even if they thought George Bush was a great lad altogether? How prejudiced she'd been! They were grand. She just needed to give them a chance. Maybe even take a gander into that church to see what all that hollering and singing was about on a Sunday morning.

But then it all went horribly wrong. It began when the men and boys peeled away from the group and set off in another direction. Ali presumed that they'd gone to do a collective pee or something. 'And they think women are bad?' she'd joked to the female half of the group, receiving some polite, if puzzled, smiles back. Still, most of them were still trying to work out her accent. '*What* did she say?' had been the murmured refrain all morning.

When the men didn't come back, Ali wondered whether they were, in fact, constructing some kind of a camp, and would surprise the women with wonderful, three-storey structures made of wood and sticks, which they had hewn with their teeth. Perhaps a fire would be aglow under a tasty pot of beans, if that wasn't a contradiction in terms, and somebody might produce a bottle of something warming, and they would all gather round and have a little singsong. Ali herself had stashed a naggin of whiskey at the bottom of her rucksack, under the baby's bottle, in case anybody wanted to let their hair down later on. Some of these churchy types could be wild when they were let out. Look at the Irish; for centuries now, they had managed to seamlessly combine extreme godliness with rampant drinking and sex.

She was just about to suggest that they crack open the whiskey now when a terrible blast filled the air. Guns, just like on the telly. The blast was followed by another, and another, until Ali felt she was trapped in a Martin Scorsese movie. 'Hit the dirt!' she yelled, diving to the ground and covering little Jack's downy head. Clearly they had walked into some kind of drugs war. And on the side of a remote mountain too! She was outraged.

Then she saw that the other women had gathered round her, chuckling and cooing in great amusement. It was only when the lads arrived back, strutting like Hollywood studs as they carried between them a beautiful buck deer, oozing blood and guts like something out of an episode of *CSI*, that she realised what had happened. They had shot it.

'What's happened, honey?' Kyle said in alarm when she arrived home half hysterical.

When she told him what had happened, he laughed. 'They were just hunting. It's what they do around here.' He shrugged. 'Personally, I'm not into it, but if you're going to live here, you'll have to get used to it.'

She had looked at him askance. Her Kyle — the man she'd thought of as a gentle giant — was really no better than the murderous nutters who praised the Lord on a Sunday morning and went out to slaughter half his creatures that afternoon.

She felt foolish. She hadn't even noticed that the group had been carrying guns. Well, she *had*, but she hadn't looked too closely, and they were kind of the same shape as golf clubs, weren't they? She'd been thinking maybe a little pitch and putt after the picnic. At no point had it registered that half the jolly picnic group was walking along with enough armoury to wipe out a small town. Even the boys. The *little* boys.

'We're never going back to that playgroup,' she declared, clutching her precious baby to her chest lest he be ripped from her and brainwashed before his bedtime bottle.

'You can't go around getting offended the whole time,' Kyle told her. 'Last week you were bitching about all the four-by-fours in the town, and the goddamn ozone layer.'

She was really outraged now. 'You have a son. Do you not care that by the time he grows up, you'll have polluted every breath he takes?'

'Here we go,' Kyle said, throwing up his hands.

Meanwhile his parents were sitting in the front room in front of Fox News, eyes rigidly trained away from the rowing couple. The whole house was strewn with baby paraphernalia — nappies and dirty baby-gros and toys and general crap, and there was a smell of puke in the air.

Ali took a deep breath.

So did Kyle. 'This isn't all my fault, you know.' He sounded pinched.

'I know. But it isn't mine either.'

★ ★ ★

31

'Are we nearly there yet?' asked Anto from the back seat.

'We're only on the outskirts of the blooming town.'

Silence for a moment.

'I feel sick,' Erin announced.

'How could you be sick? We're only in the car ten minutes.' Finally, the freeway ahead. 'Will we sing a song?' Ali said chirpily.

In the rear-view mirror she could see them looking at each other like she was a crazy woman. And maybe she was. Maybe if she were to pull over to the side of the road right now for just a minute, and thought about what she was doing, *really* thought, she might chicken out entirely.

Still, when had she ever stopped to think about anything? Oh, she did plenty of thinking *after* the fact, but rarely before. It must be some genetic fault or something, or else all that anaesthetic that Dad came home reeking of from the surgery had somehow leaked into the drinking water. But then look at Emma. The most clued-in, forward-thinking person Ali had ever met. Emma would never fuck up her life to the extent that she had to make a hasty escape from it in the middle of the night with her kids still in their pyjamas.

Anyway, what was Ali going to do? Go *back*? Not likely.

So she put her foot down, turned her headlights on (oops) and kept on driving.

'I have a biology test today.' Finally, Jack spoke. Or, rather, squeaked. The poor lad's voice was breaking, and he could hardly get a sentence out without sounding like an opera singer with croup.

He sat in the passenger seat beside her, all six foot one of him. He was the spit of Kyle, pre-paunch: broad shoulders, proper American teeth (white and plentiful), and hair like a Labrador puppy's. He had inherited nothing of Ali's, except a tendency towards in-grown toenails, and the way he would scrunch up his eyes when he laughed.

'Have you?' she said calmly, while her brain went, *fuck*. What biology test? Hadn't he done one only last week? At least, she remembered cobbling together dinner in the kitchen — probably tuna casserole again; she only had three recipes, which she rotated — whilst being grilled about the whereabouts of her clavicle.

'It's my shoulder bone,' she'd announced Wow. She'd even surprised herself. Something at school must have sunk in during her time with the nuns after all, even though she used to transport herself mentally to Barbados.

But it was the wrong answer. Or, rather, it was the *right* answer, but he'd have preferred if she hadn't known and he could have shown off his superior knowledge. So she duly pretended that she hadn't a breeze where her kidneys were, or what the precise function of her pancreas was. And she didn't, either.

'Today, you say?' she clarified now, frantically buying time.

'Yes, Mom. *Today.*' There was that new tone in his voice again, the one that said, you're so

33

thick I can't believe they allowed you to give birth. Ali found it very upsetting. OK, so Erin had been speaking that way to her for years now, but Ali was used to it, and besides, she spoke to everybody that way. Jack had always been so normal up to this point. So lovable. Of their three mistakes, he was definitely the most forgivable. Although technically Anto wasn't really a mistake; more a misfire, after Kyle had drank those cocktails he hadn't really been able for.

Placating Jack, Ali said, 'I'll ring Miss . . . ' What was her name? Kyle would know. Kyle knew the names of every one of the local high school teachers. He'd necked with most of them, according to local lore. Granted, he'd been fifteen at the time and so had they, but it was still mildly unsettling to be talking to, say, Miss Parkinson or Mrs Lewinsky, knowing that they knew exactly how her husband kissed. 'It's still the same,' she often felt like telling them grimly.

'Miss Walker,' she said to Jack. Phew. Her memory was on top form these days.

But Jack only glared at her. 'And what are you going to tell her?'

Ali kept her eyes trained on the road. 'That you're not going to be in today.'

'Are you going to lie that I'm *sick*?'

Well, actually, yes, she had been going to. She could hardly tell the truth: that they were, in fact, leaving the country. That they'd have left on Monday and missed Jack's English test too had Ali been able to find her blasted passport. Eventually it had turned up in the front of

34

Anto's backpack. Anto had scratched his head at length when confronted by an angry mother. 'I can't explain it,' he'd said eventually, very nicely. 'I haven't been in that pocket in months.'

Blame seemed to just slide off him. Broken windows, missing money, doughnut bags actually *in* Hal's car, on the front seat, along with greasy napkins — none of it was ever Anto's fault. And if he *was* pinned down, he always had an extremely plausible explanation. The money was just sitting there, and he was afraid that if he didn't take it and put it somewhere safe, like his pocket, then it might be stolen by a burglar. The doughnut bag had been a joke on 1 April, and it was an awful shame that Granddad didn't have a sense of humour like everybody else. 'Well, yes,' Ali and Kyle would end up having to admit, and suddenly the whole thing was Granddad's fault, even the broken window, while Anto was a rock of sense and reason.

'I think I'm afraid of him,' Kyle had whispered to Ali once.

Jack, on the other hand, was a typical first-born: responsible, protective, diligent, and no doubt worried now about his biology test and the fact that his mother was driving too fast on the freeway in the middle of the night and had snuck a suitcase into the boot of the car when she'd thought he wasn't looking.

She met his eyes briefly. This wasn't fair on him. But she was doing him a favour in the long run. 'I'll explain everything at the airport.'

'We're going to the *airport*?' He was aghast now. He was giving her the same look that Kyle often did: there she goes again, doing something crazy, off her bloody rocker.

She pretended she didn't notice. 'I know, isn't it great? I wanted it to be a surprise.'

'Where are we going?' he demanded.

Ali smiled her first genuine smile in what felt like months. 'Home!'

2

Emma

Working in television wasn't half as glamorous as it was made out to be. This was especially true if you worked in breakfast television, as Emma did, and had to get up at the ungodly hour of 4 a.m.

Rise and shine! Rise and shine! Rise and shine!

That was her alarm clock. Instead of beeping, it shouted the above at her in a manically cheerful New York accent. It had been a present from Ali the week that Emma had landed the job.

'Shut up,' she shouted at it, with a wild lunge to turn it off. She collapsed back on the pillows in fright. Her heart was thrashing around worryingly in her chest. If ever she didn't turn up for work, they would find her dead in the bed, one fist clasped to her breast in a futile attempt at self-administered CPR, the other one jammed on that blasted alarm clock.

OK, first things first: what day was it? Thursday. Good. Great! Only one more morning of this hell and then it would be Saturday, and she could sleep in till ten. Till *noon*, if she felt like it. In her more extreme fantasies, she slept the whole day long, only getting up in time for dinner.

But, of course, that never happened. At

precisely 3.59 a.m. her eyes would snap open in the dark, and she would be awake — wide awake — the way she never was on a weekday, when it would actually have been handy. No matter how late she'd stayed up the previous night, or how many glasses of wine she'd sunk, some ironic inner clock would tug her to full consciousness just as milkmen all over the country were getting up. Then began the battle to go back to sleep: she would toss and turn and punch the pillow and count sheep and then, in desperation, subtract sheep, until eventually she ended up on the couch in her massive fluffy dressing gown, the one that made her look like a baby polar bear, drinking cocoa and watching the poor souls who were pulling the night shift on Sky News.

'It sucks, doesn't it?' she would sympathise with them.

That morning she felt particularly fuzzy, and so she dragged one foot out from under the duvet and plonked it on the chilly wooden floor, just in case she was tempted to nod off again. She had only once turned up late for work, and that was because she had driven into a deer. It had been awful. She'd staggered from the car just as the deer was getting back on its feet. It hadn't seemed hurt, thank God. They'd stood in the middle of the dark road at 4.30 a.m., looking at each other in shock and fright. And a hint of blame, from the deer.

'I'm really sorry,' she told it at last. 'But I'm going to have to go to work.'

Live television waited for no man or woman, or animal for that matter. The show must go on, no matter what kind of personal disaster might befall you. Emma had gone to work with the flu, the mumps (awful — her neck had swelled up like a tree trunk) and hangovers so vicious that she couldn't see straight. She'd gone to work the morning the pipe had burst in her bathroom, flooding the whole place, and on Dad's second heart attack three years ago. The shame was still with her. But the alternative had been ringing up the front desk, and saying something utterly outlandish like, 'I'm sorry, but I'm not going to make it in this morning.'

Lying there in bed, idly wondering what she was going to wear — the purple dress or the skinny jeans that looked great with her new brown boots? — Emma only gradually became aware that something was wrong. It wasn't just the freakishly early hour; there was something else awry too. Something worse.

This feeling had happened every morning for the past month, and so she wasn't unduly alarmed. She just lay there quietly, waiting for the full realisation of the situation to make itself clear. The bed, she eventually knew. To her left, it was cold and empty, and the duvet was flat and undisturbed. And with that knowledge everything else began to fall into place, bit by horrible bit, until she ended up clutching handfuls of the bedding in fright, hoping to God it was all just a bad dream, and the alarm would burst into life at any second, exhorting her to *Rise and shine!* in its best Joe Pesci voice, and none of this would have happened.

It never did, though.

Work, she thought. It was the only thing that had got her out of bed these last few weeks, and it did that morning too.

★ ★ ★

Emma's decision to work in television had come as a bit of a surprise to everyone but herself.

'The *meeja*?' her parents had said fearfully when Emma first told them of her intention to put down media studies on the CAO form. The CAO was short for the Central Applications Office — a dark, hellish place in the midlands where every seventeen-year-old in Ireland with college ambitions was forced to submit their future hopes and dreams on an application form, the length and complexity of which had parents popping Valium up and down the country. This piece of paper was sent off to the hellish place, sometimes with a tenner tucked into the envelope, or a packet of fags, and about six weeks after the exams, another piece of paper was spat back out, saying, '*Medicine*? Fat chance, stupid,' or, 'I think we all know you would make a really lousy social worker, so it's Arts for you, where at least you can't do any harm.'

Emma was told by her career guidance teachers that her grades were so good that she could do almost anything. Anything, they impressed upon her, whilst palming her information on law and stockbrokerage and other high-flying jobs that would have her earning a ruddy fortune by the time she turned thirty.

'*Meeja* Studies?' They were aghast too. A half-baked, makey-uppy course, even worse than Arts. What a waste of a fine brain! 'But we only have the two channels on the telly,' it still being 1995. 'What exactly will you be doing after you graduate? Reading the news?'

The very idea of sitting in front of the nation at six o'clock every evening in an inch of pan-stick and reading an autocue made Emma go hot and cold. She was more a background sort of person, she'd always felt; the kind who kept her head while all around her lost theirs. She wasn't sure if this was a good thing or not. It might even be a disadvantage; didn't people who worked in the meeja have to be kooky and entertaining and a bit mad? But she had a hunch that this was only for the people in *front* of the camera (bar newsreaders, of course); that the people behind it were in fact the opposite. That they might actually be a bit like Emma: diligent and calm, and the ones who remembered to blow out those fecky little tea lights before everybody went to bed, the ones that Mam had taken a brief fancy to and liked to position just beneath the heavy, highly flammable curtains whenever they were 'entertaining'. There had been at least two major house fires averted in recent years, thanks to Emma.

'No newsreading,' she told Mam and Dad firmly. 'I was thinking of something more behind the scenes. Like producing.'

They digested this. There were no producers in the family on either side. Only dentists and structural engineers.

'So, theoretically, you could end up working with, say, the likes of Gay Byrne?' Dad began to deduce carefully.

You could see his eyes start to shine. Dad's 'weakness' was current affairs. He fancied himself as being very up on them, what with having the radio on in the background all day in the surgery while he extracted teeth and did root canals and the like. He knew of all the broadcasters, and had great respect in particular for Gay Byrne, a man he often declared 'knew what he was talking about'. If Gay said something, well then, it must be true. Often he would bore the socks off Mam by telling her, word for word, what Gay had said on the radio that day. She'd be so addled by the crisis in the Middle East or whatever that she would end up burning the blessed shepherd's pie.

But now there was a chance that Gay might actually be *in their lives*, through Emma.

'I'd love to know what he eats for breakfast,' Dad said suddenly. 'Or what he buys in the supermarket.'

'What everybody else buys,' said Mam impatiently.

'He's a national figure,' Dad argued. 'He can't be seen stocking up on a sixteen-pack of toilet roll like everybody else.'

'You think he's the only man in Ireland who doesn't do a number two — '

'Don't you dare,' Dad cried.

Mam didn't care about celebrities, although she was prone to irritating Dad when he was trying to watch the six o'clock news by idling in front of the telly and pondering, 'I wonder what age she really is? Not forty-six, anyway, like she told that magazine. I'd say more like fifty-six. Look at her neck. It's worse than mine.'

In the end she declared that she was just relieved that Emma was going to college at all, and so was unlikely to enter into early motherhood, not like Ali. Mam was only now getting over the shock. 'I was too liberal with them,' Emma had heard her sobbing to Dad in the kitchen the night of The News. 'Letting them think that sex was all right if you were in a loving, committed relationship.'

'It's all right,' Dad had comforted her. 'A lot of people believe that.'

They were making a big effort to accept things. Mam had started to knit something in the evenings — a baby cardigan by the looks of it — although she kept getting distracted by the telly, and one arm was looking quite a bit longer than the other. And Kyle was 'a lovely lad', according to Dad, although this was always said through slightly gritted teeth. No *truly* lovely lad took advantage of a young girl in a foreign country, an innocent girl, miles away from her family.

This was always met with great hilarity from Emma and Liam, but Dad persisted in his suspicion of Kyle as 'fast'. The fact that he had married Ali, and rented an apartment with her in Boston, and even bought a Volvo estate, did nothing to lessen his alleged fastness. The die was cast.

'You mind yourself now, love,' Dad warned

Emma as he dropped her off at college on her first day. He'd taken to driving her places and picking her up afterwards. Emma was suspicious it was an attempt to stop anybody impregnating her.

She got lost in the media building trying to find her first lecture. She pressed herself in tight against the wall as bleached-blonde people in dungarees and multicoloured Doc Marten boots clattered noisily by, shouting luvvy things at each other such as, 'Lindsey. Missed you, babes! How was your summer? Mine was crud.' (These people would end up on children's television, she would later find out.) She felt horribly drab and boring next to them, and began to wonder whether she didn't properly belong over in the science lab or the business studies building after all.

Then she saw her: another girl pressed against the wall, wearing jeans and a hicky sweatshirt just like Emma's, and clutching a Tupperware box of what looked to be brown rice.

'I have no idea where we're supposed to go,' the girl said cautiously (she would turn out to be Hannie). She looked down the corridor after the would-be children's television presenters. 'But I think our job is to follow them.'

★ ★ ★

Fast forward fourteen years and Emma was now the producer of Wake Up Ireland. 'Ireland's most popular breakfast television show', as it liked to bill itself. In truth, it was Ireland's only

44

breakfast television show, but in a country of four million there were only so many unemployed people, insomniacs and night-shift workers out there free to lounge in front of the telly at seven in the morning learning how to get the most from their foundation (yesterday's featured guest had been a Hollywood make-up artist).

When Emma arrived at the studio that morning, Hannie was already there, unpacking her usual selection of Tupperware boxes. The first one always contained fruit, cut up — 'one of my five a day'. The next one had porridge in it: grey, lumpy, horrible-looking stuff, made by Hannie herself, and that had everybody else retching and moaning, 'It's half-past five, put it away.' The last Tupperware box was always a little surprise, even to Hannie herself. Every Sunday night she made up an assortment of these boxes, popping a breakfast bar in one, nuts in another, a mini muffin in a third, et cetera. Then she jumbled them up in a bag, and each morning she would scrunch her eyes up tight and put in her hand — 'lucky dip!' — and so she never knew what she was going to find in that third box until she opened it at work.

'It helps to keep me interested,' she maintained.

'I'd love to take a photo of her with her hand in that fucking bag,' Phil, who had a desk behind hers, once said venomously.

Every office needed a Hannie: scarily organised, obsessed by detail, and anally retentive (although never for long in her case, with all that roughage). So what if she irritated the hell out of the other assistant producer, Phil, who got by on fags and strong coffee until it was time to send someone to the Spar for a bacon roll, no ketchup — oh, and twenty John Player Blue while they were at it. Hannie would perkily pass him by at dawn every morning, Tupperware boxes rattling, as he was hunched over in the rain outside the television building, sucking desperately on a sodden butt.

'You're going to die at forty-nine,' she'd tell him viciously.

'I'd rather be dead than be *you*.'

There was a bet on in the office as to when they would start sleeping together. Some people thought never, others said the following Friday night after a session in the pub.

'Twenty-two minutes and counting,' Hannie chortled now as Emma pitched up at her desk.

Every morning Hannie kept track of how long Patrick, the co-presenter on *Wake Up Ireland*, spent in make-up. He always got in before everybody else, carrying a latte and an armful of newspapers, and got worked on by his 'girls', Trish and Wendy. Admittedly, they had quite a task. While Patrick was considered gorgeous by some, he was also very dark and extremely hirsute. Rumour had it that he got a back, sack and crack wax every six weeks, along with the backs of his hands, but even at that you could see wiry black hairs creeping out from under his shirtsleeves and over his wrists by about week four. Someone said that Trish and Wendy beat his eyebrows back through regular plucking, but they refused to either confirm or deny this. Patrick was clever; he ensured their loyalty and silence through massive L'Occitane hampers at Christmas and exclusive concert tickets at regular monthly intervals in between.

Anyhow, he emerged every morning from make-up buffed and glowing and expertly covered in the finest pan-stick money could buy. There was scarcely any time left for Alannah, his co-presenter, and God knows, if anybody needed a bit of colour in their cheeks it was her. She was one of those English-rose types, and because she never gave Trish and Wendy anything at Christmas, she sometimes came out looking suspiciously orange, or with two crude dollops of blusher on her cheeks, like Mr Plod.

Patrick had got there first that morning too, it seemed.

'Vainer than Ivana Trump,' Hannie declared, looking at her watch again to see if the twenty-two minutes had turned into twenty-three.

But when Emma failed to raise a snigger, and hadn't done for weeks now, Hannie looked at her and pulled a very sympathetic face and said, 'Why don't we lay off Patrick for a while? Just until you're feeling a bit better?'

Emma tried to look grateful, as though feeling better was actually a possibility, even in the distant future. She simply couldn't imagine it. But you got used to anything, didn't you? In six months' time she'd be waking in an empty bed and it wouldn't knock a bother out of her. In fact, she might even enjoy it. 'What's in the papers?'

Very brave, Hannie had called her in the pub last Friday. To keep giving a shite about what was in the papers, after what had happened. *She* wouldn't do it. She'd be at home with her head in the cooker. Well, probably not. But she'd be devastated. She'd probably have to take a week off work and fly somewhere sunny and drink her head off. And she didn't even *drink*. Well, she did, but only socially, not like the other animals around here who sucked Searson's dry every Friday afternoon — not naming anybody, but Phil and Loose Lucy were prime examples. You vould think the way they downed gin and tonics 'at they were producing documentaries on, say, 1cer or children in care, instead of blooming 'kfast telly — no offence, but it was hardly ' to win an award for the most meaningful of television ever made.

rally, she didn't say any of this in front of Patr or Alannah, and especially not Adam O'Reilly, the Controller of Programmes, and therefore of all of their lives.

Emma, on the other hand, had heard it many times before. She and Hannie had remained friends since the day they'd met in college. They'd gone on to share a flat together — a disaster, given Hannie's dietary habits and her love of true crime documentaries — before working together on and off for six years on various programmes. There had been a brief separation when Hannie had emigrated to Australia, only to arrive back within six months,

48

traumatised by all the sun. And then *Wake Up Ireland* had thrown them together again.

'Sometimes I feel like I'm your lover,' Hannie often complained. 'I have absolutely no impetus to go out and find a boyfriend, because I always have you to offload emotionally on, and for bitching sessions. If I end up old and single, it'll be all your fault.'

'We can be old and single together,' Emma always assured her, 'because I have no boyfriend either.'

But that was before Emma had met Ryan, and had 'dropped all her friends', according to Hannie. It wasn't intentional. She'd just fallen so hopelessly in love that she'd barely noticed anybody else. She started to do things she'd never done before, like giggle helplessly to herself at work, and wear the colour pink. 'You're making a fool of yourself,' Hannie had hissed the morning she'd worn a jaunty hat into the studio. But of course Hannie was completely pissed off at having been unceremoniously dumped for the gorgeous Ryan. She'd put on a brave face for a month, but when it became clear that the love affair was going to last longer than that, there had been unseemly scenes of petulance and jealous rage. Hannie had to accept it in the end — she had no choice; Emma and Ryan were in love. Hannie had even begun the grim task of finding a boyfriend of her own. It wasn't pleasant, it wasn't easy, but it had to be done.

Then came the announcement of the engagement, and they barely seeing each other six months.

'Are you mad?' Hannie had demanded.

'Probably,' Emma had said doing that giggling thing again. Oh, if only everybody could be as happy as she was!

'You just said that out loud,' Hannie had pointed out, coldly.

Emma had tried to tone it down a bit after that, swallowing back her manic giggles, especially at budget meetings with the Financial Controller. But all she could think of was Ryan, and the great big rock on her finger (he never did things by halves) and whether he would want a white wedding and all that lark. It turned out that he did.

Then, suddenly, a month ago, the whole thing went belly up. They hadn't even got round to discussing the honeymoon.

'Are you *serious?*' Hannie had been shocked. So shocked that it hadn't occurred to her yet that Emma was single again, and thus available for nights out and impromptu mad weekends away.

'It was mutual,' Emma said dully. She'd said it so often in the last few days that she was nearly starting to believe it.

'*Mutual?*' Hannie screeched. She knew a big fat cover-up when she heard one. 'Come on, Emma, this is *me*.'

But Emma didn't say any more. Not even when Hannie took her off to the pub and poured gin and tonics down her, and said encouragingly, 'I never liked him anyway,' even though she had.

'Look, Hannie, I know you mean well. But I just can't talk about it. Not yet.'

'I understand. Take your time. No rush.'

But that was a whole *month* ago. And Emma still hadn't spilled the beans. Hannie was nearly bursting. She kept darting concerned (in other words, rabidly curious) glances at Emma, and she had a box of tissues strategically positioned on the edge of her desk, in case Emma should break at any moment. She probably figured that if she bided her time, all the nastiest, juiciest details, the what-that-fucker-said, and the what-I-said-back, would eventually be hers. What crockery was thrown, that kind of thing. It was just a question of time.

And Emma often wished it had been as simple as that: a few chipped mugs chucked at each other, a few insults along the lines of, 'I'd rather have sex with my Rotating Rabbit any day,' and maybe a door taken off its hinges on the way out. Just your normal, clean, old-fashioned break-up. Emma would have cried for a bit, and put on half a stone. Then, about a month or so later, she would have dusted herself off, no real harm done.

But no, Ryan couldn't have done the decent thing and slept with her best friend, or siphoned off ten grand from her savings account. She could have handled that. Well, perhaps not, but at least she'd have had twenty girlfriends to whom these exact things had happened, sometimes simultaneously, and she could have sought their advice, and cried her heart out, and got over it.

Ryan didn't do simple. Everything had to be complicated. Have ramifications. And now she was left with a broken engagement, a pile of curious friends and relatives, and she had no idea how to get her own head around what had happened, never mind explain it to them.

'The papers?' she prompted Hannie again, ignoring the box of tissues Hannie was discreetly pushing towards her across the desk. She just didn't take no for an answer.

'Oh. Right.' Hannie sighed. She rooted about through the pile of broadsheets and tabloids scattered about her desk and extracted a short, typed list that went as follows:

Thirty-four-stone man too heavy to get to
the shops has to be winched out through
second-floor window.
Nineteen-foot pet python by the name of
Fluffy escapes from house in Limerick.
Public are warned not to approach it.
Pineapples may hold the key to impotence.

'They're absolutely awful,' Emma declared.

'I know,' Hannie said, delighted.

Just after the seven o'clock news on *Wake Up Ireland* every morning, Patrick and Alannah went through the newspapers, picking out stories of importance or interest that Hannie had already briefed them on. The policy was to 'go easy' on (in other words, avoid) anything involving recessions or budgets, as that tended to put people in a bad mood for the day. Instead they stuck to the weird and wonderful, embracing crazy new diets and multiple-birth stories.

'Five babies! I'll tell you, I wouldn't do it, Alannah,' Patrick had confided on air that particular day. He had delicately crossed his legs and flashed a pained look at the camera. 'Not since I've had the operation, anyway.'

He'd played it perfectly; just enough to get the laugh, but not enough that people thought they were watching an episode of *Benny Hill*. Alannah, meanwhile, had looked at the camera with one thinly arched eyebrow that said, 'See? This is the kind of stupid, laddish crap I have to put up with on a daily basis,' but always with a twinkle in her eye. Well, she was supposed to, anyway. Recently she had lost her twinkle a bit; a lot of the time she looked like she meant it. Emma must have a little word; tell her to lighten up a bit.

Her phone rang. She knew without looking that it was Ryan. He knew her routine too well — what was the best time to get her, what was the worst. Recently he'd taken to phoning her just before they went on air, no doubt hoping that that she'd be so frazzled that she might answer it without checking the caller display.

As if. When she'd said she never wanted to speak to him again, she'd meant every word of it. She carefully scrutinised her phone, while Hannie pretended to mind her own business.

'Is it him?' Hannie could never last long.

'No.'

Emma didn't recognise the number. Maybe he was using a different phone. And maybe, just maybe, she was getting a tad paranoid.

'Hello?' she said into the phone, frosty just in case.

'Emma? Emma, is that you? Can you hear me? There's an awful lot of — '

'Ali? Is that you?'

There was a scuffling sound in the background, and possibly a yelp of pain. 'I'm back! Look, I'm sorry to be ringing you at work.' She sounded a bit strange. Wired, or excited or something. 'The thing is, I have a bit of a favour to ask.'

Emma loved Ali. Adored her. Sometimes she still woke in the middle of the night and automatically looked across towards the window, as though Ali was there in her narrow, single bed. But when Ali rang up looking for a favour, which she'd done many, many times over the years since the rat episode, it was usually not a good thing. The fact that she was downplaying it to a 'bit of a favour' was actually more alarming.

'Yes . . . ?' Emma said.

Out of the corner of her eye she registered the clock. Five minutes to six. In thirty-five minutes the show went on air.

'The thing is, we've decided to come back for a little break, me and the kids.' Ali had on her chirpy, bright voice, the one she'd been using since childhood to hide a big, fat mess. 'And I was wondering — if it wasn't too much trouble — whether we could stay with you?'

Emma's mind ricocheted from the studio clock to her apartment: had she thrown out those leaflets on the coffee table, the ones Ryan had (helpfully) left for her? Could she bear to walk into the spare bedroom, and clear out the rest of his stuff, which she hadn't got around to yet? And what about sheets? For *four* people. Where would they even sleep?

'Where are you now?' she said, buying time.

She couldn't handle this. Not now. Not with everything.

There was a sheepish pause. 'Outside your flat.'

3

Ali

'Don't touch anything,' Ali warned Erin and Anto. 'Don't even *look* at anything. Just sit quietly on the couch until Auntie Emma gets home.'

They did, for about two minutes, looking around, wide-eyed. They'd been in Emma's apartment before, of course, but rarely beyond the little lobby area at the front in case they broke any of the lovely vases decked around the place, or trod chewing gum into the tasteful cream carpet that ran throughout the flat. Ali would hold them back like a bouncer, while they hopped up and down behind her trying to catch glimpses of the fabulous wonderland that was denied them; plasma tellies, electric reclining chairs, a big bowl of jelly beans on the coffee table, and — wait for it — *a jukebox in the corner that played real music*. It had been part of the studio set of a youth programme Emma had worked on once, and she'd bought it from them when the show had finished. It was from the 1950s, the real deal, and, according to Kyle, who fancied himself a bit of an expert on these things, had probably cost a small fortune. When you put one of the tokens in from the little pile Emma kept on top, the whole thing would burst

56

into life in a blaze of colours and the sounds of Billie Holiday and The Ramones. You could run a club in the place, Anto maintained, seriously.

'Have a go,' Emma would encourage the kids, naïvely holding out the tokens while Ali tried desperately to contain them in the lobby.

Poor Emma. She had no idea what children were really like. Or maybe it was just Ali's children. It would all go swimmingly for about ten minutes until Erin wondered if a marshmallow would fit into the token slot, or Anto began to charge people admission.

'Don't even think about it,' she told Anto softly now, as she saw his eyes fix on the jukebox with intent.

'I'm very sorry to bother you,' Erin piped up beside him. 'But I'm hungry.'

Ali looked at her.

'I *am*. I haven't had anything to eat since the plane. And that was horrible.'

She was still in her pink pyjamas, and managed to look both adorable and highly disapproving of the situation in which she found herself.

'Do you think you can hang on?' Ali pleaded.

She didn't want to go into Emma's kitchen. Wasn't that mad? It would feel like poking around or something. Not that Emma would have minded. After her initial hesitancy on the phone earlier, which was understandable, given that it was the crack of dawn and she was at work, she couldn't have been more accommodating. She'd insisted that Ali find the spare key that she'd attached via a glob of Blu-Tack to the underside of the electricity meter outside the apartment block.

'Anal,' Erin had commented to Anto. 'She should just leave it under the mat, like Mom does.'

Emma had encouraged Ali to settle herself and the kids in.

'Help yourself to anything — tea, coffee, have a shower if you want. Just make yourselves at home.'

Foolish words. That was practically an invitation to trash the place. Ali thought of her own house now, the one they'd finally got around to building a mile from Hal and Ethel's (though Ali would have preferred the next state). It was American-style big, with a double garage and a swimming pool out the back. Lest anybody get too excited, the pool was freezing most of the time, and there was usually green stuff floating on top that Anto loudly blamed on other people peeing. The double garage was so full of broken bikes and televisions that you couldn't even get one car in, never mind two. The latest addition was a double rowing machine that Kyle had bought in the zeal that had accompanied his New Year's resolution a couple of years back to shed two stone and get fit. 'We'll do it together,' he told Ali. 'Me in front and you in back. It'll be romantic.'

How he thought she was going to experience a rush of love gazing at his portly back as he invited a coronary was anybody's guess. Perhaps it had been said in humour. Yes. Probably. So she'd laughed like a drain and then he'd put on that whipped-dog look that she couldn't stand, and then *she* got hurt. How dare he imply she needed to lose weight? We'll do it together, indeed. She still had the same figure as when they'd met, kind of. He was the one who'd let everything slide.

So that was the story of the rowing machine. The main house contained the rest of the spoils: including overstuffed cushions, a life-sized baby doll that Erin had got for Christmas once, and an enormous fridge-freezer in the kitchen with an ice compartment and a built-in water filter, and that often took Ali both hands to open. It continually hummed and whirred in the corner like a plane about to take off. Even when Ali lay in their massive repro four-poster bed upstairs, she could hear the damn thing throbbing two floors beneath her.

You couldn't call any of it classy. Just big. And more than a little dirty since Aranchez, their maid, had left a couple of months ago to go to the McArthurs' down the block. They still weren't sure of Anto's role in that. On the plus side, with her gone, at least Ali could drink a cup of coffee without worrying that it might spill over onto the carpet, sending Aranchez into a silent strop.

'I'm afraid I'm still hungry,' Erin announced at last. 'I tried, but my stomach is rumbling.'

'Right,' said Ali, in resignation. 'Don't move until I'm back.'

★ ★ ★

59

Did Emma not have any actual *food* in her kitchen? Ali gingerly opened another press, to be confronted by boxes of raisins and two tins of chickpeas. (What *was* a chickpea, anyway? The picture on the front made them look like little arses.) The fridge was worse: a wasteland of probiotic yoghurt drinks and some kind of fancy cheese with a thick rind on it that would have Anto making loud puking noises.

Probably she should have gone to Mam's instead, as usual. But think of all the *explanations*. Where was Kyle, why weren't the kids in school, how long was she planning to stay? And then there would be the endless debate over where to sleep them all, and Mam fussing around with those white lace things on the back of the sofas, the yokes that looked like doilies. And then there was Dad and his health problems, and oh, it all became a headache.

Emma would need an explanation too, of course. But at least she wouldn't go telling Ali she was foolish and selfish, and that the best thing to do would be to go back to Texas with her tail between her legs. She hoped, anyway.

The thing was, Ali wasn't entirely sure *what* Emma would say. And that was the crux of why she was nervous at being in the flat. It was more than just a fear that the kids would set the place on fire. (Was Anto still on the couch? Yes. Phew.) It just seemed a long time since she and Emma had been close. *Really* close, the way they used to be. It wasn't that they'd fallen out of contact or anything; they still spoke on the phone a lot, and Emma came over maybe once every year or

60

two, and then of course they caught up when Ali and the family were back on the annual trip home.

These weeks were always busy, though, and flew by. There were so many old school friends to see, and relatives that might not be around this time next year. They nearly always were, though, and had to be visited, even if the greeting had now descended to, 'Uncle Paul — still here?'

And then there was Dad. Nobody ever said it out loud, but the thorny subject of How Long Will He Be Around was a constant family concern. He'd had another heart attack in September — his fifth now; he was becoming something of a local celebrity. Everyone was getting used to the breathless phone calls from Mam in the middle of the night announcing that they were in the hospital right now and they were trying to get hold of a priest. By number five, the priest had given up coming, and Mam began taking sandwiches to the hospital.

'Will I come home?' Ali had asked, on number five. She'd come home on numbers one, two and four.

'You know, I wouldn't bother my barney,' Mam had decided after some consideration.

She'd already declared she wasn't ringing anybody in the middle of the night when he had the next one, she would just text the following morning after everybody had had their breakfast.

Ali still liked to stick close to the house when she was home on holiday. Just in case. Emma would come over in the evenings, and the chat would revolve around her job in television, and any behind-the-scenes gossip she might be willing to impart.

'Noel!' Mam would reach over and poke Dad. 'She's going to talk about Gay Byrne.'

'I never *mentioned* Gay Byrne,' Emma would protest.

'Well, you're going to have to now,' Mam would insist. 'I've got him all excited.'

And indeed Dad would be trying to pull himself up in his chair, and licking dry lips; the most interested he'd been all evening. All week, really, bless him.

'We don't even work for the same television station — how do you expect me to know anything about Gay Byrne?'

'Yes, but don't you all go to the same parties?' Mam leaned over and said to Ali, with great relief, 'That one who does the clothes programme has to wear control pants, Emma says.'

Ali tried not to take offence at being sidelined. Emma *did* have an interesting job. And Ali could hardly talk about hers, seeing as she didn't have one. The last time she'd worked was back in Boston, in Macy's, before she'd got pregnant. There had been a few bits and pieces for Kyle over the years as well, like that time Louise was out for a month with a slipped disc, and Ali got to sit at her desk and say into the phone, 'Good afternoon, Peterson's Plastics!' It had been peculiarly satisfying.

'Lunch, tomorrow, just the two us?' she would say to Emma, when Mam and Dad had eventually been palmed off with a detailed account of how awful the newsreaders *really* looked without makeup, and they'd been able to escape to the kitchen for a sneaky glass of wine.

'Yes. Definitely. Tomorrow,' Emma would agree.

That was dependent on kids, of course, and elderly parents, and whether Emma had a crisis at work, which seemed to happen with great regularity.

Then last summer Emma had hardly been around. Like, at all. And with very little explanation. One minute she was there, sitting in front of the TV with Mam and Dad and the kids, and explaining to everybody how dirt doesn't really get picked up by the cameras — 'Very handy,' said Mam, enviously — and the next minute her phone would ring and she'd be out the door like someone off to collect her next fix.

'Never mind,' Ali would tell Mam and Dad consolingly. 'You'll just have to listen to me.'

'Oh,' Dad would say, bad-tempered.

'Where is she gone, anyway?'

Mam and Dad would look at each other with a shrug. 'She never tells us anything.'

Nor Ali any more, it seemed.

★ ★ ★

'She's got a new man,' Liam informed her.

Ali was stunned. Even *Liam* knew; Liam, whom everybody for years had thought was going through teen hormonal hell, only for them to realise eventually that he really was a taciturn, cynical grump who liked nothing better than to be left alone. This would have been fine had he not gone and married Tina, a woman who could be heard three streets away, and who spent her life organising rowdy get-togethers. Liam still wasn't sure how he'd ended up with her, except that when she had first laid eyes on his thin, miserable face she said she'd instantly been reminded of Oliver Twist.

That day she was throwing their summer barbecue party, and seemed to have invited most of North Dublin.

'Coming through, coming through.' Her voice was part fog-horn, part SpongeBob Square Pants. She shouldered her way through the crowd, carrying aloft a big platter of burgers swimming in blood. If it dipped just another inch to the left Mam and Dad would look like extras from *Nightmare on Elm Street*.

'Make sure they're done right the way through, will you?' she said to Ali, plonking the tray down. (Hello? Since when had Ali been in charge of the barbecue?) 'We don't want people to get food poisoning like last time.' She tugged down her shocking-pink T-shirt and hissed, 'He's just arrived.'

'Who?'

'Emma's new man. I heard you and Liam talking.'

'Radar ears,' Liam told Ali. 'If I want to have a private conversation on my phone I have to go up the Dublin Mountains.'

'Don't be stupid, nobody ever rings your phone,' Tina pointed out kindly. She turned back to Ali. 'You haven't met him yet — Ryan

— because he spends a lot of time travelling for work. He's a news photographer.' She sounded very impressed. 'He's only just come back from some assignment in South Africa.'

Big swing, thought Ali. *She'd* been to South Africa. Or, at least, she'd got all the brochures, but Kyle couldn't be persuaded; the distance, the crime rate, blah, blah. It had been Florida as usual that year.

And all right, fine, so this new lad of Emma's might have been unavailable for family meet-and-greets due to his very important job, but there was nothing stopping Emma *telling* her about him, was there? Just a simple, 'Oh, I'm going out with someone new. His name is Ryan and he seems pretty nice.' Nothing wrong with that.

Unless he was twice her age, of course. Or married. Or otherwise undesirable.

'There's nothing . . . this guy is *normal*, right?'

Tina threw back her head and laughed like a drain. Several small children looked over, worried. 'Normal as you and me, and absolutely gorgeous, isn't he, Liam?'

'Stunning,' he agreed. 'Now can we stop yapping and get those burgers on before the guests start picking on the weakest?'

Can Ali get the burgers on, he meant, while he and Tina fecked off back to the house, no doubt to crack open a nice cold beer. Unbelievable.

She was just flipping the first batch, and coughing her lungs out, when Emma came up to her in some kind of floaty pink dress.

'Is that *you*?' Ali said, through the gales of

smoke, just to be sure. Emma normally wore cool, tasteful clothes in various shades of beige.

'What are you trying to do to those burgers?' Emma enquired.

And look at her *hair*. The last place it had seen was a pillow, Ali guessed, judging by the big rat's nest wedged into the back of it.

Huh. Ryan, no doubt.

'You didn't tell me,' she said baldly. It was hard not to sound hurt.

At least Emma didn't pretend that she didn't know what Ali was talking about. 'It's very new, Ali. I didn't really tell anybody.'

'Oh, bollocks. Liam knew.'

Emma gave a big sigh. 'All right, fine, I *didn't* tell you. Because you'd have done your level best to find fault with him.'

'I would not have!'

'You did with Keith a year ago.'

'Yeah, well, with a name like Keith . . . '

'There you go!'

'And he was a gynaecologist,' Ali went on doggedly. 'I've said it once and I'll say it again: what kind of a man — '

'Oh, shut up.' Emma sounded really cross. 'I haven't had a single boyfriend in the past ten years that you haven't managed to say something bad about.'

'I liked Jerry.'

'No, you didn't. You just pretended to like him because you knew that I was going to finish with him anyway, and liking him made you look less totally unreasonable.'

Ali thought she'd been quite clever about it,

but obviously not. 'Look, Emma, you're my sister. I just want the best for you. That's all.'

Don't throw your life away on the wrong man like I did and spend the next fucking fifteen years regretting it, was what she really wanted to bawl from the rooftops. But it would be most unseemly behaviour at a family barbecue and so she went back to flipping burgers. They were incinerated on the underside. Shit. Still, nobody would notice once they were in a burger bun.

'I really like Ryan, Ali,' Emma said eventually. She was using her stern producer's voice, which always reminded Ali a bit of Gordon Gekko. 'I hope you will too.' She turned to say over her shoulder, 'And if you don't, you can bloody well keep it to yourself.'

'Sure thing. Will do,' Ali muttered, suitably intimidated, whilst thinking, yes, well, we'll see about that.

She was flinging more burgers onto the barbecue in a bad-tempered fashion when she realised she hadn't seen the kids in over an hour. Normally this would be a cause for celebration, as they were usually incapable of amusing themselves for more than ten minutes without adult intervention. But it was different in someone else's house. It was worrying.

'Erin? Anthony?' she called, raking a meaty hand through her heat-frazzled hair as she hunted through the garden. This wasn't a big job. Liam had bought at the height of the boom, and had got a modest four-bedroom semi with a pocket-sized garden for his troubles. She let out a bellow now. 'Erin!' Wouldn't you think that

Jack, at least, would have told her if they'd planned on getting a bus home? When she got her hands on them . . .

The other guests were parting like the Red Sea to let her through. Liam's sister from America, she heard someone say, as though that explained everything.

They weren't in the kitchen either, or the living room, or doing an experiment with toothpaste in the bathroom. Her hand was on the phone, about to stab out 999, when she heard the squeals of laughter.

They were in the garage, which Liam had converted into a den, and they were being attacked. Oh sweet Jesus. A man — a tall man — had Jack pinioned under him while the other hand grabbed Erin — only a baby! — and tossed her into the air like a rag doll, while she squealed dementedly.

'Stop it!' Ali screamed.

Nobody heard her. Anto, bless him, now launched himself at the bad man with a terrific cry of, 'Take that!' (brave boy!) but the man just laughed, the monster, and fended Anto off easily with one bare foot.

OK, the bare foot was unusual. You didn't normally encounter too many child-molesters with bare feet. And a T-shirt with 'Save the Dolphins' on it. But just because he had a conscience didn't make it OK.

'You want more?' the man was taunting Jack.

Jack tried to squirm free, laughing. *Laughing*. It must be the shock. He'd been fourteen then, and big, too big to engage in horseplay, and Kyle

x

68

had given up years ago, so this *must* be an attack.

'Yee-*haw*,' Anto screamed, and launched himself at the man again with a fierce karate chop.

The man smiled and brought Anto to the ground with one practised move. 'Squirt,' he said.

That was *it*. Ali filled her lungs with air and bellowed, 'Stop it right now!'

Utter silence.

'That's our mom,' Erin said, with a gloomy sigh.

She climbed off the man. Anto got to his feet. Jack unpeeled himself from the carpet. They were all looking at her like she was the anti-Christ.

'And you are . . . ?' Ali enquired of the man, even though she already knew. She knew *everything* about this guy from a glance, thanks to his bare feet and khaki shorts (if you turned them inside out they probably became a sleeping bag) and his T-shirt-with-a-conscience. He had a discreet yet painfully cool tattoo on his upper arm — probably more dolphin stuff or else the name of some beautiful girl who had tortured his soul some years back. The whole lot was topped off with spiky hair, intense blue eyes, and a tan from the searing African sun.

Poor Emma. Poor, poor Emma. He was part Boy Scout, part Indiana Jones, and had one foot permanently on a plane.

'Ryan,' he said, carefully. Well, his bush instincts were probably so well honed over the years that he could recognise naked hostility at a hundred paces. 'And you must be Ali. Emma's told me about you.'

'Really? She hasn't mentioned you.'

She had meant this as a crushing confidence-shaker.

But Ryan just countered with, 'Your kids are great.' He sounded sincere.

'Oh. You can have them if you want.'

'Someday you're going to say that once too often, and we'll leave you, and you'll be so sorry that you'll top yourself,' Erin warned her sternly.

Ryan flexed his fingers at her threateningly, and she immediately squealed in mock terror and clutched her tummy.

'Hi-yaw!' Anto shouted again from behind them, no doubt hoping to entice Ryan onto the floor again.

'I think Ryan has had enough for one day,' Ali called sternly. 'They can be very rough,' she informed him. He might look the part, but it was highly likely that once you scratched the surface you discovered his foreign assignments generally involved stays in five-star hotels, peppered with sedate tourist excursions.

'Ryan's Jeep broke down in Somalia once and they all had to live in the bush for five days,' Anto piped up.

She would swear that he did it to spite her.

'Oh. Well, I'm sure Ryan had ample supplies — '

'He didn't. They had to collect rainwater, and trap and skin rats in the bush.' This was Jack. He sounded mighty impressed.

'I'm sure rat meat isn't too bad,' Ali said in a jolly voice. She wondered what other merry tales Ryan had been filling their heads with.

'How come we only ever go to Florida? Or Dublin?' Jack said accusingly. 'There're wars on all over the world, in countries we couldn't even point out on a map.'

Ali looked at Ryan: thanks a lot, buddy.

'A lot of these places you can't go to,' he said quickly to Jack.

'But you do.'

'That's because it's my job.'

'I'm going to have a job like that someday,' Jack resolved. 'Something that makes a difference.'

Oh, great. So now he was going to head off to some hellhole at eighteen and get his head blown off. Little did he know that his father had a job lined up for him at Peterson's Plastics.

'If you're quite finished . . . ' she said to Ryan acidly, before grabbing the kids and turning on her heel.

★ ★ ★

The kids eventually came looking for Ali in the kitchen, still starving.

'I'll just have some pretzels,' Anto informed her.

'I told you, there are no pretzels. Just toast.' She'd eventually found a loaf of bread.

'Peanuts?'

'Just toast, Anto.'

A flounce. 'I wish I was at home.'

71

'You *are* home.'

It always drove Kyle wild, the way Ali forced them all to refer to Ireland as 'home'. 'The kids were born and bred in America, *this* is their home — will you stop trying to convince everybody we're only in Texas on an extended holiday?' But Ali had persisted in her relentless promotion of the auld sod. Under her auspices, St Patrick's Day became the family's biggest annual celebration, even though the kids were the only ones in school wearing enormous leprechaun hats, and were beginning to resent it. She also spoke to them occasionally *as Gaeilge*, though her own knowledge of the language was, to say the least, poor. But they knew how to say hello in Irish (*Dia dhuit*), goodbye (*slán*) and, of course, *feck*, *shite*, and *skanger*. At bathtime, when they'd been small, instead of singing 'Twinkle, Twinkle, Little Star', she had them belting out the Irish national anthem instead. The only problem was the words, which nobody was a hundred per cent sure about. In the end they just used '*Twinkle, Twinkle*', and it sounded so lovely sometimes that Ali cried.

The last couple of years Kyle hadn't come home with them. Not for the barbecue last summer, or when Dad had had heart attack number whatever the previous summer.

Emma must have noticed. Everybody else had. Yet she hadn't said anything. And Emma always knew how to handle things. She was the best handler of things that Ali had ever met. She was always pushed to the front at funerals, for instance, because she instinctively knew what to

72

say to the bereaved, usually something thoughtful and sympathetic, while everybody else looked at their shoes or blurted out something inappropriate such as, 'When exactly did he start getting into auto-erotic asphyxiation?'

Yet she hadn't mentioned Kyle's absence even once. Ali was both hurt and relieved. It would have been nice to have been able to come clean, and say, 'God, yes, I'm glad you brought it up, because do you know what? Things have been absolutely shite.' But another part of her didn't want to admit it to anybody, not even Emma.

'Move it.' Jack huffed past Anto into the kitchen and unceremoniously dumped a massive suitcase at Ali's feet. Ali had sent him out to the hire car to bring it in, like, *ages* ago.

'Hey,' said Anto, giving Jack a dig back.

'What the fuck?' Jack was really riled up now, and he got Anto in a headlock. Given that he was a foot and a half taller, and three stone heavier, meant that this was probably very painful.

'Let him go,' Ali ordered.

'Not until he says sorry.'

Anto was slowly but surely going pink. No, purple.

'*Now,*' Ali bellowed.

Jack reluctantly released him. Anto lay on the floor for moment, coughing and spluttering.

'What's the matter with you?' he complained, panting. Then, in a nah-nah-*nah*-nah-nah voice, he said, 'Jack's missing his girlfriend, Jack's missing his girlfriend — '

'You little shit!'

73

In the end Ali had to stand between them with a wooden spoon.

'Any more and you can go cool down in the car,' she told Jack. 'And watch your language, too.'

'In fairness, we get it from you,' Anto piped up reasonably.

'Out,' Ali ordered, pointing to the living room.

When it was just her and Jack, she took in his red, agitated face. 'Is there something the matter, Jack?'

They'd always had great chats, her and him. Of the three kids, she felt she had a special bond with him. She considered him more 'Irish' than the other two, even though that was daft, she knew.

He said nothing.

'Is it Anto?' she prodded. 'Don't mind him.' A month ago, Anto had been calling Jack fat and that had really got under his skin too.

'I want to know how long we're staying for,' Jack said abruptly.

Ali looked at his tense face and she smiled and reached out to run a finger down his cheek. 'It's OK,' she said. 'I spoke to your teacher.'

'What?'

'About your biology test. I called her earlier. She says it's OK, it was only a mock test anyhow, and that you're so bright that you can easily afford to miss one. So you can relax.'

He'd be delighted. He always loved coming to Ireland, and now that the pressure was off from school, at least for a little while, he

74

would give her one of his big smiles.

Except that he didn't. He glared at her. 'You're so dumb sometimes, Mom,' he threw at her, before walking out.

4

Emma

Emma had no idea what children normally ate for lunch. Especially American children. Was it all hot dogs, and peanut butter and jelly sandwiches, or would they accept plain ham and cheese on brown bread? Ali was quite liberal with them when it came to food, Emma had noted. All right, she was totally crap. She didn't seem to mind *what* they ate, or at what time. Once, when Emma had been over visiting, Ali had actually given them the leftovers from dinner the night before at breakfast time. Some kind of burrito things. They hadn't acted like this was off the radar either. Emma would bet those three regularly trotted off to school on lasagne and pumpkin pie and the occasional full Sunday roast.

'Who's for cereal?' Ali would then shout at about eight o'clock at night, just about when they should be going to bed.

Weird. But the kids seemed healthy enough, at least from what Emma could see — she could hardly peel back their lips to look at their teeth. Maybe it didn't matter if you ate dinner for breakfast, and breakfast for dinner.

Dinner. Damn. They'd need feeding that night too, wouldn't they? There wasn't so much as a clove of garlic in the fridge. Ever since Ryan had gone she hadn't felt much like eating. Or cooking. Not that she'd ever been any great shakes in that department. Ryan had always done the cooking, wearing that apron with a naked torso on the front, and singing recipes aloud to the tune of Penny Lane: 'Put the e-eggs in a bo-o-wl a-nd whip-them-good . . . '

What was worse was that he genuinely thought he was a great singer.

'You're tone deaf,' she would point out to him repeatedly and insistently.

He would look at her with great compassion. 'You just can't hear it. Listen very carefully. I think you'll find I hit all the right notes.' And he would sing it again for her benefit. In his own head, he sounded like Pavarotti, and she was the one who was acoustically challenged.

He was a good cook, though. It was all those hotel meals he ate when away: 'Chips and more chips, with the odd burger thrown in. It's great.' And he'd patted his belly with satisfaction. 'But you can't keep that up. Not if you want to see fifty. When I get home I like to eat healthily.'

'Such an old fogey. And there was me thinking that you foreign news people were always hanging out of the rafters.' She often slagged him about this.

'Believe me, I did. But my wild days are over.'

'I wish I'd known you when you were wild.'

'Me?' He did his best to pull off a rakish grin. And, actually, he was quite convincing. 'I was a pain in the arse.'

'How?'

'I don't want to tell you in case you finish with me,' he joked. 'Very unreliable. Not earning anything. And certainly not able to cook the way I can now.'

'No false modesty, then.'

He cocked his head to look at her. 'I can't imagine *you* ever being young and unreliable.'

'Hey. I'm still young.'

'You know what I mean.'

What was he implying? That she was an old fart? 'I had my moments,' she bragged.

'Really? Tell me about them.'

Now she was sorry she'd said anything. She didn't want to have to tell him about that sun holiday with Hannie when they'd foolishly drank lots of lethal cocktails at lunchtime, and then Emma had ended up being sick all over the bar, getting them both kicked out.

On balance, her wild days probably weren't any more attractive than his, and so she said, 'You know what? Let's save memory lane for another time.'

And the cooking had been abandoned while they went and untidied her bed. Ryan maintained that she was a neat freak and that it was his mission to mess up her bed as often as possible.

To her left someone prompted loudly, 'Four Boys and a Banjo?', snapping her back to the present.

It was then that she realised that she was in a production meeting, with four people staring at her, and that she very possibly had erect nipples.

She did a quick check. Yes. Lovely.

'Four Boys and a Banjo, you say?' She rustled her papers in a boss-like fashion, and wondering what the fuck the question was. Here she was, still stuck at work while her flat was being overrun in her absence by her sister and kids. Maybe Ali had taken them out to eat. At least Emma hoped so. The last time Anto had been permitted into the flat — only to use the toilet — he'd inflated one of Ryan's condoms, which he'd found in the bathroom cabinet, and twisted it into the shape of a sword.

'They're definitely confirmed?' Patrick prodded her. He was shorter than he looked on screen. He was only about five foot eight, which meant that Alannah, at a willowy five foot nine, had to do a Nicole Kidman on it, and wear flat heels. Some people maintained, always in a whisper, that that was the start of all the trouble.

'Yes.' She'd better sound a bit more excited than that. After all, it was a coup.

But Hannie did it for her. 'They're flying in this afternoon. It's very exciting.'

Four Boys and a Banjo were currently top of the charts. They were the first post-modern boy band, hence the name, even though Emma thought they looked like every other boy band that ever was — there was a cherubic blond one, a cute dark gay one, a tall macho one with pierced body parts, and one that could sing. But apparently they were chock full of irony, and they were in Ireland to sell six concert dates in

79

the O2. *Wake Up Ireland* had got their hands on them first.

Emma consulted her notes again. 'We'll do ten minutes of chat on the couch first.'

'Their PR says there's to be no mention of the band member who left,' Phil chipped in. 'Surprise, surprise.'

'Then they're going to sing their number one live,' Emma finished up.

They weren't really set up for live music. It was going to be an audio nightmare. And the four lads might find it hard to hit those high notes at ten to eight in the morning. They'd just have to go easy on the mini bar in the Merrion Hotel tonight.

'I really like that song,' Alannah remarked to no one in particular.

Across the table Patrick gave a little snort.

Emma counted to three.

'What's that supposed to mean?' Alannah demanded, right on cue. Why, oh, why couldn't she just ignore him?

'Nothing. It's just, like, their music is for eight-year-olds.'

Alannah's cheeks began to glow under the inch of pan-stick. The girls in make-up had gone at her with a heavy hand today, but she still managed to look delicately attractive, despite the deep purple eye shadow and the plaits that they had arranged over the top of her head, making her look like a member of the Von Trapp family. 'Why is it so important to you to put everything into a box?' she demanded of him.

Across the table, Hannie popped a sucky sweet

80

into her mouth and sat back to enjoy the show.

Patrick pushed back his sleeves impatiently. Then, when everybody's eyes went to the thick black rug lining his forearms, he pulled them back down swiftly. 'I just don't see why we have to *like* every fool who ever sets foot on the show. All this, 'Oh, that's marvellous!' and, 'I just *adore* your latest single/book/piece of hand-crafted pottery-that-looks-just-like-a-penis.' ' He said this in a shivery, high-pitched Alannahesque voice, complete with mincing hand movements. Oh Christ. 'Frankly, it's embarrassing.'

And he turned to Emma indignantly.

Hannie's sucky sweet went still in her mouth. This was worse than usual. Normally Patrick contented himself with a few sideways swipes at Alannah, but today he was making it into a production issue.

Emma was raging. Damn him anyway, dragging her into his petty dislike for Alannah. All she wanted to do was wrap up this meeting and go and reclaim her home.

Phil met her eyes across the table now: *Are you going to rein the fucker in or will I?*

She sent him a look back: *Calm down, tiger. I have it under control.*

'Actually, Patrick — ' she began in her big voice.

'Fuck you,' Alannah burst out. 'Not *you*,' she informed Emma hurriedly. 'At least I'm enthusiastic,' she told Patrick furiously. 'Interested! At least I'm not looking at the guests with a stupid, superior smirk on my face like they've got their skirts snagged in their knickers.'

81

Hannie's eyes were going to pop out of her head now. Alannah, being so vicious! Her purple eye shadow was actually looking quite scary now.

Other people were looking up from their lukewarm coffee. There had been rumours from the get go that Alannah Jackson and Patrick Martin didn't get on, but hey, a row in public. Fantastic. This was better than the time that Una, the weather girl, had got off with Anne Marie from HR at the Christmas party. There had been tongues and boob gropes and everything.

There were a few glances in Emma's direction too. Alannah and Patrick, even though they earned ten times what she did, were supposed to be under her control. The two of them having a public scrap during elevenses was seriously not good for her image.

She could feel Phil looking at her again. This time she ignored him. He was only the assistant producer, and sometimes needed reminding of that.

'Let's get back to the schedule, will we?' she said in her iciest voice, which actually *was* quite icy. Small children were sometimes afraid of her.

'Fine with me,' said Patrick, holding his hands up in a 'wasn't my fault, it's that hormonal head-wreck over there sipping her herbal tea' way.

If Patrick was short and had a complex about it, then Alannah was altogether too fond of flowy scarves and peppermint tea and notebooks with Snoopy on the front (she bought them on eBay). Put her next to Patrick, whose five o'clock shadow was already trying to burst through at eleven in the morning, and you had, as they said in the business, an almighty personality clash.

'We go out on Janet Willoughby,' Emma went on crisply, not giving the row a chance to flare up again. 'She's that woman who maintains that she's come back from the dead.'

It was the kind of thing they did well. Patrick would be all polite scepticism — 'The dead, you say? How dead exactly? Had rigor mortis set in? Worms?' Alannah would be wide-eyed and amazed — 'Oh my God. Oh my *God*' — and occasionally clasping a hand to her chest dramatically. This always drove the sound guys crazy, as that was exactly where they'd fixed a microphone on her earlier, and so it sounded like one of her rather large breasts was exploding.

'She's promoting her new book.' It'd be a miracle the day they got a guest who *didn't* have something to promote.

'I've got copies,' Hannie said helpfully, dishing them out. 'It's actually quite good, if you can get past the fact that she maintains Led Zepplin were playing 'Stairway to Heaven' in the background as she was dying. It's just too much of a coincidence, in my opinion.'

Patrick picked up the book, chucked it into his satchel where Emma knew it would languish until five minutes before the show tomorrow morning, and rattled his car keys. He usually went to bed for an hour or so after the show, often with whatever girl he was currently seeing; Emma had given up remembering their names a long time ago.

'I'm off,' he said, nodding around at everybody except Alannah. 'See you in the morning.'

★ ★ ★

In the end Emma stopped at the supermarket on the way home and bought a selection of things for lunch. Oh, and a packet of Kimberley biscuits for Ali. They'd been her favourite since she'd been a child. She would nibble the top off, bit by bit, then the bottom, until just the white, squishy marshmallow circle in the middle was left, which she used to waggle about on her tongue, pretending it was Holy Communion.

'Take those clothes out,' she would order the kids at the end of the annual trip home, just as they were about to depart for the airport. 'I need to fit in these Kimberleys. No, I don't care if that coat is new. This is important.'

'But, *Mom*,' Erin would howl.

Ali always managed to create a bit of aggro, even over a packet of biscuits. Ever since Emma could remember, she'd always known Ali was in the house the minute she walked in the door.

'Sister Lydia is *not* a lesbian, and I don't ever want to hear you saying that in public again,' Mam would be saying agitatedly in the kitchen, addled. 'Oh, hello, Emma,' she would say briefly, before turning back to resume the row.

In one way it was great. Emma hardly ever got into trouble, because Ali was always in so much of it. Not that Emma could be described as a rampant law-breaker or anything. But once she stole a birthday card from Woolworths. Even now the memory made her feel queasy. One minute she'd been queuing like the good citizen that she was, the next she was hoofing it out the door, the card tucked down the front of her school uniform skirt, property so hot that it scalded her knickers. She'd just wanted to know what it felt like.

'It says 'Happy Retirement' on the front of it.' Ali had roared with laughter, when Emma had displayed her spoils. 'You silly goose,' she'd added affectionately, which made Emma feel about as madcap as a tea cosy.

No doubt there was aggravation attached to her sudden visit home too. Some big story. Emma would be greeted at the door with a hug, and a, 'Thank Christ you're back! You'll never guess what's happened. No, really, you won't, will she, kids?'

A pot of tea would be made — no, scratch that, a bottle of wine would be broken open, and the kids would be banished to the bedroom with a DVD, mostly because of Ali's colourful language. Emma would listen, as she couldn't get a word in edgeways, while Ali let it all out, every last gory detail, because she had no censorship button like other people did. She would never think to hold anything back, or, indeed, spare anybody's feelings. And when she'd finished some hours later, and the kids had fallen asleep in their clothes on the bed in front of the DVD, and the bottle of wine had been sucked dry, Ali would finally put down her glass and say cheerily, 'So! Tell me about *you*.'

She didn't mean it. It was just that she was so noisy and brash and full of energy that people who weren't seemed to just melt into the background. And, in Ali's defence, when something serious *did* happen to other people, like Dad's numerous heart attacks, for instance, there was no one better. She was on that plane like a bat out of hell, sorting things out, demanding that Dad give up work, which he had, and that they get in a home help twice a week, which they hadn't. Mam wouldn't countenance another woman around the place 'taking over her spot'.

She'd be the same about Ryan. After the initial, 'How bloody awful, Emma!' she'd swing into action. She'd barge into Emma's life, whether she was wanted or not. 'There are things you need to sort out,' she'd be saying, wagging fingers. 'You can't go burying your head in the sand.' When she'd finished with the clichés, she'd roll up her sleeves, and wouldn't rest until she'd bullied and badgered Emma into things that she just was not ready to do.

The truth was that Emma didn't want Ali in her apartment right now. Unannounced. And with marital problems that Emma didn't want to be dragged into. Kyle hadn't come home the last two summers. Some flimsy excuse about work — as though any of them were expected to believe the world might grind to a halt due to the lack of plastic bags. But Emma had pretended to swallow it for Ali's sake.

The apartment looked suspiciously sedate when Emma pulled in to the front of the

86

building. There was no loud music blaring from the open windows or pizza delivery guys pitching up, which was the usual scene in Ali's house in the States. The only sign that Ali was there at all was her rental car. Emma knew it was Ali's because the driver's window had been left down, and there was a copy of the *National Enquirer* on the dashboard.

Emma rescued the magazine in case it rained. The car was a Volvo saloon — if Kyle had his way, nobody would ever drive anything else — but it was a rather tacky red. Good girl, Ali.

Then the bathroom window flew open, and there was Ali, clad only in a towel.

She waved down so hard that one of her boobs escaped the towel. 'Honey, I'm home!'

5

Ali

'You look great.'

'No, *you* look great.'

'The state of my hair.'

'There's nothing wrong with your hair. It's great. Look at my arse. I've put on loads since you saw me last.'

'You have not.'

'At least five pounds.'

'Stop it. You look great.'

'*You* look great.'

Even the kids were looking at them now, wondering how high the 'great' count would climb. Before Erin could remark on it in her usual candid manner, Ali urged them to go outside and partake of the fresh air.

'The what?' said Anto. Fresh air continued to be an alien concept to him.

'But it's freezing out there,' Erin protested. She had changed out of her pyjamas into a fluffy fleece and pink boots, and looked like an utterly beautiful angel. Her outward appearance often threw strangers; they would bend down to pat her little blonde head and say something completely inoffensive like, 'So! How are you enjoying school?' only to be rewarded with a hard look, and a sigh that said, 'Why do adults never say anything *original* to kids?' They would snatch their hands back in fright and, then, predictably, look at Ali rather accusingly. Why couldn't she have raised *nice* children?

'You'll warm up when you run around a bit,' Ali promised her. 'Jack, will you keep an eye on them?'

This was not a good time to be asking Jack for favours. He threw a look her way that was offended, confused, hurt and judgemental all at the same time. Ali could safely say there wasn't a person in this world who could make her feel worse than Jack could.

Emma may have noticed the chilly atmosphere between mother and son because she promised the kids, 'When you come back in, I'll have made dinner.'

Ali saw them exchange looks: Auntie Emma was great, but, man, *lunch*. Soup (ugh), with bits floating in it, and some kind of bread peppered with lumps that she said were wholegrains. (Were they some distant relation of nuts? Anto had enquired.) And now she was going to be cooking dinner too?

Ali tried to compensate for their lack of enthusiasm by giving Erin a little dig. *Say thank you*, she mouthed encouragingly.

'What?' Erin enquired, puzzled.

Ali swallowed a sigh. 'Have you got something to say to your Auntie Emma?'

Erin obediently turned to Emma. 'Your apartment is kind of small,' she informed her apologetically.

'No. *No*.' Ali slapped a hand to her forehead

in despair. What the . . . ? Erin was wounded. 'But when I said it earlier, before she was home, you said, 'Why don't you tell Auntie Emma that?' '

'I was being *sarcastic*, I didn't mean for you to go and . . . '

All the time she was aware of Emma, smiling politely, trying to pretend that the whole thing was great craic, when inside she must be going, what the fuck was I doing, letting this lot into my life, only to have them insult me and pour my soup down the sink when they thought I wasn't looking?

'Go out. Now,' Ali told Erin with a loving smile and a murderous look in her eye.

There were no flies on Erin. 'Absolutely,' she told her mother fervently. 'We'll stay out from under your feet as long as possible, even if it starts to rain. Do you want your headache pills before we go — '

'No. Thank you.'

Erin fairly legged it out the door, followed by Anto.

Jack paused long enough to give Ali another long, guilt-inducing look. 'We need to talk about your plans,' he told her sternly. He sounded worryingly like Kyle at times.

He went. Ali gave a laugh and said, airily, 'Teens. You'll know all about it someday.'

Emma was giving her a look; the one that said, I know you're lying your size twelve/fourteen arse off because I'm your sister, but I'll bide my time until you come clean.

God, mustn't it be great to have only brothers?

You could maintain three lovers and a robust coke habit and they'd never notice a thing.

'So!' Ali tinkled. Then, she thought, enough of this tinkling. They'd been tinkling all afternoon, covering such subjects as the flight over, and Dad's health, and then Emma would ask what mileage was on the rental car (w.t.f.?).

Emma was going to find out about things sooner or later. Probably when Kyle phoned her up, wondering if she'd heard from his wife. Ali needed to tackle that one head on.

'Look, Emma, I'm sorry to land in on you without any notice.' She checked over her shoulder to make sure the kids really were gone before she continued on. 'The truth is that Kyle and I are having some . . . difficulties.'

'Really?' Emma looked very surprised, as though she hadn't noticed the constant bickering and the snide asides and the way they sometimes referred to each other as 'fatso'. Where on earth had she been for the past year? Ah, yes. Planet Ryan.

'Serious difficulties,' Ali felt she had to add. Well, loads of people had 'difficulties'. Show Ali one marriage where there *weren't* difficulties, and she would show you a con job. Fights, jealousies, resentments, petty rivalries — these were all part and parcel of a normal, healthy marriage, at least from what Ali had deduced from friends. But she and Kyle had gone beyond that. Way beyond. It had got so bad now that they didn't even bother to fight any more.

'I'm really sorry, Ali.' Emma looked very

upset. 'What did he do?' she immediately enquired.

Ali blinked.

'He must have done *something.*' This came out sounding rather judgemental. Bitter, even.

'No . . . I mean, nothing specific.' She had a vision of him chasing some nubile secretary around his desk at the plastic plant, and she wanted to titter viciously. As if.

'Sorry. I didn't mean . . . I just assumed . . . ' The peculiar look had gone from Emma's face, and it was business as usual. 'I just can't believe it. You two have been together for so long.'

About two centuries, or at least that's what it felt like some days.

'It wasn't anybody's fault.' At least that much was the truth. 'We haven't been close in years. It was just one of those things.'

'That sounds like something you picked up from a magazine,' Emma said bluntly.

Just when you thought she was on side.

'All right,' said Ali. Obviously she would have to be clearer. 'We're completely and utterly wrong for each other. We have been from the very start.'

'That's not true.'

More backchat. Honestly. Didn't she realise that Ali was jet-lagged and, frankly, emotional, and could do with just the teeniest bit of support here? Could they not agree that men were useless feckers and head off for a bit of retail therapy?

'You were mad about him,' Emma was insisting now. 'All those letters you wrote about

92

him in the beginning, do you remember?'

'Well, yes — '

'How handsome and kind and funny he was, how you couldn't wait to marry him despite being up the duff, and what a fantastic father he was going to make?'

'I was trying to make the best of a bad situation — hey, you're not still *keeping* those letters, are you?'

'Yes, I read them every night before I go to bed,' Emma said with great sarcasm.

'Sorry. I didn't mean to suggest you had no life,' Ali said humbly.

'Thank you. Although a lot of the time I don't.'

Ali shook her head in disgust. 'Are they still making you get up at four o'clock in the morning?'

'Yes. That's why it's called a breakfast show.'

'And could you not move to something a bit more civilised? Like, say, the after-lunch show?'

'I'm very happy where I am.'

Well, if the big long miserable face on her was anything to go by . . . When Ali had told her earlier that she was looking great, she'd been lying. Check out those bags under her eyes, and was she on some kind of mad diet? Her neck was scrawny and her chest flatter than Anto's. Ali felt like a rhino sitting at the other end of the couch, which, she was only now noticing, was listing embarrassingly in her direction. And she was *normal* sized. Well, by American standards, which were always comfortingly more elastic than anybody else's.

'If you're having problems with Kyle, should you not, like, be at home trying to sort them out?' Emma enquired. Instead of gadding about the globe and keeping her kids out of school, she might as well have added.

Feeling under attack, Ali sat up as straight as she could on her end of the sagging sofa. 'I didn't want to have to say this,' she began with dignity.

'Oh, just spit it out.'

'Fine. Kyle and I are divorcing.'

★   ★   ★

Talk about a conversation stopper.

Emma was still looking shocked five minutes later. No doubt she'd thought that Ali had had a petty row with Kyle and had flounced off home in a temper until he begged her to come back.

But a divorce . . . well, that was serious. It was break-open-a-bottle-of-wine time, which, thank God, Emma did now, in silence.

'Are you OK?' she asked Ali quietly, as she poured two humongous glasses.

'Yes. I'm fine. It's been coming for a long time really,' Ali said very philosophically. 'Cheers.'

And then she burst into tears; big, horrible hiccuping sobs, complete with runny nose and snorts. She had, unfortunately, never cried in an attractive way.

Not that that mattered now. Her marriage was over. This wasn't the first time she'd realised it — she'd had an inkling on her wedding night when Kyle had turned on the television after

94

they'd had sex — but it was the first time she'd really cried over it. There hadn't been a chance in the sixteen years before, what with giving birth three times and doing the weekly grocery run and, in recent years, Kyle's mother, who had broken her hip and had to be washed and dressed every morning because her home help was a *man*, and Ethel wouldn't let him near her.

'I'm so sorry, Ali.'

And then Emma leaned over and put her arms around Ali. No doubt she'd thought it would be a normal, brief contact, finished up by a squeeze of the shoulder, maybe. But Ali clung onto her like a drowning woman, and when she tried to get away, Ali just squeezed tighter, a bit like a boa constrictor. Emma was far too polite to pull away, so she just sat there quietly while Ali mauled her person and bawled into her shoulder.

'It's going to be all right,' Emma tried again.

'No, it's fucking not. It's a disaster.'

She buried her head in Emma's neck again. The familiar smell of her was great. Ali remembered it most keenly from the times they would huddle together in the same narrow single bed and talk about which of the Hardy Boys they fancied more — Parker Stevenson, definitely. The other guy looked a bit of a wuss. Emma refused to have any truck with either of them, and insisted she fancied Nancy Drew instead. Ali remembered that Emma always smelled of Palmolive soap and, curiously, lemons, although they only ever had them in the house at Christmastime in case any callers wanted a gin and tonic.

Ali opened her nostrils now and gave a deep sniff. So comforting, even if the Palmolive and lemons had been replaced with Molton Brown (Ali had had a good root in the bathroom presses earlier).

'O-K.' Emma was trying to foist her off now.

Ali disentangled herself reluctantly. 'Sorry.'

They drank their wine in silence for a minute. Well, Ali sank hers, while Emma, bless her, took occasional teensy sips so that Ali wouldn't feel like a total lush.

'You never know,' Emma said. 'You might work things out.'

Yes, in Teletubbyland, maybe. This was the real world. But Ali had to remind herself again that Emma was engaged, and so on a different planet altogether. Let her say that in ten years' time. Or maybe five, when the gorgeous Ryan still hadn't learned the art of picking his underpants up off the floor and putting them into the laundry bin.

When Ali didn't bother replying, Emma took a different tack. 'How about the kids? How are they coping?'

This was a tricky one. Ali was tempted to sugar-coat this, too. But what if Emma came out with something in front of them? Not that she would. All the same, Ali couldn't take the chance of them discovering that they were, in fact, from a broken home over Emma's awful soup.

'We haven't actually told them yet,' she confessed. Before Emma could condemn her, she said, 'We only came to the decision ourselves last week. There just hasn't been the right time.'

She had always planned that they would do it together; sit down all civilised at the family table after dinner some night, and confess that Mom and Dad just didn't want to be married to each other any more, and from now on would be living in separate houses. Hey, wouldn't that be fun! They wanted the kids to know that it was absolutely nothing to do with them, especially Anto, and that they would continue to be the most important people in Mom and Dad's life. And they would see lots and lots of Dad (more than they might want, even), as he would be taking them to his new house for cool sleepovers all the time . . .

Or not. Around this point the plan had become somewhat unstuck. Derailed entirely, in fact. The cosy chat never happened. Kyle upped in a fit of rage and unreasonableness and went to his parents (he could bloody well wash and dress Ethel in the mornings), refusing to have anything to do with the arrangements Ali had wanted to put in place.

This whole thing was his fault. Ali was in no doubt about that. If he hadn't decided he was going to throw the head and say all those things he'd said, then she wouldn't even be in Ireland right now.

'Look,' Emma began, 'I'm not a parent — '

'No. You're not. I know you mean well, Emma. But things are difficult, all right? I'm just waiting for the right moment to tell them. You know what divorces can be like in the States. Contentious. It could get messy.'

97

As if it hadn't already.

'I came home for a couple of weeks to get my head together. Give us both a chance to calm down. In the meantime I'll tell the kids we're having problems.'

Which they must have deduced in the past week already, what with Dad suddenly working massive overtime in the office, allegedly, and being too tired even to drive the short distance home to sleep, although he managed to make it to Granny's. They'd only seen him twice in the last week. Both times Ali had had sudden and urgent appointments and had been unable to join them.

It would take Erin about two and a half minutes to put the whole thing together, if she hadn't already. Jack already knew something stank. And Anto? He would probably just wait and see what way things panned out before getting involved.

'Anyway!' she said, with a shaky smile. She didn't want to talk about it any more. It was done now, she'd got on that plane, and she certainly wasn't going to start questioning her decision at this early stage. 'I hope you don't mind us crashing here with you.'

'Not at all.'

'And maybe you could, you know, not tell Kyle if he phones.'

A pause. 'You want me to tell Kyle you're not here?'

'No, no! Don't be silly. Just to, maybe, fudge things. Say I'm not in at the moment. Or, better still, just put your answering machine on.'

'Ali . . . '

'Oh, look, I don't want to talk to him, Emma. I just want some peace and quiet. I have a lot to think about, and I won't be able to if he's on the phone four times a day.'

Emma didn't like it. Not one tiny bit. But in the end she said, not bothering to hide her misgivings, 'OK. I'll leave the machine on. For the next day or two, anyway.'

'Thank you! You're a star.' Filled with relief, Ali was anxious to move the conversation on now. 'So!' she said, looking around. 'When is Ryan home?'

When Ryan would be home was about the only thing that Jack had showed any interest in since their arrival back in the country. No doubt he was looking forward to more tales of derring-do from the action man himself. If Jack ended up in the marines at seventeen, Ali would know exactly who to blame.

Emma put down her wine glass carefully. 'I'm not sure.'

'Well, is he in the country?' Ali enquired.

'Oh, I think so, yes,' she said vaguely.

Imagine having a fiancé where half the time you didn't even know what continent he was on. Ali thought Emma was marvellous to be so casual about the whole thing. But apparently Ryan had warned her in the early stages, right back when they knew it was serious between them, that he might be sent anywhere in the world at very short notice, sometimes — and Ali always thought this a tad dramatic — *dangerous* places, and if she couldn't handle that, then there was no point in them carrying on. No doubt the lighting had been low at the time, and both of them had been wearing very little, if anything.

'Oh my God, how romantic,' all Emma's girlfriends had moaned. They were engaged to electricians and bank managers and the like; it would be great if they ventured somewhere more dangerous than the local pub once in a while, they maintained.

And yes, it was romantic, but it also had an element of like it or lump it, in Ali's humble opinion.

'He's not like that at all,' Emma had insisted when Ali had put this to her. She'd looked appalled at the thought that anyone might think Ryan, well, horribly selfish to be shagging off to war-torn Wherever in the middle of Sunday lunch, leaving the love of his life to put the bins out and service the car, and probably drive herself to the labour ward sometime in the future to have his kids. 'He's going to give it up.'

'Oh?'

'Once we're married. He's going to look for something closer to home. Maybe set up his own photography business. Portrait work. That kind of thing.'

Somehow Ali just couldn't imagine Ryan contenting himself with weddings and the odd First Communion photograph.

Emma had lifted her chin defensively. 'It's his decision. I'm not going to make him give up something he loves just because it might suit everybody else, you know.'

Time to drop it. Nothing worse than falling out over a man. Especially one who was destined to be her future brother-in-law.

Still, Ali was pleased now that Ryan seemed to be off on another job. With any luck they'd be gone from the apartment by the time he was back, and Jack's head wouldn't be filled with stories of how Ryan had eluded seventeen guerrillas in Sudan, and defused a roadside bomb, using just a soup spoon.

'When's he coming back?' she enquired, just to be on the safe side.

Emma looked a bit peculiar again. Was she coming down with something?

'He isn't,' she said.

It was only then that Ali noticed that her engagement ring was gone.

6

Emma

Mam had been devastated. Not so much about the broken engagement, but about the manner in which she'd heard.

The story (told often) went something like this: there she was, doing her grocery shop as usual, bombing up and down the aisles with her trolley — difficult to control at the best of times, but even more so at twenty miles an hour and one-handed. The other hand she was using to grab things, usually random, and hoof them into the trolley, and to shoo small children aside in the nick of time before she ran them over. The reason for this weekly frantic dash was Dad, who couldn't be left unattended in the car for any length of time. Well, he probably *could*, as he rather tetchily pointed out. How bloody likely was he to croak it in Tesco's car park while she was gone for seventeen and a half minutes? Sixteen, if she parked near the door. And would she please stop going on about what the consultant said? He was a fool if ever there was one — forbidding Dad's fry-ups, as though there was anything else exciting left in his life.

So grumpy these days, Mam would often sigh to Emma. It was like living with Victor Meldrew. She didn't know whether it was those new pills he was on, or else just the strain of waiting for the next heart attack. He was always in great humour in the days after he'd had one. Probably the relief of having survived it. But he'd go downhill just as soon as he got home; sour and short-tempered, like everything was *her* fault. Honestly, for two pins . . .

Anyway, the whole supermarket thing was stressful enough without bumping, literally, into Anita Black. Mam only knew her vaguely and flashed her a smile as she prepared to gather speed again before entering the frozen food section. This was always treacherous, as glass doors had to be opened and closed whilst moving, and several times now she'd nearly lost an arm.

But didn't Anita Black stop her in her tracks by announcing, 'Sorry to hear about your Emma and Ryan.'

Mam, to her credit (her words), didn't gawp like a fool, and blurt, 'What the blazes are you talking about?' Instead, quick as a wink, she said, 'Oh, I know, but I suppose these things happen.'

She said that in her confusion and shock it had struck her then that maybe there had been a terrible traffic accident, that the hospital had been ringing and ringing the empty house fruitlessly, that Anita Black had somehow just come straight from the scene to do her shopping, and that maybe 'these things happen' mightn't be the most appropriate response.

'Still. I'm sure she won't be long finding someone else,' said Anita Black sympathetically.

('What did she mean by that?' Mam had fumed afterwards.)

Mam had left her trolley right there and walked out. They didn't even miss the shopping afterwards, she said, mostly because the trolley had been full of things like firelighters and rice cakes and bags of granulated sugar, grabbed in her frenetic dash.

Emma's engagement off! And she had to find out two weeks after the event from someone who had met Ryan's mother at a bridge tournament purely by chance.

Oh, the scenes at home afterwards. 'I can't believe it,' Mam kept saying, stunned. Her upset was understandable. Well, it was more selfish than anything. One minute she'd had a lovely wedding to plan for, and now, kaput. She even had all her catalogues marked and everything, ready to show Emma some mother-of-the-bride outfits. It was a toss-up between a mauve dress with an 'edgy' matching bolero jacket, and a more traditional two-piece. It wasn't ideal, ordering from a catalogue, but she couldn't get into town any more, for fear of having to resuscitate Noel on the 39A bus.

Now there was no wedding. She was back to sponge-bathing her husband and waiting for the next heart attack. The dogs in the street had more fun.

'I'm sorry, Mam.' It wasn't that Emma had deliberately kept it from them. Well, maybe she had. Her whole life had just had a nuclear bomb dropped on it. Could she not be given five minutes to pick herself up before traipsing

104

around all her friends and relatives to admit, 'Actually, yes, you were right to be suspicious of him all along — no, no, don't protest — he turned out to be a feckless, useless turd after all.'

Although that had only been Ali. Everybody else had liked him. Loved him, even.

'He's got it all,' Hannie had raved, once she'd got over her initial resentment and fury. 'Good looks, commitment, sincerity, a really cool job. He even stayed around and nursed you through that bout of the plague, remember? Most guys would have run a mile.'

At ten past eleven one Friday morning, just as they wrapped up the post-production meeting, Emma had broken out in a series of weeping sores. 'Jesus Christ,' Patrick had said in alarm, and legged it in case it was contagious. Hannie maintained it was some form of the plague, because she'd seen something like it on a documentary once. Emma's GP very firmly said it was most likely an acute allergic reaction to something she'd eaten. They never identified what that might have been, but she ended up spending the whole weekend in bed being nursed by Ryan, while the sores spread to every part of her body, including her face. At one point she could hardly prise open her eyes, but when she did, Ryan was always there, perched on her bed and holding a damp facecloth.

'I have no idea what I'm supposed to do with this,' he finally admitted. 'Also, I've boiled some water and torn up some sheets.'

'I think that's for childbirth.'

He slapped his forehead. 'Of course. Let me

see — broth, perhaps? Or I could lance your boils?'

'Thanks, but I'll pass.'

He leaned over and kissed her very tenderly on the forehead; actually *on* one of her bumps, that was how lovely he was.

'I hope you don't catch it,' she said.

'Anything of yours I'm happy to have,' he said gamely. 'Within reason.'

He was marvellous in a crisis. It was probably all that time he spent in war-torn Wherever. Nothing fazed him, ever, and it was that same calmness that had endeared him to Mam and Dad, as he'd been the one to stumble upon the scene of heart attack number five.

This wasn't planned. It wasn't some trick to test his character. He'd officially been invited over for lunch, to meet her parents for the first time. Emma was already there, tussling in the kitchen with Mam over the cooker, trying to give a hand but not being let.

'I'm only doing pasta,' Mam insisted, 'I'm fine.'

She didn't look that fine. She'd always been a great woman for her appearance; hair set at least once a week, always on some faddy diet that Ali told her about, to keep her figure and that kind of crack. Recently she looked a bit thrown together. But then look at the amount of time it had taken her to get Dad in and out of the shower earlier. She really was a saint. Although Emma could have sworn she heard the word 'fecker' through the walls.

In fairness, Dad was hard-going. All the time

106

they were trying to cook lunch, he was complaining loudly in the living room; his glasses had fallen, the room was too cold, what time was lunch anyway because he was hungry? Was it pasta? He didn't like that cream sauce. It gave him indigestion. He'd have tomato sauce on it instead.

'Oh, just leave him, he can wait a minute,' Mam said on the fifth demand for help from the living room.

'Are you sure?'

'Drain the pasta, quick. I think that's your fellow after driving in.'

And it was. Emma waved at him through the window, far too enthusiastically, probably. He smiled back, an enormous smile that lifted her heart. Mam, meanwhile, nipped off to the loo with a yelp of, 'My hair!' leaving Emma to rescue the pasta from oblivion.

And so it was Ryan who discovered poor Dad thrashing about on the living-room floor, in the throes of another heart attack, and being completely ignored by his family.

'Hello, Mrs Murphy,' he said with a lovely smile when Mam walked in. 'I'm Ryan. Very pleased to meet you. Something smells lovely! Listen, I wonder would you ever go and give an ambulance a buzz while I perform a bit of life-saving CPR?'

That was according to Mam, anyway. She marvelled at his calmness and cool head. Just like something out of those medical dramas on the telly. And such strong, square hands. She'd noticed them while he was performing the CPR.

You could always trust a man with hands like that. After that she doted on him, and Dad had no option but to dote on him too, as without him he would be toast, as Mam repeatedly and insistently told him.

And now Ryan was gone, just like that. When Mam had got home from the supermarket, and Emma had been summoned round, they just shook their heads in hurt bafflement.

'What happened, love?'

'Just . . . things.' There was no use saying 'nothing'. If nothing had happened, then they would still be together, arguing (lightly) over whether to have a big or a small wedding. Besides, it was best to give people a reason. Then they went, 'Ah', and shook their heads knowingly, and then shut up about it, which was nice. So far, when backed into a corner, Emma had told people that they'd rushed into the engagement and had broken up by mutual consent. But then she began to think, why protect him? None of this was *her* fault. So she began declaring that he'd cheated on her with a Swedish lap dancer. Then she thought, sod that, and downgraded it to an insurance saleswoman. With moles. She'd even told one of her neighbours that Ryan had admitted that he didn't want kids, that he *hated* kids, in fact, and that she'd better not start wanting any after they got married, because he was going to get his bits snipped whether she liked it or not, so there. What choice had he left her, only to finish with him?

'We rushed into things,' she eventually told

108

Mam and Dad. She didn't want to get into lap-dancers or vasectomies or anything like that. 'You said it yourself, that we got engaged too soon.'

'Well, yes . . . but you seemed so sure.'

'I know, but you think you know someone, and then you discover that you don't at all.' At least that much was said with conviction.

'Just so long as he didn't hurt you, or he'll have me to answer to,' Dad rumbled threateningly, just like he used to. Then it was time for Mam to help him to the toilet. 'Quick,' he urged her.

'Maybe you're better off,' she said to Emma in passing, with a long-suffering sigh.

* * *

And now here Mam was again, listening to another tale of a broken relationship, only this time it was Ali's.

'At least I'm not in the supermarket,' she said. 'At least I'm in my own kitchen.' She flopped back in her chair, looking at Ali in bewilderment. Possibly they should have picked a better time to drop the bombshell on her. The district nurse had been round that morning and Mam had had to clean the whole house and then get Dad into fresh trousers, despite his protestations that the ones he had on him were fine, even though there was, she told Emma and Ali, wee on them. Wee. She repeated this three or four times, making sure that Dad could hear her.

'*Divorce*,' she said now, in despair. 'Dear God. Are you sure, Ali? What about the kids? Where *are* the kids, anyway?'

At that point she began to look around nervously.

'Here, Mam, have a cup of tea,' Emma said briskly. 'It'll make you feel better.'

She put a tray down on the kitchen table containing a teapot, cups, and two plates of rice cakes and stuffed vine leaves, which was all she could find in the kitchen presses, thanks to Mam's frenetic weekly shop.

'Lovely,' said Mam, tucking in.

Emma saw Ali looking at her gratefully. Emma hadn't wanted to come round at all, as she felt this was Ali's private business, but Ali had insisted that Emma's mere presence would cast Ali in a better light. 'You can steer them away from any specifics, like when the divorce is going to happen, or when I'm going back,' Ali had instructed.

This last one was easy enough, as Emma had no idea either. Ali's plans were fabulously vague. Meanwhile, her and the kids' stuff, at first strictly confined to the spare bedroom, was spreading out over Emma's flat like lava. Every so often Ali made attempts to clean up, but Emma would still find the boys' socks in her underwear drawer.

'I suppose you want to move in here,' Mam said. In fairness, Ali normally had an ulterior motive.

'Certainly not,' Ali announced. 'I wouldn't impose upon you and Dad.'

110

'We wouldn't mind. In fact, I'd quite enjoy the company.'

'I wouldn't do it to Dad. Not with his health,' Ali insisted nobly.

In other words, moving in with Mam and Dad would be too much like hard work.

Erin came to the kitchen door now. She'd been banished to the living room before any talk of divorce reared its head. 'Mom, can I borrow your lipstick?'

'What do you want it for?'

'Nothing.'

This was so unconvincing that they all swung around to look past her. There was Dad, having a sleep on the sofa, as yet unaware of Ali's divorce revelations. ('Oh, don't wake him,' Mam had insisted. 'Let's enjoy the peace and quiet.') With all the medication he was on, he slept often, and deeply. But not usually with a pair of large pink sunglasses on, two bright spots of blusher high on his cheeks, and with his comb-over arranged in racy kinks.

Emma waited for Ali to thunder, 'Erin!'

But she just said, half-heartedly, 'Don't put lipstick on Granddad,' not seeming to mind that a man with a heart condition was going to wake from a lovely sleep to find that he'd turned into Danny La Rue.

Mam, meanwhile, was drinking her tea meditatively. 'I suppose you'll have great freedom now, the two of ye, to be gallivanting around Dublin without husbands and fiancés to hold you back.' She sounded nearly jealous.

Emma was appalled. 'We're not exactly

111

looking at all this as a shopping opportunity, Mam.'

'Absolutely not,' Ali chimed in. 'Our hearts are broken. We can barely find the energy to break open a bottle of wine in the evenings, can we, Emma?'

She managed it all the same, even if she had to use her teeth. Her idea of being broken-hearted seemed to involve imbibing copious amounts of (Emma's) wine and food, peppered with trips to the park with the kids, and noisy games of karaoke in the evenings courtesy of Emma's jukebox. In between this, she would throw on washes, clean Emma's kitchen, or half-clean it anyway, and get into deep conversations with the postman, a man Emma wouldn't even recognise.

Jack and Anto clattered in from the green across the way now, where they had been kicking one of Liam's old footballs about. They descended upon the tea tray with delight, only to rear back when they saw the vine leaves and rice cakes.

'I just can't get used to this traditional Irish food,' Anto said with a sigh.

Mam, meanwhile, was marvelling to Jack, 'The height of you!'

Fair play to her, she always tried to make a little conversation, even if it was the same one they'd had every year since Jack had been a toddler. 'You must be what, five-foot-eleven?'

'Six-foot-one,' he answered politely, but not elaborating. Still, what else was there to say?

'Six-foot-one!' Mam said valiantly. American teenagers always seemed more polished and worldly than the yobs in the streets around Mam, she'd confided in Emma earlier. With them, you could just shout, 'Damien Ward, leave that car alone or I'll be up to your mammy so fast it'll make your empty little head spin.' They would hurl some abuse back, and so on and so forth until they had quite a conversation going.

'And what class are you in now?' she said. She was close to exhausting her list of topics by now, Emma could tell.

'We don't really call them classes,' Jack corrected her very nicely. 'In high school, we say — '

He was interrupted by the sound of someone breaking wind. Loudly. Unmistakably.

Everyone froze. Finally, Anto looked up from studying the milk carton as though he had just noticed. He sniffed. He turned to look at Mam.

She went puce. 'But I . . . it wasn't . . . '

Emma saw her confusion set in: could it possibly have been . . . ? She was under such stress these days, and so used to blasted bodily functions, that it was entirely credible that she had done it without noticing. Emma could see her mind travelling to other, more public events that she had attended recently, and her mortification deepened.

'Anthony,' Emma snapped.

He gave her a wide-eyed look. 'Yes?'

She let her eyes bore into his: I know your game, sonny. You might have fooled your mother and father and the world at large into thinking you are directly descended from the Angel Gabriel, but you and I know differently. And I will be on your back every moment you're under my roof, got it?

He did. He gave her a look back that clearly said, Game on.

★ ★ ★

When they got home, Ali proceeded to hustle the kids into baths and showers, amid shouts of, 'Don't skip any bits because I'll know.' She then forgot all about them and went to ring Mam to tell her that she'd meant to say it earlier, but she was going shopping tomorrow and would Mam like to come if they could palm Dad off on someone? What, there *wasn't* anyone? Disgraceful! Oh, and if by any chance Kyle happened to ring, would Mam mind telling him that she hadn't heard from Ali in a while? It wasn't a lie, it was just to give her some space, that was all.

Emma watched from a quiet corner of the room, hoping not to be noticed. How did Ali do it? How did she keep putting one foot in front of the other, when inside she must be in meltdown, if the amount of tears and snot she'd produced that first night was anything to go by?

Emma, on the other hand, woke every morning to find that all the black clouds in the northern hemisphere seemed to have converged over her head. She would reach over in the dark and futilely pat the empty bed beside her, not knowing whether grief or anger was the appropriate emotion. Everything just seemed so mixed up.

Then the miserable trek to work, and the

miserable tussles with Patrick and Alannah, and the miserable drive home again. Was it any wonder the children kept asking Ali, ostensibly out of her hearing, 'Why does Auntie Emma look so *miserable* all the time?'

'She was born that way,' Ali would tell them soothingly. 'Wednesday's child. Full of woe.'

'Ah,' they would say.

It was a great relief at the end of each day to say good night to Ali and the kids at nine o'clock, and slouch off to bed. Tonight she nipped off while they were still drying off in the bathroom. She lay there in her big empty double bed, listening as they then decamped to the living room, and had their usual bedtime snack of cereal. The walls were so thin that she could hear the clink of spoons against the sides of the bowls.

'Anthony.' Ali's voice. 'Don't go *near* that jukebox. You know that Auntie Emma has to be up at half-past four in the morning. So we all have to sit here quietly until she falls asleep.'

Fifteen seconds passed.

'Do you think she's asleep yet?'

'No.'

Another fifteen seconds.

Then, the usual question, 'Mom, why is she so miserable all the time?'

Emma waited for the Wednesday's child explanation. But tonight there was a big long pause, then: 'Ryan is gone.'

'Gone where?'

Emma held her breath. Even she didn't know where he was. The last phone call, a good few days ago now, had shown up as a long string of numbers on her caller display; she wasn't sufficiently up to speed on international dialling codes to be able to tell what country it signalled. But he wasn't in Ireland at the moment. She didn't know whether that made her feel better or worse.

'I don't know,' she heard Ali admit, and she deflated. Ridiculous to have thought that Ali had some kind of insider information that Emma didn't. 'Look,' she carried on. 'Ryan and Auntie Emma are not seeing each other any more.'

Emma thought she could hear a collective intake of breath.

'Don't be stupid,' she heard Jack say roughly. He'd always been a little star-struck by Ryan. 'They're getting married.'

'Well, yes, but these things don't always work out. Engagements.' A pause. 'Marriages, even.'

Emma turned over in bed then and wrapped a pillow around her ears. She didn't want to be privy to Ali's laying of any groundwork to explain her own situation. She lay there for a long time, trying to blank out her own thoughts, but it was no use. In the end she flung the pillow off. The apartment was silent now. They'd all gone to bed. She wondered should she go into Ali's room. She wondered whether she might be upset, after everything.

But then again, Ali was so self-sufficient. Such a survivor. Emma was afraid that if she *did* go in to Ali, she would be the one who'd break down uncontrollably.

116

In a way it would be a relief. But then, if she said her fears out loud, they would become real, and right now they were nicely contained in a little box called denial.

She turned over and tried desperately to go to sleep.

7

Ali

They'd never really had a chance. Everything had been a mistake, right from the first positive Wal-Mart pregnancy test.

'Shit,' Kyle moaned, running around the flat Ali shared with June and Eileen, and clutching his head in despair. 'Shit, shit, *shit*.'

Ali sat there with it in her hands, feeling peculiarly calm. Maybe she just refused to believe it. She was only eighteen. She was going to a great party that night where someone said there would be lethal cocktails; she was looking into night-time college courses; this just couldn't be happening to her.

'Sometimes they're wrong, aren't they? These tests?' Kyle said, in a sudden rush of hope.

'Yes, but I think it only works one way. As in, it's possible to get a negative test and still be pregnant but not the other way around, if you know what I mean.'

'Fuck, fuck, *fuck*.' He flung himself on her sleeping bag in despair.

I don't know anything about babies, was all Ali could think. Not a blind thing. Sometimes she saw them in Macy's, all trussed up in their buggies and being dragged around the various departments by their mothers. A few of the girls, like Donna, would lean over the counter to them, and say, in this coochy-coo voice, 'You look so *cute* in that hat! Are you helping your mommy?'

Ali never coochy-cooed over the counter. To tell the truth, she wasn't that keen on babies. It didn't bode well.

'What am I going to tell my parents?' That was Kyle again, buried somewhere under a pillow. 'They'll kill me. Whatever else you do, use a condom, Dad said to me. And I did! And it didn't fucking work!'

They'd joked that his willy was too big for condoms. Unhappily, it seemed that it had turned out to be true.

'Four times! Four times we had sex! What kind of lousy, rotten luck is that?'

Indeed. They'd have had a lot more sex if he hadn't lived on campus with Dorky Dave, who never left the dorm room after 7 p.m., and had Ali not shared an apartment with two other girls, both of whom had recently split from boyfriends and were taking comfort in reruns of $M^*A^*S^*H$ and giant bags of Doritos. Bringing back boys to the apartment to shag was against house rules, according to Eileen, especially if everybody else had to go without.

And so every date would end in the back of Kyle's old car, with lots of groping and snogging. Kyle would usually have to pull away several times to take deep, calming breaths. 'Jesus. I don't know if I can hold on much longer.'

Ali, ever open to new experiences, would have been quite happy to have had a go right there on

119

the back seat, but Kyle seemed to think it was cheap and not done by nice girls.

In the end they'd gone to a motel, and were signed in as Mr and Mrs Peterson (ah, the irony) by the somewhat sceptical clerk. Kyle had thoughtfully brought some chocolates for her, and a cheap bottle of wine, which they'd drunk before they'd jumped on each other enthusiastically.

They did it twice that night, and would have managed a third time had he not had an early lecture the following morning, and they had to walk out past the very same clerk, both of them looking as though they'd been dragged through a hedge backwards.

How they'd laughed in the car on the drive back. And why not? They were young, good-looking, with money in their pockets (mostly Ali's, from her job at Macy's). Nobody ever said they were going to carve each other's initials into their buttocks or anything like that. It was just a bit of fun.

The fun continued apace the following Wednesday when she nipped home to the empty apartment during her lunch break at Macy's to have sex a third time. Even better than times one and two, Kyle declared.

The fourth time, they would later deduce, was probably the culprit. He used a different condom, clearly of inferior quality and much, much smaller than usual (or so she kept consoling him in the difficult months that followed). Plus, they'd been in a hurry, as June was expected home at any moment, and it was entirely possible there had been some slippage or breakage or other natural disaster that had gone unnoticed by either of them at the time.

There was no more sex after that because Eileen came down with the flu and lay about the apartment for a week like a bad-tempered slug. Just when she got better Kyle had to go back to Texas for a family funeral and ended up staying ten days.

Meanwhile Ali's boobs seemed to be on some kind of growth spurt. It was curious. They constantly felt like they were on the verge of exploding. In the end she had to go and buy a new bra from the lingerie department at Macy's at a staff discount of ten per cent.

It was only in the changing room trying on some enormous padded yoke that she noticed the veins: big blue ones travelling in a spider's web all down her chest and over her gigantic breasts. Almost simultaneously, she realised that her period was late.

Oh sweet, divine Jesus.

'What the hell am I going to do about college?' Kyle was now in a foetal ball on the sleeping bag, rocking back and forth, all six foot two of him. 'I can't look after a — ' he almost choked — 'a *baby* as well as study. I live in a dorm, for fuck's sake. What am I supposed to do, ask permission to move a cot in?'

Ali threw the pregnancy test at him with all her might.

Her aim was good.

'What the hell?' he yelped. 'You nearly took my eye out!'

121

She stood over him, hands on her hips. 'You selfish git. All you've done so far is go on about yourself. What about me? I'm three thousand miles from bloody home!' And a good thing too. Mam would murder her. 'How do you think I feel? I'm the one who's pregnant, not you! All because of you and your cheap condoms!'

It wasn't the most rational argument to have made. But right now she didn't feel rational. She felt helpless and trapped and she didn't know what to do.

'Ali, I'm sorry,' he began.

She threw her bag on her shoulder and grabbed her keys.

'Wait — where are you going?'

She didn't bother answering.

★   ★   ★

When she got back it was dark, and Kyle was still there. He'd tidied up and made some dinner — spaghetti hoops and toast — which he put down in front of her as a peace offering.

'Where are Eileen and June?' Tonight was *M*A*S*H* night. June had got in the Doritos and everything.

'I told them we needed to talk.'

'Fantastic. So now they know I'm up the duff too.'

'I didn't tell them anything!'

'You didn't have to. They're Irish.'

He sat down opposite her. 'Look, I'm sorry about earlier. I just got an awful fright. Not that that's any excuse.'

122

She took a tiny nibble of the spaghetti hoops to signal her softening.

'I haven't been able to think about anything else all afternoon,' he admitted.

'Me neither,' she said.

She'd wandered around the streets in a daze, in between nipping into coffee shop toilets on a foolishly optimistic knicker-watch. Please God, please God, she'd begged each time before whipping them down. She promised Him she would even find a church in Boston and go to Mass. But He clearly only responded to bribery of a higher nature, because each loo trip ended in disappointment.

She was still pregnant, only five hours more so now. The embryo had probably doubled in size in the interim, if her hazy memories of biology classes were to be trusted. Didn't they grow at some ferocious rate in the beginning? The thought made her feel queasy.

Kyle took her hand in his. 'This is going to be OK. I promise you. I'm not going to run for the nearest hill, or anything. Even if you want me to.'

He gave her a crooked smile and she felt tremendously relieved. He was a lovely guy. He was just too young for all this. And so was she. It wasn't anybody's fault.

'I suppose the first thing is to go to the doctor and get it confirmed,' she said.

'Absolutely. We'll go together. There's a guy in college we can probably see.'

'OK.' Maybe this wasn't going to be as awful as she'd thought. 'And then I suppose we have to, you know, decide what we're going to do.'

This was really only politeness on her part. As he was the father, he *should* be asked. But out on her walk, Ali had already made up her mind. Things might have been different had she been at home, and not across the Atlantic in some strange city with a guy she barely knew. It might have been different too if she'd had someone to confide in, like Emma. But what could she do? Ring her up at home, with Dad hovering in the background?

Anyway, if she was being really honest with herself, whether she was here or back home or on the planet Mars, she'd still do the same thing. She was only eighteen. This was not for her.

'Will you marry me?' Kyle blurted out.

Ali laughed. She couldn't help it. It was just so . . . ludicrous.

'I'm serious, Ali.'

She stopped laughing. 'This isn't the flipping Middle Ages any more, Kyle. You don't have to marry me just because you got me up the spout.'

Kyle had on that plodding expression that she would become very familiar with in later years, God help her. 'I'm not doing this out of duty.' He thought about that. 'Well, maybe I am a bit. But it's more than that. I *want* to. I love you.'

'You hardly know me.'

'I love the bits that I know.'

'Kyle, stop. *Stop*. This is crazy. We are not going to get married.'

124

'So, what, you want us to just *live* together?' he demanded.

Well, no, actually. She was quite happy with Eileen and June.

'What kind of security is that for a child?' he went on. He sounded worryingly like her parents.

'Kyle . . . ' She looked at him pleadingly. 'Do you not see? I don't want a baby.'

'It wasn't exactly high on my to-do list either.'

'I mean, I'm not having this baby.'

The penny dropped finally. He released her hand fast. 'You can't be serious.'

She forgot sometimes that, for all his cool clothes and college course and his apparent sophistication, he was really a small-town boy from Texas. She was only a small-town girl too, relatively speaking, but already she suspected she was aeons ahead of Kyle. That didn't bode well either.

He swallowed hard, as though stepping up to the plate. 'We made a mistake, Ali. But it's done now. We have to deal with it. We can't just refuse to take responsibility.'

She admired him for it. Really, she did. It took guts to stand up for what you believed in, especially when you knew your girlfriend was in the driving seat and had no intention of listening to you.

'It's not about that,' she said.

'I know,' he said sadly. 'It's about you. And I don't blame you.'

'I'm not even legal here,' she said. It sounded a bit like she was making excuses. And maybe she was, but they were also realities. 'I have no healthcare, no proper job. I don't even have a *bed* in my room. How do you think we'd bring up a baby?'

It was the wrong thing to have said. She had given him an opening. After that, it was just a case of him wearing her down.

'Well, my parents would help,' he began. 'Financially. One phone call and we'd have the cash to rent our own place. They'd cover the medical bills too, I'm sure they would. And the stuff for the baby. Buggies, nappies. Crèche care, if you still wanted to work.'

'Kyle . . . ' But it was futile.

'I'll still have to study, of course, in the first couple of years. But when I graduate, then I'll stay at home with the baby while you get your chance. I know you dropped out of college back home, but you could start over here if you wanted. I'd support you. I swear.'

He made it sound so plausible; like her life wasn't going to stop at all, that in fact having this baby could be the gateway to a whole new set of opportunities. That she would be foolish *not* to go ahead with it.

She had no doubt that he believed everything he said. And maybe she did too, or at least enough to get sucked into his grand plan.

'My parents will go mad,' she said. 'Me, shacked up with some guy in America at eighteen. Having a *baby*.' They'd be on the first plane over. In fact, Dad may well ring up his 'contacts' in America in advance; a couple of dentists who he'd trained with and who'd emigrated to the States. They might turn up on the doorstep armed with dental implements, and demand that she comes to her senses.

'So let's get married,' Kyle said. They can't object if you're married, can they?'

Object? They'd go loony altogether.

'This is their grandchild. They're going to want to see you settled. Just like mine will.'

OK, she was getting a headache now. Intuitively she knew his plan was wrong, but was it any more wrong than pitching up at some abortion clinic, with several hundred grubby dollars in her hand? If she had her way, she'd hop on a bus somewhere — anywhere, just so long as it was far away from Boston — but this time she would only be taking the problem with her.

And there was Kyle, so unwavering, so sure of what they should do.

'People marry young here all the time,' he told her.

'Is that supposed to persuade me?'

'It isn't that crazy, that's all I'm saying. It's not like in Ireland where you all live at home until you're thirty-five and then you might start thinking about getting hitched.'

Nothing wrong with that. But *eighteen*.

All Ali could see was Emma's face, quietly appalled.

'Look, I know this isn't ideal. It's going to take some getting used to.' He took her cold, clammy hands in his. 'But it's going to work out just great. We're going to have a baby — just imagine. And I just bet it's going to be a girl, just

127

like you.' (The eejit was wrong about that too.) 'You and me, we're going to have our own little family.'

He was looking . . . *excited* was the only word for it.

Great. She'd only gone and got herself pregnant by the one guy in America who actively wanted to settle down and have a baby at the age of eighteen.

★　★　★

She was going to have to ring him. They'd been gone from home for almost a week now. So far he'd left eighteen voice messages on her phone, each one more irate than the last, even though the content was more or less the same: 'Where the hell are you . . . how dare you . . . I want to see my kids now . . . my attorney says . . . my other, more expensive, attorney says . . . having an urgent meeting with both my attorneys . . . ring me now.'

Erin came in. She was in her pyjamas, ready for bed, which meant the left side of Ali's double bed. Anto slept on two cushions on the floor. At some point during the night Jack would come in and silently climb into a sleeping bag over by the door. Anto fretted about oxygen levels and smells, and insisted on leaving the window open all night.

'Who are you ringing?' Erin asked.

Ali quickly put down her phone. 'Nobody. Just listening to a voice message.'

'You look kind of sad.'

No sense in lying to her, a junior FBI agent in the making. 'Maybe I am a bit sad.'

Erin climbed up beside her and gave her a hug. It was unexpected and lovely, and Ali clung to her thin little body hard, breathing in the gorgeous smell of her. (Hmm. Molton Brown?)

'Do you miss Daddy?' Erin enquired.

Ali smiled brightly. 'Yes.'

'Me too.' Erin looked gloomy, as though she didn't treat Kyle like her unpaid personal servant most of the time.

Ali gave her a last hug. 'Go tell Anto to come to bed.'

'I'll try. But he says he's not tired.'

Of course he wasn't. He hadn't got up until nearly eleven that morning, having stayed up playing video games half the previous night. 'Yeah, but we have no school,' was his argument. Each day was one long holiday for him and Erin, with no routine, no commitments, and free rein of a gorgeous apartment.

Jack was the only one spoiling the fun. He went off on his own for long walks, rain or shine. When he got home he would put on his headphones and listen to music for hours on end, shutting her out. He wasn't even going to pretend that he was having a good time.

He hadn't said a thing about Kyle; just given her many long, suspicious looks. He wasn't buying it; any of it.

But what could she do? She'd had no chance to prepare them. Not with the way things had turned out.

And to think that she'd thought they would

discuss the divorce in some kind of mature fashion. In fact, she'd thought Kyle would be relieved. God knows, she was. The pretence was over. They could finally admit what they'd both known all along: that they were fundamentally unsuited in every way imaginable, and that it would be a kindness to their marriage to put it down.

'I want a divorce,' she'd finally plucked up the nerve to tell him.

'Tell me something new, babes,' he said, not taking his eyes off the telly (the baseball was on).

And, in fairness, she quite often threatened divorce, usually when his parents had been around for dinner, or when he went off with 'the boys' and didn't come back for two days. Or sometimes when she just looked at his face. He always let these idle threats wash over him, immune to it after all these years. She was forever bitching, she'd heard him tell one of his friends once; man, she could give you a headache.

But to keep watching the TV, to not even *look* at her . . .

Something snapped in her then. Really, something did; she heard it, right under her breastbone. And she opened her mouth and it all came tumbling out: her unhappiness, her disenchantment, her lack of fulfilment, her feelings of being buried alive in a small town, and also some extraneous stuff such as the fact that he never ordered anything other than pizza when they ate out. Not once in sixteen years, except in that steak restaurant, and even then

130

he'd spread tomato ketchup all over the steak and topped it off with some cheese. OK, maybe she shouldn't have, but she just couldn't stop herself.

She must have been quite animated because when she'd finished he'd gone completely white.

'Jesus Christ, I had no idea you were suffering so terribly all these years. You should have said something, instead of keeping it all inside.'

She tried to ignore the sarcasm. But Kyle was a bit like the McArthurs' slobby old porch dog. The kids would tease it and tease it, and it would completely ignore them, until they went that bit too far and then it would be forced to defend itself with surprising vigour.

'Kyle, can we just talk?' She didn't want this fight, even though she'd started it. She didn't want to hurt him.

'About what? How much you hate it here? How I dragged you up the aisle, kicking and screaming? Forced you to have three kids against your will?' His voice had risen. 'Change the record, Ali.'

She tried to keep her cool. 'This isn't what we want, either of us.'

'Don't tell me what I want.'

Well, it wasn't her, she was damned sure of that. He hadn't really looked at her properly in a decade, nor her him.

'Let's not stay together just because we're too settled and lazy to do anything about it, Kyle.'

'Oh, I didn't realise divorce was something you'd dreamed up to get us off our butts.'

He hated change. That was his thing. He was

131

slowly tuning into Ethel and Hal, with the narrow mindset that comes of never really having pushed yourself, never opening up to any new experience, especially if it involved travelling outside state lines.

He was thirty-four and it was like he was twenty years older.

She did something silly then. Instead of backing down and leaving him time to get used to the idea, which was usually the way he came round to things, she lost patience and said, 'Well, you can't stop me. I'm going to file anyway.'

The whole thing kicked off then into a fully fledged row, the likes of which they hadn't had since Anto had been a toddler, and they'd been sleep deprived and despairing and, as usual, got more comfort out of bickering than pulling together. They should have ended it back then, instead of limping on for another ten years. But then they wouldn't have had Erin.

Kyle was crying in the end — they both were — and accusing her of pulling the family apart.

He packed his stuff then. His parting shot at the door had been, 'You're not getting the kids.'

8

Emma

Dear Emma,

DON'T STOP READING. Please. I'm not trying to change your mind, OK? No sorry shit, no please-take-me-back. I know we're past all that, and I don't blame you.

But you can't stop me worrying about you. You won't take my phone calls and I'm fairly sure you're deleting my emails without reading them first. And if you don't mind me saying so, for a smart woman you're being pretty stupid. I'm enclosing (again) the details of someone that you can see, absolutely confidentially —

Emma tore the letter up into paranoid pieces, and then *more* paranoid pieces, until in the end it looked like confetti for very little people. Damn him, anyway. She had a shedload of kids in the house, not to mention her very canny sister, and he had to go writing a letter to her that had lain on the kitchen table all day while she was at work? Anybody could have opened it. Well, Anto, anyway. She'd a suspicion that he'd steamed open one of her bills last week, or else the envelope-licker had been having a very bad day.

She resisted the urge to burn the miniature confetti pieces in a pyre out the back, and instead tipped them into the bin. This was harder than you might think, what with all the pizza boxes stuffed in there, and the juice cartons and God knows what else.

Almost immediately she was sorry she'd torn it up. He might have said something about himself in it. If he was all right. He'd *looked* all right when she'd last seen him, but then again, they'd been breaking up at the time, and her judgement had probably been a tad impaired.

And, to be honest, she hadn't cared a whole lot. He could have crawled off pathetically on all fours, as far as she'd been concerned. She'd thrown him out in such a magnificent fit of moral outrage that it would have been a definite weakening of her position if she'd suddenly stopped to enquire, 'By the way, how are *you* in all this?'

Weeks had gone by since, though. It was hard to keep up all that anger. Draining, actually. Most nights now as she lay in bed listening to the karaoke competition going on in the living room, she was too wrecked to be furious, and her mind, treacherous thing that it was, would eventually wander in the direction of his welfare. He was a coper, Ryan, not given to hysterics over, say, a head cold, but come *on*. He must be knocked for six. And he was on his own now. Fiancée-less. Nobody to hold his hand, to assure him that everything would be fine; to sit up with him talking about the future, or to look up the Internet with him in the name of research when they'd both plucked up the courage, only to log off just as fast when it scared the life out of them.

She would eventually make herself cry with these thoughts; just small, blubbery noises. She couldn't risk anything more because, knowing her luck, there would be a lull after 'Only the Lonely' in the living room, and they would all stop singing (which was putting it charitably) and come stampeding in to find out what was making miserable Auntie Emma even more miserable than usual. Whenever her crying threatened to get out of control, she would make herself think about Patrick and his hairy arms for five minutes until she was unsentimental again.

Ryan wasn't her responsibility, she reminded herself sternly. Being engaged thankfully didn't come with the 'for richer, for poorer' stuff. You were only on a trial run, and could bail out as and when, no harm done.

She hoped not, anyway. Presumbably not. Unlikely, statistically. Well, with a bit of luck.

Still, every morning now she stood in front of the mirror, turning this way and that, looking for signs. Of what, she didn't know. Some kind of disintegration, maybe. But she always looked so crap at half-past four in the morning that it was hard to tell. Did big black rings under her eyes count? Or bloodshot eyes? Nobody on the Internet had mentioned them. The only thing she'd noticed were some dry patches of skin that were maybe an indication of something. More likely, though, they were merely the result of all the rubbish food she was eating recently, now that Ali had taken it upon herself to ensure that the fridge was always full.

Common sense told her that she couldn't go on like this. Apart from anything else, she was in danger of being late for work if she spent much more time in front of the mirror in the mornings. Maybe, just maybe, it would be no harm to have a useful phone number. Not that she had any intention of using it. But just in case.

'What are you looking for?'

Ali. Usually you could hear her a mile off. She must be wearing slip-on shoes today.

'Nothing!' Emma took her head out of the bin so fast that she nearly collided with an overhead press. 'Just . . . putting the rubbish out.'

'Let me. Most if it's ours anyway.' And she bustled past, taking the bin liner from Emma and giving it a violent shake. 'There. Plenty of room now.'

'Lovely,' Emma murmured, watching as the little bits of Ryan's letter were scattered to the four corners of the bag. Ah, well. She'd only been fooling herself anyway; she wasn't really going to ring anybody.

'I wanted to ask you something,' said Ali, casually. 'Do you know of any good solicitors over here?'

'For what?'

'Well, you know, with the divorce coming up, I thought I might as well start getting a bit of advice.'

It sounded sensible enough, even if planning ahead wasn't exactly Ali's forte.

'But isn't divorce law completely different in

America? I mean, I don't know how much use an Irish solicitor would be,' Emma pointed out.

'You could well be right. Never mind. It was just a thought,' Ali said airily.

Emma wondered when they were going to stop telling each other porkers. Oh, it was all very chummy over a glass of wine every night, when they discussed such intimate things as the pubic hair that Ali had spotted growing on Anto the other night in the shower, and her urge to clip it all off because she could hardly handle him as a child, so him as a *teenager* . . . Emma in turn had confided her desire to completely refurbish the flat now that Ryan was gone, maybe in pinks and pastels and frills, something completely unlike her, even though she had no intention of starting until Ali and the kids had gone back as there was no point in doing it twice.

But all the time the air was blue with other things being firmly kept under wraps. Sometimes Ali's cheeks would be puffed out as though she was going to burst, but somehow she managed to keep it all in, a miracle in itself. And as for Emma . . . having grown up in a house with Ali and Liam, she'd got very good at keeping things to herself.

'No problem,' she told Ali now, and they both nodded and smiled and said 'Great,' about fourteen times.

*　*　*

Emma met Ryan at a film and TV awards bash in the centre of town. She normally ran a mile

137

from these things, as it always involved procuring some class of a long dress, which was a week's work in itself, and having to make small talk with loads of arsey film types.

'Some of them are quite cute,' Hannie pointed out. She was wearing a long red kaftan thing with fringed sleeves, and looked like a member of a remote tribe. A good-looking tribe, though, she pointed out.

'You can't be serious.' Emma was aghast.

'I'm just saying — '

'Hannie, we *hate* filmy types.'

This wasn't just some kind of silly personal prejudice. This was *policy*. In Emma's experience the problem with a lot of filmmakers, and for that read young(ish) men entirely dressed in black and with or without a ponytail, was that they tended to look down on people who worked in television. Oh, they never *said* it, but they harboured a deep-rooted snobbery about people who produced soaps and talk shows and the odd drama for the masses, while they, the arrogant custodians of culture, produced edgy films for an audience of about fifteen.

And the films weren't even any good. The plot usually ran like this: two lads in their mid-twenties, hilariously funny (i.e. still living with their parents) yet socially relevant (unemployed), who inadvertently get caught up in a crime (a bank robbery is always handy) and go on a madcap car chase around Dublin, bonding over guns (also hilariously funny). Occasionally there's the odd female lurking in the background for a bit of colour (the mammy, the girlfriend).

The whole thing usually ends up with them having a 'character moment' (cue bad lighting), and then the reviews at the weekend (nearly always written by other young men) would hail the film as hilariously funny and socially relevant.

But tonight was different. Tonight Emma didn't mind sharing the same air as the filmmakers.

'I still can't believe it,' quivered Hannie. She was always good for a bit of drama in these instances.

'Me neither.'

'Oh, stop trying to sound cool.'

'I'm not!'

She couldn't hide her excitement even if she tried; *Wake Up Ireland* had been nominated in the Best Live Television category. If they got the gong, she'd be the one taking a walk up on that stage to accept it, and she might even throw two fingers at the film lot while she was at it: *we might broadcast shite in your opinion, but it's award-winning shite.* Or else she might lose the run of herself entirely and start crying before thanking her mother and her piano teacher and the stray cat that sometimes sat on her windowsill.

It was a tremendous kick. She'd worked on award-nominated shows before (well, two) but as researcher and assistant producer. Never as the head honcho. And *Wake Up Ireland* had only been on the air less than a season.

But hang on. Reality check. They hadn't won yet. And, in truth, they weren't likely to. In all probability they'd only got the nomination at all because they were new, in a field as tired and predictable as the chicken vol-au-vents now doing the rounds.

Hannie looked at them, appalled. She put her arm round the teenage boy who was handing them out. 'I'm a vegan,' she confided in him. 'Have you ever seen one before? No? Anyway, I wonder would you mind popping back to the kitchen and getting me some suitable snacks? *Muchas gracias.*'

Meanwhile, Patrick and Alannah were over having their photograph taken near a water fountain. Given the night that was in it, Alannah was in five-inch heels, and towered over Patrick who, though pretty darn sexy in his tuxedo if you liked that sort of thing, could have done with a couple of serious shoe lifts. Perhaps out of spite he had worked it so that she was nearest the fountain, and she kept giving little flinches as spots of cold water hit her bare back.

'Could we get a little closer, folks?' the photographers asked innocently.

And so they put their arms around each other's waists, but below that, their bodies never touched. In fact, both of them were holding their hips (his snaky, hers wide and voluptuous) so far away from the other person that the impression was that they were shit-faced, and propping each other up.

Honest to God. Why couldn't Emma have got landed with *normal* people?

'Nobody ever takes our photographs,' Hannie said, visibly irritated.

'Here, I will.' It was Phil, looking rather smart in a monkey suit, and without the ubiquitous cigarette. He took in Hannie's bizarre tribal outfit, and aimed a small digital camera. 'Especially as you're the two most attractive women in the jungle.'

'Oh, vomit,' Hannie said.

'*Try* and be a lady,' he advised her kindly. 'Just for tonight. And leave some of those sunflower seeds for the rest of us.'

Emma regarded them indulgently, like a maiden aunt. She would let them go at it until it got nasty, and then she would step in and tell them to either cool it or get a room.

Hannie was looking at the door now, and giving Emma a dig in the ribs. Her elbow, honed on porridge and sprouting alfalfa, was so skinny and sharp that it was like a bread knife into the ribs. 'Look who's walked in.'

'Colin Farrell?'

Well, there had been rumours.

'Brian *Costello*.'

There he was, stuffed into a suit made for a smaller man, his goatee quivering on his plump little chin. He was the producer of *Afternoon Tea* over on TV2, which, despite the terrible name, was quite a good show with the usual mix of chat, reviews, fashion and cookery. He'd won the award for the last three years in a row. Apparently he'd been most surprised — *most* surprised — to find that *Wake Up Ireland* had been nominated in the same category. Well, what category had he expected it to be nominated in? Best lighting?

'Good luck tonight,' he called in passing.

'And to you!' they parroted back. 'Good luck!' Then, the minute he was gone: 'What a fucking phoney.'

'God, yes. He thinks we haven't a snowball's chance in hell.'

'We haven't,' Emma pointed out.

'If he wins he'll be on the phone first thing in the morning to tell us how humbled and surprised he is, blah, blah,' Phil said bitterly. 'I don't even want to be in the same *room* as him.' He looked at his hands. 'They're shaking,' he marvelled. 'I'd better go have a fag.'

But there was no chance to feed his addiction because here came the station's Controller of Programmes, Adam O'Reilly, and it would take a bigger man than Phil to walk off on him.

Everybody wanted to be around Adam. Naturally, this was because he was the boss man, and the person you were hauled in to see if your programme was going to be axed, or if you'd been caught spiriting off station toilet paper for your personal use at home. But apparently this last bit was just a vicious rumour put around by Resources.

He didn't just give out, though; there was something else about him too, something wise and caring. He had a beaten-up kind of face, like he'd seen every horror known to mankind (he'd come from the BBC) and the experience had made him more human. He was tall and slightly stooped; he always listened before he spoke, and when he did, it was in a very, very quiet voice. So quiet that the whole room would go on red alert, with people clutching each other and demanding fiercely, '*what* did he say?' and generally behaving as though they'd missed the Second Coming.

'Sometimes I feel like he's my father,' Phil blurted one day, having met Adam in the corridor and instead of making a little joke, had inexplicably found himself telling him all about a strange lump he'd found in his armpit in the shower, and that he was too afraid to have investigated, but which had been giving him sleepless nights.

'He told me to go and see the doctor just to put my mind at rest,' Phil said. His eyes were burning. 'And you know something? He was absolutely right.'

It turned out that most employees had found themselves in his office at some point or other, crying over their gas bill or their mother's clear preference for their sister Marie when they were children, and the terrible scar it had left.

' 'Evening, all,' he said now, in a quieter voice than usual. Emma had noticed that the more noise there was, the quieter he spoke.

'Hello! Hi, there.' Phil and Hannie were squirming in pleasure and looking at their shoes. Daddy was here. In a minute they'd ask for a lollipop.

He kissed Emma on the cheek, a warm, dry kiss, and said, 'Congratulations. I hope you know that you deserve it.'

Emma was now grinning too, massively, and tried to stop, but she couldn't. She'd never been a protégée, but given the chance she'd have

143

chosen to be Adam's. Imagine having him looking out for you: you couldn't go wrong.

But when she'd joined the station the previous year, she'd been thirty; she was already established, and besides, there was nothing worse than an ageing protégée. It was like wearing a miniskirt when you were sixty-five.

'I don't suppose we'll win,' she said. 'Not up against *Afternoon Tea*.'

'I don't suppose we will,' he returned.

She hadn't expected him to agree with her. She'd hoped he'd say something heart-warming and wise like, 'In seventy-two per cent of awards ceremonies, the underdog wins,' or, 'I have a feeling in my waters.'

But then he said — heart-warmingly and wisely — 'Awards don't count. Ratings do.'

She beamed at him and he nodded around at them all and went off to the bar. It was only when he'd gone that she got the sting in the tail: *Wake Up Ireland*'s ratings hadn't been great. They were fine for a show that had been on air only a year, but she knew that hopes had been higher. It wasn't building as much as it should.

Damn, he really *was* wise.

'We need to have a meeting,' she told Phil and Hannie.

Hannie laughed merrily. She was on her third gin and tonic.

'I mean it. We have to look at ways to get people out of bed in the morning.'

'Put Phil in beside them?' she suggested.

'Stop fantasising about me,' he chided her.

Emma cut across him. 'After the show

144

tomorrow we're going to sit down. See what we can do. In other words, don't get off your faces tonight. See you in a while.'

'Where are you going?'

'The loo,' she lied.

She was going home. The feel-good factor had gone; they hadn't a hope of winning, the ratings were poor, and she had no intention of hanging around to hear Brian Costello's acceptance speech. Far better to go home and deal with that nagging feeling she'd had for a while now that something about the show just wasn't gelling.

She squeezed by two filmmakers hunched over pints of Guinness and earnestly trying to fit the pitch for their next project onto the back of a postcard. 'I know! How about a guy who wakes up one morning and discovers that the world has suddenly moved on fifty years, and he doesn't know if it's a dream or if it's for real?'

'That's a load of shit.' Pause. 'How about *two* guys wake up one morning and discover that the world has moved on fifty years?'

'Class.'

Oh boy. With great relief she flung open the double doors of the ballroom and made her escape.

⋆ ⋆ ⋆

'Bloody hell, you nearly killed me.'

For a minute she didn't know what was happening. There was someone, a man, hopping about in front of her, clutching his shoulder and yelping in pain. Then she thought she knew:

145

another drunken nominee, not looking where he was going. It appeared that she had opened the door on him.

'Sorry,' she said frostily.

And, oh God, he was a filmmaker. Some of them didn't dress entirely in black, but went more for the grungy look. This specimen here was wearing faded jeans, a striped, slightly hippie, hoodie top, and a battered pair of Converse runners that could have done with a run through the washing machine.

He was rubbing his shoulder hard. 'Thank you for your heartfelt apology. I think I'll just about survive.'

He was making a bit of a song and dance about it, she felt. Probably after compensation, which he would then use to fund his next caper about two lads in Dublin who get involved in a robbery.

'Do you want to sit down?' she said a bit guiltily. He actually looked a bit pale. She'd probably given him a right whack.

He hobbled to one of the sofas in reception. Wanting just to leave him there, but feeling that she couldn't in the circumstances, she sat down gingerly at the other end of the sofa.

'You're very strong,' he commented.

She wasn't sure how to take this. It didn't sound like a compliment.

'Look, do you want an ice pack, is that it? Or can I pay for a taxi home for you or something?' she said defensively.

'I just want to sit here for a minute. You can go if you want.'

Except that now she couldn't, of course. So she sat there, trying not to look at him as he lay back against the sofa and shut his eyes. Ages seemed to pass. At one point she wondered whether he'd fallen asleep. She was just leaning over to check when his eyes opened and locked with her; there was almost a click.

Suddenly her mouth was dry and a zing shot through her veins.

He was looking at her dress now. She endured his scrutiny, wondering if he could see how red her cheeks were.

'You're at the awards bash,' he eventually stated.

'Yes,' she confirmed. 'I'm the producer of *Wake Up Ireland*.'

She waited for his supercilious little smirk. Telly. *Breakfast* telly.

But there was no smirk. Then, from his blank expression, she realised that he hadn't even heard of it. The insult!

'Which one are you up for?' she enquired. '*Tom and Dec? Blast?*' She tried to think of what the rest of them were called. Laddish things, anyway.

But he was displaying no comprehension there either.

'You can't remember which film you were nominated for?' Maybe her first instinct had been right; he was off his face.

'I'm not in film. Or television,' he stated. He looked towards the ballroom doors. 'I thought I might find the jacks through there.'

He suddenly smiled at her, and she wished he

147

hadn't, because there went her stomach again. He just kept smiling at her, never taking his eyes off her, almost like he was memorising her face.

'So what are you doing here?' She only asked because the atmosphere was getting too intense. She didn't know if he felt it too, or it was just her.

'Me? I'm just waiting for someone.'

A girlfriend? His mother? Emma suddenly realised she wanted to tear any other female in his life apart, limb by limb, and hold her still-beating heart aloft victoriously. Holy crap. What was happening to her?

'A journalist friend of mine,' he said. 'Fred.'

Ah. Fred. That was all right then.

He looked at his watch. 'At this stage I'd say he's a no-show.'

But he didn't move. He didn't look at his watch and say, 'Well, right-e-o, I'd better go and catch the last bus.' He just stayed there on the couch, stretched out — the length of him — with his Converse-clad feet — the *size* of them — crossed at the ankles.

'Do you think you'll win tonight, Emma?' he said.

'Well, actually, no — ' She stopped. 'How do you know my name?'

'You're wearing a name badge.'

'Oh. Yes. Of course.' For a wild moment she'd thought it was some crazy intuition between them. 'How's your shoulder?'

He gingerly reached up to rub it. 'I don't know,' he said doubtfully. He shot her a look. 'I might have to have a whiskey.'

148

His eyes were an open invitation. She found herself grinning back.

'Really?' she said.

'Yes. But not here. This place is too fancy for me.'

'Let's go to McGinty's then.' It was a run-down kip around the corner, run by a mentaler called Paddy-Joe. Paddy-Joe would be all over you one night, but the next, when he was in a bad mood, he would threaten to bar you just for ordering a drink.

'You know McGinty's?' He was delighted.

It was a great start.

9

Ali

The phone rang one afternoon at about four o'clock and, as Emma was working late — could she be avoiding coming home? — Ali answered it.

'Hello?'

'Hey, there! Can I speak to Jack, please?'

The voice was so energetic, so cute and squeaky, that Ali had to hold the receiver a little away from her ear. 'Who is this?'

'Carly.'

Carly. Ali racked her brains. Nope.

The second thing that struck her was that this girl had their number. *Emma's* number. How had that happened? Nobody was supposed to know where they were.

But before she could enquire further, the girl — Carly — said, 'Oh, and thanks for that recipe, Mrs Peterson. My chocolate chip cookies turned out just great. Everybody at the fundraiser said they were the best they'd ever tasted.'

Now Ali was really confused. Apparently not only did she know Carly, but such was the extent of the friendship that there was some kind of recipe-swap going on.

Finally she began to put things together. 'Have you been at my house?' she enquired carefully.

'Sure I have!' Carly chirped.

In the last year or so, girls had discovered Jack. This was through no fault of his. He'd gone about his business as usual, studying, playing basketball, and riling up Anto when he got the chance. But he must have inadvertently been giving off some kind of high-pitched sexual hum that only pubescent girls could hear, because they started arriving at the house in droves; gorgeous little creatures with train-track braces and names like Hannah and Briony and Carly (had she been the one with the blonde ringlets or the teensy weensy denim shorts?). They would ring Ali's doorbell, clasping homework books helplessly to their chests.

'I just can't do this math,' they would confess. 'And Jack is such a whiz . . . '

Kyle had laughed when he'd heard this. 'That's exactly what used to happen to me. The amount of math homework I used to do for girls . . . '

Maybe, but he'd enjoyed it by all accounts, and had necked with most of the applicants. Quite the stud in his heyday, as he reminded her from time to time. But poor Jack was only fifteen, and an entirely different proposition from his father. He looked positively frightened when some of them would follow him home from school. And it didn't help that Anto kept shouting things like 'whoaar' at him every time one of his admirers turned up on the doorstep.

'Come in,' Ali would tell the girls brightly. 'I think Jack is busy right now, but how about *I* help you?'

How their little faces would fall. But they would come in anyway; at least they were in the actual house, they probably reckoned, and then it was only a short journey up to Jack's bedroom where no doubt they intended to strip him naked and determinedly have sex with him.

Ali never turned her back on them, not even to fill the kettle. There they would sit, eating cookies and drinking milk, while Ali, just to fill the silence while she tried to figure out what the square root of 625 was (answer: 25) would regale them with the tale of the flat tyre she'd got on the highway that morning, and how she'd had to show quite a bit of leg before a motorist would stop and help her out. (Kyle had often warned her off this practice. It might be all right in Ireland, but in America you were just as likely to get kidnapped and murdered and be found six years later in a refuse dump.)

'But don't try this yourself,' she would have to impress hurriedly upon the girls.

Most of them didn't come back a second time after an hour with her. But a couple, Carly included, had persevered, and struck up quite a rapport with her. And she *did* remember Carly commenting on her chocolate chip cookies, even if she had no recollection of giving her the recipe.

'Do you need help with your homework?' she enquired of Carly on the phone now, suppressing a yawn. Emma tried to be quiet in the mornings when she got up, but the power shower lifted them all out of it anyway.

Carly laughed again. Dear God, where did she

get her energy? 'You're the funniest of all the moms, everybody says that.' Before Ali could figure out whether this was a good thing or not, Carly was off again. 'When are you guys coming back, anyhow? I've kept notes for Jack of all the stuff he's missing in school, but the teachers are starting to wonder now what's up. And Pete and Charlie keep trying to text him, but it never goes through. He needs to call his mobile company and get that fixed — '

'Carly.' It was like trying to calm down an overexcited chipmunk. 'Listen, I really appreciate you doing that. Looking out for him at school and stuff. But he's actually in the power shower right now,' big fat lie, 'and won't be able to hear a thing.'

Poor Jack. Imagine being tracked down to Ireland. This Carly was clearly more ingenious than Kyle, who hadn't thought to ring Emma even once to see if Ali might be there. As far as she knew, he hadn't phoned her parents either. So how come Carly had outwitted everybody?

Then Carly said, 'I'm returning *his* call.'

OK. Ali put the phone tighter to her ear. '*Jack* called *you*?'

'Can you tell him to call me tonight? Thanks, Mrs Peterson! Have a good day!'

★   ★   ★

They were in the supermarket, and nothing was right.

'Not that popcorn, I don't like the taste of it,' Erin said quite decisively.

153

'You haven't even tried it.'

'Yes, but I know I won't like it.'

She was also certain that she wouldn't like Heinz Baked Beans, Birds Eye fish fingers or Colgate toothpaste, because none of them looked the same as the ones back home, even if they cost twice the bloody price.

'It's either that tube, or else you'll have to brush your teeth with charcoal, missy.'

Ali wasn't sure at what point the thrill of being back in Ireland, and having a karaoke competion every night, and dodging school, had started to wear off. But the whinge-factor had definitely upped a notch in the past few days. Earlier, Anto had thrown himself on the floor in anguish when informed that they had to do a supermarket run, and was now trailing ten paces behind, throwing scrunched-up balls of paper at the back of Erin's head.

'Anthony! One more time, and I swear . . . '

Several shoppers looked over in concern. She lowered her voice in case one of them happened to be a social worker, and ploughed on.

'Oh, look,' she said, in a very jolly voice, picking up a bag of nachos. 'Phileas Fogg. The same as home!'

Damn. She hadn't meant home. She'd meant Texas.

All three of them — Jack was bringing up the rear — looked from her to the nachos and back to her again blankly. OK, so maybe she hadn't expected them to jump up and down, but come *on*.

'Bet they still won't taste the same,' Erin

concluded eventually.

Oh, for heaven's sake. Still, with luck it was just a phase, and things would be back to normal tomorrow. They always had such a good time in Ireland, and never wanted to leave to go home. So what was with all the complaining?

In the end she bribed Anto and Erin with a fiver each to spend in the newsagents at the other end of the shopping centre. 'You can even go on your own,' she told them. They were delighted. She hardly ever let them do that in the States, because of all the abduction scares. Like anybody would abduct those two. And if they did, they'd stop a hundred yards down the road and beg them to get out.

In high spirits again, off the two of them set, telling her that she was the best Mom in the world.

'Yeah, yeah. Go on.'

Now it was just her and Jack. He had his hands stuffed deep in his pockets and was as good a specimen of teen awkwardness, belligerence and hormone-ridden angst as you could get.

Well, Ali had been there too. She wasn't so ancient that she couldn't remember those years herself. And she was easily the most clued-in parent in his class. She hadn't even *mentioned* Carly and the phone call in twenty-four hours, that was how cool she was.

She had it all worked out. The trick with these things was subtlety. No sense in barging in there and getting his back up.

And so she said brightly, as though it had just

155

occurred to her, 'Guess who popped into my mind the other day?'

Jack gave her a wary look. 'You're going to have to be more specific.'

She allowed a dreamy, faraway look to come over her. 'Someone I used to know when I was young. A boy.'

Jack misinterpreted her look. 'Did he *die*?'

'No. I used to go out with him when I was young; about, oh, the same age as you are now.' She had his attention. Good. 'He was six foot tall and his name was Nick.' It had actually been Jeremy, but she was sure he wouldn't mind. 'All the girls were after him but he picked me. We were mad about each other. Couldn't be separated. The first time he kissed me, I swear, it was like . . . like a whole load of fireworks exploded inside me at once.'

'*Mom*.' He was looking at her as though he hoped a large hole would materialise in the floor of the Personal Hygiene section and swallow her up.

'Sorry.' She did actually feel a bit hot. Jeremy *had* been a ride.

'Maybe you should be telling one of your friends about this,' Jack mumbled, desperate to move the trolley on and end the conversation. 'Or a counsellor or something.'

Ali jammed her foot firmly against the trolley wheel. She wasn't finished yet. 'My point is, I was sure, *positive*, that nothing would ever change. That we'd always be mad about each other. That we would even get married.'

His face grew rigid now. He was cottoning on

156

to where she might be going with this. He began to shake his head. 'Mom — '

'Two months later I found out he was two-timing me with a girl on my hockey team.' Bitch. How about *that* for team spirit. 'I thought I would die, Jack, but in another month I was going out with someone else too.' A couple of guys, actually, but there was no need to tell him that.

He was looking at her with great hostility now. Her little boy, who'd only ever thought she was the bee's knees. 'I get the moral of the story, OK? You think me and Carly are dumb. Maybe you're even laughing at us.'

'No!' This was backfiring.

'Well, you can laugh all you want, but Carly and me, we love each other.'

Love? Dear God. When had all this happened? She didn't even know they *knew* each other.

'You can't love someone after, what, three weeks?' She tried a little laugh.

'We've been going out six months.'

Six months? Where had she been? Clearly with her head in the sand. And why hadn't he told her?

'Well, that's good,' she said, nodding furiously. 'Obviously you know each other pretty well at this stage — '

'I've met her parents.'

He was like some stranger now, with a whole other life that she hadn't even known existed.

'We'd have liked to have met Carly. Officially,' she said, trying to keep the hurt and blame out of her voice.

'No, you wouldn't have. You'd have tried to break us up. You'd have said I was too young, and that I had to study hard and get to university so that I wouldn't get stuck in Texas selling plastic bags.'

'I never said that!' She had not. She knew damned well she hadn't.

'You didn't have to,' he said coolly.

She was floundering now, feeling like she had been found out. 'I only want the best for you, Jack. That's all. And yes, maybe I *do* feel you're a bit young to go saying that you love someone — '

'There!' He threw up his hands. 'I knew it!'

'You're only fifteen. Maybe tomorrow you'll meet some Irish girl, and fall in love with *her*.'

Just keep your options open, that's all she wanted to say to him.

But he took it the wrong way. 'You really think I'm that shallow?'

'No . . . I didn't mean that . . . just . . . well, maybe *Carly* could meet someone while *you're* away.'

She couldn't believe she said it. It just kind of came out. Most of her mistakes happened that way.

'Carly's not like you. She doesn't walk out on people,' he bit out, and then he aimed the trolley at her, gave it a push, and walked out.

There was further bad news awaiting her at the checkout, when the girl on the desk told her, quite politely considering she had just run two hundred and four euros worth of stuff through her scanner that would now have to be put back, that Ali's credit card had been declined.

158

The joint credit and cash cards had all been cancelled; the cards that were supposed to feed and clothe the children. (And also to purchase a pair of boots she'd seen in Brown Thomas that could hardly be described as a necessity, but they were such a fabulous rich brown colour, and they'd whispered to her as she'd walked past, *buy* me. Oh, why hadn't she resisted?)

She rang the credit card companies and angrily demanded to have the cards reinstated. The response was standard — terribly sorry, nothing we can do, please make a fresh application in your own name, oops, we just cut you off.

Meanwhile she had the sum total of sixty-two dollars and twenty cents in her purse.

What a fecker. What a dirty, rotten creep. To leave them defenceless like this in another country. Even if he didn't give a damn about her, what about his kids?

OK deep breath. Running out of money had not been part of the plan. But she would just have to deal with this. Finally.

His secretary Louise answered the phone on the second ring. 'Oh, hi, Ali! How are you guys enjoying your vacation in Ireland?'

Ali was momentarily blind-sided. Kyle knew she was in Ireland? His *secretary* knew she was in Ireland?

'Having a whale of a time,' she managed to sing happily. 'Fecking brilliant! Is, ah, Kyle around?'

'He's in a meeting.'

Thank Christ. It would give her time to regroup. All this time she'd thought that, unbelievably, she'd pulled the wool over his eyes. Almost laughing at his dimness. Clearly he wasn't that dim after all.

'No problem. I'll try again later.' Or not.

'He told me to let him know if you called,' Louise insisted. 'One minute.' It didn't even take a minute. He was on the phone fourteen seconds later.

'Ali. I'd a feeling I'd hear from you today.'

It was a bit of a shock to hear his voice. Well, it had been a while. And he sounded so smug and *righteous* that she wanted to slap his face for him.

'Hi, Kyle,' she managed through gritted teeth. 'I need you to reinstate my cards.'

'Hell will freeze over,' he told her pleasantly. 'How's the weather over there? Wet and miserable as usual?'

Now she *really* hated him. 'What did you have to do, hire a team of private investigators to find me?' she said, intended as a direct hit on his intelligence.

'Didn't need to. Not when you were running up credit card bills all over Dublin. Anyway,' he said, 'you always go back to Ireland.'

He sounded kind of sad for her, that she didn't have enough imagination to flee to, say, Madagascar or the beaches of Phuket.

'You're dishonest,' she told him.

'No, you're the one who's dishonest. Sneaking off in the middle of the night without even telling

160

me. Sneaking off with my *kids*.' He was making sure that she knew it was them he was concerned about, not her.

'It was an early flight,' she flung at him.

'I thought something had happened to you,' he burst out violently. 'I kept ringing and ringing your phone, then the house . . . Then I go around and the whole place is closed up and your stuff is gone. I nearly called the *police*, Ali.'

He sounded really upset. She had to remind herself that it was entirely his fault that she had left.

'Maybe you shouldn't have said the things you did,' she told him coldly.

He was just as cold. 'When you go and do something harebrained like this, it makes me all the more determined to get my kids.'

Ali laughed, but there was a strange tone to it. It sounded like fear. 'I'm not going to be threatened by you.'

'They're missing school,' he pointed out. 'They should be in their own house.'

'The kids are absolutely fine,' she told him haughtily. 'Having the time of their lives, in fact.'

'That so? How come Erin was getting all teary this week about her new bike left behind in the garage?'

Ali nearly dropped the phone. How did he know about that?

'Jack phones me.' He didn't say it with any pleasure. 'And it's only that he does that I'm not on a plane over there to get you back.'

All right, so maybe Ali *did* feel a little bad about the kids in all this. But he'd just gone and made them destitute. Two wrongs didn't make a right, but as far as she was concerned they cancelled each other out.

Besides, the 'getting her back' thing wasn't going down well.

'You've made quite enough threats in all this,' she told him furiously. 'Make another one and I swear, I'll leave Emma's and move somewhere else and you won't find us next time.'

Silence now. She'd got to him. When he spoke again he sounded worried. 'When are you coming back?'

'I'm not. I'm staying in Ireland. Me and the kids.'

10

Emma

It was unprecedented to get called in to work on a Saturday. Worse still, they were made to wait in the canteen for a full fifteen minutes before finding out what might be wrong.

'Well, they haven't called us in because something is *right*,' Phil said. His hands were shaking. He didn't dare go out for a fag in case he was missing when they were called up.

'Anybody for a dried apricot?' Hannie asked, rooting in her handbag.

'No.'

'A brazil nut?'

'No.'

'A — '

'Fucking *no*.' Phil let out a tense breath. From the smell of it, he'd been out on the batter the previous night. And why not? It'd been a Friday, and there was no 4 a.m. start the following morning.

Instead there came a phone call from Adam O'Reilly — personally — asking each of them if they would mind coming in to the office. Phil had actually been on the job with some girl he'd picked up the previous night, and he said it was like Adam could actually *see* down the telephone line. Sometimes he got a bit

163

confused between Adam and God.

Hannie had been carrying on as normal: making a Saturday morning green smoothie from spinach leaves, kiwi, that kind of thing. There were still bits of it stuck between her teeth. She never minded this, as it gave her something to chew on all day.

Emma had been in the bathroom, in her pyjamas, examining her tongue in the mirror. She was wondering whether that layer of whitish stuff at the back was normal. It was difficult to know, with tongues. It's not like you could compare it with anybody else's. And was it, overall, slightly *grey* looking? In the end she went to give it a good scrub with her toothbrush, hoping it might bring a more lifelike appearance to it, only to find that there was no toothpaste left, only a tube of Erin's violent pink, sickly sweet stuff that left her breath smelling like cheap chewing gum.

Her tongue was fine. Absolutely fine. There was no need to go reading anything into it, just because it had all the colour and attractiveness of a slab of uncooked tuna.

Fine, fine, fine. She repeated this to herself now in the chilly canteen. But the stress was starting to get to her. In normal circumstances she'd have laid her head on Ryan's solid shoulder, and he'd have held her close and said, comfortingly, 'Don't let the miserable, rotten, dirty bastards get you down.'

Unfortunately now *he* was the bastard. And he was gone, and she felt like she was missing an arm, her right one at that, and she kept looking around for it, wondering where the blazes it had gone.

And when was it going to get better, anyway? All this angst, and upset, and missing-arm business? A month, she'd read in some magazine. Two months, somewhere else. Then, very pessimistically, someone else said a year. A whole *year*. Dear God. She'd be dead from grief by then. Or else from that white stuff on her tongue.

Shite. Now she was back thinking about that again. And was it *normal* to have little white flecks in one's nails, or was it a sign of something sinister?

'I know!' Hannie hit the table with her fist, making Emma jump. Phil held his head. 'Maybe he's going to tell us that we're getting pay rises.'

She knew this was stupid the minute it was out of her mouth. She gave a little sigh. 'Sorry. It's just my innate optimism.'

'Have another dried apricot,' Phil encouraged.

Eventually they were called up to Adam's office. He was sitting very still behind his desk, his fingers pressed together in a little pyramid under his chin. He looked a bit like a Buddha, only, in his dress-down jeans and polo shirt, a groovy one.

'Have you seen the papers?' he asked in a very, very low voice. No hellos, no, 'Was the traffic bad?'

Hannie leaned forward. She hadn't quite caught him. 'The papers, you say?'

'I have,' Phil blustered immediately. Because his dial was permanently set to self-survival, this kind of shameless lying came easily.

Adam leaned forward intensely. 'And what did you think?' he whispered.

The word 'fuck' ran across Phil's face. He opened and closed his mouth several times. 'Well . . . naturally . . . these things can be taken both ways . . . '

While he was busy extracting his foot from his gob, Emma's eye was caught by the stash of newspapers that were trapped under Adam's elbow. 'Man Has Twenty-Seven Wives', 'Bigger Breasts Can Mean Higher IQ'. Surely he hadn't called them all in to discuss *that*.

What was he doing, reading the tabloids, anyway? He'd often been spotted with a copy of the *Irish Times* or the *Guardian* tucked under his elbow, but rarely the *Irish Sun*.

Then she saw it. A photo of Alannah and Patrick, quite a big one, over some headline she couldn't read.

That in itself wasn't alarming. Both of them graced the pages of the tabloids on a regular basis, either in connection with the show or at some social event, or else, in Patrick's case, anyway, talking about the challenges of balancing work with a hectic beauty regime. Actually, that was just a joke that Hannie had made. The real article had been about the modern Irishman's busy life or some such rubbish.

Emma even recognised the photo. It was a stock studio one, taken back when the show had just launched, and before Patrick and Alannah realised they disliked each other quite so much. They looked almost chummy. The dimple in

Patrick's chin twinkled rakishly, and Alannah for once didn't look like she had bad wind.

Adam caught her looking.

'Yes,' he said. Then, in case she hadn't quite cottoned on that the photo signalled something less than benign, that in fact it meant something *bad*, he said. 'Yes,' again, even quieter than before.

Better to face it head on. 'Has something happened?' Emma enquired calmly, even though her stomach was flip-flopping unpleasantly. The ratings, she knew. The bloody things had gone down. It was the only explanation for a Saturday morning emergency meeting. The tabloids loved stuff like that: 'Morning Show Hits Rock Bottom!' or some other spin. 'Only Two People Watching, Polls Confirm!' — Emma could write the headline herself.

Adam didn't answer. Instead he flicked the paper across the desk, Frisbee-style. On either side of her, Phil and Hannie scrabbled to catch it. They missed, and it landed squarely on the desk in front of Emma.

It was there in one inch headlines: 'TROUBLE ON SET OF *WAKE UP IRELAND*'.

For a minute, she thought they were talking about her, and the cup of tea she'd knocked all over a camera last week, and how everybody had gone mental (no liquids were allowed on set). How in the name of God had the papers got hold of that? And, why?

When her eyes flicked down it, she saw that of course it wasn't about that at all. The article, which was no more than a hundred words — out of all proportion to the size of the photo — went on about 'rumours' that were floating around regarding 'antagonism' between the co-presenters of *Wake Up Ireland*, as told to the paper by 'unnamed sources' at an 'unidentified location'.

'Why isn't the location identified?' Phil wondered, reading over her shoulder and completely missing the point.

This was bad. Very bad. For all of them.

'They didn't contact the programme,' Emma told Adam fiercely, hating the defensive whine that was colouring her voice. 'They didn't even give us a chance to reply before going to print.'

It was low. Normally they at least got the right to rebuff nonsense like this. But this time, nothing.

Adam, unfortunately, didn't share her moral outrage. 'And what difference would that have made? From what I hear, it's true. Isn't it?'

He was very pissed off. Emma knew this by the little white ring around his mouth. He had given her this programme and, barely two years into it, it was descending into a public mess that he would have to explain to the board of directors.

'Isn't it?' he enquired again.

Phil and Hannie sat like mice beside her now. Not a word out of them. Emma didn't blame them. She was the producer, on a much bigger salary than they were; it was her problem and she would just have to suck it up.

'There are some ... differences between them,' she admitted.

He just waited. There was going to be no

168

soft-soaping of this one.

'All right,' she said. If he wanted the score, he could have it. 'They don't seem to be able to stand each other.'

Some movement at last from her co-producers. 'That's right,' Hannie murmured, while Phil piped up helpfully, 'They hate each other's guts.'

Adam gave them all another sweeping look, and then relaxed back a bit. 'I see,' he said heavily.

He looked quite sympathetic. Well, what could any of them *do*? It was nobody's fault that Alannah and Patrick heralded from different planets, one swirly and perfumed and slightly odd, the other hairy and opinionated and given to volcanic explosions at the mere mention of the word horoscope. How anyone had thought it would be a good idea to pair them up on a programme together . . .

But Emma would say nothing. No doubt on paper they'd looked good. And it was up to Adam to wrestle with his own conscience on that score.

'We've been having problems for a while,' she said diplomatically, not wanting to make him feel worse. 'Tensions, minor squabbles, that kind of thing. They just can't seem to leave each other alone.'

Maybe he would get them on the phone too. Haul them in, tell them to cop themselves on.

The more Emma thought about it, the more indignant she became. It was lack of profession-alism, pure and simple, and it was unfair to make everybody else take the blame. Hadn't she

169

enough worries of her own, between a broken heart and a dodgy-looking tongue without having to make excuses for Patrick and Alannah's bad behaviour?

And perhaps Adam was dying for a good old bitch himself, because he asked Hannie and Phil to leave the room. Best not to do it in front of them.

'So what you are going to do?' Emma asked, when they were alone. There was a kind of sick excitement working its way up in her. This could be a blood bath.

'Nothing,' said Adam.

OK, it wasn't exactly the kind of plan Emma would have come up with, but he was the boss. If he wanted to let Alannah and Patrick slug it out amongst themselves, it was his decision.

'I was wondering what *you* were going to do,' he said.

So it was right back at ya. Fine. She could handle that, even though she felt her face flame at the implied criticism 'If you want me to take responsibility for that article — '

'I do.'

'Right. Well, I'm sorry.' She'd never been dressed down by him before and it was horrible. She felt weak and small and a total failure. 'I'll have a word with them. It won't happen again.'

She was on her feet and striding to the door in mortification and shame when he called her back to sit down again.

'How are things with you?' he said.

She looked at him blankly. What did he mean? After such a horrible conversation, surely he wasn't trying to finish things up with a chummy, 'So tell us, what's the crack at all?'

But his face was worryingly kind. She guessed what he was going to say a second before he said it.

'Listen, Emma.' Here it came. 'I heard about your engagement.' There was no need to insert the words 'broken' or 'banjaxed' or 'fecked'. They were both on the same wavelength here.

For some reason she found herself smiling like some lunatic in a toothpaste commercial. 'It's not having a detrimental effect on my work, if that's what you mean,' she said chirpily. Well, the alternative was throwing herself upon his shoulder and weeping hysterically down his polo shirt and, horrors, maybe even asking him to take a quick peek at her tongue.

It would be all over the station in an hour. Her credibility shot to hell. And there was hardly any need to mention that her job was all that she had left. Well, along with her apartment, her car, and the stray cat she informally shared with next door (put like that, some people would think she wasn't doing too badly).

'I didn't mean that, Emma.'

He cared. He really did. Bloody hell. Why couldn't she have got a nasty, cold boss who said things like, 'Get your house in order or it's the door for you, Miss Broken Engagement (not that I give a shit)'?

She stood quickly before her emotions got the better of her. 'Look, I'm sorry about what happened with the papers. But I promise that it won't happen again. And as for my engagement,

171

I'm completely over that.'

On that whopper, she walked out.

★ ★ ★

She wanted a glass of wine, a bath and some movie with Colin Firth in it, in that order. She'd spent the day trudging around town, mulling gloomily over Ryan, Alannah, Patrick and, most of all, Adam — that horrible look of sympathy, like she should consider compassionate leave and maybe a short course of antidepressants. Now all she wanted to do was shut out the world and curl up on the sofa, and have a good cry if she felt like it.

'Just in time for charades!' Ali called as she let herself in.

It was all happening in the living room. Anto was splayed on the carpet like a dead body in a police crime scene, his eyes rolling back in his head. He hissed out of the side of his mouth, 'I've just been sawed in two.'

'You're not allowed to talk,' Erin insisted. 'You're only allowed to mime.'

'Is it *Night of the Living Dead?*' Ali tried.

'No.'

'*Scream? Friday the Thirteenth?*'

He shook his head and erupted in a loud rr-rrr-rrrrrrr noise.

'He's doing it again!' Erin protested hotly. 'You're not allowed to make sounds!'

'I know!' Ali was on her feet. '*Texas Chainsaw Massacre!*'

'Yes!' Anto sat up and grinned. 'Can we rent

172

that out again, Mom?'

Jack was hunched on the furthest corner of the sofa, looking too big for the room, his eyes firmly fixed on the ceiling as though he had no connection whatsoever with these people.

Emma knew the feeling, kind of. She too had the sense that she was an alien, standing there in her own apartment. Not that it looked anything like her apartment any more, what with the lines of underwear and socks drying on the heaters, and the unidentifiable stains that were appearing over the furniture and carpets at the rate of one a day. Shoes, bags and toys lay in doorways and hallways like booby traps. And if they didn't get her as she fumbled around in the dark at 4 a.m., then the wires that charged various phones and music gadgets certainly would. She'd nearly decapitated herself with one last week when she'd bent down to get something from the fridge.

But mostly it was the people who made her apartment so weird. The kids and Ali. They were too loud and full of life for her quiet little home. Didn't they know that she was miserable? Well, clearly they did — they commented upon it often enough — but wouldn't you think that at least they'd go around with big long faces in sympathy? She was putting them up, paying the astronomical gas bill and going around after them with bottles of Cif; the very least they could do was allow a moment's silence whenever she walked in the room, in deference to her general level of misery.

Not a bit of it. 'You cheated, you jerk,' Erin

173

told Anto, jumping on him with a couple of well-aimed blows to the head.

'Stop it, you stupid kids,' Jack shouted, trying to drag them apart. He joined in with a few blows of his own. There would be blood in a minute; gallons of it, the way Anto was fighting back.

And now here was Ali bustling in from the kitchen. She scarcely gave the mini-riot on the carpet a glance. 'I kept you some dinner.' She held out a plate — newly chipped, another one. What did she do, hurl them against the wall before putting them in the dishwasher? On it was some kind of tuna casserole thing that looked pleasant enough, by Ali's standards anyway, but that immediately got Emma's back up more.

'I don't like tuna,' she said. Well, she didn't.

'Oh. Well, OK, I can make you a ham sandwich if you'd prefer. Kids! Did you eat all the bread earlier?'

'It wasn't me,' Anto said immediately.

'I don't like ham either.' Emma had to raise her voice to be heard over the mêlée. 'Don't you know *anything* about me?'

Ali was looking a bit pissed off now. 'What do you want, a full Sunday roast?'

Emma, stupidly, felt tears sting her eyes. 'There are only two foods that I don't like. Tuna and ham. Only two. And you're so wrapped up in yourself that you can't even remember that!'

She sounded about seven. But suddenly the kids were silent — imagine, Auntie Emma blowing her lid like that. And all over Mom's casserole (which hadn't been great, in fairness).

Ali just watched her worriedly. 'What's wrong, Emma?'

'What's *wrong*? What do you think is wrong?' Her voice had gone right up now, worse luck. She was furious, yet sounded like Minnie Mouse.

'Right. Let's do this someplace else.' Ali, bossily, twirled her round and pushed her in the direction of her bedroom. Emma tried to resist but it was futile. 'Anto. Erin. Stop it now,' Ali ordered. 'Jack, put on the telly, please.'

Then they were in the bedroom, with *The Simpsons* blaring busily in the living room, although Emma suspected that at least two of the kids had tumblers stuck to the wall, hoping for some kind of cat fight.

'Sit down,' said Ali.

'Oh, just stop it. Please.'

'What?'

'I'm sorry for my little outburst, OK? But I'm fine now, so you can go back to charades and stop trying to sort me out. Which you were never that good at, to be honest.'

Ali wasn't a bit offended. 'Is it work? I know something happened this morning when they called you in.'

'I don't care about work.'

'Yes, you do. You've always been very . . . conscientious.' She looked like she didn't fully grasp the concept herself, but admired anybody who did.

'This is not about work, Ali, OK?' Stupid thing to have said, of course, because Ali now scurried further down her check list of calamities that might have befallen Emma.

'Ryan, then. Your heart is still broken.'

'You're on the ball today.'

'Emma, I'm just trying to help here, that's all.'

If she really wanted to help, she'd pack up her myriad belongings, and take herself and her out-of-control kids to Mam's, and leave Emma in peace and quiet.

Actually, Ali had stopped mentioning leaving altogether. A few weeks ago, she used to say regularly, 'We'll be out of your hair soon.' Now they were using her address to register new mobile phones, and for what looked suspiciously like a form for the dole.

'I know it's shite when relationships go wrong,' Ali said fervently. 'Look at me, for heaven's sake. Three kids and sixteen years together, and now we're living on different continents!'

'For the moment,' Emma reminded her. 'Speaking of which, isn't it time you booked your flights back?'

'Don't try and run from the pain,' Ali told her gravely. 'You're going to have to face it sooner or later.'

'Oh, shut up, Ali. I hate all that touchy-feely American crap.'

'So do I, but you can't get away from it over there,' Ali said with a sigh. 'I've tried to fight it but it kind of seeps in.'

'Well, it doesn't suit you, and it's not going to work on me anyway, so you might as well go back out to the kids.'

Ali was looking very hurt now. (Somehow this had become about her again.) 'I know something's wrong. I just have to look at you, Emma. Something happened with you and Ryan and I'm not leaving this bedroom until you tell me.'

Emma shook her head incredulously. 'You can't march back here after sixteen years away and demand that everybody lets you in on every intimate little detail of their lives.'

'Not everybody, Emma. Just you. I told you all about Kyle.'

Ah, yes. Hardly a night was complete without some gory story of his misdemeanours, the last one being his penchant for corduroy trousers and red check shirts. According to Ali, all he was missing was a ten-gallon hat and a bumper sticker that said 'Redneck'.

Each story, one layered upon the other, sounded suspiciously like Ali was laying down a defence. Against what exactly, she had yet to say.

Emma pinned her with a look now. 'So you want me to tell you all about Ryan, and what a creep he is, and that'll make us both feel better? Well, I'm sorry, but it doesn't work that way.'

Ali looked like she'd been slapped. 'I just want to make you feel better, that's all.'

'You can't. Nothing can make me feel better.'

Ali looked frightened now. She sat down beside her and tried to take her hand. 'What's wrong? For God's sake, just tell me what's wrong with you.'

It was getting harder to keep up a tough front. And Ali was patting her back now, not exactly

177

gently, more like she was burping a baby, but Emma could feel more treacherous tears starting to choke her gullet. She tried to blink them back but it was no use. 'I'm afraid, Ali.'

'Of what?'

'I don't know.' She couldn't say it. The words were compacting in her throat, refusing to be let out.

And now there was Ali, pushing, pushing. 'Just describe how you feel.'

'I can't! What do you want to do, look at my bloody tongue?'

Ali looked baffled. 'What's wrong with your tongue?'

'Nothing! Nothing. Just leave me alone.'

'Have you got a bit of a fever? You look hot.'

She could not have said a worse thing. Fever. Heat. It was what they said to look out for. Oh God. It really was happening.

'You had to say it, didn't you?' she shouted into Ali's startled face, pushing her away and storming for the door. 'You just bloody had to.'

11

Ali

'Is Emma all right?' Ali asked Mam. 'Like, she's not sick?'

'She had a bit of a cold last week — sneezing, runny nose, that kind of thing — but that's about it,' Mam said. And, she regularly maintained, she knew sick when she saw it, having to look at Dad all day long, languishing in his chair, alternately blue or white, or else red when he was doing a number two (he liked her to be there for those too in case his heart gave out in the middle of the exertion). 'Did she say what her symptoms were?'

'She didn't say anything, really. She looked a bit off.' They were in Mam's kitchen, drinking tea. Erin and Anto were in the garden, walking around the square of green aimlessly. Jack was on his mobile phone, no doubt composing a text message to the lovely Carly. Ali had come across one yesterday when she'd picked up his phone to charge it. It had started with, 'Hey babes. Missin u lodz.' And they said romance was dead?

But back to Emma, and her very strange mood, and her increasingly erratic bathroom habits. After their spat last night, she'd locked herself in the bathroom for an hour. Erin maintained, having looked through the keyhole, that she was staring into a magnifying mirror. It was all very strange.

'She's probably just pining after Ryan,' Mam said. 'She looks all right to me, apart from being miserable, but sure, we're used to that.'

'I suppose.'

Mam was right: Emma looked like always, with her shiny hair and her lovely, unlined skin (that was no kids for you), and her general classy and groomed air. Heartbroken or not, she still managed to look marvellous, and every time she walked into the room in her skinny jeans and little tops, Ali wished she had packed fewer velour tracksuits and more high heels.

'You could always ask Hannie,' Mam said. 'She tells her everything.'

Mam didn't mean anything by it. But it hurt just the same. Ali wondered whether Emma wasn't right; that all that time away meant that things had changed, and no matter how hard they tried, they'd never again be the way they were.

'The tea,' said Dad. They'd nearly forgotten he was there. He was looking into his cup in a crotchety fashion.

'What's wrong with it?' Mam had taken to speaking to him in a loud, highpitched voice, like they do in hospitals with very old people.

'It's too weak.'

'You like weak tea,' she shouted at him.

'Not this weak.' He looked a bit bewildered now as well as half-deafened.

'I'll get you another one if you want. You want a fresh cup, is that what you want? Is it?'

You would think he was after the crown jewels. Ali wanted to cover her ears now at Mam's bellows. She looked into his cup. Dad was right; the tea was nothing more than brownish water.

'I'll get it for him, Mam.'

'No, you won't. Sit down. I'll get him another cup.' She grabbed the cup off him and threw the tea down the sink before pouring another one in an ill-tempered fashion. 'He has me crucified,' she said, as though he wasn't sitting two feet from her. 'And now he'll be widdling all night long, after two cups of tea.'

Dad hung his head in shame; a man who, up to a few years ago, used to go for five-mile walks around the neighbourhood, chatting with people he met, and admiring their teeth, if they were his. 'Holding up beautifully, those dentures,' he would assure people proudly.

'I'll stay over, if you want,' Ali offered. She felt sorry for Dad, even though she knew he did get up several times a night, and so, therefore, did Mam. Maybe they both needed a break from each other. It must be claustrophobic, being cramped up in the house all day long, except for supermarket dashes, and Ali or Emma calling in.

At least now Ali would be around more. A lot more. She wouldn't break the news to Mam just yet, not until she'd worked out the logistics, such as where they would live, et cetera. She didn't want Mam to insist that they all stayed there at the house. They might never escape.

Mam brushed off the offer of help with a, 'You will not stay over,' and Ali felt a guilty relief.

Mam plonked herself back down again. 'Keep

181

an eye on Emma, won't you?' She looked worried now. 'It's not like her to get all mysterious and storm off about things. Not like you.'

'Thank you, Mam.'

'You know what I mean. When something's wrong with you, we all know about it. And thank God for that, I say. But Emma . . . a terrible one for bottling things up.' When Dad looked at her blankly, she shouted, 'BOTTLING THINGS UP.'

'I'm not deaf, you know. I can hear perfectly.'

Mam jerked a thumb in his direction. 'He'll put me into an early grave,' she told Ali gloomily.

*   *   *

'Where are we going now?' Anto complained in the back seat. Having been bored rigid in Granny and Granddad's, it now seemed that they were being taken on an unscheduled trek to the very outskirts of the city. There had been some excitement when they'd passed several horses running wild on scrubland, and a car that had been set alight, but now they were driving through several shiny new estates that seemed to have been randomly dropped from the sky onto the middle of said scrubland.

'Wait and see,' said Ali. She was lost. Damn. All the roads looked the same; all the houses, too. Anonymous semi-detached jobs with a tiny square of manicured garden in front and every driveway empty.

'Where are all the people?' Jack wondered.

182

At work, probably, to pay the mortgage, while their kids went to the crèche. Every now and then there was a little pink or red bike strewn on a lawn, abandoned and forlorn-looking.

'I don't like it here,' Erin decided, looking out warily as though it were Amityville.

Ali sensed trouble brewing. 'But look at the lovely big green area to play on,' she said very enthusiastically. 'And there's a basketball hoop and everything. And look! A bus stop!'

The kids dutifully looked out at the lone bus stop standing in the middle of nowhere. Luckily they didn't know that it was an eight-mile journey into town; one of the reasons why rents were so reasonable on the estate.

'Man, I'd hate to live here,' Anto commented.

'Yes, drive away quick, Mommy,' Erin recommended.

Feck them anyway. Why couldn't they just, for once, make her life a little easier?

'You could at least give the place a *chance*,' she burst out, startling them. 'Lots of people live here and I'm sure they're very happy! We can't bum off Auntie Emma for ever, you know! Someone drank all her probiotic yoghurt drinks last week and didn't even tell me so that I could replace them. Has it occurred to any of you that maybe she might want us out of there?'

A suspicious silence fell over them now. A very suspicious silence.

'If she's getting sick of us, why don't we just go home?' Jack enquired, his eyebrows burrowing together warily, just like Kyle's did sometimes. 'We've been here weeks.'

183

'We have,' Erin concurred. 'Much longer than we normally stay.'

Ali gripped the steering wheel hard. She wished now she'd explained things to them as they'd gone along. Maybe she'd hoped that it would be easier once they'd acclimatised. That they'd be delighted at her decision. But looking at their faces over her shoulder now, it all felt horribly like entrapment.

'Look, it turns out that we're going to stay a bit longer than planned.'

Anto was the first to react. He looked out at the estate, with its numerous 'To Let' signs, and then began to thrash about in the back seat as the implications sunk in. 'No! Not out here! It's a *dive*. There's not even a shopping mall, just that stupid Spar and a dry cleaners.'

Erin met Ali's eyes in the rear-view mirror and warned her, 'I'll stop eating.'

She'd done it once before, when they'd refused to let her give up ballet lessons after only two weeks, and they having bought all the gear — a tutu and slippers and tights and a little pink wrap-around cardigan and a pink bag to put it all in. The whole lot had cost a fortune before they'd even paid for a single lesson. 'She'd better turn out to be Shirley bloody Temple,' Kyle pronounced grimly (she was the only dancer he knew). But then Erin decided she wanted to give it up. And Kyle decided that she would continue to go. That night she refused dinner. No big deal. She'd eat her breakfast next morning. Except that she didn't. 'All right!' shouted Kyle. 'Give the damn thing up!' But Ali intervened, insisting

184

they must stick to their guns. So they sent her to school with no breakfast, and didn't the little witch go and faint in gym class. Kyle had raced to the school like she needed life support. By the time the pair of them had got home, not only had Kyle agreed to let her give up ballet, but also piano, swimming and possibly school, if the authorities agreed. 'You fool,' Ali had hissed at him coldly. 'It was pizza for dinner tonight. She'd never have held out.'

She met Erin's eyes squarely in the mirror now. 'You go right ahead.' She wasn't dealing with her father *now*.

She didn't look at Jack. She was afraid to. He was just sitting rigidly beside her in the passenger seat. It was hard to know whether it was from shock or rage. But how was she to have known about Carly? If only he'd *told* her, then . . . then nothing, actually. She couldn't change all their plans for a little blonde fifteen-year-old who was mathematically challenged.

'Let's just look at the house,' she begged them. 'That's all I'm asking.'

All three of them completely blanked her as she took another wrong road, was forced to turn round, and then finally found Park Drive amongst all the crescents, avenues and places. The road looked exactly the same as all the others, except that there was an estate agent's car parked outside a particularly anonymous-looking house that bore yet another 'To Let' sign.

'Hello!' The estate agent hurried over with a wave. She was young and fresh-looking, God help her. 'Hi there, kids!'

Nothing. Just vicious glares.

'Um, right,' she said, only slightly taken aback. 'Would you all like to take a look inside? It's open.' Some fatalistic streak made her pick out Anto, of all of them. She winked — actually winked — at him and said, 'There's a really cool playroom in the attic; you get a great view from the window!'

Anto looked out his own window, at the industrial warehouses and desert-like land that ringed the estate, and then he threw back his head and roared at her, 'I-am-not-living-in-this-shitty-dump.' He kicked the back of Ali's seat methodically with each word. 'I-want-to-go-home. Home as in Texas, not home as in Dublin.'

The last bit he bellowed at the back of Ali's head; she could pretend all she liked, but he was done letting on he was a wee Irish lad.

At the mention of Texas, Erin suddenly broke out in sobs. 'I miss Daddy.'

Jack just folded his arms across his chest and looked at Ali. She recognised the look; Kyle had bestowed it upon her many times over the years, and it said, what a mess. What a god-awful, stupid mess she had got them all into. Again.

The estate agent, meanwhile, took a step back from the car, probably for her own safety, her clipboard held up like a shield.

'I'm terribly sorry,' Ali told her, and drove off.

★ ★ ★

She took them to Pizza Express. Anto at first refused to go, but it was either that or stay at

186

home with Emma, and he plumped for pizza.

'It's not that I don't *like* her,' he said. 'It's just that she looks at me strangely sometimes.'

Erin sipped at her orange juice, lacklustre, her eyes still red. She would break your heart.

Jack sat between her and Anto like some kind of protector. He would be the one with all the questions, Ali knew; the one who would need the most handling.

She began with the 'Daddy and I like each other but don't love each other' speech. It would have been nice had Kyle been there for that bit too, for corroboration, if nothing else; to assure them that while he too, liked Mom, in reality she drove him cracked, especially the way she played the Furey Brothers and Johnny Logan at half-past seven in the morning, and if they didn't split up soon, it was entirely possible that he might end up in some kind of monitored accommodation.

Then, part two. 'It's nothing to do with you,' she assured them. Not even Anto, she impressed upon him. These things happen. Sometimes it was nobody's fault. People fell out of love for no good reason (except, maybe, that they had never been in love in the first place, just up the duff). And while things might be different from now on, it didn't change the way they felt about their kids.

'How different?' Jack butted in just as she was about to dispense reassuring hugs and kisses. 'We get stuck here?'

'I wouldn't exactly call it stuck.' Ali was a little stung. Ireland was a great place. Lonely Planet said so. She'd been reared here and there was nothing wrong with her, was there?

'Are we orphans now?' Erin interjected, perking up.

'No. Of course not.' Ali gave a little laugh, but inside it was like a knife twisting.

'I want to go back to Texas,' Anto announced. He seemed to think that if he repeated this often enough she would say, 'OK, sure!' and pack their bags.

'Well, we can't. Not for the moment.'

'Why not?' Jack demanded. 'So you and Dad are getting divorced. Fine. Well, obviously, it's not fine, it sucks. But why can't we just go home?'

She had known this question was coming, had known from the moment she'd stepped on that plane in Texas, yet she still wasn't ready for it. 'Because . . . because your father won't move out,' she blurted.

She watched as they puzzled over this for a bit. Even she was surprised. But it was the first thing that had popped into her head.

'He won't move out of our house?' Anto clarified. 'That's kind of . . . petulant, isn't it?' He saw no irony in calling anybody else petulant.

'I know. He could live in the garage,' Erin offered brightly. 'We could move all the broken bikes and stuff, and put in a TV for him, and some beers.'

Jack rode in to Kyle's defence. 'Dad's not like that. He would never put us out of our house, no matter what you say about him.'

You have no idea what your daddy is capable

188

of, sonny, Ali felt like bawling at him. Give him a couple of overpaid lawyers, and his old bitch of a mother whispering into his ear, and horizontal, check-shirted Dad can turn into a right little bossy-boots who thinks he can take what he likes.

Well, he wouldn't. Looking at her kids now, her beautiful kids, she knew she would do anything in this world to stop him. Even if they hated her for doing it.

When the waitress arrived to take their order, Ali sent her away. She looked at each of the kids in turn very seriously. 'We have some things to work out, your Dad and I. I can't explain everything now. But there are . . . legal problems at the moment that make it difficult for us to go home.'

'What 'legal problems'?' Jack thought she was making it up; she could tell by his face.

She wasn't entirely sure herself; in her wilder moments, she had visions of their plane being met by a posse from the sheriff's office upon arrival, and someone shouting through a loudspeaker at her, 'Step away from the kids, ma'am! Your husband is taking them away.'

She put on her haughty face, the one that said 'parent'. 'I can't tell you that right now. And I'm sorry that you don't like it here.' She let a very disappointed and hurt expression flit across her face. (Good. Anto looked guilty.) 'But there's nothing I can do about it at the moment. We have to stay.'

189

12

Emma

Ryan didn't do boring. Or routine, or domesticity, much. He was far more likely to say, 'Will we head off to Paris for the weekend?' than, 'What day do the bins go out?'

Luckily Emma was the kind of person who knew exactly what day the bins went out. Not that she did it herself; she would poke him with her toe until he got out of bed, naked and still sweaty from early morning sex (about 3.30 a.m.), and he would put on her dressing gown, a pink frilly affair, and go give the neighbours a thrill, if any of them were up.

At first she was afraid he would find her boring. He came and went at such odd hours, while she was all curled up in bed in her jimjams at nine o'clock every night with Mr Teddy.

A lot of guys couldn't handle it. 'What time?' they would say, aghast and no doubt thinking, not much chance of sex there.

'I can't see you mid-week,' she told Ryan when they'd first started dating, but he was always popping around anyway, worming his way in with seductive offers of back rubs and promises to watch reruns of Sex and the City with her over a glass of wine in bed.

'I'm a girl at heart,' he often assured her.

'That's why women rarely find me a threat.'

He didn't look much like a girl, sprawled across Emma's bed. He was tall and wiry, and there were tufts of hair poking out from all kinds of nooks and crannies, but not in a horrible way. He also had lots of smooth, sallow skin that was extremely touchable. His grandmother was Italian, he'd confided in her. It also accounted for his fiery temper.

'What fiery temper?' Emma had enquired.

'You mean you haven't noticed?' he'd cried angrily.

Ryan, angry? That'd be the day. He was the most laid-back person Emma had ever met. She thought it was just the way he'd been born. He was the youngest of seven, after all, and, according to him, had been routinely left to get on with his own nappy changes and feeds. It had made him very independent, he maintained, and he'd been bitten by the travel bug as far back as the age of three, when he'd wandered out onto the motorway outside the house, and had followed the cars to see where they were going. The experience had also honed survival instincts that would later come in extremely handy in the forests of Burma. He'd left home as soon as he could, at seventeen, and hadn't really put down roots since.

'I was a right scut. Didn't even go to college. Bummed jobs in every country I landed in, just for the experience.'

He didn't go into too much detail on these 'wild' experiences, as previously alluded to, but some of them had involved tattoo parlours, and a small love heart with the initial B in the middle of it.

'Brigitte,' Emma guessed.

'No.'

'Bethany?'

'No.'

'Barbara . . . Briony . . . Brandy?'

'*Brandy!*'

'Who then? What was her name? Tell me, I can handle it.'

'Bernadette.'

'Bernadette?' It didn't sound very racy. But a name told you nothing. She could be a six-foot blonde with a 40DD chest and a neat line in bondage.

'My mother,' he said proudly.

Such a sweetie. But he wasn't a mammy's boy either. Not a bit of it. He had a look in his eye of someone who had been there and done that.

'I want to know everything that happened to you before we met,' Emma insisted. This wasn't just prurient curiosity. Well, maybe a bit of it was. But mostly she couldn't bear to think of all that she had missed.

'There isn't that much to tell. I had a girlfriend or two — and no, not as many as you think — and a bunch of us used to get off our faces at the weekends. Pretty much what you probably got up to here.'

Emma was fairly sure Dublin didn't offer the same nocturnal delights as Bangkok, where he'd lived for a year in his mid-twenties, or New York, the city he'd eventually ended up in at the age of twenty-nine, living in a one-bedroom flat with six others, and completely broke. She got the impression that this was the wildest period of his life, mostly because he seemed unable to remember a lot of the finer details.

'I guess we partied a lot of the time. Then a friend got me a job in the mail room of a newspaper — totally crap job, don't ever do it. But then one of the staff photographers let me mess around with his camera one day, and the rest, as they say, is totally boring to everybody else except me.'

'And me.' It was embarrassing how into him she was. She could spend hours and hours just snuggled up beside him, listening to his accounts, always funny, of the shittiest hotel he'd ever stayed in (the Majestic in Goa, where he and the journalist he was travelling with had to share a single bed. The other fellow was twenty stone). Some of the places he'd been to Emma couldn't even point out on a map.

Thank God for the guy who'd given him that camera. He often said that. He'd never taken a photograph in his life before, except on a disposable camera his mother had given him at a wedding once. He'd a knack for the unusual, for looking at things in a way that nobody else did. He'd gone out and taken some really quirky photos of homeless people in New York, trying to make people see them differently. 'Trying to give them a voice,' he said to Emma, taking himself off. 'Talk about being up your own arse. I sent them into the newspaper, expecting that I would win some kind of prize.'

He heard nothing back. He went on and did a

photography course, got a qualification, started chasing freelance work. Then one Friday night out of the blue he got a call from Mike, one of the photo editors in the paper, asking him could he go to Afghanistan that very night as a one-off to cover events over there, as the regular guy was in hospital with appendicitis. Ryan could, he did, and the rest, as they say . . .

'Our Jeep hit a landmine on the first morning. We were in the open for a day until someone came to get us, with three bottles of water between us. I was scared shitless, got down on my knees and started praying. The other guys laughed their heads off at me, just lay around smoking and ringing their girlfriends on their satellite phones. When I got home, I thought no way am I ever going abroad again. But then I got another call, and off I went. I haven't stopped since.'

A thought occurred to Emma then. 'I hope you don't think . . . you and me, I hope you don't feel like I'm trying to tie you down.'

'I'll find a bit of rope,' he said, looking excited.

'You know what I mean.'

They'd seen each other four nights on the trot that week, despite Emma's protestations that she needed her sleep. But Ryan had been persuasive. 'I won't talk. I'll just lie quietly beside you and look at you.' Of course, it was all very flattering. No guy had ever been so determined to sweep her off her feet.

Ryan was silent for a minute. Shit. Had she just given him an in to say, 'Well, actually, now that you mention it . . . '? Maybe all this cosiness in her flat had merely been a diversion for him; a break from his exciting life of airports and exotic locations. His next job should be coming down the line soon. It was a perfect opportunity for him to tell her that it had been nice while it lasted.

Instead, he thought about things for a minute, and then looked rather cross. 'What exactly do you take me for?'

He'd never got antsy with her before, not even when she'd picked up one of his cameras and inadvertently deleted some photos.

'You think this is just a bit of fun and games for me? Or maybe it is for *you*.'

'No . . . of course not . . . '

Suddenly things were very intense. They hadn't spoken before of where things were going. Nobody had got drunk and blurted out, 'I love you!' inappropriately. Maybe they were afraid they'd jinx things, when everything was going so good.

'Can I move in?' Ryan asked suddenly.

Emma blinked. 'Here?'

'Yes.' He thought for a bit. 'And it isn't because I'm sick of travelling and crappy hotels and want a base where there's a cold beer in the fridge.' He thought about that some more. 'Well, I *do*. But that's not the reason.' He raked back his hair so that it stuck up more than usual. It was a nervous gesture, she was beginning to learn. 'In my humble opinion, we probably need to live together for a bit first before we can decide if we want to get married.' He paused. 'Am I going a bit fast for you?'

Yes. Bloody hell. And she'd thought he was laid-back?

But of course he wasn't at all. It was just the front he put on when things were very important to him. Like his work; the photographs, some of them of children with their ribs sticking out from starvation, or bloated corpses after some natural disaster or other. He'd shown some of them to her quite dispassionately, calmly, had even handed her a tissue to mop up her tears afterwards, but the very fact that he went back to those places again and again told her everything.

'Do *you* think we're going too fast?' she said, throwing it back at him. He was the one who'd started this. She'd thought he'd just come around for a game of Monopoly (he was worryingly good) and an 'early night'.

Without any suspicious pauses, he said promptly, 'No. Other people might, but I know how I feel.'

The question was: did she?

She must have let her hesitation show because he said, persuasively, 'We're good together. We're *great* together.'

'Yes, but we only know each other a wet weekend. I don't even know what you like for breakfast. I've never even seen you *have* breakfast, because I'm always gone to work.'

'Weetabix,' he told her gravely. 'And two fried eggs on the weekend.'

'You don't know anything about me either. About my slightly obsessive streak — and I would stress the word 'slightly' — or the way my

196

hair won't lie down at the back unless I wet it, or
. . . or *anything.*'

Suddenly she felt like she couldn't breathe.
She wasn't the sort of person who moved in
with somebody after two months. *Two
months.* You had to have a certain lack of
caution for an act of foolishness such as that;
a dangerous impulsivity, and Ali had already
bagged the family's share of that for herself.
But as for Emma? She still practised the Safe
Cross Code whenever she crossed a road, for
heaven's sake.

'How can we move in together — never mind
get married — when we're practically strangers?'
she flung at him. She was quite cross now. The
nerve of him, to ask her to marry him (sort of)
like that! Clearly he didn't know the first thing
about her, which proved her point.

But he was rising to the challenge. 'You're
talking about details here,' he argued. 'We have
years to talk about all that yet. I'm talking about
what's inside. Feelings.' He jabbed his chest to
illustrate the point. 'And I've never been surer of
mine.'

Oh, so now she was some lightweight,
incapable of feelings as profound as his.

'Me neither!' she said huffily back. 'I've never
felt about anybody the way I feel about you.
From the very first moment I knew you
were . . . ' Dear God. She'd nearly said 'The
One'. 'We're perfect together!' she insisted
strongly.

'Good,' he said vigorously. 'So what do you say
we move in together?'

197

Not so fast.

'How do I know you don't have a wife and two kids in Bermuda?' she shot at him.

He looked momentarily taken aback. 'How do I know *you* don't?'

'If we're going to make this big commitment based on feelings and not good, solid information — ' in other words, if she were to go totally against the grain here — 'then there had better not be any surprises waiting down the line for me.'

'Like the wife and two kids?'

'Or a criminal record in Nairobi.'

He took her face in his hands and looked at her for a long moment. Second thoughts? But then he laughed and said, 'Look at you. You're petrified. But you're giving me far too much credit here. The only thing I want to do right now is settle down with you, maybe buy a house in the country, and raise four kids.'

'Four.' Now she really was aghast.

'One or two anyway. Now come on. Can I get any more boring than that?'

Maybe she should have held out longer. Kept him at arm's length until they knew each other inside out. But he was too gorgeous, and too in love with her, and she with him, plus he was prepared to come to bed with her at nine o'clock every night without bitching.

So she put her considerable powers of reason and logic on the back burner and said, 'Move in.'

★ ★ ★

Patrick was doing a very good impression of outrage. 'You think *I* went and told the papers? What good would that do me?'

Fair point. None of them had come out of it smelling good. The whole thing was a bit of a mystery.

'Nobody's accusing anybody of anything,' Emma said firmly.

'Good.' Patrick crossed his arms huffily.

'In relation to the leak, anyway.' She looked from him to Alannah. Quite a vicious look, too. 'But we need to talk about the atmosphere on the set.'

Over in the corner, Hannie lifted her pen officiously and held it poised over a thick notebook. She'd been drafted in to put the shits up Alannah and Patrick by writing every single thing down, as though it might possibly be used against them in a court of law. In reality the pages were destined for Hannie's bin, but it seemed to be doing the trick, because Patrick cast a nervous glance over at her.

'What atmosphere are you talking about?' he tried to ask in a casual manner.

Alannah, meanwhile, looked worried. She wasn't as long in the tooth as Patrick; she'd only done a couple of gigs before *Wake Up Ireland*, mostly over on the Irish language channel where she'd got to be a rather enthusiastic judge on a worthy reality TV programme where people would break into *Riverdance*-style routines or the ancient art of keening. '*Marvellous*, Donnacha,' she would say, redfaced with pleasure. 'I thought for a minute there I was watching Michael Flatley!'

But things were different in Dublin. There was none of the cosiness of special-interests television. You had to watch your back at every moment.

All of this played quite openly across her face as two high spots of colour formed on her cheeks, clashing with the garish blue eyeshadow the girls in make-up had slathered on her earlier (Emma would be having a word with them next).

Emma felt quite protective of Alannah. It wasn't really her fault. If Patrick could just stop needling her, then she wouldn't have to retaliate. At times Emma had had to resist the urge to pull her aside and say, 'Listen, girl, that prat is a borderline bully, and if you want my advice, I'd go straight to HR and let them know.'

There wasn't enough there for a formal complaint; Patrick was too clever for that. And then there was the fact that Alannah retaliated a little too enthusiastically to his barbs, like the way she'd waggled her little finger at him that morning in front of the whole crew . . . Thinking about it, Patrick himself could have gone to HR for that one.

Emma decided now she had no sympathy for either of them. She was determined to confront the problem head on. Everybody else had been sent home and they were in one of the meeting rooms, with a tray of coffee and cakes. Apart from Hannie poised like a bulldog in the corner with her pad, and glaring rather too enthusiastically at the pair of them, the whole setup was quite cosy and intimate.

Emma soon put paid to that by saying, 'Listen up. Adam is steaming. The board has been informed. And, in case you need reminding, your contracts are up for renewal at the end of the year.'

Patrick looked at her rather sulkily, and said, 'So is yours.' He couldn't resist shooting a glance at Hannie. 'And yours.'

Emma refused to be side-tracked. 'Thank you for pointing out the obvious. So let's all pull together here, stay out of the papers, and concentrate on making the show better.'

There was a little pause, in which she presumed they were reflecting on her words and formulating some kind of an apology for her.

But then Alannah piped up, 'It's not entirely down to us.'

'Sorry?'

'The ratings,' Patrick said silkily.

Emma felt colour rush to her cheeks. 'Nobody said it was.'

'We're working as hard as we can, but there's only so much we can do.' He was nailing her with a look now. The shit.

It had evidently been agreed by them beforehand that Alannah would be the good guy. 'It's not that we think it's *your* fault,' she said hastily. 'I guess we're all just a little frustrated that the show isn't doing as well as we'd expected.'

Emma wasn't standing for that. 'So you're trying to tell me that it's dissatisfaction with the show that's behind your inexcusable behaviour towards each other?'

They had the decency to look slightly shame-faced.

Patrick regrouped quickly. 'Obviously we have to take responsibility for our admittedly robust relationship — '

'Glad to hear it,' Emma cut in coldly.

'But Alannah has a point. And we're not the only ones frustrated.'

Emma could guess who he was alluding to: Phil wasn't a million miles from her mind at that moment.

She caught Hannie's eye. Hannie was pure disgusted. She threw up her hands as if to say, you might as well give up.

Well, Emma hadn't finished with the pair of them yet. 'You might like to describe it as robust. The station thinks otherwise. Now, if I were you, I'd tone it down, because the next time something like this reaches the papers, you'll be dealing with him, not me.'

Another little look ran between them, wary this time. Good. Maybe the point was starting to sink in.

Their point had certainly sunk in with her.

★   ★   ★

Ali was waiting for her when she got in.

'I don't want to talk about it,' she said immediately.

'Well, I do. I love talking. So sit down there and let's get this over with.'

It had been inevitable, really, and Emma

202

didn't bother to protest when Ali put a big pot of tea on the table and went into the living room. Emma heard coins change hands, lots of them, and then Ali's warning: 'Jack is in charge. Do not stray out of his sight, OK? Be back in half an hour.'

There was some more shuffling, and then the front door opened and closed. Blessed silence for a moment. Emma sat there, wallowing in it. There hadn't been this much silence since . . . well, since Ryan had gone.

'Now.' Here was Ali back. Blast. Part of Emma had hoped that she'd gone out with the kids. But she didn't protest as Ali fixed her a big, milky cup of tea, turned on the heating, and engaged in various other maternal faffings around. Normally Emma wasn't that compliant, but she just felt so tired all of a sudden. Drained from the worry of it, and from keeping it in.

At last Ali sat down, squarely opposite, clearly full of determination to get to the root of things. She looked tired too; wrecked, and Emma supposed that some of that had to do with her.

Ali took a breath and began. 'When I said you looked a bit feverish last night, I just meant you looked a bit worked up. Obviously I'm not a doctor — although if I had my time over . . . Sorry, sorry, different discussion. Now, what's this business with your tongue?'

To spare them both a rundown of her symptoms, and the ruling out of flu, strep throat, or the evil arthritis that was eating poor Aunties Jane, Nuala and Alice alive, and was now poised to ravage another generation, Emma said, 'I

203

think I might be HIV-positive, OK?'

It was like a bomb hit the kitchen. Nobody moved for at least sixty seconds. Emma stared fiercely into her mug. She felt like she was in a movie or something. It didn't feel real. HIV-positive. For a minute she thought she was going to laugh, and say, 'Sorry, bad joke.'

But she didn't laugh.

And neither did Ali. Instead, she looked at Emma, saucer-eyed, and said, 'HIV? HIV? Are you *crazy*?'

You'd think it was a lifestyle choice Emma had made, or something she'd got on impulse-buy in the supermarket. 'I didn't know, OK? I didn't know he had it! He didn't either.'

Ali's face went the colour of putty now. 'Ryan,' she bit out.

'Yes, Ryan! What did you think, I'd been sleeping my way from here to . . . to . . . ' She tried to think of the most depraved place she'd ever been. 'Majorca?'

There was another awful silence.

'HIV,' Ali whispered.

'Yes.'

'I can't believe it.'

'Do you think I can?'

'When did you . . . ? When did he tell you?'

'Nearly three months ago now, I suppose.' She'd never forget it. The minute he'd walked in the door she'd known something awful had happened. 'He had to have a medical. Some insurance thing for going abroad. He had no idea, Ali.'

But that seemed to ignite something in Ali.

She stood up so fast that her tea nearly went flying over. 'My God, Emma. I warned you about him!'

Emma was momentarily taken aback by this assault. She knew it was only shock on Ali's part. Her first reaction had been to blame him too; it had lasted weeks. But she didn't want to hear it now; she wanted Ali to cluck her tongue in horror and sympathy, to tell Emma what awful luck it was; not to point out what a fool she'd been. As though she didn't know that already.

'You did not. You never said anything about him!' Ali had never had the bottle; just contented herself with dirty looks in his direction and digs about his unreliability. Fat lot of use that was to Emma now.

Ali was pacing now. 'Anybody could see what he was like! It didn't take a genius!'

'What, to see that he had HIV? I hate to break the news to you, but HIV-positive people don't go around with a big stamp on their foreheads.'

Ali brushed this off. 'Condoms. Have you ever heard of them?'

'Have you?'

'Ours broke,' Ali said coldly.

Three times, it seemed, but Emma let that pass.

'We were engaged,' she said. 'We were going to get married and have kids. Maybe we felt that it was OK to dispense with the condoms.'

'Before you'd both been tested?'

As though Emma hadn't been over and over this whole thing herself already. The what-ifs, the why-didn't-wes. Whole nights had gone by in the same endless round of questions. Telling Ali was like being back at square one all over again. 'Did you?' she fired back. 'Did you march off to get tested before you and Kyle had sex? What about Kyle? Did he visit his nearest STD clinic before he whipped his trousers off?'

'This is not about us,' Ali said primly. 'What amazes me is that you're sticking up for Ryan. Trying to make excuses for what he's done to you.'

That stopped Emma in her tracks. Was she? A month ago she'd have walked over his dying body in the street.

'He didn't do it on purpose.'

She really meant it. Up to now it had been much handier to believe that it was all some dastardly plan on his part to hand her a life sentence; it made it much easier to hate him. If she didn't hate him, then she'd have to have sympathy for him, and she just couldn't do that yet.

Also, she would have to admit her own part in it; that, clearly, Ryan had been less than circumspect about certain aspects of his life. And she had let him be.

Ali began to run out of steam now, thankfully, and quit all her dramatic pacing around the kitchen. She sat down heavily at the table, and looked at Emma with a horrible mixture of sympathy and despair. Emma thought she'd prefer it if she kept pacing.

'Oh, Emma,' she said, in a voice full of doom and gloom.

'Don't start the 'my little sister' stuff.'

'I wasn't going to.'

'You were. I can tell by your face. I couldn't bear it.'

'If only I hadn't left . . . '

'What, you should have stayed in Ireland and taken up a position at the foot of my bed?'

'I always thought you were so clued in.'

'So did I.'

'HIV.'

'Don't keep saying it like that.'

'Like what?'

'Like I'm dying. Although obviously I will some day.'

She had meant it lightly, as in none-of-us-will-get-out-of-this-alive. But didn't Ali erupt into big noisy sobs. Jesus, Mary and Joseph. Emma had never known anybody to better Ali's mad crying fits.

'No 'my little sister' shit,' Emma warned her, pushing the kitchen roll towards her.

'Sorry.' Ali ignored the kitchen roll and blew her nose on a tea towel. She tried to quieten down, clearly not wanting to steal Emma's thunder. 'I just can't believe it. I thought it was going to be arthritis.'

'Maybe I'll get lucky and have both.'

Ali was aghast. 'Stop all this unseemly joking. My God, Emma, we're talking about a very serious disease here!'

So have a little respect, she meant. Clearly the only correct response was to have a massive cry-in, possibly also involving the kids when they came back, and then they could all go around dressed in black for a month.

Emma was wondering why she felt so calm about the whole thing. Maybe because she'd lived with the sheer horror of it for weeks and weeks now. She'd already read the worst the Internet had to offer, from skin lesions to a nasty death by pneumonia. It was weird watching Ali's face now; seeing her shock and upset and panic. Her own face must have looked like that for ages. It was a wonder nobody had guessed.

Suddenly Ali said, 'Do you know for sure?'

'Well, no — '

'You mean you haven't taken a *test*?'

'Not yet.' She'd been too petrified. It was one thing worrying like crazy that you might be HIV-positive. It was another entirely finding out that you actually were.

Ali threw down the tear-sodden tea towel crossly. 'All this worry and drama, and you haven't even taken a test!'

'Sorry.' Now Emma felt a bit like a time-waster. She could at least have had the decency to be glaringly positive, Ali's face said.

'Right.' Already the colour was coming back into Ali's cheeks. 'The first thing to do is to get you to a doctor.' She checked her watch. 'We might still make it today if we hurry.'

'No, Ali.'

'What do you mean, no?' She was in full bossy mode now, exactly what Emma had been dreading. 'The sooner we know, the better. They have all these drugs now, don't they?'

'Some, yes.' Emma strove for caution.

But as far as Ali was concerned, she was already cured. 'Exactly!' Impulsively, she came

208

around the table and threw her arms around Emma. 'Now, no more worrying, OK? You don't have to deal with this thing on your own any more. I'm here now.'

It sounded more like a threat than anything, but Emma nodded dutifully anyway.

And actually, she did feel a bit better.

13

Ali

'We're not moving out to that estate after all.'
'Great!' Then, 'Why not?'
'Because Auntie Emma has decided she likes the company.'
'*Ours?*'
'Yes.'
'But you said she hated us.'
'I did not. I said that maybe she needed her own space.'
'So why doesn't she need her own space now?'
Honestly. The Spanish Inquisition had been less thorough. 'I can't say.'
Big mistake. 'Has she got a secret?'
'No!'
'You always say we're not to keep secrets. So why are you and Auntie Emma not telling us what's going on?'
'There's nothing going on . . . ' Time for diversionary tactics. 'Did you see the brochures I got for that school?'
'We're not going to a new *school.*'
'If you don't go to school, the Government will come after me and prosecute me.'
'You deserve it.'
'It's a nice school. Look here. It's got a gym and everything. And lots of children who look very nice.'

'They don't, they look horrible, and anyway, they're only models.'

'We're going to visit it tomorrow.'

'Aaarrgh!'

'Anto, get up off the floor. Erin, where's Jack gone to?'

'*I* don't know. Probably to ring that stupid Carly.'

'Don't talk about Carly that way.'

'You don't like her either. I heard you telling Auntie Emma about her shorts, and how half her bottom was hanging out of them, and how Jack couldn't possibly love her, that he was only thinking with his d — '

'That's enough. Now, get your stuff.'

'Why? Where are we going?'

'Over to Granny and Granddad's.'

'Aaargh!'

'*Anto*. Stop that now. It's only for an hour, then I'll be back.'

'Why, where are you going?'

'I have an appointment.'

'For what?'

'Nothing. Hurry up.'

'How come nobody is telling us *anything* around here?'

★ ★ ★

Ali knew where he lived. That was because she'd been sneaky, and had gone through the pile of post on the hall table, and it was just as she'd thought: there were several letters for him — only bills and things, nothing worth steaming

211

open — but Emma had drawn a line through the addresses and written down a forwarding one. Clearly she hadn't got round to sticking them in the post box yet. Though, in Ali's opinion, it was far too considerate of her to be forwarding on post to someone who may have given her an incurable disease. She'd have sent anthrax.

Looking up a map Ali saw that he'd decamped to an apartment not far away. The fool. As though by sticking close by there was a chance that Emma might actually take him back.

Ali had the letters in her bag now, on the seat beside her as she drove away from Mam and Dad's. She kept telling herself she might as well drop the letters by; she was in the area anyway. Why *shouldn't* she have booked a hair appointment, not at her usual salon, but in a little place just around the corner from Ryan's new apartment? It was probably a great hairdresser's. It was good to try new things; there was no reason in the world to stick with Brenda, who always cut her hair when she was in Ireland. There could be a better Brenda out there; she'd never know unless she sought her out.

But it was difficult to think about hairdos when she was foaming at the mouth. And it wasn't just those green Skittles that Anto had insisted on sharing with her earlier.

Poor Emma. Poor, stupid, foolish Emma, having a bareback ride with a fecker like Ryan, who had clearly dipped his lad in places he shouldn't have.

Ali could have told her. Oh, yes. One look at him, with his too-blue eyes and his too-low jeans

212

Emma's pain was her pain, if that didn't sound too dramatic. They would tackle this thing together.

'You're not coming to the doctor with me,' Emma had said in alarm, as their conversation had finished up that night.

'Oh, yes, I am.'

'Oh, no, you're not,' the kids had chimed in gleefully.

Damn them. They'd snuck back in while Ali and Emma were engrossed. The conversation had been abruptly terminated and the kids were told that Auntie Emma had a sore throat and would be going to the doctor's the following day.

But Emma had gone off to work this morning without saying anything, though nobody had exactly been keeping an eye out for her at 4.30 a.m. No note on the table, no 'Ring you later'. She had no intention of going to the doctor's at all, Ali bet.

★ ★ ★

'Excuse me?' she called to a passer-by, winding down her window. 'Can you tell me the way to Raven Woods?' She held out her map helplessly and did a bit of eyelid fluttering. Kyle always said it was pathetic, but the truth was she didn't get lost half as often as him.

The man looked over. He was carrying a pint of milk. 'You're in it,' he called.

Then they each did a double-take.

'Ryan?'

'Ali . . . ?'

and she could have told Emma that he'd kept a woman in every port. And why stop at ports? She might as well throw in airports too, and train stations. And what about those anonymous hotels that he regularly seemed to be languishing in on some far-flung continent, complaining often and loudly about the 'loneliness' of being there without Emma, the love of his life?

Horseshit. He'd probably been delighted to get away from his fiancée so that he could indulge his penchant for unprotected sex with ladies as dubious as himself. And, again, why stop at ladies? God only knew what his sexual tastes ran to. There could be threesomes, foursomes, partner-swapping, and whatever-you're-having-yourself. Who was going to stop in the middle of all that and say, 'Sorry, gang, just got to slip on a Durex Extra Strength'?

And then he came home to Emma, with the smell of mad (unprotected) sex barely washed off him, and immediately swept her off to the sack for more mad (unprotected) sex.

'When he's been away, we can't keep our hands off each other,' Emma had confided once. This was back when she'd been in her giggly phase and was wont to come out with all kinds of out-of-character statements.

Oh, Ali had Ryan's measure all right, even though she herself had been stuck in a monogamous — or should that be monotonous — marriage for sixteen long years, with not even a fling with the pool boy to her credit. But just because *she* didn't partake in seriously dodgy sexual looseness didn't mean that she didn't recognise those who did. Given the opportunity, most men were at it like dogs, and Ryan was no exception. She'd had her suspicions about him from the beginning. It was nothing he'd specifically said or done; more an aura. Or was it an odour? It could simply be her sixth sense, which may have no basis in science but which she swore by. As far as she was concerned, Ryan was a rat.

HIV. Ever since Emma had broken the news she felt like she had a brick in her stomach. She still couldn't take it in. Well, it just didn't happen to people like Emma, did it? Not that it should happen to *anyone*, but you could just about understand poor old Freddie Mercury getting it. When you looked at Emma, you saw a middle-class professional woman, schooled by the nuns, who drank probiotic yoghurts in the morning and flossed at night before going to bed at 9 p.m . . . well, it was just plain *wrong*. As diseases went, she and a mild dose of ME would be far better suited, or maybe some intermittent fibromyalgia. Both of these brought their own misery, but were not, as far as she knew anyway, *life*-threatening.

Not that HIV was. Not in the near future anyway. Or even the distant future, as Emma had been at pains to point out over a stiff whiskey, which Ali seemed to need more than Emma. Talk about calm! It was unnatural. If it was Ali, she'd be weeping and wailing and immediately drawing up a will on the inside of a bread wrapper (Anto would be in danger of getting nothing).

But not Emma. She seemed almost cheerful as she listed out the symptoms. And some of them didn't actually sound too bad; tiredness, for example. Ali was constantly wrecked as it was, so she'd have been able to handle that one, no problem. She wasn't so keen on the possible skin problems — apparently, a simple boil had the capacity to spread — but a heavier foundation than usual might take care of that. But then Emma went on about opportunistic infection and spots on your tongue and possible lung issues, pointing out, far too casually for Ali's liking, 'in endstage disease, it's often pneumonia that gets you.'

'Stop. Stop, stop, *stop*,' Ali had begged at that point, having visions of Emma in a scene from ER, with rakes of tubes sticking out of her and someone shouting, 'She's gone into cardiac arrest!' (preferably George Clooney. Mm). 'Stop talking like you have it! You mightn't at all.'

'I know,' Emma said, unconvincingly.

'I mean it. You haven't even taken a test.'

'Yes.' But she had a horribly calm, fatalistic about her, like she already knew the thing was running rampant in her veins, reproducing quicker than rabbits.

'The test will be negative,' Ali insisted.

It had to be. There was no other option. Emma simply had to be all right. The idea of anything happening to her, of her not being . . . Ali couldn't even go there. Couldn't imagine it. Even though they'd spent all of adult lives four and a half thousand miles Ali still felt they were an extension of each

He half started towards her in greeting, the way you would automatically do if you knew someone, especially if she was the sister of the alleged love of your life. But then he stopped in his tracks, frozen.

Very wise move. Another foot towards her and she'd be able to reach out and rip his balls off. One problem solved.

His face was a gas, if you were in the humour for a laugh. Did she *know*? Yes. Clearly she did. Was she horrified/aghast/unforgiving? Clearly she was. Had she come for revenge? Just take one step closer, baby . . .

The pain on his face was pretty intense. No doubt there would be acres of explanations and excuses: I-didn't-know, wasn't-me-guv, could-have-happened-to-a-saint (although unlikely). Then he would probably ask her not to pick on a sick person.

Not that he looked sick. He seemed in rude good health as he trotted along with his milk and a paper under his arm, like nothing had happened at all. He was even wearing some T-shirt with a cause on the front. Infectious diseases, probably. She couldn't even bear to look. She kept her eyes on his face, beaming all her blame and rage and fear into a point somewhere in the middle of his forehead.

Finally he spoke. 'How's Emma?'

How was Emma? How was Emma? How did he bloody well think she was? Walking around having a fantastic old life?

'That's none of your business any more,' she told him icily.

But if she stuck to that line, then she would have no other reason for being here, and she would have to drive off without telling him what a thorough piece of shit he was, which was why she was there in the first place.

'She's going for a test this week,' she added in a voice full of blame.

He smiled at that. Actually smiled! What planet was he on?

'Good,' he said, sounding enormously relieved. 'She refused to go when I first told her. Said she'd rather not know. Nothing I said would change her mind. Then we, um, broke up — '

'Obviously,' Ali could not stop herself interjecting.

'I kept trying to ring her. Sent her phone numbers of people to see: counsellors, doctors. The sooner she knows the better. You know, so that she can start getting monitored, and begin the medication in time and all that.'

'I know all about the medication,' Ali said haughtily, even though she hadn't a breeze. But Emma had mentioned antivirals. Apparently they were marvellous. You took two or three of them together, and when you got the right combination it was almost like there was nothing wrong with you at all.

Except that there was.

'All I can say is that I hope this didn't happen while you were engaged to her,' she threw at him. As though it made an iota of difference now.

'What?'

'I hope you didn't sleep around while you were together.'

He looked a bit stunned. It seemed almost genuine. '*Emma* told you that?'

'Well, not exactly.' There seemed little point in outlining to him her piercing sixth sense. A lot of people looked sceptical when she explained it, so she just said, 'But you didn't catch it from a toilet seat.'

That didn't go down well. He looked at her as though the jibe had been distasteful, and she felt a bit small and cheap. 'It's not any of your business, to be honest.'

Oooh. The gloves were off now. She clawed her way up the seat a bit — the hire car was compromisingly low compared to the monstrous 4×4 she drove at home in which you could look down on people from a great height — and glared out at him. 'Even if you didn't care about the risks you took, what about Emma? Imagine putting her in danger like that! If you cared one whit for her you'd have covered up your willy.'

A woman passing by looked over, startled, and then hurried on.

'You don't have to lecture me.' Ryan looked white-faced now. She'd only ever seen him being his happy, casual self; this upset, stricken Ryan was new to her.

He stepped up towards the window and bent down so that he was almost on eye level with her. 'What happened was a mistake. I can't undo it, no matter how much I'd like to. Every time I think of her being infected too, I feel sick. All I can do is hope and pray she's not, and keep trying to get her to take a test, even though I know she never wants to see me again. But go on. Have a pop at me if it makes you feel better.'

Well, what could she say to *that*? All she'd wanted was a little decent back-and-forth about what a proper bastard he was, but he had to deny her that, too. She decided she disliked him even more.

'Do you have the number of somebody?' she ended up asking grudgingly. 'A doctor.'

It appeared that Emma's own GP was a year away from retirement and got a bit squeamish even around smear tests, so it was debatable whether he was the man for the job when it came to serious sexually transmittable diseases. Also, he was very friendly with their parents, and it wasn't the sort of thing you wanted popping out down in the Parish Hall.

'Sure,' Ryan said.

It was all civil again now, as he straightened and took a notebook out of his pocket. She watched as he thumbed through it until he came to a page with a list of names and numbers. He tore it out and handed it to her.

'There are three or four numbers there. Two of them are for women, if she'd prefer.'

Ali didn't look at the page, just put it into her bag, and said awkwardly (it wasn't like he was doing her a favour), 'Thanks.'

What else was there to say? 'Take care,' maybe, or 'Stay well'? She just wasn't there yet.

'I'm sorry you had to come home for this,' he said suddenly.

'What?'

'You don't normally come home till the summer. But I'm glad she told you. I kept telling

220

her she should. That she needed a bit of support.
I knew you'd come home as soon as you knew.'

'Yes,' said Ali, and revved the car before he
could elaborate further on her saint-like
qualities, and the alleged closeness of the sisterly
bond.

'Tell her . . . ' He was a picture of misery now.
'I hope she's OK,' he ended up saying quietly.

Ali just nodded and drove off.

★　★　★

Another day ended crappily when she got back
to Emma's flat and found a heavy cream
envelope with her name typed on the front and
an airmail sticker attached.

'Maybe it's from our school, wondering where
we are,' Anto said, turning it over, and examining
the markings on the front.

'It's probably just coupons or something,' Ali
said casually, snatching it from him.

'What happened to your *hair*?' he asked.

The new hairdresser hadn't quite been up to
Brenda's standards. At one point her scissors
appeared to have slipped. Ali self-consciously put
a hand to the back of her head. 'Nothing. Now,
go wash your hands for dinner.'

Not that dinner was anywhere near being
ready. In fact she had yet to decide what they
were going to have. Would they balk at tuna
casserole for the third night in a row?

'In a minute,' Anto mumbled. That was his
standard response to any request ever made of
him. Ali seemed to spend the entire day

221

reiterating requests and demands, only to be told, 'In a minute.'

And now Erin wanted a drink.

'So go and get one,' she told her.

'But I'm too tired.'

'Erin . . . '

'I've been watching TV in Granny's all afternoon, and I'm *exhausted*.'

Ali got the drink for her, told Anto three more times to wash his hands, and was hunting around in the kitchen presses for a can of tuna that wasn't there when Jack — her lovely boy, or at least he had been up until recently — walked in.

As usual, since she'd broken the news of their extended stay in Ireland, he utterly ignored her and went to get the charger for his mobile phone, which was only out of his hand when he went to the bathroom.

'Jack?' she said in a very pleading voice.

He refused to even look at her. 'You've completely ruined my life,' he remarked.

'Yes, I know, but I wonder would you run to the shop and get me a can of tuna?'

Erin and Anto heard her in the living room, and howled, 'Not tuna casserole *again*.'

'You want me to go to the shop for *tuna*?' Jack said. He was looking at her now all right, but in the way you'd look at a two-headed monster.

'Just one can.' It wasn't that she was oblivious to the havoc she'd wreaked in his romance with Carly, but if she didn't get dinner on now then Anto's blood sugar would drop, and then they would all be in trouble.

'Is that all you can think about? Dinner?' Jack said, his fists balled up now and his face puce. It looked like he was gearing up for a full-on scene, and honestly, after the day she'd had, she just wasn't able for it.

'All right, then, chips,' she told him in a placatory fashion.

'Yeah!!' Anto and Erin cheered in the living room.

But she didn't have enough money. She had no money, in fact. She'd had to put a tenner of petrol into the car and there was nothing left in her purse except for a few coins.

'I want to know when we're going home,' Jack said loudly.

He was standing up close to her now, and he was much bigger than she, and she didn't like it.

'I told you. I don't know yet.'

And now with Emma's situation, things had got even more complicated. But how could she explain that to the kids?

Jack stuck his face into hers, and he shouted, 'You don't give a damn, do you? You don't care about us, or what we want! All you want to do is get back at Dad!'

He'd never spoken to her that way before; never shown her any kind of aggression, and she felt afraid.

It was touch and go for a minute, but then she pushed herself sharply away from the worktop, and he was forced to step back. She put her hands on her hips and made her voice loud and clear.

'Don't you dare speak to me that way. Go and

cool down.' When he still didn't move, she ordered, 'Go. Now.'

He gave her another furious, filthy look, but then he dropped his eyes and slouched out, mobile at the ready, no doubt already texting Carly about what a bitch his mother was.

'You two can go to your room and have some quiet time too,' she told Anto and Erin, who had come to the kitchen door, agog at the excitement. For once Anto knew better than to say, 'In a minute', and they went out after Jack.

Alone, Ali sat down at the kitchen table. She found that she was shaking: no tuna, no money, no lovely Jack any more, no close sisterly bond like Ryan assumed, and a big fat letter on suspiciously expensive paper.

She took it out now, even though she knew it would only upset her further. Her normal course of action when confronted with such things was avoidance; she hadn't opened a credit card bill in years, for example, and had managed to avoid Ethel's birthday party celebrations (everyone had to come in fancy dress) for at least the last five. Why go wrecking your karma unless you had to? was her motto. Life really was much sweeter if you let someone else deal with the tax authorities, or step onto that committee in school that seemed to do nothing but organise bake sales.

That person, of course, had always been Kyle (not that he'd have been caught dead at a bake sale). She guessed he was the one behind the heavy cream envelope.

So she took a deep breath and opened it.

Inside was a letter, on more cream paper, so thick and luxurious that it took some effort to wrest it from the envelope. In the end she gave up, ripped the whole envelope apart and finally unfolded the letter.

It was from someone called Calvin Crawford and he called her Mrs Peterson. 'Dear Mrs Peterson' to be precise. He told her that he acted for Kyle Peterson, her estranged husband. That took her back at bit. 'Estranged.' What a weird word. It made him sound like he had two and a half heads, and a forked tongue.

Anyway, her estranged husband had informed Calvin Crawford that Ali had, 'without his knowledge or consent' removed her children from the state, and further, from the country. Technically speaking, she supposed she had removed them from the continent. If the moon was open for business yet, she'd have gone there.

Calvin Crawford told her that this may well be some misunderstanding, and that Kyle was prepared to give her the benefit of the doubt. It was entirely possible that she had got confused and gone on her annual holidays earlier than normal, and merely neglected to mention it to her estranged husband. Modern life was hectic, after all, and three children could certainly send your brain spiralling into confusion and forget-fulness. (It was she who added this last bit, not Calvin. Calvin probably didn't have children. Or else he had a wife to look after him, who was as confused and forgetful as Ali.)

If this was the case, then fine. No harm done. It was simply a question of rectifying her spectacular act of forgetfulness and rudeness, and returning home on the next available flight.

But if it *wasn't* the case . . . Well, that was a whole different story, wasn't it?

She imagined Calvin putting on his big voice now. And it seemed that at this point the typeface got bigger and blacker as Calvin's disapproval grew.

Basically, if she didn't return to Texas with the three kids in tow, then Calvin would take an altogether dimmer view of things. He might have to start warning her that she was in breach of all kinds of things. He might have to write another letter reminding her about courts, and family law, and illegalities performed on her part.

At no point was any bad behaviour apportioned to Kyle. He was the knight in shining armour, waiting to rescue his kids from the ditz he'd had the misfortune to marry.

Calvin Crawford expected Ali to respond to him by return post. He expected her to assure him that her children were on their way home from Ireland to the world of Peterson's Plastics, refreshed from their little 'holiday'. If — if — he did not hear from her within seven days he would, regrettably, have to take further action.

In case that wasn't enough to intimidate her, at the bottom of the letter it stated that he had offices in Oregon, New York, Toronto, Bangkok, London, Paris, Rome, and Crete (he must have a holiday home there).

Well, well. Kyle had gone and got himself a

real-life whirlwind, a man who could threaten people from the four corners of the globe.

She carefully folded the cream letter back into its original folds. Then she reached over and threw it in the bin.

14

Emma

Ali was driving her cracked.

'Are you all right?' she asked for the fifth time.

'Yes.'

'Are you sure?'

'I'm fine.'

Pause.

'Would you like a mint?'

'No, thanks.'

'It might calm you down.'

'I'm perfectly calm.'

'Are you sure?'

'Yes.'

Pause.

'Is it all right if I have one? A mint? It wouldn't bother you or anything?'

'No.'

'Are you sure — '

'Oh, just eat one, Ali!'

Ali looked at her with great concern. 'I knew you were upset.'

Then she popped a mint into her mouth and rolled it around noisily. She sighed. She checked her watch, and then checked the clock on the surgery walls. She began tapping her foot nervously against Emma's chair. For two pins now Emma would kill her.

There had been no stopping her that morning, unfortunately. She was NOT allowing Emma to go to the doctor's on her own. It was out of the QUESTION. Supposing she couldn't FIND the place? Supposing she lost her nerve and didn't go IN? And then there was the STRESS of it. She would need emotional support. BUCKETS of it. This was possibly the most aPPALLing thing that would ever happen to Emma in her life, and by God, Ali would not abandon her in her hour of need.

Besides, Ali had made the appointment, and clearly felt she had a right to go along.

Emma supposed she should be grateful that at least the kids weren't there too, drawing lots as to whether she would turn out to be positive or not. They were at Mam and Dad's again, both of whom had looked rather reluctant, but Ali promised they'd only be gone a couple of hours.

'Where?' said Mam.

'Shopping,' said Ali.

'You don't look like you're going shopping,' said Mam suspiciously. Well, they probably had big miserable faces on them. 'You look like you're off to the dentist, or to see about a mortgage or something.'

So then they had to act all jolly, and Emma had said, very falsely, 'We're going to kick off with a cappuccino!' but that only seemed to make Mam more resentful at being left in a house with a sick man and three brats, and she had shut the door on them rather smartly.

Then, as if Emma's nerves weren't shot enough, the surgery — not her normal one, but some place Ali had heard of — had no record of her appointment.

'It was made for half-past eleven,' Emma had said, trying to keep the wobble out of her voice. Behind her sat two rows of people, all listening avidly, with no radio playing in the background to distract them, and only copies of *Hello!* magazine from 2006. It was very, very tempting to leg it out the door.

'I'm sorry.' The receptionist kept shaking her head.

'It's no problem. I can come back another time.' And the awful sick feeling in her stomach began to lift at the idea of putting off this whole thing for another week, or maybe even more.

But then Ali pitched in from parking the car, probably illegally, and the confusion was explained; she had booked the appointment under her own name, Ali Peterson.

'Insurance reasons,' she'd hissed at Emma as she guided her to a seat at the very back, even though there were plenty free at the front.

'What?'

'Sometimes these things can be held against you if anyone's ever looking for your medical record. A GP has to note down on your chart the fact that you went for a — ' she lowered her voice further — 'HIV test.'

Did they? Emma felt ridiculously naïve. 'But this isn't my normal GP.'

'I know,' said Ali with great satisfaction. 'It's unlikely anybody would ever find out. But all the same I decided it was best to use my name. That way you're completely covered.'

No doubt all this was intended to make Emma feel better. Another, more subtle person, might have given the information in a way that didn't inspire an urge to sink down further in her chair and turn up her collar in shame.

Still, Ali's heart was in the right place. And if it had been left up to Emma, they wouldn't be there at all that day. It was Ali who'd presented the options to her: a private test at a GP's, or else she could queue up at one of the dedicated STD clinics in the city. 'On the plus side,' she'd said doubtfully, 'it's free, and everybody else there would be in the same boat.'

The implications in her voice were clear: there they would all be, sitting on plastic chairs, some of them no doubt with itchy bits which they would be trying to scratch surreptitiously. Others may have the wild, panicked look of people who'd drank nineteen pints of cider one weekend and got into bed with that little brat with the leather trousers who'd allegedly slept with most of South Dublin, and now their willies had turned a strange colour and were starting to shrivel up. There would be one or two with tracks on their arms, probably, and an incessant sniff.

And at the end of the row would be Emma, with her Louis Vuitton bag and new brown boots, fresh from a production meeting for Ireland's most high-profile breakfast show. (Ireland's only breakfast show, but who was arguing?)

'I wouldn't either,' Ali had said promptly, not

even bothering to hide her distaste. 'We'll go private.'

Emma hadn't argued. What could she have said? She was a snob about it too, although God knows she had little to be snobbish about. But wasn't going to one of those places the same as wearing a big stamp on your forehead that said, 'Well Dodgy'?

In the end she'd been cowardly and let Ali book her into this busy, impersonal surgery comfortingly far away from either Emma's home or her place of work, and that would do an HIV test, with counselling beforehand.

'How do you know about this place, anyway?' Emma asked now, suddenly suspicious.

'Oh, I just did a little digging,' Ali said vaguely.

So there they were, skulking at the back, while the people around them gave phlegmy coughs, or clutched their backs with a grimace. Ordinary people with ordinary ailments. And there was Emma, with her stomach swirling around like a washing machine, and possibly with a time bomb ticking in her veins.

The fact that she was having a blood test had no influence over the outcome. It would simply tell her whether she was positive or not. Getting tested didn't *make* her positive.

So they said on the Internet. It was full of pithy advice for the potentially infected. You couldn't swing a cat for the number of support groups and forums. When you ran the letters HIV through the search engine and it came back with about sixty-two million results, you'd be forgiven for thinking that you were the odd one

232

out if you *didn't* have it.

Where were they now, all those virtual people ready to support Emma? Where was Big Bill, who was the one who had preached the thing about the test not making you positive? Or SweetNell13, who was making it through, with the help of Jesus? Not one of them was around when Emma truly needed them. Instead she was stuck beside her mint-sucking sister and a load of people with chest infections. Not that Ali wasn't great in her own way, but when Emma had assured her that she was absolutely fine, Ali had actually believed her.

The white door to the doctors' inner sanctum opened now, and Emma felt the breath freeze in her lungs. A doctory-looking type stepped out and looked around the waiting room. Her gaze seemed to hover somewhere around Emma.

Then she said, 'Mr Quinlan?'

Thank you, God.

But her turn would inevitably come. There was no putting it off. In a few minutes' time she would be summoned through that white door, and blood would be taken from her arm and be whisked off to some lab somewhere, where it would be examined for antibodies to the virus. It had been almost three months since she'd last had sex with Ryan, so they would show up by now, if they were there at all. Then in a week, or maybe two, Emma would get confirmation as to whether her life had changed for ever or not.

'Hmm. I see you've been engaging in high-risk activity,' the doctor would say with great disapproval.

233

Well, he wouldn't. He wasn't allowed to. But he'd probably be thinking it. He'd probably take one look at Emma, and his eyebrows would shoot up into his hairline before he could stop them.

But she hadn't. She desperately wanted to explain that to the doctor. She wanted to tell him or her that she hadn't slept with strange men or used intravenous drugs. She had simply made love with her fiancé.

She could even remember the first time they'd had unprotected sex. They'd been away in a hotel for her birthday, and he'd forgotten his condoms. Of course, they could just have gone without, or been otherwise inventive, but the fact that she didn't have to get up at four o'clock the following morning had made them randy as hell, and they were both starkers and at the point of no return before Emma had said, 'But what about contraception?'

Because that's all that had been on their minds, bless them: not getting caught out. They were engaged at that point, but babies hadn't entered the equation in any concrete way, except that they'd like 'one or two' sometime further down the line. Not in nine months' time.

But then Ryan, piddly-eyed and emotional, had looked deep into her eyes and said, 'I'd love a baby with you.'

So sensitive! So grown-up! What a marvellous catch he was, she distinctly remembered thinking just before she let him throw her down on the bed and have his wicked way with her. Twice.

She hadn't got pregnant. She'd even been

slightly disappointed. So had he.

'I wonder if there's anything wrong with my lads?' he wondered, jerking a thumb down towards his groin. 'They might be poor swimmers. They might need lessons.'

'It wasn't even the right time of the month,' Emma told him reassuringly.

She was sober by then, and had done a little forward thinking regarding babies, and now was definitely not the time for them, even if the idea of them was nice. She'd really only just got her teeth into *Wake Up Ireland* — she needed to get the show through a couple of seasons anyway before disappearing off on maternity leave. No, they would stick to the original plan. Marriage first, and a year of 'enjoying each other' and then they would go at it with all cylinders firing.

'Does this mean I have to wear condoms again?' Ryan had asked, a little crestfallen. He'd got a taste of freedom now, and didn't want to give it up. He also wasn't very good at putting them on. Emma suspected his eyesight was at fault; either way, he would sigh and groan in the dark, and there would be much snapping of plastic and the occasional yelp of pain. On one fraught occasion, he'd been left with a little bald patch, and the pain was so acute that she'd had to massage some cream into it.

'Hey!' he said in relief after five minutes of this. 'It's still working!'

It would be great to dispense with the things altogether, but what would they use instead? Emma wasn't keen on going on the pill, and messing with her hormones, and why should she, anyway?

'Maybe we can go without them during the second half of my cycle,' she said, relenting.

This meant some very careful calendar-watching on her part. But she was good at that sort of thing, and never took any chances. 'Not tonight, buster,' she would tell him firmly, on days when she didn't feel it was safe.

She wanted to vomit when she thought about it now. There she'd been, taking responsibility for both of them, when all along he hadn't given a damn about her. It didn't help that he'd been distraught afterwards. It was too late then.

Shit. There were the tears again. She closed her eyes tightly. She would not make a holy show of herself in the middle of rush hour at the doctor's.

'People live with it, you know,' Ali said suddenly beside her.

'I'm fine,' Emma began to say automatically, but it came out all croaky and pathetic.

Ali reached over and took Emma's hand. She'd never done that before; like, *ever*, and it felt weird and uncomfortable. Also, a bit sticky, either from the packet of mints or one of the kids.

'Obviously you'll have to be monitored,' she murmured fervently. 'And take your medication, when the time comes. But, like, you're not going to *die*.'

The woman in front of them with the phlegmy cough stopped hacking her lungs out and turned her head slightly to see whether Emma had an open artery or a limb hanging off.

Ali released Emma's hand and said to the woman, haughtily, 'Can I help you there at all?' The woman swiftly turned away.

Honestly, she would mortify you. It reminded Emma of when they'd been back in school, and those big hard lads from the boys' school up the road had stolen her lunchbox. It had had a picture of Donny Osmond on the front, and possibly had some resale value. She'd been going to tell the teacher — had been quite excited about kicking off some kind of criminal investigation — but Ali had got there first, by marching up to them and unleashing a string of language so foul that the hard lads had to go home and ask their parents what some of it meant.

But suddenly Emma found she was glad for her now; glad of her misguided overprotectiveness, of her bolshiness.

'I hope you're not staying because of me,' she blurted out.

'I told you, I'm not leaving you here on your own — '

'I meant Ireland.' When Ali looked evasive, Emma went for the more direct approach. 'Look, I heard the kids talking about a new school.' Or, that 'crap new school', as they'd referred to it.

A doctor's surgery just minutes before an HIV test was hardly the time or the place to be discussing Ali's family affairs. But Emma was glad for anything that might take her mind off what lay ahead. Besides, Erin had told her all about the big family chat they'd had in Pizza

Express, and how her mommy really liked Daddy, so much so that she wanted to get him his very own house, but for some reason Daddy liked the old one so much that he was refusing to move out, and so they still had to stay in Ireland with Emma. The word she'd used was 'stuck'.

But apart from the housing situation, she didn't appear that bothered about the divorce. Half the kids in her class had parents who were divorced; four times in Annie Long's mother's case. 'She gets great presents at Christmas from all her daddies,' Erin had told Emma enviously.

Ali rubbed her eyes now. She looked for a long time at the back of the coughing woman's head and said, 'I'm not staying because of you. No offence, obviously.'

'None taken,' Emma said. 'I think.'

'You might as well know. I can't go home.'

'Of course you can. You just don't want to.'

Ali never seemed to recognise her own *modus operandi*: when the going got tough, she usually got on a plane. Often it didn't matter where the plane was headed, just so long as it was away from whatever pile of trouble she'd left behind.

'It's not that.' She was suddenly fierce. 'Do you think I *liked* taking the kids from school with no notice? Do you think I'm enjoying imposing upon you, and sponging off Mam?' Emma hadn't known about Mam, but now that she thought about it, she had seen money changing hands in the kitchen earlier. 'If there was any other way of doing this, then I wouldn't be here, I can promise you that.'

The woman with the cough was now sitting

238

very still, with the air of someone who had enough gossip to keep her going for a decade.

'Of doing what?' Emma prodded. Honestly. It was like trying to crack some cryptic code.

'Keeping the kids.'

'What are you talking about? You *have* the kids.'

'Kyle wants custody.'

Kyle? The man who had once brought over a selection of plastic bags for them all to admire?

'He said that he's going to try to take them from me.'

'Oh, Ali, I'm sure he was just angry. It was probably an idle threat — '

'That's what I thought too. But he's not going to back down, Emma. He's got solicitors and everything.'

It all began to make sense now: Ali's sudden appearance in Ireland with only enough underwear to keep them going for a week.

'But you can't just . . . run off with them, Ali.'

'Why not?'

'Technically, isn't it, like, kidnap or something?' Well, someone had to say it.

Ali snapped upright in her chair fiercely. 'You think I should have stayed, and got hauled through the courts over there, and maybe end up seeing my own kids every second weekend?'

'That wouldn't happen. A judge would never take them from you.'

'I don't know that for certain, though, do I? Kyle's got this divorce attorney that costs a fortune, and I don't have anybody!'

Just then the white door opened. Another

doctor came out, a man this time. He looked around and called, 'Ali Peterson?'

For a minute Emma wondered wildly what was wrong with Ali, apart from Kyle trying to take her children from her, and what could a doctor do about it, anyway?

Then Ali was poking her in the side urgently and saying, 'That's you.'

15

Ali

The woman behind the counter was very nice. 'Do you have a CV with you?'

Ali gave a little laugh. 'A CV? To work in a shoe shop?'

The woman laughed too, as though agreeing that it was, indeed, ridiculous. Then she said, 'We've had twenty-two applications for the job so far. We really need a CV.'

'Oh. Right. Of course.' Talk about wiping the smile off someone's face. 'I'll do one up and drop it in to you.'

They nodded and smiled at each other a bit more and then Ali left the shop with the confident walk of a woman for whom the world was her oyster. It was only once she was sure she was out of view that she dropped her strut and collapsed onto the low wall that ran the length of the shopping centre.

Twenty-two applications to measure people's stinky feet. Bloody hell. What was the world coming to?

And to think that Ali had gone into this realistically. It wasn't like she'd marched into an employment agency in town and demanded a job, immediately, with a starting salary of 50K. She'd known her limits and had chosen her targets carefully: the shoe-shop with the sign in the window; the supermarket with the cashier's job. Both low-key jobs, where no great qualifications were necessary except competence and a good manner, and where Ali felt she could learn quickly on the job. She'd thought it would be best to dress nicely, in a skirt and top of Emma's that she'd managed to beat herself into, and present herself in person for the job. Let them see what they were getting. But the manager of the supermarket had been unavailable, and the girl — the *child* — snapping gum behind the information desk told her to write in, but that they were after having rakes of enquiries and basically not to hold her breath.

'Fuck you,' Ali said. But not out loud, obviously; only in her head, privately, whilst she told the shop girl cravenly, 'I'll do that, thanks for your time, no harm in trying!'

And she walked away feeling completely ancient and totally irrelevant.

At that point her gung-ho was starting to flag a bit. And she'd started out that morning so optimistic. Cheerful, even, at the thought of reentering the workforce and providing for herself and the kids. Kyle leaving her destitute could actually be, without being too Oprah about it, the best thing ever. Look at what her life had been like in Texas! All that shopping and sitting around on her arse drinking skinny lattes. Actually, it didn't sound too bad now. But think of her *brain*. Once a fine thing, or fine-ish anyway, it had practically atrophied due to lack of use. For over a decade now she'd been

242

embroiled in domesticities and petty arguments with Aranchez over the sheer amount of cleaning fluids she used. No wonder she'd lain in bed some mornings wondering bleakly, was this it?

But Kyle had never been all that encouraging when she'd mentioned going back to work:

'But what would you *do*?'

All right, fine, so it was a valid question. She was hardly qualified for the next space run to the moon, but whose fault was that? If he hadn't knocked her up, she might have gone on to college at night, like she'd threatened, and she could be a CEO now. Well, why not?

But it was the look on his face that got to her. So sceptical.

'I don't know. *Something*,' she'd say back defensively.

'Get a job if you want. Just so long as the kids don't have to go into some kind of day-care.'

That was the crux of the matter — his dull, conventional, old-fashioned brain, where he brought home the bucks and she looked after the kids. Sometimes she felt he wouldn't care what she did on her own time; she could take up lap dancing at the local club if she wanted (Cassandra's, up by the church), just so long as she was present and correct, and holding a plate of milk and cookies, the minute the kids walked in from school.

'I will so,' she'd told him viciously. 'You just watch.'

But somehow she didn't. The nearest she'd got was an interview for a job as an usher at the cinema, but the kids said they would be

243

mortified when they went there with their friends on a Saturday afternoon, only to meet their mom dressed in some stupid uniform and waving a torch.

'Can't you do, like, something *better*?' Jack had asked.

It was the first time she'd realised she was an embarrassment to them. You'd think their father was developing a cure for cancer, instead of flogging plastic bags. But he made money. That was the difference.

Well, it was time for a wake-up call now. They were broke. And the newsagent had a sign in the window for an assistant. The kids would just have to live with it.

Except that the job was already gone. When Ali enquired, they told her they'd had thirty-four thousand applications or something like that. By now her gung-ho had completely shagged off, and she flopped down on the low wall again, wondering how Liam was fixed for a loan. He was the only one she hadn't hit on yet.

'He can't do that. He can't just cut off your credit cards and your access to a joint account,' he'd said, outraged, when Ali had relayed her tale of woe.

But then apparently Emma had set him straight on the full facts, and he got back on the phone straight away.

'You *took* the kids without asking him? Jesus Christ, Ali, what were you thinking?'

'But he's going to file for custody — '

'That doesn't matter. You're acting like a crazy woman.'

244

'He's trying to take my kids from me!' Did he have a problem with his hearing or something?

'So fight it through the courts, like other people do. But don't drag them halfway across the world. It's not fair on them.'

What did he know, anyway? What did *anybody* know, who wasn't in her situation? She would bet he'd use any trick in the book if it were his kids who were going to be whipped away from him.

They'd parted on bad terms. Maybe he wasn't the best person to ask for a sub after all.

It was depressing. Everything. How was she supposed to keep up this fight? Everything was stacked against her. Kyle had the lawyer, the money, the tasteless but massive family home. She, on the other hand, was stranded in her sister's two-bedroom apartment with nothing but the clothes on her back, and the generosity of her family. Oh, and her kids, of course, who didn't even want to *be* in Ireland, and who were, right now, looking balefully at her from the hire car parked in the car park. She wouldn't even have the bloody hire car later; she had to give it back due to lack of funds.

Erin wound down the window and called over, 'I'm hungry.'

Ali ignored her. Her next step now was the dole queue. She could only imagine how Kyle would use that against her:

'She can't even support the children, mi'lud (or whatever). I, in contrast, am the proud owner of a plastics plant, and can buy them anything they want. Within reason.'

She might as well face it: it wasn't looking good for her. She could hang on for as long as possible, but sooner or later she would be forced home. And God only knew what would happen then. Kyle would probably meet her off the plane in a fit of moral indignation.

'I said, I'm hungry,' Erin called a little louder.

Right now he could bloody well have them.

Oops. She didn't mean that. Not completely, anyway. She was just tired and stressed, and she had a pain in her stomach from Emma's skirt, which was biting painfully into her spare tyre (although there could be more than one). Lord, but that girl was skinny.

But of course she would never say that to Emma. God, no. The last thing she wanted was to send her scurrying off to the bathroom again to examine herself in the mirror. Apart from anything else, it caused a huge tailback in the hallway, what with three children needing to use the toilet approximately once every two and a half minutes. Besides, Emma had only just stopped sticking her tongue out at odd moments and having a good gawk at it in her compact mirror, and Ali didn't want to kick-start all that again.

No, it was very important that nothing be said or done that might add to her distress. The kids had been warned to be quiet around the place, or at least quieter than usual, and not, *under any circumstances*, to touch Emma's probiotic drinks. She needed as much nutrition as she could get, Ali had explained to them. She'd been secretly buying them in the supermarket (she

246

went without shampoo herself) and slipping them into the fridge, in the hopes of building Emma up. She didn't like the look of her recently. Again, not that she would dream of saying this. It was a terrible strain having to constantly think before she spoke, but she felt that, after thirty-four years, she was finally getting the hang of it.

And still no results. What the fuck were they doing with all that blood they'd drawn from Emma's arm? Drinking it? Because they certainly weren't ringing her up with a result.

'When will you know?' Ali had asked anxiously when Emma had come out of the surgery.

Emma had just shrugged and said, 'I suppose whenever they have a result.'

Whenever? Ali would have got the doctor by the throat and held on until she'd got a date, and then, an exact time. How could Emma possibly have walked out of there without at least finding out when she would know her fate?

It was denial, of course. Anybody could see that. Ali could tell just by looking at her that Emma was fit to burst with the strain of it all, only she wouldn't let herself. She'd always been like that, of course. You could never get a good, satisfying fit of hysterics from her. Whenever everybody else in the family was going around shouting their heads off about, for example, mad Auntie Jane coming to stay for two flipping weeks, Emma would just give a resigned sigh and suggest that they put her up in the attic (in fairness, it was converted).

'She's always making me feel like a right

bitch,' Mam often complained bitterly.

Emma was putting her best face forward this time too, even though it was much, much worse than Auntie Jane coming to stay.

Ali wished she'd do the healthy thing and let it all out: cry, scream, set fire to little effigies of Ryan in the back garden, anything. Ali had even stocked up on wine in the hope that Emma would want to get completely pissed some night, and maybe go over to Raven Woods and trash Ryan's gaff, but no. She'd confined herself to her single glass every night, leaving Ali to horse back the rest of the bottle, and end up with a thumping headache the following morning. In the end they'd stopped opening wine altogether because it put too much pressure on them both. So they sat there night after night, on opposite ends of the sofa, without even the cheery clink of a glass to fill the silence.

Ali couldn't even go on too much about her own situation. Well, it wasn't fair to complain about what a shite Kyle was, when Ryan was so clearly a far superior class of shite. Also, Ali felt that Emma severely disapproved of Ali's running off with the kids, although Ali preferred to think of it as rescuing them. She hadn't said anything since that day in the doctor's surgery, but she kept darting what could only be described as concerned looks in the kids' direction. Honestly. As though concerned looks were going to bother Ali, when she had a crack attorney with offices in several major cities gunning for her.

The seven days must be up now. Ali hadn't exactly been keeping count, what with Emma's health crisis and the escalating seriousness of her own financial situation. But very possibly the seven days were up. She'd rescued the heavy cream letter from the bin but hadn't read it again. Seven or eight days anyway. Possibly even ten.

The really ironic thing was that Calvin Crawford wouldn't be the one to force her back to Texas at all. It would be her inability to buy a packet of cornflakes to feed the kids.

'Mom!' Erin again, from the car.

'I heard you! I'll get you something in a minute! You're not going to blooming starve!'

In mid-bellow, she became aware of a woman exiting the shop opposite and approaching her, before slowing in minor alarm. Terrific. How come nobody ever caught her when she was being *nice* to the kids?

Ali threw a beaming smile in the woman's direction, hoping she didn't come across as psychotic.

'Um, hello,' the woman said. 'You were in with me a few minutes ago?'

It took Ali a moment to recognise her. She was the woman from the shoe shop, the woman who had laughed with Ali.

'Yes?' said Ali, thinking, what had she done now?

'I was just watching you through the window and I was admiring your boots,' the woman said girlishly.

Great. Another lunatic. But hang on — she *did* work in a shoe shop, so clearly had an appreciation for fine footwear.

Anyway, Ali couldn't resist extending a leg. 'Jimmy Choo.'

'I knew it.'

'I got them in the sale in Brown Thomas just recently.' She was bragging now. They *were* lovely, even if she sometimes wondered . . . 'You don't think I'm a little too old for them?'

The woman considered the shiny boots with the six-inch heels and the row of S&M-style buckles running down the back, and informed her, 'Absolutely not.'

'Thank you!' There were some people left in the world who knew what they were talking about.

'The thing is,' the woman confided, 'none of the other twenty-two applicants for the job wore any kind of decent footwear.'

Ali's self-interest snapped to attention. 'Wouldn't you think they *should*, for an interview in a shoe shop?'

'One of them wore Crocs.'

'Abomination!' cried Ali, even though she had several pairs herself, including a sick-green pair with multicoloured flowers on them.

'Look, I'm not the boss,' the woman said, 'but he's in later to look over the applications. Basically he goes with whatever I say. And if you still want the job, I'll recommend you.'

Ali gave her a massive, semi-delirious smile. 'Yes, please.'

★ ★ ★

There was nothing from Calvin Crawford when she got back to the flat; no cream-coloured envelope lying on the mat waiting for her. So much for his threats to launch all kinds of legal proceedings upon her. Full of hot air, just like Kyle.

But maybe it was just a game. Maybe the pair of them were making her wait, knowing that her nerves would grow more and more frazzled. Or maybe they were trying to rustle up some class of international arrest warrant, although Ali wasn't sure she'd committed a crime. Maybe she had. She didn't know any more, except that she lived in dread of coming home, and putting her key in the front door, for fear of what the postman may have brought her.

But nothing today, thank God. But that wasn't to say that Kyle wasn't working furiously behind the scenes to try to snatch her kids from her, throwing money at whoever would be the most aggressive on his behalf. What a fine man he was. What a champ.

No post for Emma either. No official-looking letter that might conceivably have come from a doctor's office, if indeed that was the way they'd tell her. It was only when she felt herself relaxing a bit that Ali realised how much worry she'd been carrying around with her on Emma's behalf too.

It was a good day. She'd got a job, Calvin Crawford appeared to be ignoring her for the moment, and in Emma's case, no news was good news.

'Jack!' she said very warmly when he came into the kitchen.

He looked at her warily. 'What?'

'Nothing. Just . . . it's nice to see you, that's all.'

'Sure,' he said, still looking at her like she was screwy. He began buttering two slices of bread. Good. For a couple of weeks there she thought he'd lost his appetite. Maybe he was finally coming round to his new situation.

'How's Carly?' she ventured.

His face went closed. 'Why?'

'No why. I'm just wondering how things are going with you two, that's all.' Hmm, how to put this delicately? 'She hasn't been phoning the house as much.'

Every night for about a month there, she would ring the landline and Jack would disappear off into the bedroom and have a long, intense conversation with the teeny-shorted one.

'You're right, Mom. She hasn't.' But he didn't sound angry. Well, not too angry. 'There didn't seem an awful lot of point, what with you making me live in Ireland, and her back home in Texas.'

'Oh, Jack.' She hadn't meant for it to be over Well, she had. Might as well be honest here. But not so swiftly. She'd thought that things would fizzle out gently over time, and after he'd enjoyed a little long-distance romance first. Nice and safe, both of them having a little fun, until in the end it'd fall apart because neither of them could remember whose turn it was to send the next text.

252

She hadn't meant for anybody to get *hurt*.

But Jack clearly didn't want her sympathy. 'I'm fine,' he said.

And he *looked* all right. He began tucking into his sandwich with reassuring gusto. He had colour in his cheeks, and she realised that today was the first day in a while that he hadn't knocked the stuffing out of Anto simply for looking in his direction.

'You'll have a great life here,' she told him impulsively. 'You just wait and see. You won't be sorry we moved back, I promise you.'

She was going to give him a hug too, but then thought better of it.

'I know,' he said politely, then he took his sandwich and went on out to the living room, where the other pair were looking at the telly. A second later she heard him say something to them, and they all laughed; a wonderful, innocent sound, and her heart rose further.

Truly, this day rocked.

16

Emma

The phone call came through to the studio at a quarter to nine on a Friday morning.

The timing couldn't have been worse. They were experiencing 'slight technical difficulties' with the cookery segment of the show — in other words, the flame kept going out on the hob. Emma was filled with dread as she watched Patrick and Alannah stir around saucepans of scrambled eggs that, due to lack of heat, refused to set.

'Are yours stiff yet?' Patrick enquired of Alannah in despair.

Gamely, Alannah looked mildly shocked. Good girl, thought Emma. Clearly her stern conversation with the pair of them had paid off. There had been several sideways swipes at each other before the start of the show, but nothing vicious. Now, on camera, they were playing it by the book.

'Patrick!' she squealed in reprimand, whilst simultaneously giving a cynical roll of her eyes at the camera, but in a playful way. Was it?

'It's playful,' Hannie confirmed in a whisper beside her. She was watching the pair of them too, eagle-eyed for any misdemeanour.

Playful, Emma assured herself. Thank God.

Patrick, in turn, gave the camera a laddish 'Was it something I said?' look.

Emma wondered with a shock how she'd ended up producing such shite TV. And it *was* shite. The worst kind. Formulaic rubbish, presented by two people who were paid to act like they were in a *Carry On* movie.

Did Hannie see it too? But Hannie was looking at the hob in horror, and clearly wondering what Plan B was. Everybody else in the studio was doing the same, petrified that Patrick and Alannah wouldn't get to finish making their eggs Benedict.

Eggs *Benedict*. As though there was anybody left on the planet who didn't know how to make eggs Benedict. Why had Emma listened to that stupid consultant chef whose idea it had been to show people how to make normal, everyday food? Dull, dull, dull. No wonder they hadn't won that bloody television award.

'I'm going to check the gas supply,' Hannie whispered in a panic beside her.

That was a good idea. Probably pretty essential given that the cookery segment was in danger of going belly-up.

'Fine,' said Emma.

Hannie looked briefly surprised at Emma's lack of panic (why worry about a malfunctioning cooker, when the entire show was shite?) before hurrying off.

Now the crew were starting to turn and shift anxiously too, like a herd of spooked gazelles. Fucking hell, Emma thought. What were any of them even *doing* here, working on stuff like this?

Maybe they were all frustrated too, like Patrick and Alannah had alleged that day. She was beginning to wonder whether they hadn't been right.

But then she saw that it wasn't the cooker at all that was drawing their attention. It was Arnie, picking his way across the studio. He was holding one of the fluorescent pink Post-its that only ever meant one thing: an urgent phone call had come through. All eyes were on him as he advanced through the gloom. Fearful looks were exchanged. Martina, on sound, blessed herself. Who had died?

There was an unbreakable rule regarding phone calls to the studio while the show was live: nobody was ever put through unless there was bereavement. And then only if the deceased was in the very immediate family.

This rule was for health and safety reasons more than anything else. Because all cellphones were turned off on set — nobody wanted to interrupt Alannah interviewing a cancer survivor with a belt of the Crazy Frog — if you wanted to contact someone on the floor you had to ring television reception. There, Tatiana would give you a good going over in her clipped accent.

'Who are you? Who do you want to speak to? Who has died, please?'

If she deemed your call to be of sufficient urgency, which wasn't often, a 'runner' would be summoned from the set. This wasn't actually someone who sprinted around breathlessly in hot-pink Lycra shorts. It was only Arnie, a great lover of bacon sandwiches, whose combat

256

trousers started off the morning around his waist but usually settled halfway down his backside by coffee break.

Once located, Arnie would first have to correctly take down the details from Tatiana (a health and safety concern in itself) on a fluorescent pink Post-it. He would then have to re-enter the darkened, cavernous studio and pick his way, completely silently, through cables, cameras and people who were nearly all dressed entirely in black (health and safety concerns numbers two, three and four). Once he'd located the relevant person, the message that there was a call would have to be imparted through sign language, in the dark, leading to many more health and safety concerns, and the Post-it handed over upon which would be written the name of the caller. Finally Arnie would have to pick his way *back* through the cables, cameras and black-clad people, followed by his victim, and without bumping into the guests. That morning's were St Anne's Cheerleading Group from Coolock, who had just finished up with Alannah and Patrick, and the eleven-year-old winner of the *Young Scientist of the Year* Competition. He was accompanied by his entry, a large home-made wind turbine that was a whole health and safety risk in itself.

Arnie's final challenge was locating the studio phone to which Tatiana would be transferring the call. The studio phone didn't ring, for obvious reasons. Instead a little red light flashed on and off. Or, at least, it had until someone had crashed into it with a stepladder. Now it didn't flash, and it was black, and the studio *wall* was black, so Arnie would have to do large sweeping movements with his hands before locating it, usually knocking it to the ground, which would invite glares and sharp cutting movements across the throat from Phil.

Arnie would then hand over the phone and amble off again, leaving the recipient of the call to conduct a hissed and confused conversation into the mouthpiece.

'Tatiana, what are you ringing me for?'

'I am not, you fool. I will put you through to the bereaved. Wait.'

Today the call was for Phil. No, not Phil . . . Lucy, who was looking after the guests. But then Arnie plodded past Lucy, and then Tadhg on camera, and started making for . . . Emma.

Dear God.

She thought she was going to vomit. Then faint. Small black dots of panic and fear began to dance before her eyes, and not even in a co-ordinated fashion, so that she felt dizzy along with the urge to vomit and faint.

Could it be . . . ? She checked her watch. A lot of doctors' surgeries opened at half-past eight. Theoretically it was possible. And she had given them her work phone number. Not consciously. It had just been a box on the New Patient registration form, and she'd filled it in. She'd filled *everything* in, just to pass the time and take her mind off the test. She'd written at length about her allergy to dust mites, and how it made her nose swell up, and sometimes tickly, and how she had to carry a packet of tissues at all times.

Then she realised they meant allergies to medication, to which she had none at all, and she felt rather foolish.

Surely they wouldn't go ringing her at this hour, though, would they? But why not? They had to make these phone calls either before or after surgery. Her results were going to come in sooner or later, and it wasn't up to her to choose a time.

Even in her panic and fear, she watched out of the corner of her eye as the gas rings on the studio cooker spluttered a final time and died completely under the semi-scrambled eggs. Terrific.

'Sorry, folks,' Patrick deadpanned to the camera. 'Cutbacks.'

Alannah dutifully tittered, even as the look in her eyes said, 'What the fuck are we going to do now?'

And here was Arnie with that horrible pink Post-it. Emma tried to avoid his eye, as she gestured frantically to Alannah to turn her attention to the pile of cookbooks on the kitchen counter which they were going to review along with the idiot consultant chef who, Emma noticed, had grabbed the only working hob for himself. They hadn't planned to get to the books until the cookery demo was over, but they had no choice now.

'Emma?' Arnie hissed, when it was clear that Emma was ignoring his sign language.

'I'm busy,' Emma blurted. Maybe if she didn't take the call she would never have to find out. 'The hob . . . '

'It's urgent,' Arnie insisted, pressing the Post-it into her hand.

She didn't want to look. She wanted to scrunch it up and get rid of it; eat it if necessary, just so she wouldn't see the words 'doctor' written on it.

But with the same sick fascination that made people slow down as they passed road accidents, she found her neck bending downwards and her eyes seeking out Tatiana's scrawl.

The Post-it was blank. Nothing was written on it.

'The caller wouldn't give Tatiana their name,' Arnie whispered, in obvious admiration for anybody who'd displayed such defiance, and had *still* got their call put through. 'I thought I'd bring it anyway,' he finished up proudly.

Now Emma really *was* going to be sick. The surgery had assured her of confidentiality at all times and it seemed they were sticking to that. In one way she was grateful. She didn't want Tatiana asking her when she got off the phone what was so urgent that the doctor had to get her out in the middle of the cookery section.

How would she keep it from them all, if the news was bad? Because she had to. She had no doubt of that. If it was any other disease she could have come right out with it, even if she'd had cancer. There would be shock, but then understanding and sympathy. People would chat about her in the canteen in concerned tones, and swap stories about how their second cousin had had exactly the same kind of cancer, but had

260

pulled through it with chemo, and a three-month diet of carrot juice.

Imagine their faces if she said HIV. There would be shock all right, and the requisite concern and sympathy, but then the speculation would start, no matter how they tried to stop themselves: *Emma*. She'd be the last person you'd think. She looked great, though, didn't she? And so calm, so determined to keep working and behaving as normal. You'd never know there was anything wrong with her. Mind you, the medication they had these days was great. But still, how . . . ?

Nobody would say that, though. They'd just think it. In this day and age, you couldn't be anything other than accepting. Besides, they were artistic people, all of them, more liberal-minded, and they would be very disappointed with themselves if they treated it as anything other than a regular disease, albeit one with an unfortunate name.

But the tones in the canteen would be lower. People's second cousins generally wouldn't have HIV, so there would be no swapping of stories about juicing and the wonders of acupuncture. Other colleagues wouldn't want to discuss it at all, because they'd see it as being disloyal to Emma; they'd view it as gossip and they'd try to protect her by cutting off all talk of her health. All this would be done with the best of intentions, of course, but they'd be treating her differently without even realising it.

But she was ahead of them all in the stigmatising stakes. She hadn't even told her own parents she'd gone for a test. She'd barely told the doctor that day. In the end he'd had to ask, very politely, after she'd frantically chatted about the weather for five minutes, what she was there to see him about. She'd almost whipped off her sock and presented him with her ingrown toenail; it was only the knowledge that Ali was waiting outside like a Rottweiler that made her confess, in a shamed whisper, to the purpose of her visit.

How could she possibly tell people, her family, her colleagues, the truth?

But all that had to wait now because Arnie was turning to lead the way to the studio phone, his builder's bum gleaming whitely in the gloom.

Emma traipsed after him, a horrible, choking feeling in her throat that made her swallow convulsively. People darted little looks her way as she went past. There was no surprise there, only sympathy. Clearly her father had suffered heart attack number six and had finally bought it.

'He's in a better place now,' Lucy whispered to her.

Jesus, maybe it *was* Dad. He hadn't looked too perky the last she'd seen him. Mam had been giving out about how the doctor wouldn't let him eat red meat any more, only chicken and fish, preferably oily. 'Oily fecking fish!'

But Dad generally had his heart attacks at night. Four out of the five had been around midnight, just after Mam had fallen asleep (sometimes she carried on as though he deliberately picked the most inconvenient time possible). The only one he'd had in daylight hours had been before lunch that time Ryan had come over — just as the pasta was done, Mam had remarked complainingly at the time.

Also, Mam would phone Emma's mobile. She'd never ring the studio. No, it couldn't be Dad, although — and a part of her hated herself for feeling this way — it would have been a relief if it was, because then it wouldn't be the doctor.

'Here,' Arnie whispered, handing her the studio phone, delighted with himself that he'd managed to find it without knocking it off the wall.

'Thank you.' Emma gripped the receiver in cold, clammy hands. She'd have to tell them she'd ring them back in forty-five minutes when the show was over. She would not, could not, get news that would affect the rest of her life whilst listening to Patrick goading a squeamish Alannah into having a little bite of the semi-raw eggs: 'It'll put hairs on your chest.'

It didn't sound that playful, either.

But she blocked him out and pressed the phone close to her ear. 'Hello?'

There was silence for ages. And then a voice said back, 'Emma?'

It was Ryan. She felt a fresh shock run through her. Even in his most blatant attempts to get hold of her after they'd broken up, he'd never resorted to ringing her in the studio while the show was live.

She opened her mouth, but she needn't have bothered as nothing came out.

It didn't matter anyhow, because Ryan was speaking now, low and fast. 'I know you can't

263

talk now. And I'm sorry for ringing you at work. But I know that you took a test. I just wanted to say that I'm thinking about you.' A little pause. 'All the time.'

His voice was so familiar, once so loved, that she realised she'd stopped breathing. Now she really *couldn't* say anything.

She thought she might finally have whispered, 'Ryan,' but suddenly he was gone. All she could hear was the beep-beep of a disconnected line.

Bloody Tatiana. Emma wouldn't have put it past her to have listened in on the call, and once she'd deduced that there was nobody dead at all, she'd smartly terminated the connection.

Right, that was it. She was going to make a complaint about Tatiana. It was outrageous to cut her off in the middle of a conversation with Ryan like that! With anybody, naturally. Not just Ryan. He might have had, well, other things to say. Not that she'd intended to get into a *conversation* or anything with him. But it would have been a courtesy to at least have heard him out.

Wait, though. He hadn't exactly sounded like he was bursting to get a whole load of other stuff off his chest, had he? In fact, he'd come across very calmly, and his piece had the air of something that had been . . . prepared.

It began to sink in then that maybe he hadn't wanted to get into a conversation either. That, once he'd said his piece, he had just quietly hung up.

The bollocks!

It was an awful shock. Every other phone call

had started with his frantic, tortured plea of, 'Don't cut me off! Please!'

But *now* — now it seemed that he didn't want anything else to do with her! He hadn't even asked how she was coping; just a quick 'poor you' type of thing, and the standard, 'I'm thinking of you.' Which, she might as well face it, could mean anything or nothing at all. How many times did people say, 'I'm thinking of you,' when, really, their mind was on the fish and chips they were having for tea that evening?

Empty, meaningless phrases. And then he'd had the audacity to hang up on her!

Well, fine. No problem! It had been a positive *relief*, actually, not to have had to interrupt his apologies this time, and his stricken monologues about how he couldn't believe what had happened, how he wouldn't be able to get a single night's sleep until he knew she was getting proper medical care, et cetera, blah, blah.

He'd slept *last* night. She was sure of that. Or else how had he sounded so perky on the phone just now? Positively chipper.

Ooh, she was raging.

Then: how had he known she was taking a test?

It was a moment before she realised there were raised voices behind her. Coming from the set, to be precise.

Oh, Jesus. What the hell was happening?

Emma turned as if in slow motion to see Patrick and Alannah in what seemed to be a face-off over a cookbook they'd been reviewing. The eggs sat between them on a plate, sickly runny and toxic-looking.

'What do *you* cook when you're at home, then?' Alannah was demanding shrilly (most definitely not playfully) of Patrick. Her orange eye-shadow glowed furiously under the studio lights. 'That's if you cook at all,' she said with magnificent disparagement.

'Of course I don't,' Patrick confirmed. 'I have a girlfriend. I'm sorry if that offends your frilly feminism.'

One of them would stop this. They had to. They were professionals, allegedly, and would know that there were thousands of people watching live at home (hopefully). There was only one way this could go, or else they'd all be holding their P45s.

Cop on, the pair of you, Emma found herself shouting in her head.

But clearly they'd reached some kind of mutual boiling point. They seemed unaware of the cameras or the lights or the furious gestures from Phil to cut it out.

At least he was doing *something*. Emma herself seemed rooted to the spot.

'Cupcakes mightn't interest *you*, but think about the kids out there,' Alannah challenged him furiously, waving a cookbook about. The cover was a riot of pastel colours and cute decorated buns, the kind of thing that might have been designed specifically to annoy Patrick.

'No, *you* think about the kids, and the cuddly animals, and any other minority group that you can rustle up, and I'll think about all the sane people out there,' Patrick informed her. 'Of which I am one.'

And with that, he stalked off the set. Alannah, not to be outdone, turned and walked off in the opposite direction, the cupcake cook-book clasped to her chest with great dignity.

Someone — probably Phil, who was dashing about with great urgency near the front — had had the sense to cue up that morning's competition. They cut away to a still of a posh cookery school, and Alannah's pre-recorded voiceover:

'If you'd like to win a fantastic weekend for two in luxurious surroundings, and learn to cook your favourite Italian food, then all you have to do is answer the following question on your screen now . . . '

Then the competition was over and the final credits rolled. Normally, they would have gone back to Patrick and Alannah, who would bid the viewer a cheery farewell, finishing up with the usual threat of, 'See you back here at seven o'clock on Monday!'

Naturally, that was out of the question that day.

Everyone in the studio stood around in shock as the show's signature tune rolled over them. What the hell had just happened?

Then the studio phone began to vibrate on the wall.

Emma didn't need Arnie to tell her that it was for her.

She reached over and answered it.

'Emma?' As expected, it was Adam. 'In my office. Now.'

17

Ali

The kids' first day at their new Dublin school didn't go so great. 'What happened?' Ali's heart jumped into her mouth as Anto and Erin traipsed in off the bus, forlorn and downcast.

Quickly, she checked them over for signs of damage: had their lunch boxes been stolen? Or the money she'd given them to buy sweets in the shop after school as a treat? Had some horrid little shit put chewing gum in their hair?

It was all her fault. It was never easy being the new kid in school, but everything about Anto and Erin was different: the accent, the massive white shiny American teeth, the branded sneakers. They were practically wearing targets on their backs.

'Whatever it is, I'll sort it out,' she promised them immediately, gathering them into her arms protectively, and trying to choke back the tears. She was having horrible visions of the pair of them backed into corners in the playground, surrounded by laughing, taunting children, some of them wielding hurleys. 'I'll go in there first thing Monday.' (She'd started them on a Friday so that they'd have the weekend to get over the trauma of their first day.) 'I'll talk to the Principal, so don't you worry, OK?'

Anto sniffed gloomily. 'You can try,' he said. 'But he's not that good.'

Ali went a little still. 'You've met the Principal already?'

'He has no *clue* about how you trade cards. Like I'm going to give some kid a card for nothing.' Anto was highly disparaging.

Ali's loving touch on his shoulder tightened to a grip. 'You took cards to school?'

Anto had various caches of collectable cards that he bought in the newsagent's every week with his pocket money. His current passion was for wrestling cards. Each card featured preposterously muscled and moustachioed individuals with names like The Tank Thompson and Rip Rider. In the States, cards were banned in most schools because of unfair trading and rampant bullying.

'I wasn't even charging much,' Anto protested. 'And then he — that Principal guy — made me go round the classes and give all the money back. Like *that's* fair. Actually, maybe you *should* go in and talk to him, Mom.'

Ali felt faint. She didn't even want to ask how much he'd squeezed out of those poor, innocent children. But no doubt there would be a phone call from the school letting her know exactly what he'd been up to on his first day.

'We'll talk about this later,' she promised him.

'Good, because next thing you know, I'll be forced to take my business outside the school gates,' Anto said, shaking his head in disbelief.

It was Erin's turn now. She'd been waiting patiently and maturely to air her grievances. Ali plucked her onto her lap and gave her a cuddle, which Erin gamely endured for Ali's sake.

'What was school like for you, pet?'

Erin reflected on this a moment and then informed Ali, 'There's nothing wrong with the actual *kids*.' She gave a little sigh. 'I just don't think they're my type.'

'Your . . . type?'

'None of them watch *America's Next Top Model*,' Erin informed her gravely. 'Some of them haven't even *heard* of it.'

'Oh. Well, I'm sure you'll find something else in common with them. It just takes a bit of time . . . '

'Mom.' Erin quietened her with a look. 'They still like Barbie.' She said it as though breaking the sad news of an unexpected death.

'I see,' said Ali at last. 'Barbie's not that bad, though, is she?'

'*Mom*.'

Ali knew there was no point in pursuing Barbie's virtues, at least not with this seven-year-old. Erin and her friends had had a Barbie Bonfire last summer in the back garden, where they'd decapitated all their old Barbies and piled them up on top of a couple of firelighters, and had chanted 'Death to Barbie' as the whole lot went up in flames.

'If they were wearing white hoods you'd be really worried,' another mom had whispered to Ali.

'I just don't see how I'm ever going to fit in,' Erin said with a concerned sigh. 'Unless I come down to their level.'

'I suppose you could try it for a while,' Ali suggested cautiously.

'But you always said we had to be ourselves,' Erin pointed out.

'Well, yes . . . ' The little witch.

'It's a bit of a dilemma, isn't it?' Erin told her sternly, before climbing off her lap and going into the living room to put on a rerun of *Extreme Makeovers*.

All Ali needed now was for Jack to come home in an hour with more tales of woe. He'd been enrolled at the local community college, which had an excellent reputation, and was reassuringly diverse and multicultural in its student body. Jack, so solid and calm, so tall and good-looking, would surely find a niche for himself quickly, wouldn't he?

But when the front door opened nearly an hour later, she rushed to it, arms already outstretched to dispense big, comforting hugs.

'Hello,' said Mam, pleased at the unusually warm welcome. 'It's nice to know that *somebody* appreciates what I'm doing for them.' She gave Dad a hard look as he shuffled in apologetically behind her.

Oh dear. Something must have happened at home. Some little accident or other. They were quite frequent these days, according to Mam.

They'd come over, reluctantly, to keep an eye on the kids while Ali went to work in the shoe shop. She was only in the job two days, and already she'd been asked to come in that afternoon and cover a shift, although she'd explained quite clearly to them in the beginning

271

that she could only work during school hours.

But what could she do? A job was a job. Without it, they couldn't live. She might have to sort out better childcare arrangements, though.

'Have they eaten?' Mam asked, casting a wary look in at Erin and Anto, and drawing her cardigan a little tighter around herself.

'I'll get them something before I go,' Ali assured her. 'How are you feeling, Dad?'

He always enjoyed these enquiries because it gave him a chance to moan. 'That pain in my chest is still there. I said to the doctor the last day that I should be sent for an X-ray or something, because everybody always thinks it's my heart, but what about my lungs? So I — '

'Mind out.' Mam had taken off her coat and was bustling around the kitchen with a sigh. She always felt under obligation to tidy up, even in houses that weren't her own. Sometimes this caused offence, especially where she barely knew the owners, but she said that she couldn't help herself: she was so used to caring for other people now that she was finding it hard to stop. 'I think my off button is broken,' she had blurted to Ali one day, in some surprise.

She began whizzing around with a dustpan and brush. Dad stood in the middle of the whirlwind, trying not to stray into harm's way, or be knocked off balance by the brush.

'I just hope Emma's OK after what happened this morning,' Mam fretted.

Ali's stomach dropped unpleasantly: was there news?

Then: how did Mam know?

'If you ask me, Patrick is right,' Mam went on. 'That Alannah one *has* no sense of humour. And as for her make-up ... desperate altogether. Wouldn't you think they'd have a professional in there who would do it for her?'

'Oh. Yes.' Ali's heart slowed. It was the thing on *Wake Up Ireland* that morning that Mam was talking about, not Emma's test results. Not that Ali had seen the telly, what with having to make lunches and breakfasts and get the kids out to school for their first day. After weeks of leisurely mornings, her system was still in shock. 'I suppose that's why she's late home. Trying to sort it out.'

'Patrick is lovely,' Mam said, cheering up greatly. 'Straight-talking. And very good-looking, isn't he, Noel?'

Dad was so pleased to have a civil word thrown in his direction that he perked up too, and agreed enthusiastically, 'Oh, yes, very dark and handsome, even if a little short. I'd give him an eight out of ten.'

'Would you? I'd go for a nine. He has lovely thick hair.'

They were definitely spending too much time on their own, Ali decided, as she left to go to work. Anybody would go a bit loopy stuck at home all day long with only their better half (and she used that term loosely) to look at, the monotony broken only by the occasional trip in a speeding ambulance to the cardiac unit.

She flicked a glance at the hall table as she left. Still no word from Calvin Crawford.

273

Instead of making her feel safe, it only unsettled her more.

★　★　★

Working in the neighbourhood shoe shop wasn't as great as it had first appeared. It was much quieter than she'd thought it would be; they had only two customers in between eleven and twelve yesterday, and one of those came in nearly every day to look but never bought anything. That was according to Moira, anyway, the woman who'd given Ali the job, and who, she noticed, usually fecked off out the door the minute Ali had taken her coat off.

She did it today too. 'I'm just going to nip up to the supermarket for a few bits and pieces. If Ernie rings, tell him I'm in the loo.'

Ernie was the owner. He was never seen, but phoned in regularly, and Moira would put him on loudspeaker, and she and Ali would gather round and take his instructions. It was all very *Charlie's Angels*.

'Check if we have a size six left in that brown Oggetti sandal that came in last month,' Ernie would say solemnly over the phone. Or, in a lower voice, 'There's a consignment of Gabor coming in tomorrow. Keep an eye out.'

'We have ten seconds before this message self-combusts,' Ali had joked yesterday when he'd hung up.

'What?' Moira had said. Not the most with it, bless her, even if she loved shoes.

Ali had wondered what Ernie looked like.

What kind of man set his heart on a women's shoe shop in a suburban shopping arcade, anyway?

'Is he gay?' she'd asked.

But Moira's cheeriness had abruptly evaporated. Clearly she had some massive loyalty thing going on with Ernie. 'I don't believe so,' she'd told Ali in a smack-down voice. And then she shagged off to the newsagent's to get the latest copy of *TV Now*, leaving Ali to carry the can.

Not that there was anything much to do in the shop, except to tinker with the displays (Moira 'designed' them) and think about her first pay cheque at the end of next week.

That was the good part. Not even weird Ernie and odd Moira could dampen the thrill of having some earning power. She'd only had a tiny taste of it fifteen years ago (ah, Macy's . . .) and hadn't realised until now how much she'd missed it. Naturally, she wished her earning power was considerably more than what Ernie was paying her, but maybe that would come in the future.

And why not? She was young, free and single (despite three kids and a bunch of greying hair) and she could do whatever she set her mind to. The shackles of marriage had been left far behind in Texas, and she was going to . . . to run Ernie's shoe shop to the best of her considerable ability!

And here came a customer at last. Decent shoes, too, although far too flat, in Ali's opinion. But she fully intended to flog this woman a pair of those gorgeous, skyscraper evening shoes that Moira had just put on display that very morning.

'Hello!' she trilled as the little bell over the door pinged.

It was Emma. She did not look in the mood for new shoes. She looked furious, in fact.

'Mam told me,' Ali said immediately.

'What?'

'About Patrick and Alannah. And them walking off the set.'

'Oh. Yes.' Emma looked vague.

'Was there war?'

'I got hauled in and told I'm on leave.'

'What?'

'It's been decided that Phil's going to produce the show for a week.'

'That weasel! Hannie's never trusted him, has she?' Ali was furious on Emma's behalf. With everything else that was going on in her life, she didn't need problems at work too.

'Yes, well.' Disappointingly, Emma didn't seem to be into assassinating Phil's character at all. 'I'm actually here because I want to talk to you about something.'

That didn't sound too good. Ali's mind raced nimbly over the possible list of her infractions: the fucking probiotic yoghurt drinks again (Anto had developed a passion for them); the massive electricity bill that had come through the door yesterday; any number of stains on the cream carpet.

'You should have put down wooden flooring in the first place,' she said accusingly. Best to go in all guns blazing. 'That way you wouldn't *have* any stains!'

Emma blinked, and then brushed this off with

276

a wave of her hand. 'I'm talking about Ryan.'

'Ryan?' Ali tried to look as innocent as possible.

'You told him I was taking a test.'

'I did not!'

'You were the only one in the whole world who knew, Ali.'

Well, all right, fair enough. 'I went over to have a go at him for you,' she admitted.

Emma would be delighted; someone finally to stick up for her, and give that fucker the tongue-lashing he deserved.

Only she didn't look all that delighted. 'And who asked you to?'

'Nobody . . . but come *on*. It had to be done. Why should he get away scot-free after everything?'

'He's hardly got away scot-free. He's positive himself.'

'Well, yes, of course. But apart from that, when I saw him he was strolling along with a pint of bloody milk! Not a care in the world!'

Emma was looking all quiet and sad, the way Ali had never been able to manage with any degree of sincerity. 'He lost me. Do you not think that was enough?'

Actually, no, Ali didn't, but had to agree, very humbly, 'Yes, of course . . . he must be *devastated* . . . nothing could possibly be worse . . . ' Apart from a good kick in the nuts but there was no point in saying that to Emma. She had no idea at all of how to play it dirty. Luckily, she had Ali to do it for her.

'What does it matter anyway,' she challenged,

'whether he knows or not?'

'*Because*,' Emma threw back, 'it's none of his business! And even if it was, I'd like to have told him myself!'

'I was only looking out for you.'

'You were not. You were poking your nose in, doing what you thought was best, without ever once considering how I might feel.'

Well, Ali wasn't going to stand for that. 'If it wasn't for me, you wouldn't even have gone for that test!'

'Please don't start giving yourself medals here for meddling in other people's lives.'

Now that was vicious. And not like Emma at all. She was always so, well, *nice*. Reasonable. She'd never really said anything nasty to Ali, despite untold provocation over the years.

'I didn't see it as meddling.' Ali found that her eyes were stinging a bit. She'd been wrong, she saw. 'I saw it as trying to help you. To do the best for you — '

'Ha!' Emma brushed aside her attempt at explanation. 'Why don't you go sort your own life out first before you go fixing anybody else's?' Then she hurriedly blurted, 'I didn't mean to say that.' She paused. 'Actually, I did.'

'Oh, well, I'm sorry!' Ali threw back. 'From now on, I'll make sure to stay well out of your perfect fucking life!'

She just threw it out in a temper. She hadn't meant it as a dig.

But Emma looked at her peculiarly. 'Not so perfect now, is it? So I guess we're quits.'

This was terrible. Awful! There they were,

278

sisters who had once been so close that they used to squeeze into the same pair of pyjamas together and stagger down the stairs to show Mam and Dad — their two heads popping out of the one top, it really *had* looked quite funny — and now they were clawing lumps out of each other in the middle of a shoe shop, of all places.

Nobody said anything for a second. Ali was trying to formulate words of apology; trying to find ways of taking it all back when Emma said, in a thin voice, 'I think it might be best if you moved out of my flat.'

What could Ali do? Refuse to go? Beg for another chance? Point out that Emma was, in effect, making them homeless? 'Yes,' she agreed finally. 'We'll be gone by Monday.'

God only knew where. Mam and Dad's doily-ridden house, maybe, or some stable in Bethlehem.

Emma nodded jerkily, her face closed. Ali didn't even feel she could ask her about the test, and when they might expect the results. Emma mightn't even tell her. She might cut her out completely after this.

Oh, why had she gone to see Ryan that day? Stupid. He wasn't worth it, and never had been.

'I'll see you later,' Emma eventually said.

'Yes. Fine.'

Ah, Jesus. It was like breaking up with some fella. Ali was going to say, 'Come on, Emma, for feck's sake, let's have a glass of wine tonight and thrash this out.'

But she was interrupted by the ping of the bell over the shop door. Bloody customers. Didn't

279

they realise there was a serious family altercation going on?

'Mom! Mom!' It was Erin, racing in to fling herself dramatically upon Ali.

OK, this was unexpected. 'What are you doing here?'

Now here came Anto, and then Mam and Dad brought up the rear, puffing and grim-faced.

Oh God. Anto and Erin had done something unspeakable and Mam and Dad were washing their hands of them. It could be the only explanation.

'I didn't want to ring you because I knew you'd be in the middle of serving customers,' Mam hissed, throwing a nod towards Emma. Her face cleared as she registered who it was. 'Oh, it's only Emma.'

'Don't mind me,' said Emma, and dutifully stepped into the background.

'Anyway, listen,' Mam went on to Ali urgently, 'is Jack here with you?'

'Jack?' Ali's heart automatically went into overdrive. 'No. I told you, he'd be home from school on the bus.'

'Well, he never arrived.'

Ali checked her watch. 'It's only half-past five. He's only an hour late.'

She was trying to calm herself as much as anything. An hour was nothing.

Then: anything could happen in an hour.

'I know.' Mam was all ruffled. 'But we kept listening out for the door, and then Anto — ' she threw him a hard look — 'started telling us about some American boy who disappeared off a

280

school bus last year and, well, I won't tell you the rest but we found it very upsetting, didn't we, Noel?'

Dad nodded. He looked a bit sweaty, and had his heart pills in his hand, Ali noticed.

Anto, meanwhile, was diligently inspecting a pair of lady's shoes, and helpfully buffing them with the sleeve of his sweatshirt.

'I'm sure nothing's happened to him. He probably got chatting to some of the kids in his class. Making new friends and all that.' She was making him out to be Mr Personality himself. 'He's probably at home right now, wondering where everybody is.'

'We rang his mobile,' Erin said breathlessly. People going missing, and possibly being in mortal danger, was right up her street. 'It just rang out.'

'That doesn't mean anything,' Ali snapped. But her heart speeded up more; Jack never, ever, even if he was in the shower, ignored his mobile phone.

'What are we going to do?' Mam demanded. Her colour was very high now. 'I knew something would happen on my shift. It's always the way! Your father never had a single heart attack when anybody else was around. Not one! He's always waited until muggins here was on duty.'

'That's not fair,' Dad interjected. 'I had one when Ryan was around. You were off faffing around with your hair. That man saved my life.' He nodded stoutly several times. To Emma, he said, apologetically, 'I know you two have had your differences, but in my book he was one of the nicest fellows you could ever meet.'

'You've never slept with him,' Emma lobbed back at him.

That startled everybody. Dad clutched his pills tighter. Ali clamped her hands over Erin's ears fiercely.

'It's all right, Mom, I *know* about the birds and the bees.' Erin shook her off impatiently.

'What are we going to do?' wailed Mam.

'I don't know — '

'We have to do *something*.'

Ali tried to quell her rising panic. 'I know we do. Just let me think for a minute.'

'We don't have time to stand around thinking. Anything could have happened to him!'

Into all this stepped Emma. 'Stop.'

She didn't even say it loudly. She held up her hands, waited, and they all fell silent, one by one. Then, as they had so many times over the years, they turned to her for direction.

'Mam and Dad, go back to the apartment in case he turns up. Anto, you're to confine yourself to the spare room, and don't go near Granny or Granddad again, OK? They've been frightened enough for one day.' She turned to Ali now. 'Get on the phone. Ring the school. See what time he left. Get them to ring the bus people. Speak to his teacher, anybody you can think of.'

Everybody obediently began shuffling out the door. Wasn't it great to have someone in charge?

'Where are you going?' asked Ali, as Emma made off after them.

Emma looked back in surprise. 'I don't know,

to ring some people, I suppose.'

Ali grabbed her hand and clung to it hard. She didn't think she'd ever been so frightened in her life. 'Don't leave me. Please.'

18

Emma

By the following morning everybody had converged on Emma's apartment. *Everybody*: Mam, Dad were there; Ali and the kids, obviously; Liam and Tina and *their* three kids; Aunties Jane and Alice, although they hadn't been invited, and other assorted odds and ends. They all had mobile phones, and were ringing *other* relatives, ones who hadn't made it to the flat yet, to fill them in.

'No, no news yet . . . thank God there wasn't a frost last night . . . we were just saying, he was always such a sensible lad . . . so out of character . . . poor Ali . . . distraught . . . comforting her as best we can . . . take the next right turn, you'll have to park out on the road.'

The house phone was being left free in case Jack rang. Or, Poor Confused Jack, as he was rapidly becoming known — confused, as in emotional and hormonal and far from home, rather than sharp-bang-on-the-head confused. Well, hopefully not, anyway. Nobody could be sure until they found him and asked him how many fingers they were holding up.

A posse had already been out searching, but what was the point, when they hadn't a clue where to start? The lad hadn't turned up for school at all yesterday morning, so he'd a whole eight hours on them by the time the alarm was even raised.

The general consensus was that he'd made a break for it back to America. Well, where else would he possibly go? He didn't know a sinner in Ireland, apart from family. And, whilst nobody was insensitive enough to question Ali directly on it (she was sitting in the kitchen, not a word out of her, God love her), it was known that he'd left a girlfriend back home.

Clearly, they'd planned the whole thing, him and this Carly. Foolish, but that was young love for you. She must have been in on it too, because he didn't have any money for a plane ticket, or a false passport (his own was under the toaster, along with everybody else's). The false passport idea seemed a bit far-fetched in the cold light of day, especially as Carly was only fifteen and, on the face of it, without any mob connections, but what other explanation was there? Carly must have somehow supplied him with documents, money, and possibly even a set of clothes, because who in their right mind would try to sneak out of the country in a bright green and orange school uniform?

The guards, when they'd come to the apartment yesterday evening, had listened to all this very carefully — and had then gone and searched the shed at the back of Emma's apartment block.

'Geniuses,' Mam had said, throwing up her hands. 'And we after handing it to them on a plate.'

The guards were being very casual about the whole thing, especially when they learned that Jack was almost sixteen, and not, say, twelve or thirteen, and that he'd been very unhappy recently with some of his mother's decisions. They'd also gone through the kitchen presses, which hadn't occurred to anybody else, and deduced that he'd taken several cans of tuna with him, and half a loaf of Weight Watchers bread (Emma's). There also appeared to be a sharp knife missing, some string, a box of matches and one of Ali's thermal vests, although it wasn't certain whether this had just gone missing in the wash.

They told the family to sit tight and wait. They would circulate his description, but in their experience, these things resolved themselves sooner rather than later, and they were pretty optimistic that Jack hadn't come to any harm.

'It's still not on Sky News,' Anto announced to the gathering now, bitterly disappointed. He'd had the telly blaring all morning, unable to believe that Jack's non-return from school hadn't made international headlines amongst the stories of atrocities and banking collapses.

'Turn that off,' Emma instructed him. She found that if she used a low, threatening voice, he generally obeyed.

'Do you want a hand making sandwiches?' Tina shouted from across the room. She was already rolling up her sleeves.

'No, I think we're fine, thanks. If you could just keep Liam away.'

Tina understood immediately. 'I'll sit on him if necessary.'

Liam had had an awful go at Ali earlier, more or less saying that the entire thing was the result of her hot-headedness. If she hadn't acted unilaterally in dragging everybody home . . . Emma had pulled him away in the end. He was right, of course, but his timing was way off.

Emma fought her way through the crowd now towards the kitchen, where Mam was washing up mountains of cups in the sink.

'It's always the quiet ones,' she said with a sigh.

Over by the door Dad stiffened, wondering whether this was a dig at him, as he hadn't said anything since yesterday evening. He hadn't had a chance, what with all the keening and roaring and threats to kill Jack going on. (This was said in an affectionate way, as in, 'I'll murder him when I get my hands on him.' Nobody really meant it.)

But Mam was taking no notice at all of Dad, and Emma saw him relax. Jack's disappearance had actually had unexpected benefits for him, as Mam had laid off him almost completely, and he was able to be frail in peace in the corner.

'I'll make more sandwiches,' Mam decided now, opening Emma's fridge. She took one look and shook her head in despair. 'We'll have to go to the shops.'

Through all this Ali sat like a statue at the kitchen table, ashen-faced, and with Jack's mobile phone in her hand. He'd left it behind.

Deliberately, of course. But she hadn't put it down once, as though hoping that eventually it would ring, and it would be him.

'Nobody's going to the shops,' Emma told Mam firmly. 'In fact, it's time for people to start going home.'

'But a lot of them have only just arrived.'

There was a call from the living room. 'We're just going to start a decade of the rosary.' That was Auntie Jane. She'd been threatening it for a while.

That was all they needed now; for the place to take on the atmosphere of a wake.

Ali looked up suddenly. 'Where's Erin? And Anto?'

She asked this every ten minutes.

'In the living room,' Emma told her soothingly.

'Are you sure?'

'Absolutely. I saw both of them just a second ago.'

Ali nodded jerkily and went back to staring at Jack's phone, not even looking up when the doorbell rang. Well, it had rung so many times now, and it had never been Jack.

Mam looked out the window, addled. 'More blooming relatives.'

The way she said it meant they were from Dad's side of the family, and he duly looked apologetic.

'Go answer it,' Emma ordered Mam. 'Tell them they can't come in. In fact, tell everybody in there — she jerked her head towards the living room — tell them all to go. Tell them you're taking the kids out for a walk, that Ali's tired.'

But she wasn't fast enough.

'Hail Mary, full of Grace, the Lord is with thee,' Auntie Jane started up in a singsong voice. After about five Hail Marys she would start gathering speed, until by the tenth and final one, she would be belting it out like a commentator at Aintree, along with blessing herself nineteen to the dozen, and you'd want to stand well back out of the way.

'Now, Mam,' Emma insisted. 'Don't just stand there.'

She may have been a little too strident, because Mam said, 'Honestly, I don't know what's got into you lately. Always taking the head off everybody.'

Emma looked towards Ali. 'Not now, Mam — '

'And we've tried to be so nice to you and everything, since you broke up with Ryan.' She looked very hurt now. 'Always ready with a friendly ear to hear any problems you might have.'

That was pushing it a bit.

'But oh, no, you tell us nothing. Never have, never will. Well, we're not stupid, are we, Noel?' She was really upset now. 'We know there's something up with you. I've lain awake nights, worrying. But, as usual, you'll take your sweet time in telling us anything. I suppose I'll just have to wait and find out from someone in the supermarket.'

She let that hang there, waiting for Emma to contradict her. As if Emma was going to tell her, in this distraught gathering, that Ryan was

HIV-positive, and that she herself was waiting to find out whether he'd given the virus to her or not.

'Hail-Mary-full-of-Grace-the Lord-is-with-thee.' Auntie Jane had moved up a gear.

For once, Emma was glad for her. 'Go. Now,' she ordered Mam, more viciously this time. 'Take the kids with you.'

Mam looked at her very sorrowfully, but she picked up her coat anyway, and held Dad's out for him.

She squeezed Ali's shoulder in passing, and whispered, 'You heard the guards — it'll all be grand. He'll be back before you know it.'

Then she closed the kitchen door behind her and Dad, and moments later the praying stopped. There was the sound of chairs being hauled back, and several 'goodbyes', and then the place grew quiet as people took their leave.

She could see Mam out the window now, leading the way down the apartment steps, with Dad, Anto and Erin traipsing after her. Her back was stooped from the sheer *responsibility* of it all.

Finally, Ali looked across at her with blood-shot eyes. 'Is it just me, or is she turning into a mad psycho bitch from hell?'

'Yes. But that's another day's work.' Emma sat down opposite her at the kitchen table. She reached across and clasped Ali's cold, stiff hands, still clutching the phone in her own.

'I know we're supposed be gone,' Ali said.

'What?'

'Or at least packing. I said I'd be out of the

apartment by Monday, remember?'

Emma was stricken. 'Ali. For God's sake. Stop.' She couldn't bear to think of that stupid row. She hadn't even meant to go throwing Ali out. She had just been so mad that she'd gone to see Ryan behind her back.

Mad, and insanely curious. Ali hadn't even said what he'd looked like. How he'd sounded. If he'd even asked after her.

Not that that line of thought was in *any* way appropriate, given the current circumstances of her nephew being missing.

'I don't blame you,' Ali was going on. 'We're after doing nothing, only causing you trouble. Eating you out of house and home. Going missing and bringing the bloody guards, not to mention Auntie Jane, down on top of you. *I'd* have thrown us out.'

'Ali, stop. Look, will you have something to eat?'

Ali shook her head violently. 'No.'

'A cup of tea then.'

'I couldn't.'

'Ali, you've two other children to look after. You'll be no use at all to them if you get sick.'

'I'm no use to them anyway. Look what I've done. Driven him away.'

'He's fifteen. Hormonal. He's just having a hard time — '

But Ali jammed a hand up to stop her. 'Don't. Don't be making excuses for me. I couldn't bear it.'

They sat there in silence for a bit. Ali sniffed loudly a few times, and kept blinking very fast, but didn't cry.

'Does Patrick not make your skin crawl?' she asked suddenly.

When Emma looked at her askance, she said, a bit desperately, 'I just want to talk about something else. Anything else.'

Emma understood. She thought about Patrick; not his hairiness or his vanity, but his ego and the idea that it was OK to be nasty to people under the guise of 'honesty'. 'I suppose he does, a bit.'

'If you ask me, Alannah could take him out. I know she looks like chicken shit, with all that blonde hair and the pastel eye makeup, and that *laugh* of hers, but she's not afraid of him. I actually kind of . . . admire her.' Ali sounded surprised. But Alannah had that effect on people. A lot of people liked her. Those same people tended to loathe Patrick and everything he stood for.

'What's going to happen?' Ali's teeth were chattering, but she kept up her end of the conversation, fair play to her. 'With the show?'

'They'll probably axe it.'

'You're joking.'

'Well, nobody's *said* anything.'

Not yet. They'd limp on till June, because what else were they going to fill the schedule with at that hour of the morning? Reruns of *Fawlty Towers*? Anyhow, everybody working on the show was contracted until then, and if there was even a hint that they mightn't get paid . . . The unions would be up in arms.

But the eggs Benedict incident had only brought things to a head, Emma was beginning to realise. The show's future had been in doubt for some time now, only she hadn't faced up to it. The ratings were too low, the content too dull, and Alannah and Patrick were like two round pegs in square holes. It was like somebody had told them that, because it was so early in the morning, they had to be all happy-clappy, and cheesy, and overenthusiastic. Of course, Patrick could never handle that for very long, and his natural bluntness would repeatedly get the better of him. Alannah, similarly, could only pretend to be an airhead for so long, and her earnestness and stridency would eventually break through.

They had never, from the very beginning, suited the show.

Or maybe it was that the show had never bothered to try to suit them.

'I don't care if he's just trying to get back at me,' Ali announced suddenly now. Her eyes were very bright. 'I don't care if he's doing this to teach me a lesson. I just want to know he's OK. That's all.'

'He will be.' Useless words, but what else could she say?

'I'm sorry for, you know, telling Ryan about the test. You were right: I was completely out of order.

'Oh, Ali, stop.'

'No, let me. I've decided I'm going to apologise to everybody for everything I've ever done to them. I realise this could take some time. But I've made this pact, you see, with God.'

'Since when did you believe in God?'

'Well, I don't, obviously,' Ali said crossly. Then she remembered herself. 'I might be returning to Him, though. If we can reach an understanding. I'm going to try to put right everything I've done wrong, and in return He's going to find Jack and send him home to me. In one piece,' she hurriedly added in the direction of the ceiling, in case there was any misunderstanding.

'Right, well, good luck with that one. Will I make you a cup of tea while you're doing all this apologising?'

'I suppose. Can we consider you done?'

'Yes.'

'Great.' Ali sighed. 'Only a hundred and twelve people to go.'

She was starting to enjoy this ever so slightly, Emma could see. Even if all this was horrible gut-wrenching, diarrhoea-inducing stuff, she was still right there in the thick of it.

Well, enough of that.

When Emma came back in from the kitchen, Ali looked up, no doubt expecting a nice, hot cup of tea along with lashings of sympathy and as many gee-ups as Emma could manage.

Instead, she handed Ali the phone, with Kyle's number on speed dial. 'Why don't you start at the top?'

19

Ali

It wasn't easy, trying to explain to someone that you'd mislaid their child. But when that someone was confused and unreasonable, and there was a time-delay of two seconds on the phone, it was just that bit worse.

'The guards say they're pretty sure he's come to no harm.'

Long pause.

She tried again. 'Kyle, I said — '

'Come to no harm? What the fuck — '

' — They're pretty sure — '

' — does that mean?'

' — He's come to — please don't use bad language — '

This went on for about five minutes, with each of them overlapping the other like billy-o. Kyle's language got worse and worse until in the end his side of things was just a series of time-delayed goddamns and friggings and fucks.

Still, it was 5 a.m. on a Saturday morning over there. No doubt he'd watched the game on the TV last night, as usual, and got a takeaway pizza, as usual, and hadn't expected to be woken with such disagreeable news at the crack of dawn.

'Where were you when this happened?' he enquired.

'In the shoe shop.'

'The *what?*'

'I have a job, Kyle.'

'Selling *shoes?*'

'That's what they normally sell in shoe shops. I had to get a job because you cut off my cards, and we have no money, remember?'

'So you were working some job, and meanwhile one of our kids walks off and you don't even notice?'

'They were being minded!' He always tried to make her out to be so irresponsible. Just because he'd had a steady job since he was nineteen, and employed ninety-two people at his plastics plant, and paid his bloody taxes. Show her one person who *didn't* pay taxes in this world. Apart from herself, of course.

'I knew this would happen,' he said grimly.

He knew one of the kids was going to run away? Jack himself probably hadn't known until he'd woken up yesterday morning. But that was typical Kyle. Instead of wondering how Jack might be feeling, or how any of this could have happened (actually, Ali wasn't that keen on going there), he went and said something that was guaranteed to rile her.

'I wish you'd given me a little warning in that case,' she threw back at him.

Then she took a breath and told herself, stop. Just stop.

Jack was out there, somewhere, living on his wits and cans of tuna, and what were his loving parents doing? What they did best, of course — having a good pop at each other, even in a crisis.

'Kyle. This is really not getting us anywhere.' Her head felt like it was about to split open. She'd been up all night, and there was still no word from the guards, and every time she thought of Jack she wanted to vomit. 'We need to pull together on this one.'

From the silence on his end of the phone, it seemed like he might be taking that on board. Or else it could just be the time-delay again.

But then he said gruffly, 'What can I do? Hire some private detectives or something?'

Throw some money at it. That was his standard response, and this time was no different.

Ali felt very weary. 'Let's just wait, OK? That's what the guards say.'

'The guards.' Clearly Kyle had little faith or confidence in this approach. He was more a *Mission: Impossible* type of guy: hit 'em hard and fast, and where it hurt. If he could have dropped a SWAT team into Ireland to find Jack, he would have.

'Kyle?' she said. She stopped, not knowing what she wanted to ask. For some reassurance, maybe. For one of his confident statements that everything would work out fine, because he wouldn't have it any other way.

In the silence that followed she strove for some connection; it was Jack who'd brought them together in the first place; without him, they'd probably have parted way back somewhere after shag number ten, and if they ran into each other in the street afterwards, they'd have been hard pressed to recognise each other.

But it was just that time-delay thing again, and when he prompted, somewhat impatiently, 'What is it?' she said, 'Nothing. Just that I'll keep you informed.'

'You'll keep me *informed*?'

'I'll call you the minute I know anything — '

'Like I'm going to sit here while my son is missing somewhere in Ireland, thanks to you? Forget it,' he said. 'I'm coming over.'

★　★　★

Carly was a lot happier to hear from her, initially at least. Ali had finally tracked down her number through a series of classmates of Jack's.

'Mrs P! Hi! Oh, it's so good of you to call!'

Was it?

And then Carly burst into tears. She was crying so hard that all Ali could hear for several minutes were heartbreaking sobs and girlish hiccups.

'Carly? Are you OK?' Maybe she was crying out of guilt, for having supplied Jack with a false passport (it was starting to sound more and more implausible) and a spare set of clothes.

'I just wish he'd change his mind,' she eventually got out. She sounded so sad. 'I tried and tried to tell him that the distance didn't matter, that we could work around things, but he wouldn't listen.'

Just when Ali thought she couldn't possibly

feel worse. 'You . . . haven't heard from him then?'

'Not in weeks. I've tried calling him, but he never picks up. You know him. So stubborn. Won't budge once he sets his mind on something.'

Yes. Ali knew well. Right now he was out there somewhere, paying her back, and he wouldn't surface until he was sure he'd made his point.

And here was poor Carly, broken-hearted, and all because of Ali. Well, indirectly. All because of Kyle, really, and his determination to snatch the kids. But how could she explain that to a fifteen-year-old?

'You're a lovely girl, Carly,' she began. She tried to think of something else positive. 'And so good at math, once you try! I bet you could . . . well, you could be anything you wanted.' She meant it too. But not in those shorts. Nobody would ever take Carly seriously in those.

Carly was silent for a minute. Then she said, sounding very unlike herself, sounding rather *flat*, actually, 'I know you thought we were kind of dumb, me and Jack.'

'What? I never said that!'

'You tried to talk him out of it. That he was young, and so it couldn't mean anything.'

'Well . . . I . . . ' Then she thought, might as well come clean. 'I got married at eighteen, Carly. I don't know if Jack told you, but now we're getting divorced.'

She just wanted to share her wisdom, that was all. But she probably just came across as some bitter old slag. Ah, well.

299

Carly wasn't even listening, anyway. All she could think about was Jack. 'Is he there?' she said, pathetically hopefully. 'Do you think he might talk to me for a minute?'

'No. You see, the thing is, he didn't actually come home from school yesterday after-noon . . . '

★   ★   ★

The pact with God wasn't working. Or, at least, He wasn't keeping His side of the bargain. Ali had apologised to everybody she could think of at that stage, and still nothing. She kept opening the front door, in case Jack would be miraculously standing there, hand-delivered by God himself. After a few hours of this, and with everybody getting freezing, she took to looking out the window. Not a sign.

Then she began looking up at the skies. Maybe a message would come that way; clouds parting maybe, or an image of Jack's face or something, along with a comprehensive set of directions to his hiding place. Or a star that she had to follow, on a camel. She wasn't fussy.

After another couple of hours she developed a painful crick in her neck and, in a fit of despair, gave up entirely on religion. Feck that. She was back to being a good old-fashioned atheist, and would just have to put her trust in the guards. And if *they* didn't deliver soon, she might have to plump for Kyle's SWAT team after all.

By now it was getting very late, and she had to

face into a second dark night of the soul. She'd barely been able for the first one. And the kids and Mam and Dad and Emma were all banjaxed and had either gone home or to bed, leaving Ali to sit up on her ownio.

She thought of him out there, in the dark too, with a can of tuna with the ringpull broken off it. Sometimes that happened, especially with the cheap cans she'd been buying in the supermarket lately.

He might be trying to open it with his fingernails. The thought made her cry, loudly, and once she started she couldn't stop.

Fucking Ireland. She wished she'd never set foot back in the place. She should have taken the kids to Boston, her old stomping ground. Or to Philadelphia; Eileen had settled there, and Ali had kept up contact. She knew people in San Francisco too, and New York, New Jersey, Chicago, *dozens* of places.

But she'd always thought of the kids as Irish. Genetically, they were more Irish than anything else, as Kyle was actually half Italian, a quarter German and another quarter Russian (which went some way towards explaining Ethel). Like it or not, the kids owed more to this little wet sod of green on the outskirts of the Atlantic than the whole vast greatness of the US of A.

And look at all the family they had here! Granted, nearly all of them were old people. There were lots of second cousins scattered about the place too, but Ali never managed to get round to them on the annual summer

301

holiday, and so the kids hadn't got to know them well.

But at least they *existed*. In America, they had no family at all. Kyle was an only child. Ethel and Hal had nobody between them except a few crotchety cousins in Florida, and they were dying off like flies. In a few years Ethel and Hal would be gone too, then in a few more years, Ali and Kyle (a good few years, hopefully, but the evil day would still come), and what then?

The kids would be orphans! In a strange country! Or, at least, it still felt strange to Ali, even though she'd been there for so long now that she said tom-A-to instead of tomato and spoke about putting the trash out.

But it never felt like home. Not truly. Every time she got off the plane in Texas after a trip back to Ireland, she had a sense of disorientation that she never quite managed to shake. Even when she walked into her house, the house she'd built from scratch with Kyle, she couldn't help the feeling that she was a visitor, just putting in time until next summer when she would get on a plane back to Ireland.

Just let Jack be OK, she pleaded, and she would go back to America and never leave it again. Even for the family vacation. She would live out her days in Texas, without once bitching about a single thing.

Maybe scratch that last bit. No sense in setting herself an impossible task.

She looked up towards the ceiling: did you hear that, God? (Yes, she was back to that.) So come on. Do your magic/miracle-y thing.

But He just sent her Emma, with another pot of blasted tea. At this rate her kidneys would be destroyed.

'I thought you were in bed,' she said. She tried not to sound unwelcoming. Emma had been so marvellous this past day, taking charge of everything, because Ali simply hadn't been able to. She'd even put the kids to bed earlier, a task Ali wouldn't wish on her worst enemy.

But Ali was tired now, and riddled with worry and guilt, and the only person she wanted to see was Jack.

'I was hardly going to leave you sitting up all night on your own,' Emma said staunchly. She calmly poured the tea. Added just the right amount of milk. Then she settled down beside Ali on the couch. There was no unnecessary chatter, or idle speculation about whether they should think about dredging that pond in the park across the way. No hint from her at all that this was entirely Ali's fault.

God, it must be great to be so fucking perfect.

Emma may have sensed some of this hostility because she said, 'Let's blame Mam and Dad.'

'For what?'

'Everything.'

They looked at each other and they burst out laughing. Ali laughed harder and harder and knew that if she didn't stop, she'd be crying again in a minute.

'Bloody hell,' she said. 'You'd wonder how we ended up like this. Me with a missing son and you with . . . well, you know. Not that you have. In fact, you probably don't.' Before she could tie

303

herself up in any more knots, she said, 'No news yet?'

'I'd have told you if there was.'

'I suppose.'

Ali was thoroughly ashamed to find herself thinking, well, there's medicine for HIV. It wasn't as bad as having one of your children go missing.

Then the feeling was gone just as quickly, and she hoped to Christ Emma hadn't seen it in her eyes.

But even if she had, she probably would have understood. She was such a good person. It was hard to think that they'd both come out of Mam.

'I was only trying to do what I thought was right,' Ali suddenly told her. It seemed very important that Emma, of all people, understood that Ali hadn't wilfully put her kids in danger. 'When I brought them to Ireland. Obviously, if I'd thought for one minute . . . '

But Emma just stood and took the pot of untouched tea to the kitchen. When she came back she was carrying two small glasses of wine.

'For medicinal purposes,' she said. Then she reached for the blanket that she kept on the back of the sofa, and she shook it out over them. It was starting to get a bit chilly, actually, and Ali was glad for it.

They snuggled up together under it on the sofa.

'This is just like old times, isn't it?' Ali said, letting her head fall back, and looking up at the ceiling. For a moment she was able to stop thinking about Jack. 'Lying in bed, listening to

304

The Late Late Show blaring on the telly downstairs.'

'And Liam having a good old wank next door.'

Ali looked surprised. 'Is that what the noise was? He said he was doing sit-ups against the bed.'

'Liam? Doing sit-ups?' Emma scoffed. 'That'll be the day. No, he was at it morning, noon and night.'

Imagine young, innocent Emma knowing something like that. Ali looked at her in admiration.

'Do you think he's stopped?' she asked.

'I doubt it.'

They both burst out laughing again. It was all very childish and silly, but it gave Ali great comfort, and she bayed so hard that she didn't hear the front door open. Such was the level of snickering that she didn't even hear the *living-room* door open, until Emma gave her a sharp nudge in the ribs, and she stopped and looked up.

Jack was standing there. His new school uniform was filthy, and had a hole in the knee, but otherwise he looked unharmed. He looked *great*.

'Jack . . . ' she whispered. She was shocked, and so weak with relief that she couldn't move for a moment.

Silently, Jack looked from her to Emma. He took in the blanket, the wine, and the scenes of mirth. The look of achievement on his face, for actually having the *cojones* to run away properly, as opposed to just threatening it, died a swift and sad death.

'I've missed you so much,' Ali blurted. 'We were all so worried about you.' But it was a difficult one to pull off when there were tears of hilarity running down her cheeks. 'Jack, I'm so sorry you felt you had to do this. Please, sit down. Let's talk, just you and me.'

She scrabbled to get out from under the blanket, to push the wine aside, to make room for her missing son on the couch.

When she looked up again, Jack had turned his back on her and walked out.

20

Emma

In the midst of all this drama, Emma's own news came very quietly, in a phone call from the surgery on Monday morning at about ten o'clock, to tell her that her test was negative.

'It can't be,' she blurted. There was a mistake. There had to be.

'It's got your name on the top.' The doctor sounded a little too cheerful for Emma's liking. He was acting like everything was *OK*.

'But the three months wasn't quite up . . . I mightn't have had enough antibodies in my blood . . . I should probably do a retest.'

'From what you told me, you were only a few days shy of the three months. These tests are very sensitive. The chances of it being a false negative are, to be honest, remote.'

'All the same, I'm sure labs make mistakes.' She didn't know why she was arguing like this. It all just sounded too simple. 'I don't know if I fully explained it to you at my appointment, but the, um, situation for me was very high risk.' In other words, her and Ryan had bonked, gloriously unprotected, dozens of time.

'Well, clearly you were one of the lucky ones.' He left a little gap, as though to accommodate any rapturous cheers her end, or screams of, 'I'm alive! Praise the Lord!'

All he got was a suspicious, 'Perhaps.'

He moved on then to the customary note of caution, adopting the required gloomy tone. 'I hardly need remind you of the dangers of not using protection in the future.'

'No.' Obviously, she would be buying condoms by the kilo, good, tough ones, 100 denier, or whatever was the rubber equivalent, if she was ever to consider having sex with anyone again; which, it hardly need be said, was about as likely as her deciding to change career and become a belly dancer.

The doctor continued on an even gloomier note, 'Especially given that your partner is positive.'

For a second she thought he'd said 'Patrick', not partner. She wasn't having sex with *Patrick*. He was one of the last men on earth she'd ever sleep with, whether he was HIV positive or not.

Then she realised. The doctor meant Ryan. He thought they were still together.

She'd had to divulge to him at the appointment where she thought she'd been infected. Not that he'd put it as bluntly as that; it had been couched in terms of her reasons for thinking she might have been infected. And she'd been glad to tell him; a little too enthusiastic, really. It was her pride — she didn't want him thinking she was spreading it about all over Dublin. But obviously she'd failed to put the 'ex' bit before 'partner'.

' . . . We're not . . . '

Clearly she sounded very decisive, because the

doctor went on, 'You should both get some counselling and advice on how to protect yourself in the future. Until then, I'd advise you to abstain from — '

'Yes. Thank you. Point taken.'

'I can make an appointment for you both, if you'd like.'

'No. That won't be necessary. I mean, I'll sort it out myself. *Ourselves*.' She hurried on. 'So when can I retest?'

A pause. 'You want to retest?' In other words, you don't *believe* me?

'Yes.'

'Best to leave it another three months.' Then he went off, maybe to ring up someone who might be a bit more appreciative of negative test results.

When Emma hung up, her hands were shaking so badly that she couldn't even put the phone back in her bag.

After all the weeks and months of worry, it was finally over. She was OK. She was OK.

She sat there for a long moment in her car, letting the news sink in. Negative. She repeated it a few times, trying it on for size. The problem with the word negative was that, unfortunately, it carried negative overtones. But in this case it was good, she reassured herself. It meant her body was virus-free. There had been no repercussions from her foolishness. She had, in effect, got away with it.

It was more than good. It was wonderful, fantastic, *brilliant*.

Why, then, did she feel so flat?

It was probably just the anticlimax of the thing. For almost two weeks now she'd nearly hit the ceiling every time her phone had rung. She'd been so completely sure that the news would be bad. It was going to take a little time to adjust her expectations; to fully accept that she was all right.

Plus, she'd expected the caller to be Ali. She'd already phoned twice, fretting about Jack, and Emma had only left the house half an hour ago. Emma had answered the phone with a, 'What is it now?' without even looking at the caller display. She'd been totally knocked off guard to find that it was the doctor on the other end. Nobody could get properly excited when they felt slightly *ambushed*.

And then look at all the other crap in her life. Her apartment was the scene of continuing drama over the whole Jack thing. Every half-hour a general cry would go up of, 'Where's Jack? If that little fecker has run away again . . . ' Everybody would have to go and search for him, and when he'd eventually be located, usually in the bathroom, there would be renewed efforts to get him to 'talk'.

Naturally, he didn't want to talk. He was fifteen, for God's sake, and had no intention of sharing the particulars of his hormonal angst with anybody, or the reasons why he'd decided to spend two days and one night in a field at the back of the shopping centre, using survival skills he said he'd learned from Ryan. (Ali had gone quite red in the face at that.) Besides, it seemed obvious to everybody besides Ali why he'd done

310

what he'd done, but she kept pursuing him, and he spent most of his time trying to get away from her.

Ali herself seemed to be on an energetic mission to transform herself into the best mother in the world. This mostly involved copious amounts of baking in Emma's tiny kitchen, even though nobody wanted to eat the results, and hiding all the empty red wine bottles that had accumulated during the course of her stay. She took to wearing an apron all the time, and carrying an old dusting rag around (which she never bloody used). She broke this illusion — and let's face it, it *was* only an illusion — only to pet and kiss Anto and Erin, and call them 'darling' and 'sweetheart', with the result that they were totally disorientated, and had grown quite afraid of her.

There was one reason for all this, of course. And it was Kyle. He was arriving in on a flight today. Emma had done the only sensible thing; she'd got into her car and driven away.

But she was HIV-negative. She must keep remembering that. It was the best thing that had happened to her, probably ever.

Apart from Ryan.

But at least now she could stop hating him. Just because it took up so much energy, that was all.

★   ★   ★

Hannie had brought a selection of the weekend's papers with her.

311

'I didn't know if you'd seen them, or even if you *wanted* to see them . . . '

She obviously had no idea of the drama in Emma's house over the weekend. Sitting around reading newspapers hadn't been on the agenda.

'Hand them over.'

Hannie looked over her shoulder as though to ensure that they weren't being watched. It was risky, meeting in the station's car park like this when Emma was on leave. That didn't mean she was banned from the property or anything. Not at all. But if she was spotted, it would just look, well, sad.

Emma didn't care. She knew that once June came, she'd probably never work here again, so what was there to lose?

Hannie passed over the first page, from a tabloid. There was a big photo of Patrick, wearing an expensive suit and shiny shoes, and looking like a poster boy for style and sophistication, but with a hint of badness.

He must have paid for those shots himself, bless him. It probably took hours and hours to pull that look off.

The caption on the article underneath was 'Straight-Talking Television.'

'It'd make you puke,' Hannie confirmed. 'The article is about how 'refreshing' he was on Friday morning, and how we're all sick of vacuous TV. That was their word,' she added hurriedly. 'Not mine.' She thought about this. 'Although some of it *is* quite vacuous.'

Emma flicked through the article. Nothing surprising. Just a general endorsement of his disdain for social niceties, and a bit of a thrill at his boldness for walking off set. Written by a woman, interestingly.

'It gets better.' Hannie dug out a broadsheet now. Another picture, this time of Alannah. Clearly she'd done her own make-up this time, and looked tasteful and pretty. 'Wait for it.'

With a little fanfare, Hannie revealed the headline: 'Why Men Can't Stand Women Who Are More Intelligent Than Them'.

This was one for the girls, only better, because it was written by a lecturer in equality studies. A male lecturer. Alannah, incredible as it might seem, came across as quite the woman of the moment for putting that thick yokel Patrick in his place.

Emma was taken aback. She'd expected the kind of gossipy, sensational pieces about personality clashes and all that — and Hannie had several more of them in her lap, she could see — but *this*, in a broadsheet?

'Did Adam see this?' she asked.

'*Everybody* saw it. Patrick's face! I thought he was going to refuse to go on set at all when he read that one about Alannah being more intelligent than him. But then Adam showed up.'

'Adam was on set?'

Unusual. But, after what had happened on Friday, maybe not that surprising. A lot of the station's top brass and shareholders had probably grimly tuned into the show that morning. Nobody wanted another fiasco.

'It really pissed Phil off,' Hannie said with a vicious chortle. 'There he was, finally in charge now that you're gone, and he has Adam hanging over his shoulder. He did the only sensible thing, of course, and turned lick-arse. It was all, 'Did you think that piece went well, Adam?' and, 'Will we go for a coffee after the show, Adam?' '

Emma could just imagine it. This week must be a dream for Phil.

'Anyway, it didn't matter, because the show was still shite,' Hannie declared conclusively.

Emma didn't want to look too happy, but it was hard.

'Phil thought he'd be all deep and meaningful, and run with an analysis of the cabinet reshuffle.' Hannie flung her eyes to heaven.

Emma was wide-eyed. Politics? At that hour of the morning? 'How did Alannah and Patrick cope?'

'Well . . . ' Hannie clearly thought about being diplomatic, but it was only fleeting. 'Patrick came across as thick as a ditch. Alannah tried her best, but neither of them could wait to get on to the dog-whisperer. That went pretty OK.'

Emma had found the dog-whisperer; a fellow from Kerry who apparently could talk to dogs. All right, so it was terrible, but not as terrible as a cabinet reshuffle at seven o'clock in the morning.

'I think Adam being there unnerved them,' Hannie confided. 'Patrick and Alannah, they just weren't themselves.'

Patrick and Alannah were *never* themselves, in Emma's opinion. She idly wondered what it would be like if they *were*.

314

'And, of course, Adam was glaring at them, which didn't help.'

Naturally. They were on notice, or the nearest thing to it. The pair of them had been waiting outside Adam's office on Friday when Emma had come out. Nobody knew the full details, but contracts had apparently been gone through. Agents were phoned. Threats were made.

He could have just fired them outright, of course: one of them, or both. But that would have meant drafting in someone over the weekend, last minute, to take over on Monday. Not that it couldn't be done; there were plenty of ambitious weather girls waiting in the wings, and one of the presenters on the six o'clock news had filled in before, the time that Patrick had laryngitis and couldn't speak for two days.

But a firing would have caused an even bigger stink. Adam was probably thinking, let's just ride it out. Let the thing run till June and then get rid of the lot of them. If Emma was him, she'd do the same.

'On the plus side, we've had more calls and texts today than we've had in weeks,' Hannie said optimistically. Then she saw Emma's face. 'I know, I know. They're only tuning in to see if there's another scrap.'

She sat back in her seat with a sigh. So did Emma. It seemed like a lost cause, all of it.

'I know!' said Hannie. 'Let's set up our own production company. Make the kind of programmes we always wanted to.'

By that she didn't mean documentaries on global warming, but holiday programmes in the

315

sun. She and Emma had idled away many hours in the canteen over bad coffee thinking up titles for it, such as *I'm Here. Where the Fuck Are You?*, and *Jaysus, It's Boiling in Bilbao*.

'Imagine. I might even get a tan,' Hannie said, holding out her white arms. She was frequently delusional, despite all the brain-boosting Brazil nuts she ate.

It was a lovely idea in theory, making holiday programmes. Hannie was forgetting that, in this recession, nobody had any money to go anywhere.

'I'll think about it,' Emma promised.

'You won't,' said Hannie accusingly. 'You'll spend your week looking for a job in the BBC.'

Right again. Rumour was they were hiring. Well, what else was Emma to do from now till next Friday? Watch Ali's crash-car of a life play out in her living room? Wait around for official confirmation that her contract would not be renewed at the end of this season?

And she liked London. She liked the busyness of it, the anonymity. After everything that had happened, maybe it would be good to get away for a couple of years, to work hard, to stop thinking so much.

'Don't look for a job,' Hannie begged. 'Come on the tear with me instead. Just the two of us. We'll go into town.'

'No.'

'You have to start getting out there again. Putting things behind you.' She raised an eyebrow that clearly said, 'Ryan'.

'I already have,' Emma said evenly.

'So let's go and see if we can score,' Hannie said bawdily, though if she was put to it she'd probably run a mile, Tupperware boxes jangling.

Emma suddenly wanted to laugh. There she was, the hot recipient of a clean bill of sexual health. Was there any better time to go into town, find a nice man and lasso him with her Wonderbra? Then she could take him back to his place — hers was clearly out of the question — and have a nice night of passionate, protected sex with him.

Oops. For a moment there she thought she was going to puke.

Very peculiar.

It was just because she was out of practice, that was all. It was nothing to do with Ryan. In fact, it would probably aid her recovery if she *did* go out and pull.

But she found herself reminding Hannie, 'You have work tomorrow, even if I don't. I hate to say it, but four a.m . . . '

'I don't care about work!' Hannie declared magnificently. 'Work can go hang!' Then, 'Oh, fuck it, I'd better not. I'll never be able to get out of bed in the morning.'

No protected sex for Emma tonight then. What a relief.

★　★　★

Instead of doing the sensible thing and going online to look up jobs in the BBC, she found herself outside Ryan's new apartment instead.

And there was no point in her even acting all

317

surprised, or slapping her forehead and going, 'Shit! What on earth am I doing here?'

Because she'd known since that morning that she would come to see him.

She resisted the urge to check her make-up in the mirror, or to pat down her hair. How she looked was entirely irrelevant in all this (but she hiked down her top just the same).

He might not be there at all. He might be away working in Singapore or Pakistan or anywhere. It wasn't like she'd phoned him up to check before she'd left.

She wasn't sure what she'd do if he was gone. Leave a note, maybe. Yes, that'd do the job.

He lived in apartment number three. She took a breath and pressed the bell. Then she stood by the intercom, waiting for it to crackle.

It didn't. She pressed the bell again. Still no answer.

OK. On to plan B. She found an envelope in her bag, and a pen, but then put them back. It wasn't the kind of thing you put on the back of a grubby envelope and shoved under someone's door.

She was halfway back to the car when she heard him call her.

There he stood, in bare feet, with the door open behind him.

'Sorry about that,' he said. 'I was on the phone.'

It was the first time she'd seen him in months.

He looked the same, only different. She didn't know what it was. Then: it was just his hair. It was longer. And he wasn't as tanned. Because he spent so much time away, and war-torn countries always seemed to get that bit more sun than the rest of the planet (well, they probably had to have something going for them), he always had if not exactly a *holiday* tan, but just a bit of colour. Usually it ended abruptly at the neckline of his T-shirt, and at his elbows and knees. But she'd liked it. She'd always found it attractive. She'd found his lack of vanity, the fact that he never thought to take *off* the ruddy T-shirt, even more attractive.

He was staring at her too. But nobody said anything. The whole thing felt too weird and odd; post-apocalyptic or something.

'Will you come in?' he asked eventually.

She managed to find her voice. 'Thanks.'

She walked in past him and up the stairs, and into a bright, airy apartment. Or, rather, it would have been, had there not been camera stuff everywhere, and at least two computers on, and clothes piled on the couch. Some things never changed.

'Sorry,' he said. 'The place is a bit of a mess . . .'

He moved some stuff off the couch so that she could sit down. He sat too, not on the couch, but on a chair in the corner, and he regarded her with an expression that could only be described as wary.

But that was probably because the last time he'd seen her, she'd been a wild, shrieking thing, chucking stuff at him and levelling accusations of him having ruined her life.

She tried out a smile now, just to let him know

319

that she intended to be better behaved today. 'How are you, Ryan?'

He shot her another wary look, and shrugged. 'I'm good. Great, in fact. As you can see.'

She didn't blame him for being defensive. She would be too. But she wasn't a stranger. Up until recently, they'd been engaged.

She said nothing, just waited.

Eventually he sighed and said, 'Look, it's early days. But the doctors say there's no need for any medication yet. That my own immune system is doing a good enough job in holding it back. They're very pleased, actually. So for the moment I can carry on just like normal.'

It was so weird to be sitting there talking about Ryan's health like this; in terms of how long he would be well, when he would start needing medication.

'In fact, I'm going to Japan tomorrow,' he said.

She saw now that she'd interrupted him in the middle of packing.

'Then Kenya next month. It's going to be a busy summer, actually. I've a lot lined up.' This was said with a hint of defiance. She needn't worry about him, in other words; he was doing just fine on his own. Never better, in fact.

'Good,' she said. 'I'm glad.' But it just came out as patronising.

God, would it always be this way, even when they met on the street? Him guilty and defiant and ready to take umbrage at the smallest thing? And her, watching her every word, petrified of being condescending or overprotective?

She picked up her bag and stood. 'I just came

by to tell you that I tested negative.'

'You . . . ?' The emotions on his face were hard to watch. Relief. Joy. A lifting of guilt. Envy; terrible, raw envy. That was gone in an instant. 'Really? That's fantastic, Emma. I can't believe it. Thank you. Thank *you*.'

And then he was hugging her, hard, the way people do when they've received the best news ever. He was lifting her, twirling her around.

'Ryan!'

'Sorry.' He put her down. 'It's just so brilliant. When did you find out?'

'Today.'

He was still holding her loosely, smiling down at her, his face so open and happy and relieved, and she was smiling back — she would defy anybody *not* to, it was that kind of moment.

But then they grew awkward, and Ryan dropped his hands, and she stepped back and began rooting in her bag for her car keys.

'Anyhow,' she said, 'I felt you deserved to know.'

One less thing for him to worry about, in other words, in the midst of all his other worries. One less regret. Put like that, it was actually pretty crap for him.

'Ryan,' she blurted. 'Can we be friends? Please? I know things between us have been . . . But I'd really like us to stay in touch.'

She hadn't rehearsed this bit; it just came out.

He looked at her for a long moment. 'No,' he said.

'What?' She hadn't quite expected such a bald response.

'I don't need you feeling sorry for me.'

'I don't!'

'It's written all over your face.' He turned away now to the desk by the wall, began putting papers into a satchel, continuing his packing. 'I have enough friends, thanks. I don't need any more.'

It was a bit like being slapped. And suddenly she was angry. 'So that's it? So long? Don't call around here again?'

He straightened suddenly. A lens cap on the desk went flying to the floor. He didn't seem to notice or care. 'We were going to get married. And now that I have HIV, you just want to be my *friend*?'

'It's not that!' She was furious now. 'How dare you? In case you didn't notice, I thought I was positive until today, too!'

'And I bet it just killed you. I bet you'd rather have had anything else in the whole wide world.' His lip lifted.

Her skin felt all prickly and she found it hard to breath. 'I'm not with you any more because you lied to me.'

'Lied to you? How could I *lie* to you when I didn't fucking well know myself?' he roared.

She thought: the neighbours. Then, to hell with them.

'You didn't tell me what you got up to in New York!'

'Jesus Christ.' He threw his hands up now, in despair. 'Here we go again. Yes, I should have. Yes, I was wrong. But, I swear to you, Emma, I didn't even think. It didn't occur to me even

322

once. I was twenty-seven. I was young. I just did what every other fool was doing.'

'Well, then, you're stupid as well as dishonest.'

He was calm now. 'Fine. You keep telling yourself that, Emma; just how dishonest other people are.' He turned his back on her. 'Now if you don't mind, I've got to get on with my packing.'

21

Ali

The black shiny hire car rolled up outside Emma's apartment shortly after lunch. It *would* be black, of course. Nothing cheery like red or maybe metallic blue.

The kids ran to the window to look. 'Who is it? Who is it?'

They'd been too tired to go to school, what with the 'sleep deprivation and trauma', as Anto had put it, that they'd all suffered over the weekend due to Jack's disappearance. Besides, they knew darn well there was more excitement to come.

Ali looked over their heads. There was a pair of sunglasses on the dashboard of the car, and a discarded empty can of Coke on the passenger seat. 'I think it's — '

She was rudely cut off by the brash tooting of the horn. There it went again — beep-beep-beh-beep-beeeep.

Then a tanned arm came out the driver's window and waved at the kids, before doing a big thumbs up.

'Daddy!'

They went pure mental. Ali didn't think she'd ever seen them as excited. They were hugging and kissing each other just like they used to do when they came downstairs on Christmas morning and found that Santa Claus had been.

So, what, Kyle — Santa Claus?

Well, she wasn't going to be happy with *that*.

'Go and say hello then,' she said. She gave Jack a sharp look. 'You especially.'

After he'd finally turned up on Saturday night (apparently it had been the lack of showering facilities in the wild rather than any fear of the unknown that had finally driven him home), it had been too late to get Kyle to turn back.

'He's fine. He came home,' Ali had gibbered deliriously on the phone. 'He's safe in bed.'

'Thank God.' Kyle's relief had swamped him too, and there had been a very odd moment of shared joy.

Then he said, 'I'm still coming over.'

She hadn't expected that. Naïve, Emma had called her afterwards. According to her, it was a miracle he'd let all these weeks go by without jumping on a plane sooner. The way she'd gone on, he'd been positively *restrained*.

Sometimes Ali thought Emma wasn't on her side at all. And after all the support Ali had offered in the face of her health crisis, too! Because that's what sisters were supposed to do, wasn't it? Stick together through thick and thin? Support each other's decisions, even if you thought they were totally crap?

Emma just wasn't playing ball. She was acting like Kyle's coming over was a good and necessary thing.

Which just went to show you how much *she* knew. Ali felt quite miffed about her whole attitude.

Anyhow, there had been no stopping him. He was already on the way, one foot practically on the tarmac to get a connecting flight to Houston. Once she knew he was definitely in the air somewhere around the east coast of America, she'd broken the news to the kids as levelly as possible.

Jack had perked up massively (this was after he'd downed four sausage and bacon sandwiches, and put on a freshly washed tracksuit and donned the air of a martyr). He'd even been quite nice to Ali; what was the point in being all grumpy and teenager-y when Dad, the voice of reason, was coming to restore order to the family?

And now that the eagle had landed, the kids were stampeding towards the door. It was clearly going to be a competition to see who could fling themselves upon him first. Erin was even fluffing out her hair to look her best for the joyful reunion, and Jack had a smile on his face for the first time in weeks.

Anto stopped briefly at the door and gave her a sombre look. 'I know this is going to be difficult for you, Mom. But remember — he *is* our father, and it'd be kind of weird if we weren't happy to see him.'

'Nobody could ever call you weird, Anto,' she assured him.

They went, abandoning her, the little turncoats. She sat there, trying to drink her tea, as

326

the family endearments floated up from down below.

'Hey, buddy! You must have grown six inches since I saw you last!'

'So have you, Dad. Around the waist.'

'Erin, you little munchkin. Gimme a hug.'

'Daddy, stop, you're all *sweaty*.'

'What did you bring us, Dad? Nothing? I can't *believe* you brought us nothing.'

They were being unusually pleasant to each other. It was true: the kids had missed him, and it wasn't just for the ten dollars pocket money he doled out every Saturday morning, either. There was real warmth in their denigration and jousting, anybody could see that.

Of course, now she would be accused of trying to cancel him out; of not giving him, their father, any thought at all.

Well, of course she bloody hadn't. She'd been too busy trying to get out of the country. She'd vaguely thought there would be visits back to the States, maybe in the summer. When the kids were older, they would be able to go back by themselves, and spend a couple of months there. And Kyle would come to Ireland a couple of times a year, once everything settled down, of course. In her loose plan, her *very* loose plan, he'd be there for First Communions and school graduations, that kind of thing, smiling benignly and hopefully not too jet-lagged. And then if one of the kids ever got married — hopefully not because of an unwanted pregnancy — then they'd all meet up in Florence or Dallas or Blanchardstown, and she and Kyle would spend a jolly week together, sharing happy memories and sentences that began with, 'Oh, do you remember the time . . . ?'

So she *had* thought ahead. And in a nice way. There was no animosity on her part. Well, there was, of course, but she hadn't intended it to be that way. It was all Kyle's fault. He would deny it, of course, but was there any other reason why she was in Dublin with her kids, and he was in Texas, minus them?

The other side of the coin was that Kyle, with the help of Calvin Crawford, would wrest the kids from her, and she would be the one heading over for Communions and graduations, sitting there in a horrible blue pastel suit (she could even see the outfit), trying to smile merrily.

She could never go too far down that road because of the panic that would begin to rise inside her; the vice that clamped itself around her chest, making it difficult to breathe. The very name Calvin Crawford had the same effect on her.

Happy chatter still floated up from below. Ali had to fight the urge to hurl open the window and bellow out, 'I changed your dirty nappies, you little pups. Don't forget that.'

Kyle had changed nappies too, plenty of them, but wouldn't have the wit to point it out. He just wasn't vindictive — that was what was so weird about this whole thing. He was a genuinely nice guy, a good father, a decent if terminally dull husband, and yet the whole thing had come to this.

But there was no going back now. The

moment was here; the big confrontation. Ali wished now she'd taken Emma up on her somewhat reluctant offer to stick around for Kyle's grand arrival. Even Mam had mentioned about coming over for a bit of moral support, but then Dad discovered that he had an appointment somewhere, and that seemed to hijack her whole day. Her whole week, in fact, the way she'd gone on about it.

Ali made another cup of tea, even though she didn't want it. She sat down, but then stood up again. Her legs were jumpy, she couldn't stay still.

Fifteen minutes they'd been out there now. They'd never spent that long together in a single go before in their lives.

To hell with it. She went to the window and looked out.

They weren't there. Any of them.

She nearly had a heart attack as her eyes scudded this way and that over the empty car park. Had he . . . *taken* them? Was this his revenge?

But the black hire car was still there, and it was a hell of a walk to the airport from here. Anyway, their passports were still under the toaster.

It wasn't the most pleasant feeling, wondering where your kids had gone to. She would give that much to Kyle. But that's all.

But wait. It was grand. When she rushed to the back window and looked down, there they were, sitting crossed-legged in a circle in the communal back garden — the grass is damp, she wanted to warn them out the window. Erin was sitting chummily on Kyle's lap, her arms wound around his neck, and occasionally she would whisper in his ear, no doubt attempting to secure a new bicycle/computer/pair of rollerblades for herself.

Kyle, it seemed, was doing a lot of talking. That was quite surprising, as normally he left that sort of pesky thing to her. And the kids were actually listening. Well, they were fidgeting like crazy, and Anto was flicking daisies at Erin when Kyle wasn't looking, but nobody was playing on a Nintendo or texting on their cellphone, which constituted a very high degree of concentration.

Most of the talk was directed at Jack.

He wasn't happy, Ali could see. And why should he be? She would bet he'd had a little speech prepared for Kyle, about what a crap mother Ali was, and how she had ruined his romance with Carly, and now he wasn't getting to say any of it because Kyle had clearly prepared a longer speech on the flight over, and nobody was getting a word in edgeways.

Kyle was doing some finger-wagging at Jack now. He was giving *out*.

Who was it aimed at? Jack? *Her*?

OK, she couldn't bear it any more. Ryan had left a pair of binoculars behind in the spare room; if she could only find them, she might be able to draw on her old childhood skill of lip-reading. Failing that, she should at least be able to make out facial expressions a little more clearly.

But just as she was buried deep in a closet, she heard them coming back. Up the steps came Kyle's cowboy boots, *clunk, clunk, clunk.*

She raced back into the kitchen and took out a bag of flour. If there was going to be some kind of showdown at high noon, then she wanted to be armed.

By the time the kitchen door opened, she was at the worktop with an apron on, and holding a wooden spoon.

'Ali,' he said, behind her.

She turned and met his eyes squarely, her chin lifting. 'Hello, Kyle.'

She'd done nothing she hadn't been forced into doing, and she wasn't going to behave like she had.

He was, she noted, in his usual uniform of checked shirt and jeans held up by a belt with a massive buckle. The shirt was never enough to keep him warm in Irish weather, even in the summer, but he refused ever to wear anything over it, in case it made him look less manly. So instead he went around covered in goose bumps, like *that* wasn't uncool.

He gave her the once-over too. His eyebrows shot up at the sight of her apron and the flour. She felt herself colouring. All right, so she'd never exactly cooked up a storm in Texas, but things had changed. *She* had changed. Give her another month and she would be so accomplished in the kitchen that the kids need never eat tuna casserole again.

'Good flight?' she asked. Well, somebody had to say *something.*

He ignored this. 'Not working in the shoe shop today?'

She stiffened, furiously analysing his tone for sarcasm or blame. But he just looked back at her blandly.

'No,' she said at last. 'I've given it up. In the circumstances.'

What choice had she had? Jack's disappearance had changed everything.

'That's a shame,' he said.

She blinked rapidly again; she'd prepared herself for all manner of insult and aggravation, but clearly he'd decided the best way to knock her off balance was to be nice.

OK, she was on to him now. And she had Calvin Crawford's letter tucked down the front of her jeans all ready to whip out and throw on the table as proof of his shameful behaviour.

But now the kids were clattering about in the living room, pulling on sweaters and coats. Erin had her hairbrush out, and one of Ali's lipsticks, and was busily doing herself up.

'What's going on?' Ali asked. She didn't like this; this sense of unease, of things happening without her knowledge.

Kyle shrugged. 'I thought I'd take the kids out for the afternoon. Just spend a bit of time together. Is that OK with you?' This was said with exaggerated politeness. The subtext was, at least *I* ask before I take them.

'Sure. Great,' Ali found herself babbling. 'They'd love it.'

Actually, Anto didn't look that enthusiastic. He'd already planned that he would try and 'fix'

Emma's jukebox that afternoon. In fairness, it *had* been acting up, but Ali suspected that he only wanted to open it up to see if there was a stash of coins inside.

'We'll bring you something back, Mommy,' Erin said kindly.

'Thank you.' Ali managed to maintain her dignity as they shouted their goodbyes and clattered off out, leaving her to bake forty cookies that nobody would bloody eat except her.

Once the kids were in the car, Kyle came back up the steps. *Clunk, clunk, clunk.*

Here it came now. The war of words. The bawls of, 'And you can pack their bags while I'm gone, because they're coming home with *me*.'

But he just said, 'Forgot my car keys.'

He plucked them up off the worktop, nodded at her civilly, and was gone.

★ ★ ★

'He's softening me up,' Ali ranted to Emma when she came home. Finally. Even though she knew Ali would more than likely be in a state. And it wasn't like she'd had a job to go to, either. Very unsisterly altogether.

'For what, exactly?' Emma enquired, far too coolly.

'I don't know! Something not nice, anyway.' It was suspicious. All of it.

'Maybe he wants to get back together.'

Ali snorted so hard that it hurt. 'As if. You didn't see the way he looked at me. I can always tell these things.'

But Emma didn't get excited about that either. She'd never had much time for Ali's intuition, or sixth sense, for that matter. If anything, she seemed rather *distant* tonight.

Maybe there had been News. Certainly, her face was grim enough. But Ali found she was a bit afraid of asking.

'That doesn't mean he mightn't want to try again,' Emma pointed out.

'No.' Ali's voice was flat. 'It's pointless.' Even if Kyle wanted it, she didn't. Her time in Ireland had only underlined for her how much she wanted to be her own person again, not half of anything. She'd been waiting for this moment since she'd been eighteen, for God's sake.

If really pressed, she could probably say, with some degree of certainty, that she probably wasn't the marrying kind. For the record, she'd never dreamed, even as a little girl, of wafting up the aisle in white. The Hardy Boys were the subjects of her lust only, not any long-term ambitions of marriage and children. And she'd never really *got* all those fairy tales about princesses and frogs and happily-ever-after. 'Is that it?' she'd once asked in outrage when one of the princesses (they'd all seemed interchangeable) had realised she was sleeping on a pea, and everybody thought that this was great, and for her reward, she — wait for it — got to marry the insipid-looking prince. Frankly, it sucked.

If left to her own devices, it was entirely possible that Ali would still be single. But, then again, who knew? Knowing her luck, she'd have

334

got up the duff at some later point, entirely unexpectedly as usual; only this time the father might have been a drug dealer, or, worse, a banker. Ending up hitched to a cowboy from Texas might have looked like a blessing in comparison.

Kyle was a good guy. Or, he had been up to now. She couldn't get away from that. It was nobody's fault that they were polar opposites and, in normal circumstances, would never even have crossed paths socially, never mind ended up in a marital bed together.

'He's a good guy,' Emma reminded her. Bloody mind-reader.

'So, what? I should just roll over?' Ali demanded. 'Pretend that it's OK, what he's done?'

'No.' Emma gave Ali one of her freaky, grown-up looks. 'But you haven't done the right thing either.'

She'd been waiting to say that ever since Ali had arrived in Ireland. Just dying to get it off her chest. It was a miracle she'd waited so long. In fact, she might as well just go over to Kyle's side entirely in all this.

Ali stood amid the chaos of flour, cookies and empty cups of tea. 'Ah, fuck off,' she said.

'Ali, don't be like that.'

'You know something, you were right. We shouldn't be trying to live in the same flat. I thought coming home would be great. That you and me would get back to normal, to the way we used to be.' She'd love to stomp out of the place right now, but to be honest, she couldn't face all the packing, and so it would have to wait till the morning (she must warn Mam and Dad that they'd be moving in). 'But I don't think there's any hope for us at all. I think we just might be finished, you and I. Kaput — '

'Shut up,' said Emma wearily.

Ali did. She'd been running out of steam anyway.

'I got my results.' The look on Emma's face was so weird that Ali's bowels turned to water. It was all she could do to stay on her feet.

'I'm negative, Ali. I'm all right.'

And to Ali's great surprise, Emma collapsed into her arms and cried like her heart was broken.

★   ★   ★

The kids were back at six on the dot, just like he'd promised.

Ali was waiting for them inside the door, in her best tracksuit and high heels, fully made-up, all ready for the big pow-wow.

'Have you eaten?' she asked, as they filed in. She didn't look past them at Kyle, who was at the bottom of the steps. Let him wait.

'Yes, we — '

'Great. Now go to bed.'

'But it's only six o'clock — '

'School tomorrow. Bed. Now.'

Off they went, Anto making screwy motions with his finger when he thought she wasn't looking.

Let them think she was unbalanced. In these

336

high heels, she practically was. But she was ready for him.

Oh, yes. Enough of this pussy-footing around. If he had some things to get off his chest, then so did she. And her chest was bigger than his (but only marginally).

She was half looking forward to it, the way you do when you know you're in the right. Whereas he had to resort to solicitors, Ali had always been well able to fight her own corner. Verbally, she could run rings around him, and always had. That was part of the problem, too. He'd have been a lot better off if he'd married a quiet Southern girl who had fitted into his world, and who wouldn't keep giving him gyp every time someone tried to organise a decent, honest-to-God gun rally.

Instead he'd landed himself with a lippy, bawdy Irish girl, and he still wasn't sure what had hit him.

She'd decided that they would go for a walk. It would be better to take it off the premises in case it got heated. Emma was all lined up to look after the kids, and was in the bathroom right now patting her eyes with cold water to make the redness go away.

Weird — to be that upset about good news. And it was marvellous news, as Ali had told her over and over. She could start again. Fresh. Put the whole thing behind her. As far as Ali was concerned, she'd just been handed a Get Out Of Jail Free card, and she should put that cheating shit behind her now and move on with her life.

At that Emma had raised fierce, swollen eyes

to her. 'He didn't cheat. He *did not* cheat.'

'Fine. Whatever.'

'It was a mistake. A stupid mistake, that's all. And now he has to live with it.'

Well, yes. And that was unfortunate. But *Emma* didn't have to live with it, and that was the important thing here, as far as Ali was concerned.

But Emma had continued to cry silently, and not in the kind of cathartic way that Ali had hoped for all along. It sounded like misery, pure and simple, and now she was shut away in the bathroom, trying to hide her upset.

'Ali?' It was Kyle calling to her, as loudly as though he were on the ranch back home. Not that they'd owned a ranch, but she knew it was his dream after he retired.

It hardly needed to be pointed out that it was not *her* dream.

Ali gathered her keys and her coat and her indignation. But by the time she got out the front door, his car was turning in the yard.

'See you tomorrow,' he called out the driver's window.

And with that he just drove off.

22

Emma

The day Ryan told her, she'd just come back from getting her engagement ring made a bit smaller, if you could believe it. The ring had fitted perfectly when he'd first slipped it on her finger, but the months of getting up at 4 a.m. were taking their toll and if the weight wasn't exactly dropping off her, then it was melting away at a pleasing rate of about a pound every two weeks. *Without her having to do a thing.*

So all was good with her world, apart from a mild, nagging feeling that *Wake Up Ireland* was stagnating, but why let that ruin the perfectly good night of unfettered sex that lay ahead? Ryan was flying out early the following morning to Afghanistan for a week, to photograph American troops for an issue of *Time* magazine or one of those, and they always did their best to make up for his absences the night before.

When she walked in the door she was met by piles of shorts, socks and waterproofs. There would be a battered old rucksack somewhere, half packed, and Ryan, last-minute merchant that he was, would probably be hanging around at the tumble dryer, watching a couple of T-shirts swirling about: 'Come on, fucking *dry*, will you?'

'What's for dinner?' she called, just for the

crack. She always enjoyed seeing him in a tizzy, because it happened so rarely. But ask him to *pack a bag* and he went to pieces altogether. You'd think he'd be used to it after all these years of travelling, but no. He would do no forward planning at all, then realise four hours before his flight that he hadn't a single clean pair of jocks for the journey, and then there would be a volley of shits and fecks, and the laundry basket would be overturned in a blind panic.

And now she expected dinner on top of it all? She was looking forward to the look on his face.

But he didn't shout back in a panic, 'What? I thought *you* were bringing dinner.'

In fact it was all very quiet in the apartment. No whirr of the tumble dryer, no final phone call with the magazine about arrangements, no snapping of clasps into place as he packed away his precious cameras.

'Ryan?' Maybe he'd gone to the shops. He'd once snuck off with her travel toothpaste and very expensive shower gel in his rucksack, and had lived to regret it.

He walked out of the bedroom then, and she knew immediately that something was wrong.

'What is it?' She automatically went to him. 'Did they cancel on you?'

That happened a lot: jobs getting pulled at the last minute. When you were dealing with military personnel and unstable regions, it was even more likely that things would change overnight and the assignment would be deferred or cancelled altogether.

'No.' He didn't let her touch him. He moved

away from her outstretched arms and stood for a minute with his back to her, head bowed.

Emma was frightened then. It wasn't work at all. It was to do with her; the way he refused to look at her, the paleness of his face.

Her engagement ring, newly tightened, felt slippery on her finger.

'Ryan, please tell me what's happening.' Her voice was eerily calm, the way it always went when catastrophe loomed on the horizon. 'What have I done?'

Because she must have done *something*. Not that she could immediately think what. Was he cross over the way she'd spoken about him to Ali on the phone earlier? She'd only been defending him, when Ali had made some quip about him being off on yet another trip, when he was only home four days after the last. 'Yes, but they've been four great days,' Emma had insisted, but not entirely convincingly (phone calls from Ali always had that effect on her), and Ryan had looked a bit pinched afterwards.

Or maybe she'd just been going on too much about having the blasted engagement ring resized. His eyes had seemed a little glazed last night, but he'd assured her it was just tiredness. At the back of his mind though, a little voice might have been saying, 'God, she can bang on, can't she?'

A chill settled in her stomach now. Romances like theirs, the fast and furious kind, often burned out just as quickly. Maybe her instinct had been spot on all along; everything had been too quick, and today, for some reason, he'd woken up and wondered what the blazes he was doing, getting hitched to someone with worrying tendencies towards control freakery, and an unhealthy preoccupation with the yoghurt section of the supermarket.

He had got cold feet.

He lifted his head at last. His eyes were red-rimmed. 'I need to tell you something.'

She said nothing. Just stood there, frozen, waiting to be terminated.

'I got my test results today,' he whispered.

His test results? For a moment she hadn't a clue what he was talking about. The medical, after all, wasn't something he'd sought out himself; he'd only gone for it at all because it was free, a perk of the new contract with the Americans. He could get all his bits and bobs checked out once a year and they'd pick up the tab.

He might as well go, they'd decided, even though it was a pain to drive out to the designated clinic and give up a couple of hours' work. But his father had high blood pressure so it made sense to start looking after himself now, right? Secretly, neither of them believed for a second he had any blood pressure problems, given that he was so thin and fit and wiry. Neither of them believed he had any problems.

But he did. A huge problem. He began saying things like 'antibodies' and 'serum concentrations' and finally, 'HIV'. Emma heard the diagnosis as though it was coming through water; the words were muffled, strange, incomprehensible.

Even Ryan looked disbelieving. He actually said HIB on the first go. He had to correct himself, looking stunned that the letters were coming out of his mouth at all in relation to himself.

Emma's shock was brief. 'No,' she said. Then, stronger, 'No.'

It was a mistake. It *had* to be. Ryan wasn't a serial sleeper-arounder. He had assured her he hadn't been, and anyway, she knew from his uncertainty around her sometimes, his lack of guile, that he had not exactly pushed the far boundaries of his sexuality, no more than herself. And surely a man who'd had dozens of girlfriends would know by now that it is never, ever a good idea to buy your beloved scratchy lace underwear.

She put this to him. His sexual history. It was limited. Not in a loser way, but he was not promiscuous, right?

'Yes,' he said. He was very vague. He seemed in a daze. 'I mean, I wasn't. I *didn't*. Of course not.'

She believed him. He was not a good liar. And in his current state, she didn't think him capable of lying.

'Well, then,' she said. She felt better, now that the initial, awful shock had passed. 'Let's ring them up. Let's get this thing clarified.'

But he didn't seem as righteous as she was. As outraged. He seemed defeated, frightened. And he could not meet her eyes without flinching.

Of course it hadn't even occurred to her at that point that she was at risk too. All she could think of was him, how to make this right for him. How to make it go away.

'I did drugs in New York,' he blurted.

Emma felt the blood leech from her face.

His own was pleading now. 'Just a couple of times, Emma. Twice. I didn't even think . . . We were at a party, people were shooting up. I just wanted to see what it was like, that was all. But I didn't have my own gear.'

Gear. *Gear?* She felt the first hot spikes of anger.

'I used Johnny's.'

Who the fuck was Johnny?

He read her face. 'He lived in the flat with me. He was a decent guy, a bit wired, but OK. It was just twice. I didn't like it much. I preferred just to drink. So I stopped after that second time. I put it out of my head and never thought about it again until now.'

Emma's voice was like a whip. 'Liar.'

'What?' He was so shocked he took a step back.

He'd be wise to take another one, for his own protection.

'You knew and you didn't tell me.'

'I told you, I didn't even think about it — '

'You bloody did. You thought about it when I asked you about what you did in New York. About your wild youth. I thought you just meant drinking and doing stupid stuff like that. You let me believe that.'

'It was *twice*.'

She was so angry now she could hardly speak. 'Twice, and you've got bloody HIV!' It began to sink in properly now; her, her own situation. What he'd done to her. She began to shake.

Ryan had his head in his heads. His eyes were wild. 'Fine! So I *didn't* tell you. It was nothing to do with . . . HIV didn't even cross my mind, OK? All I could think of was that you wouldn't approve. There I was, no proper job, not like you, no apartment, no steady future. If you knew I'd done drugs you would have written me off entirely.'

'Twice,' she repeated coldly. 'Just twice, you said. You think I'm so rigid that I'd have held that against you for the rest of your life?'

'I didn't know how you'd react. We'd just met! I didn't want to risk telling you about something I'd practically forgotten myself. And then it was too late. And *then*, Emma, then it didn't matter, because we were engaged, and we knew each other well enough to know that it was going to be OK.'

'Oh, yes, it's going to be terrific! You have HIV and very possibly you've given it to me too. All because of your dishonesty, Ryan. You stupid, stupid . . . '

She had to stop then, because she was afraid she was going to hit him. He stood there, semi-hunched, like he expected it.

It was all a blur after that. She kept telling him to get out. He insisted they sit down, face this together. The more he said that, the more incensed she got.

'What are you talking about? Together? There *is* no together.'

He didn't argue with her on that one. Her face

no doubt said it all. How could she ever trust him again, after what had happened? How could she ever *look* at him, if she found out she had the disease too? It was gone, all of it. He had ruined everything.

He kept saying in a very calm voice, 'We need to get you checked. You need to take a test as soon we can organise one.'

His concern was more than she could bear. 'I don't need your advice or interference.'

'But they told me on the phone — '

'Stop.' And she actually put her hands over her ears to drown him out. She couldn't bear this. Not now. And not from him.

It all ended very quickly. She remembered bundling his stuff into suitcases, carrier bags, anything she could get her hands on. He packed up beside her in silent misery. They didn't say goodbye at the door, and she slammed it before he'd even turned away.

Later that night, as she lay curled up in a ball on her bed, listening to the blood pound in her ears, he rang for the first time.

The answering machine picked up.

'If you won't get tested for yourself, then at least do it for me. Please, call me back.'

She didn't call him back, that night or any other night since.

★　★　★

Patrick and Alannah weren't keen on meeting up with Emma. And even less so when they discovered that the venue wasn't in the television building at all, but rather a run-down pub nearby, with ring-marked tables, and dodgy-looking toasted sandwiches.

'I haven't got long,' Patrick announced, looking with distaste at the pub's lurid red banquette before lowering his besuited nether regions on to it gingerly.

Alannah wasn't pushed either. She looked tired and colourless. Phil had apparently ripped through the girls in make-up, and they'd now gone to the opposite extreme, turning Alannah out in insipid pastel eyeshadows and horrible peach lipsticks. Her hair was pinned up and lank and, honestly, you wouldn't look at her twice. Even her clothes were dull beyond words — no quirky brooches or ill-advised shocking pink shoes. She looked like, well, anybody.

'We have to get back,' she explained to Emma tersely. 'Phil isn't finished yet.'

That was another thing; production meetings for the shows were taking *hours*, according to Hannie. Phil was ruthlessly workmanlike in his approach, and everything had to be nailed down just so, even for parts of the show that featured mad people who believed they could speak to Doris Day — stuff that Alannah and Patrick could do in their sleep. But no. Phil went over everything again and again, until by the end any spontaneity and life was wrung out of it, and Alannah and Patrick came across on screen like they were reading the news.

'He's fucking *killing* it,' Hannie hissed indignantly in her nightly bulletins to Emma on the phone.

347

But that was just Hannie's opinion. She was a tad biased, and her dislike of Phil was legendary.

To Emma's own eye, the show was looking competent, if a little safe.

But safe was good. Safe was what was required, after the recent fracas.

And the word from the top was that Adam was pleased. Phil had apparently been beating a path up and down to the office, according to her moles, fervently taking Adam's advice on the smallest thing. Little lick-arse.

But that was uncharitable. He was just filling in. It wasn't like he was making a pitch for her *job*, or anything. Right?

The change that struck her most now was that Patrick and Alannah weren't even fighting any more. They weren't exactly hugging either, but Emma saw no spark between them as they sat there on the banquette in what would normally be intolerable proximity. In regular circumstances, the way Alannah was worriedly examining the back of the sugar packets now for the number of additives — 'We're all going to have deformed children, mark my words' — would have Patrick sighing and shifting, until eventually he would burst out with something like, 'Maybe some of us shouldn't *have* children. Did that ever occur to you?'

Today they contented themselves with the odd bristling look, but nothing exciting. Nothing that would make you tune in to see what Patrick might say next that would have the blood vessels in Alannah's pale blue eyes bulging with rage, even while she had to slap a big fake smile on her face, and say in a jolly, breakfast-television way, 'Oh, now, *Patrick*!'

They were beaten. Phil and Adam and probably even Hannie had got them up against a wall during the week and gave them the if-you-put-one-foot-wrong-so-help-me-God speech. Patrick and Alannah clearly were offering no resistance either. After what had happened that day over the eggs Benedict, they knew the only way forward was to agree.

A week ago, Emma might have gone along with that. But that was before she realised what was fundamentally wrong with the show.

'As you know, I'm back on Monday,' she began.

Luckily she hadn't expected a round of excited applause, because there wasn't one. They just nodded briskly and with some resignation.

OK, so it hurt. But what had she expected? She hadn't set the show alight. She hadn't furthered their careers, as they had no doubt hoped. The ratings were doggedly average. True, she was very competent and professional, and good to work for, but where was the *inspiration*? The thing that set the show apart from the rakes of other good-but-average programmes that plagued the airways?

'Before you go on,' said Patrick gruffly, 'we just want to say sorry.' He threw a stiff nod in Alannah's direction. 'Both of us.'

Emma had been expecting this apology. It could have come a little sooner, but anyhow.

Alannah took up the mantle now. 'Yes. We're aware that what happened that day was completely unprofessional.'

Patrick stirred beside her, and muttered, 'It didn't exactly just 'happen'.'

Alannah looked him in the eye for the first time since they'd arrived in. 'And what's that's supposed to mean?'

Patrick had a brief, visible tussle between knowing he should let it go, and just not being fucking able to. 'If you're going to take responsibility for something, then do it properly. Don't just blame it on the gods.'

'I was not.' Alannah's cheeks were starting up. 'And that's rich coming from you. Taking responsibility! You were so far up Adam's arse at that meeting last week that I didn't think we'd ever see you again.'

Patrick laughed. 'At least I didn't go in with carefully arranged bed-hair and a low cut top, and then refuse to use them. That's called mixed messages.'

They appeared to have completely forgotten about Emma. She might as well not exist.

'When will you ever get it into your thick head that just because a woman puts on a bit of lipstick it doesn't mean she's gagging to sleep with you?' Alannah thundered.

Patrick winked at her. 'I'm open to all offers.'

In a beautiful touch, Alannah's hair burst loose from its clip. 'You're an argument for castration, do you know that?'

'For a feminist, you talk an *awful* lot about penises. I'm starting to think you'd like one.'

At that point Emma sat forward and said, 'Stop.'

There was a little silence. Patrick shook his head, as if coming back down to earth. Then he sighed. 'Jesus. Sorry, Emma. I just don't know what gets into me.'

Alannah, too, was beginning to remember her surroundings, and was taking small, shaky breaths. 'Yes. Sorry. I just . . . oh, this is just pointless! We can't work together.'

'No,' Patrick agreed heavily.

Emma was laughing now. 'I meant stop, you're killing me.'

They were confused now. Suspicious looks flew back and forth. Perhaps the imminent demise of the show was unhinging Emma. Plus, of course, there were all those rumours about her broken engagement, and what had *really* happened . . .

'We won't do it again,' Alannah emphasised, looking a bit worried now.

Emma looked kindly from her to Patrick. 'Oh, please. You *know* it's going to happen again. Because you two can't help yourselves. You never could. Even if it's going to cost you your jobs.'

Alannah looked stricken at that; Patrick, merely resigned.

'And mine,' Emma couldn't help adding.

Patrick sat back against the dirty banquette. 'At this point, let's just agree to try to get through the rest of this series and move on to the BBC, OK?'

Emma looked at him carefully. 'You've had some interest from the BBC?'

'My agent's in contact with them. There are a couple of options on the table.'

Liar. His body language oozed confidence, but his eyes were skittering about all over the place. The BBC had presenters crawling out of the woodwork. They didn't need another shortish, laddish Irishman — one who wouldn't be coming with a glowing reference from his last job.

Alannah stuck up her chin confidently too, even though her eyes didn't quite meet Emma's either. 'I may well get my old presenting job back.'

Yes, and pigs would have a good chance of taking off from the roof of the Irish language studios where she'd started her career.

Emma reached for her bag. 'I guess neither of you is interested then in my proposal to change things radically to try to save the show.'

Patrick sat up. 'I heard you were unhappy with the content,' he said carefully. 'And to be honest, I couldn't agree with you more. Eggs fucking Benedict. And if we book one more looper on the show with supernatural abilities, I think I might have an out-of-body experience myself.'

'Absolutely.' Alannah looked surprised to find herself in agreement with Patrick. 'If we could cover meatier subjects. Be more issue-driven. If we had something to *say*.'

'I used to think the same,' Emma confided, putting her bag down again. 'Total rubbish, nearly all of it. Risible, in fact. But actually, I've since decided that the content couldn't be more perfect.'

Alannah and Patrick exchanged a small look — crazy woman, or visionary? Or maybe that

352

toasted cheese sandwich had contained some form of strepto-something that had rapidly infiltrated her brain.

'For next week, I'm going to book every mediocre boy band flogging a new single, and anybody who's ever had a near-death experience and a need to come on national TV to tell the tale,' Emma promised them brightly.

Patrick looked at her with narrow, distrustful eyes. 'And what are we supposed to do with that crappy lot?'

'Nothing.' This was very important, and she looked at them both long and hard. 'Just be yourselves.'

★ ★ ★

All week long she'd been thinking about where Ryan had been flying out to the day she'd called over with the news of her test results. Was he back yet? Had he come home, only to take off somewhere else again just as quickly?

War-torn Wherever was great if you were young and fit and healthy. It might be a different story if, say, you weren't. Well, the healthy bit anyway.

Ryan had bad luck when it came to stomach bugs; never anything too serious, but if there was a case of gastroenteritis to be picked up abroad, he was usually first in line. He'd phoned from Nigeria last year from his hotel bed — 'Hey, babes! Oops. Hang on. Just got to run to the toilet.'

Maybe it hadn't been bad luck at all. Maybe it

had been the virus, weakening him already, even though he'd said the doctors maintained he was fine; to carry on as normal.

She kept seeing his face when he'd said that to her: a mixture of pride and defiance. He hadn't wanted her sympathy. But the worse thing was, she hadn't offered it.

The house was empty when she got back from her meeting with Patrick and Alannah. The kids, Ali and Kyle had all gone, at Kyle's surprise suggestion, on a family outing to the local bowling alley.

'He loves bowling,' Ali had said earlier, as though it was an insult.

'Maybe he wants to talk.' Emma knew there had been no overtures in that direction from Kyle at all. It was deeply unsettling Ali, who went around the whole time with her shoulders hunched as if permanently prepared for battle.

'How the hell are we supposed to talk when we're going to spend most of the time looking at each other's arses?' she'd bit out.

'You never know,' Emma had said. 'You might start fancying each other again.'

It was touch and go for a moment.

Then Ali guffawed. She went on so long that tears began to roll down her face.

Emma began laughing too. 'Come on, you two always fancied each other.'

'Not in about ten years.'

'A bit of bowling, a few beers . . . '

'Oh, Jesus, can you imagine? Knowing our luck, we'd get accidentally pregnant for the fourth time — as you know, Kyle is the most

354

fertile man in Texas — and then where would we be?'

And she'd gone off upstairs to change into one of her tracksuits, in slightly better humour than Emma had seen her since Kyle had arrived over.

The apartment felt a bit chilly when Emma let herself in. The place was a total mess, of course: dirty laundry and kids' colouring books everywhere, and Ali's overflowing pots of make-up strewn across the kitchen table.

But at least Emma had the telly to herself. And the fridge, even if there was nothing left in it except the corpses of empty milk cartons and the ubiquitous bowl of leftover tuna casserole.

But she was determined to enjoy her lovely solitude now that her messy, noisy sister and her fractious kids were gone for a few hours. She would curl up on the couch with a nice glass of wine and watch people who had no talent being told by a panel of judges that they had, indeed, no talent.

She tried. She really tried. She even turned the volume up a bit louder to lighten the mood.

The feeling crept over her gradually. It wasn't pleasant, it wasn't welcome, but none the less it was true: she missed Anto.

Even more than him, she missed Ryan.

23

Ali

Nobody had mentioned Calvin Crawford since Kyle had arrived four days ago. The thick cream letter was in tatters from being carried around on Ali's person, ready to be produced at any moment with a, 'Ha! And what have you got to say about *that*, you pig?'

But there was no opportunity. Kyle made no attempt at a show down. In fact, he was being strangely and unnervingly pleasant. He came around every afternoon after school by prior arrangement, full of cheery, 'Hey, kids! Guess where we're going today!' and whisked them off to various places for hours on end. It had been the Museum of Modern Art on Tuesday, which had been absolutely crud, according to the kids afterwards. Back they had traipsed at seven, having had a very sensible dinner out, and without having been let run rampant in the museum's gift shop.

'He hasn't seen us in weeks — you'd think he'd get us at least one stupid present,' Anto had said bitterly.

Kyle had overheard. Loftily, he'd said, 'I'm here to spend some quality time with you, son. Not try and buy you off.'

Whether that was aimed at Ali or not, she

356

didn't know. But if it was quality time he wanted, then she certainly wasn't going to stand in his way. When the kids got a half-day from their new school on Wednesday, she let him pick them up and keep them until almost bedtime. They'd looked a little frazzled when they'd got home, but it was simply tiredness, Kyle maintained. Kids that age had a lot of energy and he'd burned it off with them in the park. He himself looked exhausted too, and he hobbled down the front steps like something was hurting him around the groin region.

Then the blooming bowling yesterday.

Dear God.

'I think we should do something as a family,' he'd informed Ali officiously. 'We don't want the kids thinking we're at loggerheads.'

Was he for *real*? But there he was, smiling away at her, like nothing had happened at all.

Either he was a bit dim (and, in fairness, she'd had her suspicions over the years) or else he was playing some duplicitous game, put up to it by his cunning and expensive lawyers.

'O-K,' she'd said, in an I'm-on-to-you-buddy voice.

Off he'd gone and booked an hour slot in the local bowling alley, which wasn't as big as the ones in America, and they didn't sell beer, or nachos, but they would just have to put up with it, he told the kids bravely.

So they'd bowled. All of them. Even Jack, who thought he was *way* too cool for stuff like that any more.

The only problem was the kids wanted to be

on the same team. 'It's only fair. Three kids against two adults.'

So Ali found herself sitting cosily beside Kyle, and having to congratulate him heartily when he got a strike.

Afterwards they'd gone for something to eat, all of them squeezing into a booth together like one big, happy family.

'I think I'll have the pizza,' Kyle decided after much deliberation.

'You *always* have the pizza,' Erin pointed out with a big sigh.

'She's getting more like you every day,' Kyle commented to Ali.

But the kids seemed to be having a good time, and Ali didn't begrudge it to them, and so she put on her happy face and ate her burger and engaged in meaningless small talk until it was time to go home. It was only when Kyle peeled off in one direction in the car park, and she and the kids in another, that anybody would guess there was a thing amiss.

And still no showdown. No real discussion at all of what had happened between them.

Of course, Ali was perfectly entitled to bring it up herself. Why not? She could easily tell him that they had very important things to discuss, immediately, and sit him down. It didn't have to be *his* call.

But she said nothing. Instead she kind of fluttered around him all week, even though she was not a person who normally fluttered, or at least not gracefully. She jumped nervously when her phone rang, and tensed up when she heard

358

those cowboy boots marching up the steps.

She was mad with herself. Honestly! Behaving like she was somehow afraid of a discussion! What had *she* done that was so wrong, except, um, kidnap her children?

Then, yesterday, just when she really thought she couldn't bear any more of all this phoneyness, he asked if he could stay with them in the apartment after school.

'Here?' What the hell was he trying to do? Move in? Pretend that everything was OK again?

But that wasn't what he meant at all. 'I want to have my visit here today, if that's all right. I need to do some normal things with them, too. Not just having a great time in museums and the park.'

How could she argue with that? So she had to gather her bag and leave the apartment, feeling very odd and uneasy about the whole thing. She wandered around the shops for a couple of hours in misery, thinking of them all in domestic bliss in her home. Well, Emma's home, technically, but Ali's too for the moment.

When her time was up, she rushed back to the apartment. The first thing she heard upon opening the door was — oh *wonderful* — Erin's strident voice.

'That's not the way you do joined-up writing.'

'It's the way I learned it,' Kyle was arguing back doggedly.

'Yes, but that was last century. Things have changed. Mom understands that, and she makes no attempt whatsoever to help us with our homework.'

'All right, then! Do it yourself, if it makes you happy!'

When Ali walked into the living room, Erin threw herself upon her like she was drowning. 'Thank God you're back. We're having a terrible time. Daddy thinks he knows everything, but he doesn't know *anything*. And he won't make tuna casserole for dinner because he says we have it far too often, and he's going to cook us shepherd's pie instead, from *Ethel's* recipe.' She looked like she was going to be sick.

Ah, yes. Ethel. Ali wondered how much she had to do with Kyle's sudden attempts to be Father of the Year.

He wasn't any better at it than her attempts to be Mother of the Century.

'I did Anto's homework with him.' Kyle threw a supremely defensive look in Ali's direction. 'We had all that complicated long division to do.'

'I let you help,' Anto interjected sympathetically. He was sprawled out all over the floor playing Nintendo. The constant drone of *rat-a-tat-a-tat* coming from it seemed to be setting Kyle's nerves a little on edge.

'For the fourth time,' he bit out, 'turn that thing down.'

Anto ignored him. Kyle threw another look in Ali's direction. But he was saved by Jack's appearance from the bedroom, in a pair of boxer shorts and vest. As usual, his thumb was glued to the buttons of his mobile phone.

Kyle jumped to his feet happily and lit into him. 'I thought I asked you to take out the trash?'

360

'In a minute,' Jack said, not looking up from the phone.

'If I hear 'In a minute' just one more time . . . ' Kyle blocked his way. 'Do it now.'

Jack looked at him in surprise. 'Chill out, Dad.'

Ooh. Wrong thing to have said to a man determined to show his estranged wife just how magnificently he was coping in her absence.

She cleared her throat. Of course, it would be fun to let this one play out, but the decent thing to do was to step in now. 'Kyle,' she said nicely, 'the trash doesn't normally get taken out — '

But he refused her olive branch.

'Don't interfere,' he ordered her excitedly. 'I'm in charge this afternoon. Not you.'

Ali held up her hands. Fine. No problemo. She turned and walked into the kitchen.

'You've been a right little smart ass all day,' Kyle thundered to Jack behind her, in his best alpha-male voice. 'Now stop texting that girl, or whoever it is, get your clothes on and put the trash out for your mother.'

Oh, so it was for *Ali*. Nice touch. She was impressed.

And yes, there went Jack, squaring up to him. She watched from the kitchen, whilst pretending not to. Jack was as tall as Kyle now, and in far better shape. He could take him out easily.

'And what if I don't?' he said to Kyle insolently.

Of course, Kyle had no option but to step up too, but if it wasn't for the cowboy boots with the two-inch heels, along with the bouffant hair, designed to hide his balding patch, he would have been caught short. As it was, Ali could see him standing slightly on tippy-toe.

'Do you want to push me?' he roared at Jack, whilst subtly trying to keep his balance.

Jack was quite calm. 'You can't keep ordering me around like I'm ten.'

'Hey. There's nothing wrong with being ten,' Anto commented from the floor.

Jack ignored him. 'That's all you've done since you got here. Well, I'm not a little kid any more, Dad, and if you think I'm going to jump at the chance to move in with you just because you've promised me a car next year, you're wrong.'

Kyle went pink.

Oooh, the rat. The dirty, rotten rat! Pretending to be so nice all this week, so reasonable, when all along he'd been laying the groundwork for the kids to tell some judge that yes, really, they'd rather live with Dad than Mom. What chance had Ali against that?

Kyle wouldn't look at Ali. He didn't dare, the filthy, double-dealing coward. Just wait until she got him alone.

But she got the shock of her life to discover that she wasn't to be spared either.

'Right now, the way you and Mom have behaved, I don't think I want to live with either of you,' Jack said with a damning little sniff.

In the horrible silence that followed, Erin and Anto exchanged looks.

'Well,' Erin said eventually, 'I definitely want to live with Mom, but Dad is better at weekends because he always gives us money as he knows that will keep us quiet.' And she offered him a very affectionate look.

'I don't want to hurt anybody's feelings here,' Anto announced after a moment. 'So I'm going to let you both put together some kind of a package. You know, what kind of benefits and perks are on offer, and what the deal is on chores and bedtime. I'll consider it and get back to you both.'

Into the silence that followed, by some massive fluke, the jukebox burst into life, even though it had been broken for ages.

Everybody jumped as the thing jerked and shimmied, the lights began to dance, and Elvis burst out with 'You Ain't Nothing but a Hound Dog'.

★ ★ ★

'When is he going back?' Emma asked.

'Sunday morning.'

'And do you not think you need to thrash things out before then?'

'He's trying to take my *kids* from me.'

'And, like, hello, what have *you* done?'

'He made the first threat. I merely reacted. Anybody would have done the same.'

'Run away from the problem?'

The way she said it, you would think Ali was always doing that. The nerve of her. Ali never ran away from anything unless it got too unpleasant.

But then again Emma was in a different space these days. All sort of reflective and dreamy and lots of staring at nothing in a contemplative

363

fashion. Often one of the kids would stamp on her foot, mostly entirely by accident, and she would hardly notice, because she was away with the fairies.

'What's she thinking about all the time?' Erin had demanded yesterday. While it was an improvement on her usual misery, it was quite unsettling for everybody to have someone going around the whole time like they were trying to work out the theory of relativity.

'Work, I think,' Ali had reassured Erin.

She knew this was partly true. Emma was going around behind the scenes, all Machiavellian, having covert meetings with that pair of tits Patrick and Alannah. Big changes were happening, she'd told Ali very mysteriously.

'Like what?'

'I'm overhauling the style.' All cryptic, like.

'Yeah, but what are we talking about, exactly? Big name guests? *EastEnders* actors?' Ali loved *EastEnders*. 'Or are you going to fire one of the presenters?'

That would be a change for the better in her opinion. Get that jerk Patrick off and replace him with another woman or something.

'No, nothing that big.'

'Oh.' It sounded like nothing much was happening at all. But then Emma had always kept things close to her chest, and Ali was probably lucky to have got that much out of her at all.

But definitely she'd changed since she'd got her negative test result. She didn't even get excited over the state of the fridge any more.

Everything was, 'Oh, don't worry about that,' and, 'It's not the end of the world.' She'd actually laughed at something Anto had said during the week, even though it was rude. Most tellingly of all, Ali had seen her in a pair of *elasticated pants* yesterday.

But a scare like that was bound to affect you, right? It was probably like being two minutes late to check in for a flight that subsequently crashed, killing everybody on board. Or a lump turning out to be benign. You must do a bit of reflection. A bit of thanking your lucky stars that you were alive. What was the point in beating yourself into skinny jeans any more, you must wonder, when you could just go elasticated and let it all hang out?

Ali wondered where Ryan fitted into all this reflection. Somewhere anyway; Emma's recent computer history was chock-full of HIV information websites. Not that Ali had been prying; she'd had to use *someone's* computer to look up what could actually happen to you if you refused to return your children to their country of origin (quite a lot, actually. She hadn't slept well that night).

It was survivor guilt; Ali was sure of it. Emma had got the all clear, and was feeling so bloody grateful that she was conveniently putting to the back of her mind exactly who had put her in danger in the first place. It was, apparently, a common phenomenon. Ali wouldn't be surprised if Emma made a batch of chicken soup some day and nipped over to Ryan with it, with all her HIV printouts under her arm, 'just for a bit of support'.

Slippery, slippery slope. To get saddled with a sick man, just out of a sense of duty? That may sound harsh, but that's what it would be.

Maybe Ali was jumping the gun a little. But there must be some reason Emma was boning up on HIV. And, seeing as she herself didn't have it . . .

A night out, Ali decided. That's what Emma needed. Or a holiday in the sun. Anything to broaden her horizons. She should be looking upon her narrow escape as an opportunity to go forwards, not bloody backwards.

Yes, she definitely needed saving from herself. No doubt about it. And Ali was just the person to do it, as she was so clued in and wise, and was making such a good fist of her own life. Plus, if she was out with Emma that night, and possibly Saturday night also, then she wouldn't have to talk to Kyle, and then he flew back early Sunday . . . It would work out well for everybody.

But before she could put her grand plans in place for a spectacular weekend on the tiles, Mam and Dad made a special detour on their way to the cardiologist just to attack her, it seemed.

'We're worried about the kids,' Mam announced in the kitchen stoutly. 'They're not fitting in here.'

The flipping nerve of her. 'How do you know? They're delighted to be here. They've started school and everything.'

'They hate their schools. They're only one step

366

from running away again.'

Mam just couldn't let that go. Every time she rang up she asked whether all three kids were present and accounted for. She said that the whole episode had put years on Dad.

She said this in a kind of excited way.

Dad said grumpily now, 'They're American, Ali. You can't try to pretend they're not.'

Ali looked to Emma for help. What the hell was going on here? But Emma said nothing. Just stood there meeting Ali's eyes in a way that could only be described as challenging.

The bitch. It hit Ali then: she'd been stitched up. Emma had known all along they were coming over to have a go. Why else was the bloody spare Zimmer frame out from under the stairs, that Ali had tripped over a moment ago, and nearly broken her neck?

What a horrible, horrible sister she had! Getting everybody to gang up on her like this, when she was feeling so vulnerable, what with Kyle breathing down her neck. Any normal, decent sister would have produced a packet of chocolate biscuits and rubbed Ali's back and murmured comforting things like, 'Yes, he's a total wanker, always was.'

But not Emma. Honestly, this time Ali was finished with her. No, really, she was. 'You are dead to me,' she was going to tell her later, coldly and calmly. But she must remember not to say it before she'd borrowed her car to get to the chemist for some more head-lice shampoo for Erin. Timing was everything in these matters.

'What's going to happen now?' Mam asked again. She was particularly tetchy that morning. Dad's hospital visits tended to do that to her. 'What about the carers?' she was fond of complaining afterwards. 'They never fecking well ask how *we're* doing. Never give us the time of day. And we saving them a fortune, looking after all these old, sick people for them. It'd cost a thousand euro a week to put him in a home, you know.'

Dad would try his best to look worth even half of it, but he would have to give up halfway through and have a lie down.

Anyway, she was on a right rant today. 'Is Kyle going to go home on Sunday, with nothing sorted out between you two, and the kids wondering whether they're coming or going?'

'The kids are not going anywhere.' Ali said this coldly and politely.

'So you're going to stay?'

'Yes.' What else could she say? She was being painted into a corner.

Mam looked more concerned. 'And where are you going to live?'

'Let me worry about that.' Emma might not be dead to her for another month at least.

'You can't stay here for ever.' Mam looked around Emma's kitchen restlessly. She was clearly feeling the pressure to get stuck in and give it a good clean, but knew better, what with Emma standing within two feet of her. 'And much and all as we'd love to have you — '

'We would,' Dad chimed in.

He only said it out of politeness. To fit in, the

way you do. He no more wanted Anto and Erin and Jack descending upon him than Mam did, and who could blame him?

But Mam went mad. 'Oh, and are *you* going to cook for them?'

'Well, no, but I — '

'Mop and clean and dust and tidy, and then give yourself a sponge bath?'

Dad rallied valiantly. 'I just meant that we'd have them if we were able to, but obviously we're not — '

'*I'm* able. I'm only sixty-six. There's nothing wrong with *me*.'

OK, enough was enough. Ali flashed a look at Emma. 'Let's just all sit down and have a cup of tea,' she told Mam coldly.

'Yes,' Emma concurred, pulling out a chair firmly for Mam.

But Mam didn't seem to be able to stop herself. 'Tea! Don't give him tea, unless either one of you is going to stop the car twice on the way to the hospital and try and find a toilet before he pees himself. *Tea*. Don't talk to me about bloody tea, when the two of you are over here, having a great time, and I'm stuck fighting with the Health Board to get free incontinence pads.'

There was a speck of spittle at the corner of Mam's mouth when she was finished. Ali couldn't take her eyes off it; it was like some sick fascination.

It was only gradually that she became aware of it; a quiet, snuffling noise. The sound of crying.

It was Dad. He was turned away, trying to

hide it in the collar of his coat, but his shoulders heaved and a line of snot ran from his nose.

Before anyone could think what to do, how to react — *Dad*, crying — he turned and limped out the door.

24

Emma

Emma held her first pre-production meeting that Friday afternoon before she was due to produce the show again on Monday, after her week of disgrace.

She turned up late, which didn't help. But Dad had to be taken to a 'safe house' first, as Ali kept saying solemnly. God only knew what would happen if they let the pair of them go home together, she maintained; Mam might go completely mental and next thing they'd end up as a mawkish story on the Joe Duffy show on the radio; examples of the tragic plight of carers pushed to the edge and whom the world had forgotten about.

'We haven't forgotten about them,' Emma had pointed out sternly. 'Dad is going to Auntie Jane's for the weekend, and Mam is going to have a nice rest at Liam's.'

Not that there would be much rest at Liam's, what with the three kids and Tina, and *there* was a house that needed cleaning. But Emma had given Liam strict instructions to make Mam take it easy; that she was clearly exhausted and overwrought, and that they would have a family conference next week to decide what to do.

Dad hadn't wanted to go to Auntie Jane's at all. He'd rallied almost immediately after his upset, and was back to grumping within ten minutes. 'She's too holy, she'll be praying all the time, and making me go to Mass. And her house is always cold. I just want to go home, to my own house.' He'd dug his fingers into Emma's arm. 'Tell your mam I'm sorry. Tell her I won't be any trouble. It's my own fault. I wouldn't wear the pads, you see.'

Emma was raging with herself about the whole thing; so wrapped up in her own problems that she hadn't even noticed what was going on in her parents' house. Actually, scratch that; she *had* noticed. She just hadn't done anything about it.

Ali hadn't seemed to suffer the same degree of guilt. 'We *did* offer to help. She never let us.'

Anyway, Emma had packed a bag for Dad, and fed Auntie Jane a line about Mam having a dose of the flu and not being well enough to look after him for a couple of days. Liam had come over for Mam, who had let herself be led away, eyes downcast, as though she were a convict.

'I don't know what came over me.' She'd seemed very shocked. 'I used to be such a nice person, too. I never shouted at you three when you were kids. Never.'

'Not very loudly anyway,' Liam had told her reassuringly. 'And only on weekdays, when we had to get out to school.'

'Watch her,' Ali had kept telling him out of the side of her mouth. 'I'll go over to the house at the weekend while she's away and remove anything sharp.'

The whole thing had put a bit of a dampener on everybody, and Emma hadn't felt much like heading into work, especially when Phil was waiting to hand over to her, full of efficiency and professionalism.

'There you go, boss.' He handed her a sheaf of papers the minute she arrived: schedules, guest details, running orders.

He'd never called her boss before. But he was probably just being ironic, the way so many younger people were these days.

'Thank you,' she said, eyeing him carefully, and feeling ancient.

Hannie caught her eye now, and gave her a big, encouraging smile. She'd sent her a text earlier: 'Keeping your seat warm!'

Unfortunately Phil had plonked his arse in it before she'd got there: normally Emma sat between Patrick and Alannah, but she was so late that Phil had commandeered it, and she was forced to pull up a seat on the outskirts of the group.

Still, it may not have been deliberate; he'd been at the helm of the show all week, including that day's show. He would have just sat down there without even thinking.

But all the same she made plenty of noise as she settled in for the meeting — 'Morning, morning, great show earlier,' (which was a load of bollocks, it was a rubbish show, boring as hell) and watched as Phil sat a little taller.

Patrick and Alannah gave her a couple of

bland looks back, giving no indication at all of the clandestine meeting in the pub with her earlier in the week.

Not even Hannie knew. Emma felt bad about that, but what could she do? She hadn't told Adam yet. She had yet to work out what she was going to say at *that* meeting.

'I started running through some stuff for Monday while we were waiting for you,' Phil began, helpfully underlining her tardiness. 'If you want I can continue on.'

'Why? I'm here now.' And she smiled at him.

He held up his hands in a placatory gesture.

OK, now she was sure he was being a bit too crawly. And it didn't help that Hannie was making little sick motions behind his back.

'Let's get started, will we?' Patrick said.

He was starting to look restless, which was always dangerous. And, oh God, Alannah was beginning to worry at her enormous flowery shoulder bag, taking out notebooks and dinky jars of lip salve, and finally her little spray canister of Natural Relief Remedy.

'Anybody for some?' she offered brightly, after efficiently applying two squirts to her wrists.

'Not just at the moment,' Emma said hastily. She didn't want any trouble between them today; it might spoil the surprise for Monday.

She took the top page of Phil's notes now and discarded them casually on the table. 'I've decided not to run with the feature on how to draw up a household budget.'

Phil's face fell. 'But we spent ages putting that together.'

What he meant was, it was his idea. Why did men always love financial stuff? It was mostly women who watched the show, a lot of them while they made kids' lunches or put on their make-up before going to work. They didn't want to listen to budgets, and nor did Emma.

'Yes,' she said callously, 'but it's not right for the show.'

She was aware of Patrick and Alannah playing tennis with their eyes; watching and waiting to see how this one was going to pan out.

'We got feedback from the audience this week; they want us to do more serious stuff,' Phil insisted.

'What feedback?' Emma asked silkily.

Phil looked a bit sulky. 'Some emails and things.'

Yes, she'd heard about those. Hannie recognised one of the addresses as belonging to one of Phil's mates.

She was sure now that Phil was behind the news story about the alleged trouble on the set of the show. Not that she had any proof, except his mean, sly brown eyes.

She gave him the sweetest smile and said, 'I'm replacing it instead with a woman who allegedly has the biggest breasts in Ireland, thanks to plastic surgery.'

Alannah jerked. Patrick blinked. They knew she was sticking with more populist content, but *tits*? At dawn? Was the nation ready for it?

Even Hannie took her hand out of a Tupperware box long enough to look at her doubtfully. The programme had never been particularly noted for its high taste, but at least with people who could communicate with the dead you were pretty sure nobody was going to whip them out at any moment.

Phil said nothing; just sat there with his arms folded over his chest, disapproval wafting from his every pore. Oh dear, oh dear, his expression said; what's Adam going to think of *that*?

Emma had no idea. But she was going with it anyway. Adam was away all next week.

Hoping her voice sounded more confident than she felt, she went on briskly, 'Fidelma went from a 34B to a 42VV.'

While everybody else took a moment to mentally compute this, Patrick came right out with, 'Whey-*hey*.'

The man couldn't help himself. He just couldn't.

Alannah wasn't much better. '*What* did you just say?'

'You heard me.'

She turned stonily to Emma. 'I am not doing this feature. Not with a chauvinist pig who's going to spend the entire interview leering at someone's boobs.'

'Why do you think women get them enhanced?' he challenged her. 'So that men will look. And don't give me that crap about women doing it for themselves.'

Alannah spluttered, 'Why is it crap? Why do you automatically think everything we do is for your gratification?'

'Let's ask Fidelma on Monday,' said Patrick, rubbing his hands together in glee.

Hannie was looking at her, beaming alarm her way: *This is going to be a bloodbath.*

Emma gave her a little smile back. It had certainly got off to a great start.

★ ★ ★

The rest of the weekend stretched out ahead of her. Nothing to do and nowhere to go, except wait for Monday morning, and the show. She was jumpy and nervous. The apartment didn't help, what with Ali out nearly all the time with the kids, doing 'family' stuff with Kyle. Ali had invited her along on several of these family outings, but, honestly, the *atmosphere*. In Emma's opinion, someone should lock Ali and Kyle in a room together until they sorted something out.

Mind, she was a grand one to be giving advice. Thirty-two years of age and stuck at home on a Friday night, and she didn't even have to get up at four o'clock the following morning.

Hannie phoned her up. 'Let's go out and get off our faces.'

'No.'

'Please. I'm dying to have a bitch about Phil. What was he *doing* today, squaring up to you like that?'

'I don't know. I don't care.'

'He's after your job and you don't care?'

'I have a plan.'

But she'd said too much.

'What plan?' Hannie said immediately.

'I can't say.'

377

A little silence Hannie's end. 'I see.'

'Look, I just want to see how the show goes on Monday, OK? I don't want to go jinxing things by discussing it to death.'

'You're hardly discussing it to death. You haven't discussed it at all.' Hannie was very cool now. First Emma had held back big time on Ryan, and now it was work too.

'Adam doesn't like the breast enhancement slot,' Hannie told her with great dignity.

'How did he find out?'

'I have no idea. But I imagine it was Phil. Adam thinks it's not suitable for that hour of the morning.'

'I see. Well, thanks for telling me, Hannie. I really appreciate it.'

She hoped Hannie could tell that she was trying; that she just wasn't in a place right now to go spilling her guts about what had happened between her and Ryan. It was only five days since her test results had come through. She still looked at herself in the mirror in the mornings this way and that, unable to believe that she was really OK. Surely she should look different, or something. Surely she should feel better.

But she didn't. She still went around with a dead weight in her stomach and that funny feeling at the back of her throat that used to send her running to examine her tongue in Erin's pink magnifying mirror. She still felt tired, listless, prone to tears and very sad most of the time.

Yet the doctors said she was OK. Not a thing wrong with her. She had submitted the blood that ran through her veins to the guys in the

378

white coats, and had been told that it was sterling stuff. In fact, along with her HIV test, the doctor had run one for iron levels, as she'd been so pale that day. Her iron was terrific, he'd told her on Monday. She was so loaded up on phosphate that she could run a marathon in the morning.

Well, hurrah! Except that she didn't want to run a bloody marathon. She wanted to . . . what? She didn't know what she wanted to do.

Except that that was a lie.

She wanted to see Ryan.

Oops. Had she said that out loud?

Sneaky, insidious feelings. His face, always in her mind. Him, on an aeroplane, in a tent, a hotel, wherever the hell he was on this earth.

She should never have gone to see him that day. Seeing him again had taken her right back; opened everything up again, just when she thought she might possibly be getting used to living without him.

And now she was wondering whether you could ever go back from something like this. Could you go forward? Could you just . . . stand still for a little while, find each other again, see if you still fitted, and then worry about what might happen tomorrow?

She could hear Ali now: madness. Don't do it. Plenty of healthy specimens out there. Look upon it as a sign. For God's sake, *don't*.

'Yadda, yadda,' she told the end of the couch where Ali always sat, as she jumped up and grabbed her car keys.

★   ★   ★

He was back. His battered old car was outside. He always parked it at the airport when he was away, because he was forever leaving cameras behind in taxis and never seeing them again. At least in his own car they were bound to turn up sooner or later.

She sat outside in the dark, feeling like a stalker. Her heart was in a right old state, what with the excitement. And she knew then that it didn't matter, his illness; she couldn't possibly feel this way if it did.

They could do all the talking they needed to later: how they would get through things; support each other; plan for the future. But right now all she wanted to do was see his face again.

He was ages coming to the door. So long that she grew shivery and nervous on the doorstep, and wondered whether she should just sneak away before he'd ever known she was there.

But then the door opened and there he was, in his bare feet and khaki shorts, his hair shooting up at odd angles. She knew by the unfocused look on his face that he'd been lost in his computer, collating and editing the images he'd taken wherever he'd been this week.

It took him a couple of blinks to recognise her.

'Sorry if I'm disturbing you,' was the only thing she could think of to say. So much for the glorious, passionate reunion, him crumbling to his knees amid anguished croaks of, 'My God. You *came*.'

He looked a bit crotchety, actually. 'No, not at all,' he said, a bit unconvincingly. 'Come on in.'

He stepped past to let her in. She caught a

380

waft of his deodorant and for the first time she understood what they meant in those romance books when they used the word 'unhinged'.

She certainly was unhinged. She'd be undressed too, like a shot, if given half the chance.

But then Ryan said, politely, 'Tea?'

Now he was shuffling things around — washing, and take-out cartons, clearing the couch for her.

'Sorry the place is such a mess.' He always managed to sound surprised, even though his personal space was never anything *but* a mess. 'I'm just back.'

That was it. No detail. No, 'Thailand/Bulgaria/Bognor is beautiful in this weather.' Not even a bit of bloody small-talk to break the uncomfortable silence. Instead he hovered like a maiden aunt while she settled herself, and then he abandoned her to go through to the little kitchen to make the tea.

She watched him like a thief; his high, skinny bottom, his lean hips, his long brown legs, or at least from the knees down anyway. Wide, flat feet, with the little scars on them from that time he'd tried to walk on broken glass like all the other tribal boys he'd hooked up with in some outback, only the broken glass hadn't played ball.

She watched as he overfilled the kettle, left slops of milk on the counter, hunted for biscuits and then looked surprised when there weren't any.

No changes there then.

It was all she could do not to walk in behind him and put her arms around his waist and press her face hard against his eco T-shirt.

But he was turning briskly now and coming back with the tea, and he handed her a mug in such a way that their fingers didn't touch.

'So,' he said, after a sip, 'what's up?'

What was up? Could he not see, by looking into her eyes? Could he not tell, by the rather unseemly slick of perspiration on her upper lip? She couldn't wipe it off now without drawing attention to it. And she must stop jiggling her foot like that.

But Ryan didn't seem to notice. He kept his eyes trained firmly on hers, but in a detached kind of way.

Well, what had she expected? They'd hardly parted on the best of terms the last time she'd been here. And no doubt there was a good deal of anger and blame and resentment floating around, yet to find expression.

But that was all an aside. Something to be sorted out later on. Right now only one thing mattered.

'I came about us,' she said.

He didn't say anything. No immediate jumping up from his chair with wild whoops of jubilation.

But 'us' could mean anything. She could be there to return several pairs of socks he'd left behind, or to hand over his half of the electricity bill.

'You said you didn't want me as a friend. That you had enough friends.' Her eyes darted up to his. This was painful. 'I'm not here to be your friend, Ryan.'

That was as clear as she could put it without making a total eejit of herself. Hopefully he would join the dots himself. She dived into her tea again, cheeks suddenly aflame as she realised that he wasn't saying anything.

Eventually, after about ten minutes — no, twenty — he said, in this really weird *sighing* kind of voice, 'I see.'

He saw? What did he see? Whatever it was, it was a damn sight more than *she* saw.

'Not that I'm begging or anything,' she said jauntily, trying to claw back some bit of pride.

'No, no, I didn't mean to sound . . . ' What, flaccid? Totally fucking uninterested?

And after everything he had put her through in the last three months, too. She was getting mad now. He had a cheek! Not to mention a short memory span. Up to three months ago she had been his fiancée, the love of his life. Surely he hadn't gone off her that quickly. Here she was, not only offering to try again, but also accepting whatever the future might bring, because she wasn't the kind of person who did things by halves. She'd just more or less offered herself to him through thick and thin, and he didn't mean to sound . . . what, exactly?

He may have seen steam starting to come from her ears, because he eventually stirred himself enough to say, 'Look, thanks for coming around. It's good to see you.' At least that much sounded genuine. 'But I don't think it would work.'

Just like that. Straight out, no frills. No sparing of feelings.

'I see,' she said, nice and bright. Well, she was damned if she was going to start sobbing and wailing. 'Clearly, you've thought about it.'

He must have anticipated her coming round here at some point, and making a total fool of herself. Oh, the mortification.

But then he said, 'I've thought about nothing else.'

And the room was suddenly alive with electricity.

But not for long. 'And it's never going to be the same. It'll always be there, no matter how hard we try to pretend it isn't.'

This was some rollercoaster. Before he could raise her hopes and wreck them again, she interjected, 'Of course it's always going to be there, but it doesn't invalidate everything else.'

'Brave words,' he said, in a way that annoyed her.

'Yes, they are. This is a big decision for me too, you know.'

'You see, this is exactly what I mean,' he said excitedly. 'We'd be starting out with a sense of obligation on your part, which you'd be trying to hide all the time. And I'd always be feeling guilty that I'm never going to be the kind of husband you thought I was going to be.'

It took a moment to register with him. 'Obviously, I didn't mean *husband*. It just slipped out. I meant, man. Um, boyfriend. Whatever.'

She enjoyed his puce-ridden face for a moment.

'And you don't think we can overcome your prejudice?' she asked him tartly.

That took him back a bit. Good.

'Mine? We were talking about yours.'

They looked at each other suspiciously for a bit.

'Obviously, we'd need to talk further,' he eventually declared. 'If we were to see whether we had a future.'

'Obviously,' she concurred.

They both did a bit of furious nodding.

'How about Tuesday?' he said.

'Tuesday might be good for me.'

'I'll give you a ring.'

'No. I'll give *you* a ring.' And she left.

25

Ali

In the end they went for a walk in the park the evening before Kyle was due to fly back.

It was the first time they'd spent any time alone in the week he'd been home.

'Are you sure she can cope?' he said anxiously, as they drove away from the apartment, leaving Emma to look after the kids.

After his week with them, he seemed to have developed a fresh understanding of how, well, demanding kids could be. How much work. How so much time had to be spent cajoling and placating, and making endless rounds of toast with jam (with no lumpy bits in it. Very important, that).

'Emma will be fine.' Of anybody, Emma had the best handle on them. Anto rarely misbehaved on her watch. Ali wasn't quite sure how Emma managed it, but there was a look in her eye that invited absolutely no messing.

She would be a great mother herself some day. That's if she ever managed to move on, instead of fancying herself as some kind of Florence Nightingale to ailing ex-boyfriends.

Ali had tried her best to get Emma interested in a night on the town. 'We should go out. Two single ladies like us. You never know who we might meet!'

But Emma had given her a look like she'd just suggested they walk down Grafton Street wearing thongs.

'You go if you want,' Emma had said kindly. 'But I'm going to take a little time to recover from my broken engagement before I go looking for casual sex.'

Honestly! So fucking superior! And what was wrong with casual sex, anyway? Not a damn thing (if you used the proper protection, it hardly need be said). Ali would *welcome* some casual sex.

Actually, thinking about it, she couldn't be arsed. Sex had never been the problem in her life. It was everything else that was missing.

Anyway, so there they were in the park, her and Kyle, him looking anxiously at the ground before every step. Ireland had a serious problem with dog poo, he'd maintained all week. Two pairs of cowboy boots had already been sullied.

She cast a sideways look at him. He seemed so out of place, so staunchly himself, as they passed pink tracksuited joggers and laughing young couples out enjoying the evening sun. But he'd never been that comfortable in Ireland. He'd never really been comfortable outside his home state, come to think of it.

At least *she* had given their kids a wider perspective on the world. She doubted he would agree with her, but they knew there was life elsewhere on the planet, even if it didn't always contain Hershey bars.

OK, somebody had better say *something*. It would be getting dark soon, and both of them were puffing a bit, and trying to hide it, what with the brisk pace Kyle had set them. But if Ali slowed down it would be admitting defeat, and so she trotted along beside him.

'I think — ' she said.

'The kids — ' he began simultaneously.

It broke the ice a little.

Ali gave a little laugh. 'You first.'

'I was just going to say that the kids seem to be having an OK time here.'

Well, she nearly fell over.

All right, so he didn't say they were having a swell time, but an OK time was some concession indeed. They weren't being tortured, in other words, or starved, or forced to learn *Riverdance* routines twelve hours a day.

'Thank you,' she said. She felt obliged to meet him part-way. 'It's been good for them to see you this week. They've missed you.'

Kyle gave a short laugh. 'I don't know about that.'

Another concession! Ali was feeling better and better. And to think she'd been dreading this talk. Really, all Kyle had wanted was an opportunity to unburden himself about how *right* she had been in all this.

'They have,' she said, a bit gushingly. 'It's important that they still see you, Kyle.'

She was feeling very chummy now, as they side-stepped another lump of dog poo.

But clearly she'd misread Kyle, because he threw her an odd look, and asked, in a funny, tight voice, 'Why did you do it?'

'Do what?'

He stopped dead now and faced her. And she saw that he'd been building all week to this; he'd just been biding his time. His face was volcanic red and his lip trembling. 'You took my kids away from me. I didn't see them for *six weeks*. Can you imagine how that felt, Ali?'

The longest she herself had ever gone was three days, when she went away with June and Eileen for a reunion weekend. The first day had been great. The second day she'd kept wondering what was missing. By the third day she couldn't wait to fill her nostrils with the smell of them.

'I — ' she began defensively.

But he thundered on, 'Jack's birthday is next month — am I going to have to miss that too?'

Jack's birthday. Damn. It had completely slipped her mind in the midst of everything. How terrible.

And there was Kyle, so upset, so pinched-looking. 'You had no right. I'm their father. Did you stop to think for one minute what it's been like for me, my kids all the way over here and you telling me they're never coming back?'

He sounded like he was trying not to cry.

Kyle. On the verge of tears. She'd never seen that before, ever, not even that long afternoon when he'd tried to explain the rules of baseball to her.

But this was different. She felt terrible. All those nights, when he must have wondered where they were . . . And she hadn't phoned

389

once, or even sent a lousy text message saying, '*Póg mo shón*' (Kiss my arse, in Irish). In the circumstances, his restraint this week had been quite remarkable.

Hold on, though. Before she got too maudlin on his behalf, whose fault was this whole thing anyway? And why was she just standing there, letting herself be sucked into his emotional blackmail?

'I have only two words to say to you,' she said coldly.

His eyes narrowed.

'Calvin Crawford.'

If she was waiting for him to dissolve into a puddle of guilt, it appeared she could be hanging around for some time.

'What did you expect?' he said roughly. 'That I was going to let you romp around Ireland with my kids, without doing a single thing to try and get them back?'

'So you cut off my money? Left me here with no means of support, and three children to feed?'

'You were with family. They weren't going to let you starve.' And he eyed her midriff.

She found herself pulling in her belly defensively. 'Let's get one thing straight here. If it wasn't for you, I'd never have left Texas in the first place!'

'You didn't 'leave'. You snuck out in the middle of the night like a thief.'

'I was scared!'

He scoffed at that. 'I've never seen you scared in your life.'

She was really infuriated now. 'I suppose you're going to deny it now. That you threatened to take the kids from me?'

He sighed. 'We were having a row, Ali. I was upset, for God's sake.'

He needn't think it was going to be that easy. 'You said those words. You told me that night that if I divorced you, I wasn't going to get the kids.' It was as fresh in her mind as if it had happened yesterday. 'I never thought you were capable of something like that.' She let disappointment drip from every word. 'Of all the things you could have said to me, I never expected that.'

'All right!' He raked back his hair. There was precious little of it left these days. He looked like a tired, middle-aged man who had lost his way a bit. 'I'm sorry, OK? But you had all the answers that day. You were going to do whatever you wanted, just like always, and I'd have to fit in with your plans. And maybe I didn't want to. Maybe I wanted to fight it.'

'Fight *what*, though? The end of something that you knew was coming for flipping ten years? More?'

He wouldn't look at her. She touched his arm, forcing him to turn; willing him to be honest in this. 'We've been going through the motions for a long time now, Kyle.'

He examined his boots; looked back at her. Said stubbornly, 'We have kids, Ali.'

That was Ethel speaking. She could even picture her, her bony, cross face berating Ali behind her back, asking Kyle what had he expected, marrying a flighty Irish girl who clearly had loose morals as well as knickers? He might have known that she would fly the coop eventually, with no thought at all for those poor, defenceless little children (even though both Jack and Anto topped her by about a foot, and what Erin lacked in height she more than made up for in attitude).

Oh, yes. Ethel and Hal had had a hand in this all right.

'Don't do the blackmail thing,' she asked him quietly.

'It's not blackmail! We owe it to them to at least give things a go.'

'Give *what* a go? We were practically children when we got married. Eighteen years of age. Parents when we were nineteen. We barely knew each other!'

It was a cliché, but it was true; they were different people now. Not a whole hell of a lot in Kyle's case, but as for Ali, she felt hardly any connection at all to the pale girl who'd stood in the registry office that day, a loose navy dress hiding her bump (Ethel thought white would be scandalous), holding on tight to Kyle's hand, her own cold and clammy with the uneasy knowledge that the whole thing was a gigantic mistake, only she didn't have the courage to go against it.

But Kyle wasn't in that space, she could see.

'What is it you want?' he said, looking rather bewildered. 'A job? Is that it? You can work in a shoe shop back home, if that's what you so desperately want.'

Sixteen years together, and he thought that the height of her ambitions was selling shoes in some mall? Did he not remember those early days when he'd encouraged her to go back to college; insisted, in fact, that she better herself? That the two of them would have degrees and Ph.D.s coming out of their ears? She could be a doctor, he'd whispered to her one night, or an FBI agent (she'd once expressed an interest) or the first woman in space (she'd missed that one by a mile too).

She wondered when his expectations had fallen so low. And when had her own?

'I want a career,' she clarified coolly. 'I've put in my time, Kyle. I want to move on.'

She didn't say, from you. But she might as well have.

Her face must have shown how very immovable she was. How certain. He looked at her for a very long moment, and then away. His shoulders fell. Fine, his body language said. Do what you want; you will anyway.

What he didn't recognise yet was his own sense of relief. But that would come, too. Kyle was the kind who would take a little while to get over things, but Ali would bet he'd be back on the local dating scene by Christmas.

She hoped so, anyway. She wished him nothing but the best.

'Kyle?' she prodded gently.

'Yes,' he said. 'I know.'

So that was it: them, discussion over. It had taken less than five minutes. Her eyes felt a bit prickly. But it'd be a bit rich now to burst into uncontrollable tears of regret, and so she just stood there quietly, eyes fixed on his checked shirt, red tonight, while he dug his hands hard into the pockets of his jeans, and rolled back and forth on the heels of his cowboy boots.

Eventually, she said, 'What do we do about the kids?'

There was a long silence. He said, 'Well, Jack doesn't want to live with either of us. So I guess we need to set him up in an apartment somewhere.'

She didn't get it for a moment; that he was joking.

'Oh!' She smiled. It felt like the weirdest thing. Kind of sick, yet enjoyable.

'He's after turning into an awful pup,' Kyle declared grimly. He was coming back to himself now that it was time to give out about the kids. It was the one thing that had always united them: just how to keep the little buggers in check.

'He's a teen. He'll be all right. And he needs to talk about Carly, by the way.'

Kyle took a moment. 'With *me*?'

This wasn't his territory at all. Well, he'd better start getting used to it. 'Yes. It's a male thing.'

Kyle looked alarmed. 'I don't even know Carly. Anyway, I thought it was all over?'

'Judging by the amount of texting he's doing, I'd say it could be back on.'

'Is she the one with the . . . ?'

'Shorts. Yes.'

'She's too fast for him.' This, from a man who had worn the faces off half the neighbourhood girls at the same age. Ali would bet he'd have a few tips for the bold Jack.

'He's fifteen, Kyle. He doesn't want to talk to me about stuff like that.'

'You're just trying to butter me up now.'

Canny. 'Yes and no,' she conceded. 'The point is they need us both, Kyle. Especially now that we're getting divorced.'

Horrible word. Kyle didn't like it much either. But Ali found that she was fast getting used to it. But then again, she had moved on in her head a long time ago.

It was growing chilly in the park now, and she hugged her elbows. They hadn't got to the hard part yet.

She might as well just come out with it. 'What about this Calvin Crawford bloke?' As always, the name was enough to induce a bout of nausea. 'Are you going to call him off or what?'

Kyle left enough of a pause to bring her out in a sweat.

'Yes,' he said eventually.

OK fantastic — but what did that actually *mean*? Was he taking it all back, the threat to fight for custody? Was Calvin Crawford going to remain in the background, some shadowy figure in a pinstripe suit, poised forever over expensive headed notepaper?

'I guess the kids should stay with you,' he said quietly.

It was like someone had lifted a concrete block off her chest. All the worry of the last six weeks wafted away on the breeze.

She was afraid to breathe out, in case she said

something that would piss him off all over again. So she just stayed quiet.

'You're good with them, Ali. You're great with them.' He considered this. 'In a sort of weird, chaotic way. And you know I don't agree with what you feed them. Also, if you don't mind me saying so, you need to tighten up big time on things like bedtimes. Anto totally takes you for a ride — '

'OK.' She put a hand up. 'If you've got some things you want to say, fine. We'll sit down and discuss them, come to some accommodation.'

She sounded normal but inside she was shouting at the top of her voice. He was giving in. Backing down. Backing *off*. Whatever way you wanted to put it.

He wasn't going to try to take her kids off her. It was all over, bar the niggling details about bedtimes and meals.

She looked at him with such a wave of affection, no, of *love*, that it was all she could do not to jump upon him and clamp her legs around his thighs snugly while she planted little kisses of gratitude all over his plump red face.

Still, that might just give him the wrong idea, and so she kept some physical distance; she did offer him a lovely smile, though. Almost shyly, she said, 'Thank you, Kyle. You won't regret this, I promise you. And I'll do something about all the tuna they eat. I know you have mercury concerns.'

He nodded back and, really, it was a moment of true beauty: two people, despite their hideous cultural, intellectual and emotional differences, coming together seamlessly for the sake of the greater good. She decided she felt closer to him at that moment than she ever had in her life before. He was a *king*.

'So,' he said, smiling back, 'when are you and the kids flying home?'

The romantic background music that had been playing in Ali's head came screeching to a halt.

'Fly *home*?'

He clearly didn't notice her narkiness.

'The kids have missed enough school already,' he said pompously. 'And that's nothing against Irish schools, so don't get all defensive. But they need to get back into their routine. I'll get someone in to clean the house and fix some groceries for when you get home.'

The nerve of him! Barely five minutes officially separated and already he was trying to organise her life for her — right down to *groceries*.

'Actually,' she said coolly, 'I'm not sure yet when we're going back.'

He was confused. Maybe it was understand-able. And maybe she didn't give a damn.

'I thought it would be good for them to spend some time in Ireland,' she elaborated.

'They *have* spent time in Ireland. Weeks and weeks.'

'Which isn't much, compared to their whole lives in America! This is their *home*land, Kyle.'

'It is not. Texas is their home. Why do you always have to start this?' There was that familiar irritation in his eyes; this, from someone who

397

didn't even bother to come home for the annual holiday any more, and who refused to dress up in a big green hat on St Patrick's Day. Oh, very balanced!

'I want them to know their roots.'

Another inflammatory concept. More rolling of eyes. 'Gimme a break. They're dying to get back.'

'They're settling in very well, actually.' Erin had made four new best friends in school that week. Ali wasn't sure whether they'd been won over or conquered. 'And I really think Anto has improved enormously now that he has only the local Spar at his disposal, instead of all those malls.'

'And what about Jack?' Kyle threw out.

Yes. He was a tough nut. Especially as Ali suspected Carly was back on the scene or, certainly, on his phone.

'It's not going to be for ever,' she said. 'I wouldn't do that to you. I know we have to go back eventually, OK?'

She might know it in her head; her heart was the problem.

'Just give me a bit of time, Kyle, please? You've been great today. And I appreciate it. I really do. All I'm asking for is a bit of breathing space to organise things. There's family stuff with Mam and Dad, and I'm just not sure about Emma yet.'

He knew Emma and Ryan's engagement was off, but that was all.

'Also, I don't want to wrench the kids from school just after they've started. I need to make plans in my own time and then I'll be home.'

He looked at her through narrowed eyes. For a moment she was worried that he would refuse to get on that plane tomorrow until they'd sorted out flight reservations for the rest of the family.

'I promise,' she told him.

He let out a breath. 'OK. You've got a couple of weeks. But Ali? If you let me down . . . '

'I won't.'

26

Emma

Emma was getting ready to go out a week later when Ali pounced.

'You're back with him, aren't you?'

'No, I'm not. We're just talking.'

'Nobody puts that amount of make-up on to go and talk.'

Ali had some cheek, and she plastered in the stuff herself. She put on eyeshadow that matched her tracksuit just to go to the supermarket, for feck's sake.

'*And* you stink to high heaven of Lynx,' Ali said accusingly.

That wasn't intentional on Emma's part. But her stash of Molton Brown products had been reduced to a collection of sad, misshapen bottles that somebody had tried to re-fill with Radox in the hopes of fooling her. Her perfume, also, seemed to have evaporated bottle by bottle, although Ali smelled particularly fragrant these days. The only deodorant left in the place was Jack's Lynx; normally Emma wouldn't have touched it, but needs must.

'What are you two talking about, anyway?' Ali demanded.

'None of your business.'

'It is my business. You're my sister, and I'm

entitled to let you know my opinion, even if you don't want it.'

'Ali, I'm running late, so if you don't mind . . . '

But Ali remained standing in the doorway, arms crossed. 'You know you'll never have sex in comfort again, don't you?'

'Dear God.'

'Don't tell me it's not at the back of your mind too.'

'It is not!' Emma insisted, even as her thighs twitched in an unhinged kind of way.

But there was no sex. No *hint* of sex. When she'd said talking, she'd really meant it. They talked about his work, her work, his positive test, her negative test, the future, how they would deal with it, how they might *fail* to deal with it, when he might have to go on medication, how she would cope if he got sick . . . There was nothing they *didn't* talk about. Heavy, earnest conversations over strong coffees and low-alcohol beers, with both of them desperate to be as honest as possible. After one of these sessions, they normally switched to the economy at the end just for a little light relief.

'You can't have babies either,' Ali commented.

Emma threw down her hairbrush. 'Ali, would you just go away?'

'I know you don't want to think about these things, now that you're all caught up in this reconciliation business, but someone needs to point out to you the hard facts of living with someone with that kind of disease.'

'I can work those things out for myself, thank

you. And anyway, we *can* have babies. Hypothetically speaking, of course. He can have his sperm washed.'

'You can wash *sperm*?' Ali looked intrigued.

'Obviously not at sixty degrees.' This was a dig at Ali. She didn't understand the function of the energy-saving button on the washing machine. Everything went in on a hot wash, and usually came out pink. 'You isolate the sperm, test it to see if it's OK, and then you can, you know, use it.'

Ali looked at her accusingly. 'You've researched this!'

Emma's cheeks exploded into colour. 'Well, yes . . . not actively, I just happened to come across it on the Internet.'

'That old chestnut,' Ali cried. 'That was Kyle's excuse the time I found bondage sites in his history, remember?' Then she crossly planted her hands on her hips. 'You cannot possibly be considering rearing kids with Ryan.'

'As opposed to what? A dog?'

This entire conversation was too close to the bone, because if they *did* get back together, then the future would loom; marriage and kids had been on the horizon six months ago, so why not now?

Maybe because of the reasons Ali was intent on laying out in her usual sledgehammer style.

She was off again. 'Supposing Ryan gets sick? And you have a rake of kids to look after too? How are you going to cope?'

'Not a rake. Maybe just two.'

Had she just said that? Clearly, her subconscious was doing more planning than she'd realised.

' 'Just two.' No offence, Emma, but you have no idea how hard it is to bring up children.'

Her own were, at that moment, 'baking something' in the kitchen. She didn't seem to notice at all that the smell of burning was beginning to permeate the apartment.

'I can learn from you,' Emma told her, tongue-in-cheek.

'Well, yes,' Ali conceded modestly, 'but all I'm saying is, you don't want to go saddling yourself.'

Saddle. It was a word she used a lot in relation to Ryan. It made Emma think of a three-legged nag who was one hoof away from the knacker's yard; Ryan, who was nothing like that, who was tall and strong and full of energy.

'Maybe *I* might get sick. Have you thought of that? People contract all sorts of things, not just HIV. Ryan might end up having to look after *me*. Who knows what might happen?' She knew she sounded cross but, honestly, Ali came out with pure crap half the time.

Of course, Ali had time on her hands now. Always dangerous. Or, rather, she was making time. Putting off the moment when she'd have to pack her bags and go home.

'Your chances of getting sick are much lower than his,' she insisted to Emma. 'I just think you have to look at the practicalities here, and not let yourself be swept away by emotion.'

'Like you've never done that.'

'I may have lived to regret some of my

403

decisions, yes,' Ali conceded. 'Which is why I'm imparting my knowledge to you now.'

'No, you're not. You just don't want me to get together with Ryan. Or any man, actually. You haven't liked a single one I've ever gone out with.'

'At least none of them had HIV.'

The baldness of it brought the conversation to a momentary standstill. Emma knew Ali was just trying to protect her, but at the same time there were limits.

She took a little breath. 'Please don't reduce him to just that.'

'I'm only stating a fact.' But then she leaned against the doorjamb and gave a little sigh. 'I just want you to be happy. That's all.'

'I am happy.' Happy-ish, anyway, if it was possible to be happy at all whilst in the middle of negotiations that didn't seem to be reaching a conclusion at any time in the near future. All this talking was lovely and healthy and necessary, but at some point they were going to have to make a decision, weren't they?

She began to wonder now whether Ali was right. Maybe things *had* changed, and there was no going back. They could pretend all they liked that his illness didn't matter, but what if, at the end of the day, they were wrong?

'And what about him?' Ali prodded. 'I suppose he's desperate to get back with you.'

Her tone said that it would suit him very well; that it was unlikely he'd find anybody else to take him on.

'Actually no,' Emma said coolly. 'He's not

rushing into it either.'

'I'm only saying these things because I'm worried about you.'

Emma decided it was time to throw it back at her. 'And I'm worried about you. Especially as it's been a week since Kyle went home and he must be wondering where the hell you are.'

Ali wasn't pleased. All week long she'd wormed out of this exact conversation. Her chin went up.

'Who says I'm going home? I might not be.' It had all the conviction of a toddler doing a spot of foot-stamping. 'The longer we're here, the more difficult it's going to be to uproot the kids. Erin got a star in school today, for being kind to other pupils.'

This was more to do with the fact that she divvied out sweets at break, even though they were banned, than any spectacular act of humanity.

'And Anto said the word 'grand' today. You should have been there, Emma. Someone asked him how he was, and instead of saying, 'I'm cool,' he said, 'I'm grand.' In a little Irish accent!'

'Wonderful. Of course you must stay.'

Ali looked uncertain. 'You're being sarcastic, aren't you?'

'Of course I am! Why don't you just come out and admit it? You don't want to stay here for the kids. You want to stay for yourself.'

Ali laughed merrily. 'I left for America at eighteen, remember?'

'Yes, because you couldn't think of anywhere else to go. You could just as easily have pitched up in the West Indies.'

'I love the States,' Ali said loyally. 'Where else in the world can you get chocolate fudge doughnuts at three in the morning?'

And she looked down at her hips doubtfully.

Emma regarded her affectionately. 'You're an ex-pat, Ali. That's all. There're loads of you out there, who can't stop dreaming of the auld sod, and hoping some day that you'll come back.'

Mind you, most of them stopped short of indoctrinating their children with Irish folk tales and a language nobody used any more, not even in Ireland.

Ali gave a little sigh and conceded, 'I just feel so *different* there. Imagine. After all these years.'

'You *are* different,' Emma assured her, but kindly.

'I'm having such a great time, being back. Why can't they too?' she said crossly, jerking her head towards the kitchen. 'Is something burning?'

'Yes.'

'Damn.'

And she set off at a gallop out of the room. 'Oh, and that guy Adam phoned your mobile while you were in the shower,' she threw over her shoulder. 'I picked up.'

'You answered my *phone*?'

'He wants you to call him back.' Then the kitchen door slammed behind her. A moment later Emma heard shouting, and then the extractor fan going on full blast.

So. Adam was speaking to her again. Well, to Ali anyhow, God help him. Who knew what she'd said to him: probably that Emma was in the tub having a full leg wax as they spoke, in the hopes of getting back with her diseased ex-fiancé.

Although Ali would never divulge Ryan's HIV status. Not after that argument they'd had during the week about Mam and Dad, and whether they should be told; quite a humdinger too.

'They have a right,' Ali had kept insisting.

'To what? Ryan's private information?'

'If you two get back together you're going to have to tell them. It wouldn't be fair otherwise.'

'We'll deal with that if and when it happens. But in the meantime, it's completely Ryan's decision who he tells and when, and you'd better respect that or I swear to God I'll never speak to you again.'

'Jesus. Enough of the threats. Just so long as you know that you're going to have to widen the circle of knowledge at *some* point. You don't want them finding out from a friend of his mother's again in the supermarket.'

OK, so she had a point. But not just yet; not when things were still so fragile between her and Ryan.

And anyhow, poor Mam couldn't cope with any more change at the moment. Not now that Tina had practically moved in and taken over (Mam's words).

'She was baking in the kitchen today,' she'd raged on the phone earlier. She rang most days to give out. 'There was never any agreement about baking.'

'She was making Dad's lunch. Not baking.'

'*I* make his lunch. *She* doesn't make his lunch.'

'Mam, you're going to have to stop antagonising her. She was very upset on Tuesday when you locked her out of the house again.'

Mam had been sulky. 'It was a mistake. Why will nobody believe me?'

It wasn't looking good. And to think that Tina had been Mam's idea in the first place. Tina had looked after her so well that weekend in Liam's — warmed slippers, comfy chairs, home-made brown bread — that Mam had suggested that she would be the perfect person to provide relief care for Dad.

That was the one thing over which there had been no discussion: Mam was no longer 'in a position' (everybody would clear their throats over that one) to look after Dad; it was 'too much' for one person (more clearing of throats), and everybody, particularly Mam, would 'benefit' (major coughing fits now) from having another pair of hands around the place.

They'd looked at agencies. Mam said no. She'd prefer someone she knew.

'I hope you don't mean me,' Ali had said in horror.

'Certainly not,' Mam had said, equally horrified.

As it happened, Tina's kids were all in school now, and she'd been looking around for work, but could find nothing.

Mam had been thrilled. They would be bosom buddies. And Dad liked her too, even though she was a bit loud. But then again he was used to

408

Mam shouting at him, so after a day or two he'd acclimatised. And she let him snooze on the couch in the mornings for as long as he liked, and she didn't grumble when he needed to use the bathroom three times every hour. Best of all, she had a robust interest in current affairs, or at least let on she did, and Dad was able to show off his extensive knowledge of budgetary details, and the situation in Niger.

Everybody agreed that he looked very well these days, and had even got a bit of his old boorishness back, but that was a small price to pay.

But as for *Mam*. She went around for two days calling Tina 'a miracle worker', and declaring that she now had her life back. But on day three, when Tina had apparently invaded Mam's personal space in the kitchen (she'd brushed up against her whilst reaching for a mug), all hell had broken loose. Tina had gone home, declaring that she would never set foot in the house again. She'd had to be coaxed back with a Clinique hamper and a pay rise. They'd all had to sit down with Mam and go over some ground rules: she would stay out of the house in the mornings, while Tina was doing her thing with Dad. There would be a crossover period of an hour around lunchtime, and during that time Mam would confine herself to the living room, and Tina to the TV room. Any complaints from either side were to be put down in writing, containing no bad language, and Emma would read the complaints and then mediate.

This complaints system did not preclude Mam

from ringing up her daughters and bitching bitterly about the size of Tina's backside — 'You can't get past her without pressing up against it' — or the way she held Dad's arm when he was getting in and out of the car — 'He had a big bruise on his elbow yesterday, she had a grip like a bulldozer.'

But it was only a week into the new arrangement. Time, everybody said. Time, and hopefully Mam keeping her cool. But there were no guarantees on that one.

But first, Adam. Emma put Mam, Tina and Ryan out of her head and went in search of her phone.

★ ★ ★

'What's all this about you rebranding the show?' Adam's voice was very, very quiet; possibly the quietest she'd ever heard it. She had to press the phone hard to her ear to hear.

'Adam,' she said calmly. 'You're back.'

He said nothing to this. She didn't pursue any enquiries as to whether he'd had a good time.

'On Monday you feature a woman with the biggest breasts in Ireland, and on Tuesday we entertained a swingers' club?'

'Just two members of it,' Emma clarified. She wasn't being smart. But it wasn't as though they'd hosted an entire convention, and provided double beds with black silk sheets for their convenience. 'Did you see Wednesday's show?' she said.

She knew he had. She would bet he'd watched

410

the whole five shows back to back before phoning her up. Phil had probably recorded them for him.

'We had a born-again Christian on,' she reminded him. You couldn't get much duller than that, in other words. In fact, the guest had turned out to be so boring that Patrick ignored him entirely to have a go at Alannah because she happened to mention that she wasn't so much religious as 'spiritual'.

'*Spiritual?*' He'd been magnificently derisive. 'What kind of rubbish is that?'

Alannah had retaliated, 'At least I don't trot off to Mass once a year on Christmas Eve like you.'

'Where do you go then, Stonehenge? And dance around it in your designer sandals?'

They'd almost had to be separated that day. Afterwards they'd counted nearly five hundred texts from viewers exercised by the debate. Nobody had mentioned the born-again Christian.

'You didn't tell me what you were doing,' Adam said now, worryingly quiet.

'But I didn't do anything.' Technically, anyway.

'You're being facetious now.'

'Look, I'm just trying to breathe a bit of life into this show.'

'By letting those two nut jobs at each other?'

'They're not nut jobs. They're simply polar opposites. And they make good television, if only they were let.'

'You saw what happened the last time they were 'let'. They walked off the set.'

411

'Only because they can't operate in the format we're imposing upon them.'

'It's breakfast television, Emma. We're not reinventing the bloody wheel here.'

'You're speaking like we should just settle for mediocrity.'

His voice began to rise. 'I think you're just trying to achieve a little notoriety before we get the axe in June.'

There. It was out. Adam saying they were getting the axe was about as official as it got. And in a way Emma felt better. She really had nothing to lose now. All her nerves melted away and she spoke with more confidence than she'd ever felt before. 'Patrick and Alannah were great this week. They set the screen on fire. You mightn't have liked the woman with the biggest breasts in Ireland — I wasn't mad keen on the idea myself — but I needed something controversial to kick-start the pair of them. And it did, and it worked, and that was the best show we've made in nearly two years.'

She must have sounded quite impassioned, because Adam said nothing for a moment.

Then: 'You're assuming people want to watch confrontation all the time. And sometimes they do. But not necessarily at seven o'clock in the morning, when they're just out of bed. A lot of the time they just want to catch the news headlines and maybe what's in the papers.'

And Emma felt sick again. He could well be right. She'd just run with her gut instinct this week, without putting a huge amount of thought into it. Supposing people *didn't* want to watch aggro? Supposing it was just her who found Patrick and Alannah endlessly entertaining?

'I suppose we'll have to see,' she said, sounding braver than she felt.

'Yes,' he said. 'The ratings will be in on Monday.'

She felt her stomach lurch.

'And, Emma? Don't ever do something like this again without telling me.'

★ ★ ★

Ryan had cleaned the place; at least, you could see some surfaces, and all his camera stuff was packed away so that Emma didn't have to worry about smashing a priceless lens every time she took a step.

'Nice shorts,' she said, as an opener.

He wore voluminous Hawaiian-style jobs that would nearly blind you, even though it was only about ten degrees outside.

He laughed. So did she. And then it petered out and everything was all tense again. He turned away to search for a take-out menu — 'Chinese OK for you?' — while she stood about like a plonker waiting for an invitation to sit down.

It had never been like this. With Ryan, you couldn't be anything but easy-going. He didn't do stress, or standing on ceremony. And when she was with him, she'd been the same.

But now it was there between them all the time: his 'status'. How could it not be, when the two dates they'd had in the past week had been

413

entirely about it? Tonight was scheduled for more of the same. She couldn't even remember the chosen theme; was it societal perceptions and prejudices about HIV-positive people, or just hers? Or maybe his?

'Chicken chow mein?' he asked.

He looked tired. Her mind immediately flew to his CD4 count (down?) and his viral load (up?) before she told herself to just stop. He was fine. His doctors had told him so. He would probably go for another couple of years without even having to start medication.

The most likely explanation was that he'd stayed up too late on his computer, editing photographs, which used to happen at least three times a week when they'd lived together.

But it was hard not to analyse every little cough or sigh. The last time she'd been here she found herself staring at a rash on his arm until he'd grown quite embarrassed. 'Eczema,' he ended up saying. 'I've always had it.'

Now she couldn't stop staring at the bags under his eyes.

'Chicken chow mein?' he repeated, looking wary now.

OK. This couldn't go on, not for one minute longer. Someone had to do something.

'No,' she said.

'What?'

'We're going out to eat.'

He didn't want to. She knew by his face. Him, the one-time party animal. She knew that he'd barely set foot out of the house since his diagnosis. He didn't need to explain that he felt

414

different; marked; she'd already guessed that.

'Where?'

She had no idea. She just wanted to get out of here; to get away from the elephant in the room.

'The beach.'

'But . . . it's seven o'clock in the evening.'

She looked him in the eye. 'Six months ago you'd have been well up for it.'

'Six months ago you wouldn't have suggested it.'

'Well, I am now. Do you want to come or not?'

He thought about it for a second. 'Fine. I'll get the rug.'

And he did, and two pink buckets and spades belonging to his nieces, just in case she got bored, he said, and they set off in her car, stopping for the takeaway *en route*.

'It'll be cold when we get there,' he remarked.

That did it. She swung round in her seat. 'Since when did you turn into such a moan?'

'And what about you? Miss Conviviality all of a sudden.'

'I think it suits me, actually.'

And he started laughing. 'Yeah, till Monday morning and you have to get up at four o'clock and *then* who'll be a big fat moan.'

She put her foot down then and drove quite fast, the way Anto was always urging her to do. If only it was a sexy convertible, and not a Ford Focus, they could have had their hair blowing in the breeze, like in the movies.

Most movies didn't have potentially terminal illnesses lurking in the background, though. Ah, well. You couldn't have everything.

The beach, predictably, was deserted when they got there. They sat on the rug, freezing, as they ate cold noodles, and Ryan kept drawling, 'Great idea. No, really, one of your best.'

'Shut up.'

In the end, the breeze got so stiff that they had goose bumps all over their arms and legs, and they had to huddle together for warmth, like the penguins in the South Pole.

There was no awkwardness in having to snuggle up. It was raw necessity.

'Well, this is romantic,' Ryan remarked after a minute, plucking a stray string of cold noodle from her hair and flinging it at a nearby seagull.

'At least we're not talking,' she said.

'I know. It's a relief. I wouldn't mind if I never spoke to you again. If you know what I mean.'

'Yes. Definitely.'

'Come on. Let's make a sand castle.'

'Are you mad?'

'We're not admitting defeat and going home yet.'

So they kneeled on the sand, with the pink buckets and spades. Ryan, typical man, began to construct a fortress-like job with moats and walls and all kinds of complicated-looking fortifications. He got terribly excited about it, and kept urging her to 'look how big mine is'.

She ended up abandoning her own efforts and going in search of shells to decorate his castle, and feathers and stray ice-lolly sticks to put on top. 'How did I end up being an accessory?' she grumbled.

'Yes, but you do it so well,' he assured her.

416

Eventually, just as it was getting dark, he seemed satisfied. He stood back in his psychedelic shorts and appraised it. 'What do you think?'

'Magnificent,' Emma assured him. 'Now, can we go home?'

'In a minute. You still haven't told me what you think.'

She realised then he meant them. She kicked at a bit of sand and looked back at him. 'I don't know. What do *you* think?'

'I think,' he said, 'that maybe you don't realise what you're getting into.'

'What, because you've got some disease that might or might not make you sick some day?'

'It's not just some disease. Can we please stop pretending that it is?' He looked at her a little desperately. 'I've been afraid to even kiss you in the last week.'

'Let's do it now then. Get it over with.'

'How flattering.'

'I mean it. We're going to have to do it sometime. And we're going to have to sleep together too, so we might as well get that over with as well.'

He looked horrified at that. 'When we do it — *if* we do it — it certainly won't be on a freezing beach with sand getting up my arse.'

She smiled and he smiled back. He went on, 'And certainly not without getting some kind of — God, I hate this word — *counselling*.'

He was probably right. 'I suppose,' she said.

'I heard that.'

'What?'

'You gave a little sigh.'

'I did not!'

'You did. And I don't blame you. All this stuff is a pain. Having to be careful. To think before we do anything. Always thinking of the future. If I was you, I wouldn't bother.' But the jokey bit at the end was only for show; to cover how serious all this was.

'I'd rather you didn't have it, yes,' she said slowly. 'But you do, and nothing can change that. And convenient and all as it might be, I can't turn off my feelings just like that.'

If Ali was here she'd kill her. Because that's exactly what she wanted Emma to do. But it was impossible. One look at Ryan's face told her that.

'Well, you can't say fairer than that,' he said at last.

'Meanwhile, you've said nothing at all.'

'I have!' His brow crinkled. 'Have I not?'

'No. Not a word about being crazily in love with me, and desperately wanting me back. Nothing.'

'I'll amend that immediately.' He put his arms around her and held her close. It would have been very romantic had both of them not been slowly turning blue with the cold. 'Thank you,' he whispered.

'I could say the same.'

With the water lapping gently at their feet, and setting the container of cold noodles afloat, they kissed.

27

Ali

Mam and Dad were very pleased about the whole thing. 'Well, I suppose if they broke up because they rushed into things, then they must be dead certain the second time round. We always liked Ryan, didn't we, Noel?'

Dad nodded vigorously. He was less grumpy these days now that he was being waited on hand and foot by Tina. Or maybe it was because he and Mam got a break from each other for four wonderful hours every morning.

He might be less pleased with himself if he knew the full truth about Ryan, but of course Emma was doing all that touchy-feely business of letting Ryan break the news at his own pace, blah, blah. She'd insisted that their getting back together again was enough for Mam and Dad to digest at the moment.

A total cop-out in Ali's opinion, but who ever listened to her?

'It's nice to see one of you settled,' Dad remarked.

Honestly. She'd just about had enough of today, and it was only 9.30 a.m. 'Much and all as I'd love to stay married to Kyle just to make you and Mam feel better, we're still going to get divorced,' she told him sarcastically.

The word always made Mam flinch, and she didn't disappoint today. 'Still, I suppose it's for the best,' she said with a sigh. 'Lots of people get divorced these days. Even older people.'

Dad stiffened; was that a dig at him? But Mam was looking serenely at the needlepoint in her hand. She'd taken it up on Tuesday mornings in the Community Centre, mostly out of desperation, because there were only so many walks you could take in the rain.

'Oh, here,' she said now, getting up and going to root in a press. 'I got you some holy water to take back with you. Nellie Jackson got some in Knock when she was over there.'

Ali looked at the litre-bottle of water, with bits of unidentifiable stuff floating around in it. 'Mam, I haven't a hope of getting that past airport security.'

Mam shook her head in disgust, as though the people who worked hard to make the world a safer place were nothing more than a bunch of misguided fools. 'Ah, well, never mind,' she said (she had got altogether more sanguine since she didn't have to change Dad's diapers whenever he had an accident). 'I was only trying to get rid of it anyway. I've been doing a bit of a spring clean in the attic in the mornings while the rest of my house has been out of bounds to me.'

So that explained why the holy water looked about ten years old. She put it back in the press now, no doubt to pawn off on someone else, and said, 'Are you all packed?'

Why did everybody ask that? It was like they could think of nothing better to say. 'How long will it take you to get to the airport?' was another old chestnut that Ali must have been asked about ten times in the last twenty-four hours. 'Is the flight long?' would usually be hot on its heels. She felt like printing out little cards with all her travel and packing information on them, and handing them out.

But if she did that, then they'd all have nothing to talk about, would they? Because nobody, it seemed, was going to enquire how she actually felt about going back (very upset); whether she was going to miss her family and friends (terribly); and whether her heart was going to be broken by the whole thing (yes).

Instead they all went around pretending that she'd only come home for a short hop, like she did every summer, and that now she was heading off back just like normal.

None of it was normal. She was going back to life as a single mother, in that bloody enormous tasteless house, with not a soul to comfort her in her time of need. Oh, and a swimming pool with a load of green scum floating on top.

'Will you come and visit?' she blurted out now.

Mam and Dad looked startled. She could read their minds: visit? They hadn't visited since before Dad's first heart attack. Well, how could they? And all that distance, too. And then there was the language barrier. On their first time over Mam had been asked outside the airport by some taxi type (typically, Ali had been late to pick them up) whether she needed some wheels, sister.

Plus, Mam didn't like Ethel. In fairness,

nobody did. But it had been a terrible strain trying to make small talk in Ethel's front room that time, especially with that enormous stuffed moose head over the mantelpiece glaring down at Mam. She'd subtly changed chairs, only to find a deer's head waiting for her over there. It was like being in some horror museum, as she'd told everybody afterwards.

'We'll try,' said Mam, hesitantly. In other words, Ali wouldn't see them for dust.

She put a big smile on her face anyhow as she took her leave. 'See how it goes,' she said cheerily. Well, there was no point in being miserable. Nobody gave a shite.

Although that wasn't strictly true. Emma had been marvellous in the last few days, despite being horribly in love all over again. It would sicken you. But she'd managed to extricate herself from Ryan's arms long enough to help with the travel arrangements, and wind up things like bills and the school stuff. Ali was amazed at how settled they'd become in such a short space of time. In some ways, it was like uprooting all over again, even though they were going home.

Kyle had been good too. She hated to admit it, but he had; surprisingly so.

'I've got the house all fixed up for you,' he'd told her on the phone last night. 'I did some painting, and put the door back on the shed. And I got someone in to change sheets and dust the place and stuff. You should be able to just walk back in.'

She knew he would have fresh milk in the

422

fridge too, and frozen pizzas (what else?) in the freezer.

He was making an effort. And she had to, too. 'That's great, Kyle. The kids are really looking forward to seeing you again.'

He was suspicious. 'Are you just saying that?'

'No! Anto even got a bit tearful last night.' Mostly that had been to do with having to leave Emma's jukebox behind, even though it was broken, but there was no need to tell him that. 'And Erin, she's already spending the pocket money you're going to give her on Saturday.'

He gave a bit of a chuckle at that. 'I spoke to school. There's no problem about them going straight back in. Miss Walker in particular was real pleased Jack's coming back.'

Ali wouldn't bother telling Jack that. He was already showing unrestrained delight at heading home, and the news would only make him more unbearable. His mobile was practically smoking from all the texts flying back and forth between him and Carly. She couldn't resist a peek at one of them while he was in the shower, and immediately wished she hadn't, because it started off with, 'The woman has finally seen sense.'

'I guess I'll see you Tuesday,' Kyle finished up with.

There was a bit of a question in his voice. She had, after all, left it till the eleventh hour before booking the tickets home. He must have been wondering whether he'd have to go and give Calvin Crawford a nudge after all.

'Yes,' she said, sounding very sure and

423

decisive, even though half of her wanted to stick the kids into Emma's car and make a break for it to Donegal. He'd never find her up there, especially around those mountain lakes. They could disappear for years. Mind you, they'd have to live on any fish they could catch or rabbits they could trap and skin.

She might as well face it: there was nowhere left to run. And even if there was, she couldn't go. She'd always been the kind of person who'd find some eejit to take her in, but things were different now; she had three kids, and she simply had to put them first.

Plus, of course, they wouldn't go to Donegal with her. Not a chance. No matter what she tried, they *would* persist in having minds of their own, and there was no way they were staying in Ireland unless she actually chained them up, which would be no fun for anyone.

So, home they were going. She had hung on as long as she could, had eked out those two weeks, but her time was up, and they were flying out tomorrow.

And no, she hadn't the bloody packing done. Not even half of it. Plus, she'd promised Emma they would leave the apartment exactly the way they'd found it. So she had a lot of broken plates to glue back together that afternoon, and a set of curtains to mend and put up in the living room, not to mention some serious work to do with a bottle of carpet cleaner.

The kids were singing Simon & Garfunkel's 'Homeward Bound' when she got back to the apartment. They'd finished school on Friday, and Ali had been assured by the Principal that they'd left their mark. He hadn't been smiling, either.

Anto was playing air guitar while Erin sang lustily, and Jack directed the whole thing from his favourite position on the couch.

There was a little moment before they noticed her at the door. Then their voices petered out.

A little silence followed.

'Sorry, Mom,' Erin said guiltily. 'We were just having some fun.'

Oh, and they couldn't have fun while she was around? They had to wait till she was out of the apartment?

'We know you hate going back,' Anto clarified, carefully putting away his imaginary guitar.

Ali managed a laugh. (Shit. Was she that transparent?) 'Don't be ridiculous.'

But they all looked at her solemnly. 'Don't tell lies, Mommy,' Erin said sternly.

'Just admit it, Mom,' Jack piped up.

Now she felt a bit under siege. And she'd always been so careful to conceal her loyalty to her roots, too. Well, tactful, anyway. And if not exactly tactful, then . . . oh, at least she was *honest* about things.

'I do not hate America,' she stated calmly. 'It's just that I'm Irish. All my family is here.'

That never made much of an impression on them. As far as they saw it, Granddad was some sick old dude, and Granny had got more freaked-out over the years. Emma was OK, though, Anto had magnanimously declared last week.

'You have family in Texas,' Erin said, trying to make Ali feel better, bless her.

'You mean Dad's family,' Ali clarified. 'Ethel and Hal.'

A gloomy little silence fell over the group. However bad Ali's family was, Ethel and Hal were way worse. Everybody had always acknowledged that.

'You have us, though,' Erin tried now valiantly. Her little face would break your heart.

'Oh, pet.' Ali crossed the room and took her in her arms. How could she have let her little girl think, even for a moment, that she wasn't enough? 'Of course I do. You're the most important thing in my life.'

'What about me?' Anto asked, more curious than anything else.

'And you!' She caught him in a huge hug too, and held him tight until his face went red with pleasure. Then it was over to Jack, who was already squirming and going, 'Aw, *Mom*.' But she threw her arms around him anyway, and slapped a big kiss on his cheek, and told him he was wonderful.

'Does this mean that, like, everything is cool?' Anto enquired.

Ali made a decision there and then: they had enough to cope with, what with their parents divorcing, without having to carry her (transparent) discontent on their shoulders as well.

And so she put on her biggest, warmest smile, resolved that it would remain in place until they were all at least eighteen, and announced, 'We're more than OK. We're great!' Then, before it all got too Disney, she grumbled, 'Now, if we don't get packing we're going to miss our flight tomorrow, and then you'll be stuck here.'

★ ★ ★

She only got really emotional when she was putting out all the wine bottles into the recycling. It wasn't the number of them, although there were definitely too many. It was the thought of all the nights she'd sat on the sofa with Emma, even if they'd been in a snit with each other. Brought together after all these years by Chardonnay.

She could hardly believe now how apprehensive she'd been about moving in with Emma when they'd first arrived. Wary, of her own sister! And look at how things had changed. Granted, she was still wary, but she felt she'd broken down some of Emma's reserve, mostly by sheer brute force and determination. If you could help each other through kidnappings, divorces, incurable diseases and warring parents, then you were pretty tight.

And now it was all going to end. Who was going to sit with Ali on Tuesday night, on her porch, and drink wine with her, and argue and have a laugh? Nobody, that was who. She'd be there all on her ownio, while Emma would be here, no doubt wrapped around Ryan.

She'd be replaced. It hurt. Oh, she would do while Emma was single and heartbroken, but now that Ryan was back on the scene Emma would probably be delighted to have her apartment back so the pair of them could get loved-up all over again.

But Emma was loyal. She'd stay in touch. They'd email, and there would be the weekly telephone call, and of course Ali would be back every summer as usual. And now that she wasn't tied to Kyle, she might be able to stay a little longer each time, dependent on whether the kids could be bribed or not. Emma would send over highly unsuitable presents for the kids' birthdays every year (Anto usually flogged his on eBay) and then she would announce, out of the blue, that she had a window in work and she'd be flying in at the end of the week.

It wouldn't all be gone, Ali tried to convince herself. Just because they were going to be on different continents once again didn't mean all the closeness would evaporate overnight.

No, it would probably be a slow bleed, the way it had gone the first time round, nearly seventeen years ago. The time between emails would get longer, phone calls would get shorter, and within a couple of years the annual holiday would be about visiting ancient relatives again.

Bloody hell. Now she was *really* depressed. And she hadn't even started to glue the broken crockery together yet. Still, she had all night, as it seemed that Emma wasn't even going to bother coming home on their last night in Ireland. Out with lover boy again, no doubt, not giving Ali a thought.

Then she saw Emma's car drive in.

OK, so she'd been wrong.

And who got out of the car? Emma and Ryan.

This was even worse than Emma staying out. Now Ali had to look at the pair of them snogging on the couch while she packed. Ignored and left to drink that fecking Chardonnay on her own — it wasn't as though she had any choice; she'd already opened the bottle.

She was on the verge of tears when Emma finally came in.

'Hi,' said Emma, sounding altogether too happy for someone who was, if you thought about it, going to lose her sister in the morning. But hey, let's not make a big deal out of *that*. 'The kids in bed already?'

'Yes.' It was an early start tomorrow and she'd packed them off. Emma was pleased, no doubt, that they wouldn't interrupt her dalliance with Ryan. 'If you give me five minutes, I'll have my stuff out the bathroom so that he can move his in,' Ali said stiffly.

Emma crossed her arms. 'What are you on about now?'

'Ryan.' She looked past Emma. Where was he anyway?

In the living room, actually, with a toolbox spread open, and taking the front off the jukebox as quietly as he could.

He met her eyes steadily. 'Hello, Ali.'

You'd never think they'd clawed lumps out of each other the last time they'd met.

'Hi,' she said back, rather ungraciously.

He looked all right. He looked great, actually. But that was the love of a good woman for you.

'Emma was telling me how much Anto misses the jukebox,' he told her. 'I said I'd see if I could

429

fix it so that he can have a bit of a song before he goes tomorrow.'

It was all a bit too cute. He didn't even like Anto that much. Jack and he had always got on best.

'We probably won't have time,' she said.

But now here was Emma, looking a bit mean and nasty. 'Cut it out, Ali. Now, I'm going to get a glass of wine from that bottle before you finish it, so I'd appreciate it if you'd stay here and help Ryan.'

It was a ruse, of course, to force them to make up, so that everybody would be happy. So Ali gave a big martyred sigh, and picked up a screwdriver and held it out.

'What's that for?' Ryan said.

'I'm helping you, as per Emma's instructions.'

'I don't want that one. Hand me a wrench.'

Great. Like she was supposed to know what a wrench was. She put down the screwdriver rapidly and did a kind of slow retreat, hoping he wouldn't notice.

'So,' she said. 'You're back together.'

She had no time for small talk; she had a plane to catch in the morning.

'That's right,' he said. 'I hear you disapprove.'

So he was going to throw it right back at her. Fine. She lived in a place where they taught kids to shoot before they toilet-trained them; she was able for him.

'I'm just worried about her future.'

'So am I. Nothing's certain in this world. But if I deteriorate at some point in the future then we'll just have to face it when it comes.'

Oh. She'd been prepared for a few euphemisms but he was being quite direct.

'At the same time,' he went on, 'the chances that I'll outlive you are pretty good.'

Well! That was just plain cheeky.

'Look, Ali,' he said, 'I know you're just trying to protect her. I'd be the same. But she's big enough to know what she's getting into. Don't make her feel bad about it; if you've got a problem, then take it out on me.'

'Yeah, like I'm going to attack a sick man.'

He looked at her evenly. 'I am not sick.' He put down the wrench. 'If I had something else, like MS or cancer, would you be saying the same thing?'

Yes! No. Maybe. Oh God, what would she say?

'It's not the same thing, though,' she argued.

He let it go. 'I'm going to look after her too, you know. It's not going to be a one-way thing, no matter what you think.'

He went back to the jukebox. As far as Ali could see, he did damn all to it, but when he screwed the front back on, and tried a button, it came to life.

'Turn it off,' Ali began.

'Sorry,' he said.

But it was too late. The bedroom door burst open. There were the kids, in various states of sleepiness, looking out.

'Ryan,' said Jack, delighted.

'The jukebox!' Anto roared. He stampeded over Ryan to get to it, pausing briefly to tell him, 'I love you, man.'

431

It was 2 a.m. by the time the kids went to bed and Ryan went home. The whole thing had descended into a full-on party, with Emma putting on frozen pizzas in the kitchen, and Ryan mediating between Anto and Erin, both of whom insisted that they were in charge of the playlist. At one point, after several glasses of wine, Ali had ended up dancing with Ryan. *Laughing* with him. No doubt she would cringe about it in the morning.

'You should go to bed too,' Emma advised her. 'You're up in five hours.'

'Stop, I don't want to talk about it.' She just wanted to hang on to the buzz for another few minutes. They would have to leave soon enough.

Emma, fair play to her, sat down and poured out the rest of the wine. They were probably on bottle number three at this point.

'Was fixing the jukebox your idea or his?' Ali suddenly asked suspiciously.

Emma looked indignant. 'Mine. I wanted it to be a surprise for Anto in the morning.'

'Did he say thank you?'

'Actually, now that you mention it, no.'

Ali took a slug of wine and gave a big sigh. 'I suppose you'll forget about me once I go back.'

'See, I knew you'd get like this. All maudlin and silly.'

'I just want to know.'

'How could I forget about you, when you'll be on the phone every second day, giving out about something? I hate to put it so bluntly, but you're

432

not an easy person to ignore.'

'You make me sound like a pain in the arse.'

'You are. A lovable pain in the arse.'

'Warm words indeed, coming from you.'

Emma laughed. 'We'll email, and you'll be back next year, and I'll go over.'

'Yes, but it won't be the same.'

'I suppose it's a question of making an effort, Ali. Like most things.'

'How did you get to be so wise?' Ali chided.

'I don't know. I was born ancient.'

Ali said very magnanimously, no doubt mostly because of all the wine, 'Ryan isn't a bad dancer.'

It was best to stick to non-contentious issues, she felt.

'I'll be sure to tell him that,' Emma said gravely.

Ali felt she had better go the extra mile. 'And, you know, I hope things work out for you two, if you will insist on getting back together.'

'Is that approval?'

'Certainly not. More a grudging acceptance.'

Emma said nothing, but she gave Ali a grateful smile.

'Will we have another drink?' Ali said. That half-glass seemed to have disappeared awfully fast.

'No,' said Emma sternly. She gave a huge yawn. 'Come on. Time for bed.'

Grumbling and giving out, but feeling a bit better, Ali let Emma link her arm and hustle her off to bed.

Epilogue

To: planet.peterson@savvy.com
From: Emma@TV5.co.ire
Hi Ali,

You forgot your phone, foundation, earplugs, shower gel and the fake pint of Guinness you were going to bring back for Kyle.

Love Emma xxx

To: Emma@TV5.co.ire
From: planet.peterson@savvy.com
Dear Emma,

I still don't know which end of me is up. We finally found Anto in the airport that day, and Kyle has threatened him with boot camp if he does it again. The kids have settled back into a routine and seem to be doing OK, although the big reunion between Jack and Carly is now entering its third week. Now, I'm not easily shocked, but Jack asked me on Monday if I would consider letting Carly have a sleepover. *In his room.* He said that as they'd both turned sixteen in the past month, legally they could have sex if they wanted, but it would be more convenient and safer if they had my approval!

Had to go have a lie down for two days. Am considering telling Kyle, but you know what he's like. He'd probably give Jack a wink and tell him he was a chip off the old block. Of course, if it was *Erin*, he'd be reaching for one of those shotguns in his new glass cabinet (did I tell you about the house he's rented? It's got a Jacuzzi and a motorbike bay out the front. I think this divorce may prove more traumatic for him than I'd thought).

As for me, I'm rattling around the place, still trying to unpack. And thank you for all the Kimberleys! I discovered them in Erin's suitcase. Oh, and she seems to have brought home a handbag of yours by mistake — that nice one you got in town the weekend before we left. Sorry! How are Mam and Dad? Mam sent me some awful thing she'd made in that needlepoint class. Honestly, I think she's cracking up altogether. Could you not encourage her to change over to cookery or basic French?

You do know what you're doing, don't you, letting Ryan move back in so quickly?? I'm not trying to preach or anything, but it's never a good idea to give in too easily — take it from me. Oh, and how are those plans coming along for him to quit flying off to unstable regions and set up a company doing wedding photos? Just thought I'd mention it in case you'd both forgotten . . .

Anyway, I'd better go. Kyle and I are going roller-blading with the kids, and then, if we don't end up taking somebody to the Emergency Room, we're going out for a pizza to talk about the divorce. You wouldn't believe how quickly the whole thing gets sorted here in the States, especially if you both agree. Kyle reckons that it should all be finalised as early as September — sooner, he says, if I would just stop insisting that everything in the garage is his.

If you want to know the truth, he's being a little bit freaky. Or maybe it's just me. But he seems to have gone from wanting us to stay together to being quite excited about his new life as a single man, all in the space of, like, *weeks*. He's taken up jogging (I know, I laughed too) and got a new, younger haircut. Anto said that when they were out with him last week, they went into this tattoo parlour and he got a brochure. Of course, Anto wants a tattoo now too. He says he wants a shamrock, which I think is meant to flatter me, but he didn't say where.

I hope your apartment has recovered. And sorry again about the carpet.

Ali xxx

PS. The weather here is a nice change from the rain and cold in Ireland. I'm not saying this to rub it in; I've made a resolution that every day I will think of something positive about living away from home. Yesterday, it was hot fudge sundaes with whipped cream — yum.

PPS. Well done on the ratings, missus. Very impressive. And a nice description of how green Phil's face was. Can you not fire him or something?

To: planet.peterson@savvy.com
From: Emma@TV5.co.ire
Hi Ali,

This is a short one as we're off to the airport in an hour, and you know the way I can never relax until I go around turning everything off and unplugging all the electric appliances. Although Ryan says I've relaxed a hundred per cent since having you lot living with me. He says he can't believe how calm I am now about things like the lid being left off the jam. I'm laughing the whole thing off, of course, but heard him say 'obsessive compulsive disorder' to you on the phone last week and am quite annoyed. Especially when you didn't seem to disagree with him.

Anyway, will have to throw caution to the winds over the next few weeks — Ryan says that I can forget about my fancy toiletries as we'll be living in tents and eating goat meat. Although I'm hoping he's joking about that last part. But he's probably being overly dramatic. How difficult can it actually be to get to Everest base camp? And we'll have all these fellows called Sherpas to carry our stuff and generally wait on us hand and foot. And I'll probably have plenty of time to relax and read while Ryan is off taking photos. He thinks he wants to branch out a bit more into travel photography (heavily encouraged by me. I'm not trying to mammy him or anything; I just think he has enough challenges in his life now without getting run over by a tank). This trip is a chance for me to finally see what he does for a living, and for us to bond

— stop making puking noises — and anyway, I've always wanted to climb to Everest base camp. Yes, I have, you just weren't listening.

Thanks for your card. Although there was no need to stick in the word 'again' under the 'Congratulations on Your Engagement' bit. It was very nice of Anto to offer to be a pageboy for us, but he's probably a bit old, and you might want to mention to him that there wouldn't be any payment.

We haven't set any date yet, although I know you're anxious to book flights early so that it's cheaper. But this time we're definitely not rushing into things, although Mam is mad for a bit of excitement. The French course is going quite well for her, and she's doing a bit of practise around the house. She calls Dad, '*mon ami*', which is the nicest thing she's called him in years. Anyway, there's a gang of them from the class thinking of going to France to 'brush up on their accents'. They're all over sixty-five so it'll probably be safe enough. She keeps going on about how worried she is about leaving Dad with Tina, but he's fine, no sign of another heart attack this year yet. He's getting a bit grumpy about it — you know him, always a stickler for time-keeping.

So glad to hear that your divorce is coming along well. It was generous of Kyle to throw a pool boy into the settlement, although I presume the purpose is to remove the green scum from your pool as opposed to anything else. And I was *not* being negative about your new job; it's just that you were full of plans to go back to college,

438

and I don't know how you're going to manage that if you're working five mornings a week in Just Shoes. I also don't know why you even asked my advice, because you'll do whatever you want to anyway, regardless of what anybody else tells you.

We had the *Wake Up Ireland* summer barbecue yesterday. Patrick got drunk and started rubbing himself up against Alannah. Unbelievable. Afterwards he pretended that he'd banged his head on the set and suffered momentary confusion. But she didn't take too much offence, mostly because of the news that we're back in September!!! And don't say you told me so — none of us knew until the boys upstairs made their decision yesterday. Adam said, a bit grudgingly, that they were prepared to 'give the show another chance'. In other words, the ratings are up again. Hannie is a bit disappointed as she really thought we were going to branch out on our own and make documentaries on Ibiza, researched by her. Patrick is already saying that he doesn't know if he can commit to a new series, as he's had a hot offer from the BBC — like anybody believes *that*.

I have, though. Remember I applied during my week 'off'? But not a word to anybody. Ryan is mad keen for me to take it, so that we could both move to London. But I've only just got *Wake Up Ireland* back on the radar and I'd feel so guilty about Alannah and Hannie and everybody else. I know you don't understand the concept of guilt, but I'm full of it.

Also, I've had enough change in my life, without being too dramatic about it. I'll stick around here for another while and see how it goes.

Lots of love to the kids. Erin's drawing was great. I've stuck it on the fridge with magnets. Ryan thinks it's very Picasso.

Love Emma xxxx

PS. The place is very quiet without you. Very quiet.

To: Emma@TV5.co.ire
From: planet.peterson@savvy.com
Hi Emma,

I hope you're sitting down for this. And no, I'm not accidentally pregnant again, you wagon.

First, let me set the scene: Kyle pitched up at the house yesterday evening in new cowboy boots. No surprises there, as I'd actually sold them to him in Just Shoes last week, at staff discount, only don't tell anyone. Anyway, over the cowboy boots he was wearing these new jeans. You know the really tight ones that are stretchy and that stick to you like glue? Yes. I swear, you could see every bulge, it was mortifying. And the whiff of aftershave nearly knocked me sideways. In he struts, finds me in the kitchen and says, very intensely, 'Have you time to come out for a cup of coffee?' At that the kids burst out into shouts of jubilation and celebration, and start singing, 'Hurrah! They're going to get back together! We're going to be a

440

proper family again!'

And I have to admit, I was a tad worried myself for a moment. But Kyle just laughed and said to the kids (in quite a callous way, I thought), 'Don't be stupid.'

I was a bit hurt then. I mean, I'm not *that* bad, am I? At least two husbands flirted with me in the shop last week, while their wives were hobbling about in shoes that were too small for them, only they wouldn't admit it. And Kyle had always been up for his conjugal rights after two bottles of Bud Light, so for him to go on now like I'm the back of a bus . . .

Let me be clear on one thing: I'd rather sit on barbed wire than sleep with him again, but at the same time it would have been nice to have been given the opportunity to turn him *down*.

In Starbucks he broke the news. He 'didn't want me hearing it from anybody else', but he was 'seeing someone new'. He hoped that I would understand, and that he hoped I would 'enjoy a new relationship too, in time'.

Miss Walker, Emma. Miss Maths-Teacher-Walker! Talk about on your own doorstep. Apparently now that he's collecting the kids from school two days a week he's been rekindling all his old friendships with the various teachers that he snogged two decades ago. So himself and Miss Walker — she never married, and he hasn't said it but I know he thinks it's because she never got over him — have been quietly dating, and things have been going so swimmingly that he felt it was time to let me know. 'I hope that's OK with you,' he said, very

441

solemnly and maturely.

I wanted to slap his face. Really, I did. But he'd only think I was jealous and so I had to nod and smile and wish him all the luck in the world (and Miss Walker too. Wait till she sees his spotty back). And then he gave me a hug at the end of it all and told me, quite emotionally, that he felt closer to me now than when we'd been married!

Seriously, though, is he the thickest man that was ever born? Or are they all like that? (Apart from Ryan, of course. When I heard how he'd tenderly massaged your frostbitten toes at the foot of Everest . . . You two think you're in a movie or something.) Anyway, I went home and ate a gallon of Ben & Jerry's, and slowly, the epiphany came over me: it really was over. I need never worry about that eejit again. No more turning myself inside out, wondering that he was lonely/hungry/overweight/had high cholesterol on his last test. I could hand the whole thing over to Miss Walker. I was free!

I rang him up immediately to tell him this, but he sounded very out of breath and I realised then that he was in the middle of nailing Miss Walker, God help her.

Jack's livid, of course. The kids in school found out and are making his life in school hell, making kissy-kissy noises whenever he goes past. But as I explained to him, this could equally be to do with the fact that he and Carly were caught necking in the girls' toilets last week.

(She had the sleepover. I took his door off the hinges beforehand. It's safe to say there was no nooky.)

442

Got to go, shoes to sell. I didn't mention it because I know you look down on my job, but I'm Assistant Manager now due to the sheer volume of footwear I've shifted in the past month. So up your bum. And I've got a name badge and a uniform which I'm half ashamed to say I like.

Love Ali xxx

PS. Hi to Ryan. I don't really have anything else to say to him. Just, hi. In a friendly way.

To: planet.peterson@savvy.com
From: Emma@TV5.co.ire
Dear Ali,

I didn't put her up to it, I swear to God. She just announced that she'd bought her ticket, and she was off, just like that. Liam and I think it's the France trip; far from wandering around rustic towns picking up accents from the locals, they were having boozeups every night on cheap wine, and playing games of truth and dare. They all came back wrecked, but have another trip planned already for next Easter. And then she announces *this*. But there's no danger of her boozing every night, not if she has to look after Dad on her own again.

Anyway, I don't know what you're complaining about. You're always giving out that nobody visits you. Won't it be nice to have company on your first Christmas on your own? And Mam will probably cook the turkey and everything, so you can kick back and drink wine for the day, which you probably would have done anyway. I'll probably head over in February. We're mad busy at the moment, what with Phil gone (he resigned; I didn't fire him) and no sign of anybody decent to replace him. And Patrick and Alannah are totally unbearable since their nominations for TV Personality of the Year. It'll be a bloodbath if one wins and not the other. Adam is thinking of banning them from going along to the ceremony on the night. With all the drama, nobody's even thought to say congratulations to the rest of us for our nomination in the Favourite Live Programme category (except you, thanks), although Adam invited me to lunch yesterday, and I accepted. Hannie says that lunch with Adam means that you're the hottest property in the station, but how come I ended up stuck with the bill?

We finally put an offer in on the house — the four-bed semi which I know you think is very boring, but we didn't feel the thatched cottage was us. We set Dad to work on the estate agent, and he bitched so much about the plumbing and the heating and the design — he was in there a good hour — that they knocked three grand off the sale price. Dad was chuffed with himself, but completely exhausted afterwards, and Mam took him off home for a rest.

Re: the Kyle issue, I'd have a quiet word with him. Explain to him that while you completely understand his urge to explore his new-found freedom, it's not appropriate to work his way through his kids' teachers. In other words:

444

school's out of bounds.
    Love Emma xxxx

To: Emma@TV5.co.ire
From: planet.peterson@savvy.com
Dear Emma,

So glad to hear Ryan is out of hospital. Jack sent
him a book in the post, I hope he got it.
    Ali xxx

To: planet.peterson@savvy.com
From: Emma@TV5.co.ire
Dear Ali,

He's up and about today, and eating again,
which was great. He's a little worried, even
though he won't show it, and so am I, but his
consultant said that lots of HIV-negative people
get pneumonia too, and that it's most likely bad
luck. All the same, his viral count is slightly up,
and we've made the decision to start treatment.
It's a little sooner than we'd hoped, and he was
all for hanging on as long as he could, but what's
the point? I told him that he'd be seeing more of
hospital unless he copped on, and he was quite
meek about it in the end.
    Thanks for all your phone calls and texts. I
don't know what I'd have done without you.
    Love Emma xxx
    PS. It was great to have Mam and Dad gone
during all this, even though I know they drove

you cracked. You know how Mam's been since we told her, fussing over Ryan like she does with Dad. I don't think I'm going to tell them about the pneumonia at all now, so maybe you wouldn't mention it either.

PPS. Not that it's important in the middle of all this, but we won the award. Patrick and Alannah were both trumped in the TV Personality of the Year by some little shit (Patrick's words) over on RTE. I smuggled in a bottle of champagne to Ryan's ward and we had a glass on the sly.

To: Emma@TV5.co.ire
From: planet.peterson@savvy.com
Dear Emma,

Forty-eight hours to New York! I can't believe I'm so excited about a weekend away, even though it's only with June. But she was delighted at my suggestion, as she's just split up from her husband too (if you saw him, you'd understand), and we're going to have a proper girls' weekend away. Am completely wrecked from watching back-to-back box sets of *Sex and the City*, and now June's petrified that I'm going to dress up in slips of things and insist that she trawls the bars with me looking for cheap sex. As if I'd have the energy. I just want to do Times Square and maybe catch a show — *that's* how old and sensible I've got.

Kyle keeps saying how much he's looking forward to having the kids for four days. He's quietened down a bit on the dating front, which is just as well. He was looking absolutely wrecked there for a while, and we were all concerned for his health; some of them were so much *younger* than him. He's gone back to his normal jeans, and has taken up drinking beer and watching baseball again. Anto's developed an interest too, and they sit on the sofa together discussing rules and tactics, and it's quite sweet sometimes.

The big news here is that Jack's been invited to go on summer holidays with Carly's family. They adore him, much more than we do, he says, and he wants to go with them rather than coming home to Ireland. I don't know what to do yet but I'll need to book our tickets soon. Also, there's this camp Erin really wants to do — she said it was arts & crafts, but when I looked at the brochure it seemed to be all about singing and dancing and how to dress like a hooker. Kyle says that they just look like gym clothes to him. That man is so innocent.

So, to answer your question (or was it Mam's question?) I don't know for sure yet when we'll be home. You could always come and visit me, hint, hint.

Love Ali xxx

PS. What are they putting in those drugs?? And don't jump down my throat, but are you sure it's all right for a man in Ryan's condition to be running a half-marathon?

Hi Ali,

It was not a setup, I swear. I just thought you and June might be at a loose end in New York, so I gave Ryan's friend Jim your number as he knows all the best places to go. I did not instruct him to hit on you. Besides, he didn't have to try too hard, from what he told us. Joke! But I'm glad you got on well, even though I can't believe you wasted four days in New York drinking pints in Irish bars. You're a disgrace.

Dad's OK, so you're not to rush home. They're just keeping him in for observation for few days. He doesn't really want to see anybody except Mam, not even Tina. They got Mam a comfy chair and she's staying in nights. I tried to get her to come home for some rest but she won't budge. She says it's her job now and that's that.

Ryan's ferociously busy but he refuses to turn anything down. It's like he's trying to prove something. I've told him it's going to be very difficult to get married at this rate, as it's unlikely he'll ever be in the country long enough. But to be honest, I don't really mind — he's tolerating the meds so well, and is in top form. He doesn't have to go back to see the consultant for another six months.

Hannie's going to produce *Wake Up Ireland* while I'm on holidays this year. She's discovered that the way to deal with Patrick is to shout at him. So everything he says, she just roars, 'Shut up, I'm producing this show now.' And he listens too.

Emma xxx

PS. I know this is out of the blue, but I fly into Texas Friday. Hope you've got a spare bed.

To: Emma@TV5.co.ire
From: planet.peterson@savvy.com
Hi Emma,

I know this is the third email in two hours, but are you sure Anthony is OK? More to the point, are *you* OK? If he does anything — and I mean anything — to your new house, you're to tell me straightaway and we'll cover the damages.

We were just saying (Kyle's here for a beer) that we hoped you weren't lying when you said that you could do with the company while Ryan was away in Australia. And we were only joking when we said you could take Anto back with you. On the plus side, we think it could be the making of him, especially with all the educational outings you seem to have lined up. We're sure he'll enjoy the Natural History Museum, although Kyle is not sure if his boredom threshold can handle more than an hour of the Chester Beatty Library. You might want to cut that one short. Anyway, I'll be over on 19 July with Erin as planned. Can't wait to see you again. And thank you for saying I'd lost weight, even though it was a big lie.

Work is mental. I never knew it could be so

stressful selling shoes. I was awake till 3 a.m. last night wondering whether I'd ordered enough of those stripy wedges. I wish they hadn't promoted me to buyer. I haven't a fecking clue — one of these days they're going to realise that and fire me. Although free shoes are a great perk.

Tell Mam not to be fussing about cleaning out the spare bedrooms for our arrival, as we're going to stay with you.

Ha, got you going there for a minute. Wouldn't dream of infiltrating the love zone. We'll bunk down with the terrible two, and endure Mam's awful Italian (what's she going to *do* with all these languages she's learning?) and Dad's grumbling. Great to hear that he's back on form, and giving out yards. Let's just hope that Tina doesn't find another job, or go and get herself pregnant again, or Mam might take an axe to him.

I still haven't told Kyle about Jim, although he nearly caught Jim buck naked the other morning when he called around to pick up Erin. First reason: I don't even know if me and Jim are serious. He only seems to fly down from New York for sex. Which is fine in my book, but it's hardly a life-long commitment. Second reason: now that Kyle's finally stopped bedding half of Texas, how's it going to look if *I* suddenly start at it? And no, I don't agree with your observation that Kyle is spending too much time here. His kids live here, of course he's going to be around if he's dropping them off or picking them up. You

450

have a very cynical mind, if you don't mind me saying so.

I'll ring tomorrow to talk to Anto. Remember what I said about the Chester Beatty Library. See you on the 19th!

Ali xxxx

To: planet.peterson@savvy.com
From: Emma@TV5.co.ire
Hi Ali,

You forgot your toothbrush, support socks (sexy), and fake tan. At least you remembered Anto. Tell him I was only pretending to lose at Quasar.

Oh, and put 11 November in your diary. We're getting married. I know it's a terrible time of the year, and Mam is already giving out because we'll all have to wear big coats and scarves, but we both like stormy weather, so there! Ryan is talking about trekking in South America for our honeymoon. So much for two romantic weeks on a beach . . . sigh.

Emma xxx

To: Emma@TV5.co.ire
From: planet.peterson@savvy.com
Hi Emma,

I phoned Dad again today, and I really hope it's sinking in with him that he's not to blame. Mam, of course, couldn't resist getting a dig in about

451

the fry-up he had the morning before the wedding — as though things would have been different if he'd had muesli. He's very upset at you having to spend your wedding day in the cardiac unit, but I said it gives us all an excuse to get together again in a few months' time.

Ryan looked gorgeous in his tux, and I don't say that lightly. In fact, for the whole week I forgot there was anything wrong with him. Sorry if that sounds very crude, but I think you'll know what I mean. And thanks for your kind words about Carly. I don't know where she gets her outfits from, I really don't. I'm very surprised at things lasting this long with Jack. Usually at that age they get through half the class by Christmas. All the same, I'd give it another couple of months and I'd say Jack might want to follow in his father's footsteps and sow a few wild oats.

The kids don't mind Jim, which is the best that can be said, even though they think he's ancient. Kyle's still in a snit, and won't come around the weekends that Jim's here. And he's got very territorial about things like hosing down the driveway. The two of them nearly came to blows over the water pump yesterday. It's all très flattering, as Mam would say.

Ali xxx

To: planet.peterson@savvy.com
From: Emma@TV5.co.ire
Hi Ali,

Thank you SO much for all that information. When it's your first time you just don't know what to expect. When we saw the heartbeat we just burst out crying, the two of us, and couldn't stop. We probably looked like we'd just given birth, instead of only being seven weeks' pregnant. But the IVF was so stressful, and then the screening, and then the news that we had only one embryo that was clear . . . But, like you said at the time, it only takes one. I never realised until now just now wise you are. (Yes, I'm laughing.)

Ryan's already decorating the spare room and making all kinds of rash promises to look into wedding photos again as a career. I'm happy enough if he just cuts down a bit. There's no way I'm going to be stuck at home while he's having a great time by himself. And no, I won't change my tune. You don't know everything, just because you've had three.

Mam keeps on and on about us getting married. It's made me more determined not to bother at all, just to rile her.

If you want my advice on the Jim thing, refuse to make a decision. If you insist that he relocates from New York, he'll only blame you if it goes wrong. Throw it back at him. If he's sure about you, he'll want to move.

Love Emma xxx

PS. Can you send me some more Oreos? Have

developed a terrible addiction to them. The ones you get here just aren't the same.

To: Emma@TV5.co.ire
From: planet.peterson@savvy.com
Hi Emma,

Anto's come up with some names for you: Damien, Carrie, Hannibal, Darth. He's started taking bets on how long you'll be in labour. But for God's sake don't go early, as I won't be there until tomorrow week. The kids are staying here with Kyle. Jim's offered to help out, but Kyle told him, magnificently, that he could cope perfectly well on his own. I just wish those two would go get drunk together, and discuss the cellulite on my thighs. Then we could all be friends.

Well done on the award for *Wake Up Ireland*. How many is that now? And I know you won't claim credit because Hannie's been in charge. You'd want to watch your back there.

Ali xxx

PS. Will bring over some of those new orthopaedic shoes for you. God knows you need something, what with those varicose veins.

PPS. Will Ryan be in the delivery ward? I just don't know if the room will be big enough for both of us. And I'm your sister — he's only the father.

To: planet.peterson@savvy.com
From: Emma@TV5.co.ire
Hi Ali,

Here's my advice: don't freak. Don't put your foot down and say no. Because you know from history that Jack will probably just pack up and run away.

Plus — and here's the important bit — you can't stop them. They're both eighteen. If they want to get married, there's not a single thing in the world that can stop them. And you demanding that Carly take a pregnancy test was a bit out of order. Especially as it was negative. Nobody's forcing anybody this time. It looks like they want to get married because they love each other. Do try to get your head around that one.

Beatrice finally produced a tooth. Ryan says it's the cutest tooth he's ever seen. (I know, I know, it's typical first-child stuff. You'll have to forgive him.) Am completely wrecked. Don't know if I can handle this working/being a mother thing at all. You were right — Hannie is only dying to steal my job. And I might just give it to her.

I went and put flowers on Dad's grave for you for his birthday. Mam keeps it very well, even if I had to stop her putting a doily on the headstone last week. She's getting out a bit more now. I'm trying to persuade her to go to France with the gang this year, but she says it's too soon. But she's definitely coming out with me and Beatrice and Ryan in October. She says that this time she wants to stay in a hotel, so don't take offence. I just think she likes the peace and quiet, and when your kids get together with mine . . . By the way, don't worry about getting a travel cot for Beatrice, she'll just sleep in the bed with us. I can't wait for the kids to see her for the first time. And no, she's not going to make Jack and Carly all broody. And even if she did, you'd make the best-looking grandma in Texas. To be honest, I'm more worried about you — didn't you tell me that Jim was just mad for a baby . . . ?

Tell Erin she looked absolutely beautiful on the television (thanks for sending the CD on). She was head and shoulders above the rest of them, and I'm inclined to agree with her that there was some corruption afoot amongst the judges that didn't see her advance to the next round. But wish her the very best of luck in the upcoming auditions for America's Got Young Talent.

Love Emma xxx

To: EmmaTV5.co.ire
From: planet.peterson@savvy.com
Hi Emma,

Hope you get this before you set off for the airport. Can you bring some proper teabags? The ones here are shite and Mam doesn't like them. Oh, and Kyle's going to come over and do a barbecue for everybody, so brace yourself for lots of red meat.

Have a good flight, see you tomorrow.

Ali xxx

We do hope that you have enjoyed reading this large print book.

Did you know that all of our titles are available for purchase?

We publish a wide range of high quality large print books including:
Romances, Mysteries, Classics
General Fiction
Non Fiction and Westerns

Special interest titles available in large print are:
The Little Oxford Dictionary
Music Book
Song Book
Hymn Book
Service Book

Also available from us courtesy of Oxford University Press:
Young Readers' Dictionary
(large print edition)
Young Readers' Thesaurus
(large print edition)

For further information or a free brochure, please contact us at:
Ulverscroft Large Print Books Ltd.,
The Green, Bradgate Road, Anstey,
Leicester, LE7 7FU, England.
Tel: (00 44) 0116 236 4325
Fax: (00 44) 0116 234 0205

Other titles published by
The House of Ulverscroft:

GOING IT ALONE

Clare Dowling

Newly-weds Millie and Andrew have been so busy enjoying themselves that making babies hasn't entered their heads. But as friends turn forty, one by one, Millie gets a rude awakening. Suddenly she wants a baby, and she wants one now. Cue her obsession with fertility charts, pregnancy tests and black negligees. But all that sex would wear anybody out, and Andrew is soon flagging under her gruelling regime. Then he drops his bombshell: he's just not ready to be a father yet. Millie takes matters into her own hands. Determined to go it alone, she sets off on a package holiday to a fertility clinic in Spain. But, surely, it takes two to tango . . . And what happens when the sumptuous Simon arrives on the scene?

NO STRINGS ATTACHED

Clare Dowling

Judy is getting married on Saturday and it's going to be the happiest day of her life if it kills her. It's a military operation, but it'll all be worth it because marriage is for ever, right? But the night before the nuptials, fiancé Barry goes missing. Then his credit card shows up two days later in a nightclub in the south of France. A case of cold feet? Or worse, is it because he's being frog-marched up the aisle? Fanning her fury and grief is Lenny, Barry's best man. Lenny argues that relationships aren't permanent and that commitment ruins romance. With her fiancé romping around France, Judy just might be in the mood for a little romance — with no strings attached, of course . . .

MY FABULOUS DIVORCE

Clare Dowling

Jackie Ball knows that happiness is hard to find, so when Dan Lewis jogs into her life with his skin-tight shorts and sexy smile things start to look up. But when he presents Jackie with a diamond ring and suggests he trade in his BMW for a people carrier, there's a fly in the ointment — her first husband, Henry. Jackie considers her marriage over, so she engages the services of a solicitor and sets about moving on. But Henry has some old scores to settle and the divorce papers hitting the dog-haired mat are the excuse he needs. It's not that he still loves her, but Jackie walked out on him without even leaving a note and now he wants to know why . . .

RSVP

Helen Warner

Four women, one wedding. Anna's world is rocked when she receives an invitation to her ex Toby's nuptials. Toby was The One, The Love of Her Life, The One That Got Away. So will attending his Big Day give her the closure she craves, or re-open old wounds? Clare is Anna's best friend — little could she know that Toby's wedding day would change her life forever. Ella is a classic femme fatale who loves and leaves men without a backward glance. Yet Toby has never fallen for her charms — is it too late to attempt to win his heart? Finally, Rachel is the blushing bride-to-be. This should be the happiest day of her life. Why is it then, she feels only a terrible sense of foreboding?

SUMMER CIRCLES

Sarah Jackman

With her unusual appearance and shy nature, Hannah Ruland leads a content, sheltered life. She lives in the heart of the Fen countryside under the protective eye of Ella, her mother, and elder brother. But Ella faces her own demons and is becoming increasingly secretive; disappearing for hours and neglecting her beloved garden. So Hannah turns to a young stranger, Toby, for company. Together, they befriend the crop circle followers encamped by a local wheatfield where mysterious patterns have appeared. Then Hannah's middle brother returns home unexpectedly, and soon Kirsten, his old girlfriend, arrives on the scene. Desperate to be accepted by the close-knit family, Kirsten stirs up conflicting emotions and resentments. In the long, hot summer days, secrets thrive — and a confrontation seems inevitable . . .